Stopping with my hand on the door, I sneaked a peek left and right, worried someone I knew would recognize me, then I took a deep breath and stole inside. Need I explain? This is a small town.

My eyes took a moment to adjust to the dark. One girl wearing a thong—thank goodness she wasn't anyone I knew—was on stage. Mr. Hot Head sat at the bar with a tall beer, foam on top, glass full. Looked like he had just been served a fresh, cold one, and this early in the day, too. I backed out the door, ran for the tow truck, and zipped back to the alley as fast as I could.

I angled the truck in front of Hot Head's Jeep and muscled the dolly wheels over to the rear end, crouching low to the ground, getting a whiff of the rank dumpster. Hot Head couldn't see me from inside the building, but he had a sixth sense about me, and I was determined to keep under his radar. I jacked up the first dolly wheel and was on my way around the back bumper to jack up the second one, when *bam!*

I stumbled right into Hot Head.

He had a tire iron in his meaty fist.

Local Author! Fun book.

Toes on the Dash

by

Karen C. Whalen

The Tow Truck Murder Mysteries, Book 1

This is a work of fiction. Names, characters, places, and incidents are either the product of the author's imagination or are used fictitiously, and any resemblance to actual persons living or dead, business establishments, events, or locales, is entirely coincidental.

Toes on the Dash

Contact Information: info@thewildrosepress.com

Cover Art by *Diana Carlile*

The Wild Rose Press, Inc.
PO Box 708
Adams Basin, NY 14410-0708
Visit us at www.thewildrosepress.com

Publishing History
First Edition, 2022
Trade Paperback ISBN 978-1-5092-4106-4
Digital ISBN 978-1-5092-4107-1

The Tow Truck Murder Mysteries, Book 1
Published in the United States of America

Dedication

To Tim, my number one fan

Acknowledgments

I have been blessed with family, friends, writers, and editors who helped to make my writing career possible. First, Tim, Drew, Astrid, Garred, and Joy. Next, fellow writers Rhonda Blackhurst, Rachel Weaver, Anita Halvorssen, Becky Martinez, and the Sisters in Crime writers. My first readers Sandra Hilger and Sunny Sanders pointed me in the right direction. Also, Russ VanHouten, for his law enforcement advice, developmental editors Jessica Cornwell and Zachariah Claypole White, for their expertise, the Brighton Police Department, master mechanic Brent Claudin, and Elite Towing for answering my questions, and those who gave me encouragement, including Deb, Keith, Mary, Dean, Pete, Barb, Michele, Dave, Sunny, Bill, Russ, and Sandy. I can't forget my webmaster Chris Love for all his work. And last, thank you to my readers and my editor, Ally Robertson, at The Wild Rose Press.

Chapter 1

I kicked the black tires with my pointy-toed, high-heeled shoes. Isn't that what you did when you bought a car? Only I wasn't buying, I was inheriting. And it wasn't a car, it was a tow truck.

A heavyset man, pushing fifty or sixty, stepped out of an open auto bay and strode over. "Hello, there." His deep, striking voice was at odds with his mechanic's overalls and dirty work boots. His eyes swerved down to my heels. "Ya' here for the truck?"

"I am." Me, all of five-foot-two, weighing in at 110 pounds, wearing my skinny jeans and slingback stilettos. The man probably thought I couldn't handle such a big rig. He was probably right. My freckled face was certain to have turned crimson to match the single red braid down my back.

I offered my hand. "I'm Delaney Morran."

"Byron Oberly." He returned a hard handclasp, his fingers rough and cracked with dark oil stains. "So, you're Del's girl. When the lawyer told me you were comin' over, that's the first I heard a' you. Your dad didn't say anything to me 'bout a daughter, but I can see the resemblance. Sorry for your loss."

I stared hard at the truck. The rig was a faded white with "Del's Towing" painted in navy blue on the door. It appeared fairly new and only had a few scratches.

"Thanks." My chest felt tight, but I gave the man in

overalls what I hoped was a confident smile. "I understand you bought the building and most of the equipment." The truck I had inherited, but the autobody shop had been sold to Mr. Oberly.

He pointed toward the worn sign, "Del's Motors," above the three-bay garage. "I'm changin' the name to 'Oberly Motors' once I get the painter to stop by."

The front door on the concrete block building faced the street, and the auto bays overlooked the parking lot. Only one bay was open; the other two were shuttered behind closed garage doors. A tall, red tool chest and a brown sedan up on blocks could be seen in the open bay. No sounds drifted over. No booms of tires hitting the ground or the whoosh of air compressors. It was dead quiet, which gave the auto shop a sad feeling of abandonment, like a playground overgrown with weeds or a vacant house with broken windows.

I returned my attention to the truck, reminding myself why I was here. "So, where's the big hook that goes on the back?" A large metal crossbar in the shape of a "T" hung from the rear end of the tow truck, but no big, metal hook thingie.

Chuckling, Byron slapped his thigh, and a strong smell of engine oil flew up from his coveralls. His smile revealed a gap between his two front teeth. "This here's a Fulcan Xtruder, a self-loader, not a wrecker, the best in the industry. You don't know anything about the car-haulin' business, do ya'?"

Even at the ripe age of twenty-eight I had never changed a tire, let alone towed a vehicle. I was sort of a wuss. A cream puff. When my girlfriends took rock climbing lessons, I studied ballet. When they joined the lacrosse team, I tried out for cheerleader. So, no, I didn't.

I held up a hand. "I'll be fine." My voice within laughed at this, but I tamped down that thought and stole a peek at my watch. "I'd better head out or I'll be late for work."

"Here ya' go." He dropped the keys into my palm. "Give me your number and I'll set you up with an experienced tow man who can show ya' the ropes, you know, how to operate the rig." He extracted a short pencil nub and a weathered yellow receipt from his pocket. "If you're willing to get your hands dirty and work hard, that is."

I said, "I'm willing to work hard," although I wasn't sure about the dirty hands part. Gripping the cold keys, I rattled off my number and Byron wrote it down. I asked him, "Is it okay for me to leave the truck here for now?"

"Yeah, that's fine. And that tow driver, he'll be a real gentleman. I'll make sure of it."

"Sounds good. Thanks."

He went inside the autobody shop, and I raced across the street to my silver Fiat 500 as fast as my flapping slingbacks could take me. I fell into my tiny car and stowed my purse on the floorboards. I eased out from the curb, then sped down Fifth to zip over to the newer part of town. I had to stop at a light, so I took in the snow-topped mountain peaks that could be seen from every direction under a cloudless blue sky.

The warm spring air blew in through my open window. A man and a woman cycled toward the trail along the river. Runners in jogging gear, mothers pushing strollers, and teens chatting together cleared the crosswalk. Spruce Ridge served as the gateway to the mountains and ski areas. A desirable and affluent location between Denver and Vail, the town offered a superior mall with trendy boutiques.

Roasters on the Ridge Coffee Shop was located on the corner of Pine Street and Eagle. There wasn't a drive-through service, but it had a charming, calm atmosphere. Around the entryway were pots of flowering geraniums, scented pines with new growth, and aspen trees sprouting green leaves, forcing the fuzzy catkins to float on the breeze. Inside, quaint signs greeted the customers, "Coffee makes everything possible," and "Humanity runs on coffee." Antique skis and poles, snowshoes, and ski boots graced the walls. Distressed-wooden shelves held beans, mugs, and syrups. Epic, inspiring music played at a soft volume. And my boss was a purist who roasted her own beans, so I took *half-a-mo* to breathe in the smell of the brew.

After kicking off my heels in exchange for the comfortable high-topped sneakers I kept in a drawer, I whipped the café's clean, black apron, embroidered with a swirl of steam over a coffee mug, around my waist and nipped the strings down low to ride on my hips. I crowded behind the counter next to Kristen Guttenberg—a soul sister and a great boss all in one. I'd known my friend since elementary school, and when she asked me to help her open her coffee shop, I jumped at the chance. Seven months later, I was still working as a barista.

"Well, I did it. I picked up Dad's truck." I gave Kristen a wide-eyed, flat-lipped duck face.

She said, "Everything's going to be fine, you're going to be fine," using her big-sister voice. "Just wait and see, you'll be quitting here soon, you'll be so busy with that tow truck."

Yes, I'd decided to give the towing business a try. I mean…make the towing business a *success*—but quitting my barista job? I think not! I held both hands in front of her face. "No, no."

"Yes, yes. Before long I'll be saying, 'I told you so.' " She sponged milk from the edge of the worktable, then snagged a paper towel to wipe the coffee splatters off the tops of her bright yellow clogs. I wouldn't be caught dead in plastic shoes, even though Kristen insisted they were the most comfortable and practical shoes on earth. But everything else about her outfit was cute, especially her fashionably torn jeans. With her build, she looked good in anything. I always wanted her long legs. Not that I was envious…well, maybe a smidgeon.

With my fists out in front of me gripping an imaginary steering wheel in the two-ten position, I said, "You can picture me driving a tow truck? Right?" I gave her a hopeful grin.

Kristen said at once, "Sure I can." My friend always believed in me, even when I doubted myself. "And I'll need to train somebody else to open the store. You're the only one who knows how to open other than me."

"Job security. Ha! You can't replace me yet." I gave her shoulder a clasp, and I gave the other employees a mental assessment. The perky, pink-haired teenager loading the dishwasher in the back or the English Lit major clearing an empty table outside…which one would make me redundant? I didn't relish the thought of Kristen training anyone else to do my job. Not yet.

"Now, you prayed about this, didn't you?" She wrung out the rag at the sink.

"You do enough of that for both of us." I hugged my friend, four inches taller and ten times a better person than me.

Several moms with toddlers shoved through the door, so Kristen stepped behind the register. "Let's go out to celebrate tonight," my friend said to me out of the corner of her mouth, then to a woman with a baby on her hip, "Good morning. What can I get started for you?"

The day flew by, and once Kristen turned the "Open" sign to "Closed," we got busy scouring equipment, washing down tables and floors, and emptying garbage. An hour later Kristen locked the door behind us and we headed to the employee parking lot.

"I'll come and get you around five-thirty." Kristen tucked the bank deposit bag under her arm and strolled in the direction of her car.

"I'll be ready," I called to her departing back.

I climbed the exterior stairs to the two apartments above the coffee shop. One was mine. The other was Kristen's. When I agreed to help my friend open her business, she offered me the apartment rent-free in exchange for a paycheck. Kristen had started to pay me a salary last month, and it was time for me to give her rent or move out. I needed to pull my own weight and quit depending on Kristen. The free food at the coffee shop needed to end, too. I had to get a handle on the truck and start to make a living.

I nabbed a hardboiled egg out of the refrigerator, and a picture of me and my ex-boyfriend floated to the floor. My brown freckles stood out in the photo, but I was actually having a good hair day when the picture was taken. But him. His eyes no longer looked dreamy and his five-o'clock shadow did not hold any more appeal. I stripped the group of snapshots from the fridge and stuffed them into the garbage can under the sink along with the one that had fallen on the floor. Good riddance. Why hadn't I thrown the pictures away before this? I was starting over in more ways than one.

Time to consider the next step in my grand plan. I had a tow truck. Now what?

My laptop had been sleeping on the kitchen counter, so I opened it and stared at the screen, peeling the shell from the egg. Might as well pull up the *YouTube* video and watch the *how-to-tow* demo for the tenth or twelfth time. Starting a business like this felt a huge undertaking to me, but I was determined to figure it out. The web had informed me the other tow companies in town employed only men. I would be the lone female. But I could do this. And I would do this. And if I kept at it, would the *moola* roll in?

Yes, I told myself. Whoot! Whoot!

Kristen said something similar over drinks at the Ale House, one of our favorite hangouts known for craft beers and better-than-average bar food. The interior had a trendier tone than the cabin-like exterior. A long counter crowded with pour handles took up the left side of the room, gray-stained concrete made up the floor, and scattered square tables filled up the rest of the space. All four walls displayed glossy photographs of the Rocky Mountains in every season.

"Here's to success." Kristen clinked her glass with mine. "You're a hard worker, Delaney. You'll make this happen."

I took a big swig of my super-hopped IPA, then said, "Right on, sister." I hooked my jade stilettos over the stool's bottom rung and leaned in. I'd changed into the green heels because green meant new growth and renewal. New beginnings. A clean slate.

My cell phone rang with an unfamiliar number and I gave my friend an apologetic look.

"Go ahead and take it." Kristen sipped from her glass of soda.

A man's voice came over the other end. "Hello, Delaney, I'm Tanner Utley. I got your name from Byron. Can you meet me right away?"

"Who did you say?"

"Tanner. Byron gave me your name. Byron Oberly. Maybe I have the wrong number. Is this Delaney?"

"Yes." *Duh, hello? Earth to me.* "I just didn't expect you to call so soon."

"Well, I have a job right now. If you want to see how it's done, get over to 913 Third Street. Bring your self-loader."

His words yanked my heart into my throat, but I croaked out, "Okay. I'm coming," and flashed Kristen a look of fear. All my bravado had gone out the door. Was I ready? I hadn't even taken the truck out for a test drive.

She mouthed, "*Whaaaat?*"

"He hung up." I tossed my phone into my purse and slid off the stool before I could talk myself out of it. It was now or never. "I'm sorry we just got here, but I need to get my dad's tow truck and meet this guy on Third Street."

Kristen set down her glass. "Right. Let's go."

"You don't have to come."

"I drove you here, remember?"

"Oh, yeah. I'm a little flustered."

We buckled ourselves into her car and ten minutes later arrived at my dad's old autobody shop, now Byron's. Kristen said, "You go, girl," before she took off.

I fished the keys out of my purse, unlocked Dad's truck, and hoisted myself inside for the first time. The upholstery felt hard and stiff. The cab smelled like engine oil and dust and the normal truck-odor of diesel exhaust. A fleeting thought went through my mind that my dad had sat in this same seat, breathed in this same scent. I inserted the key in the ignition, adjusted the mirrors, and pinched myself to get going. But it took another minute to determine how to release the parking brake. A foot lever on the floor of the cab in case you wondered.

The engine rumbled with an irregular hum, a low moan with an occasional ting, and I was off. The steering wheel felt gigantic in my hands and the hood seemed to stretch out for a mile. Good thing I was in such a hurry I had the green stilettos on my feet because the extra inches helped me reach the pedals.

Once on Third Street, I glanced around but did not see another tow truck. I did spot a cute guy about my age in front of a closed garage in the alley. Tall—somewhere over six feet—slender, dark blond hair, and heavily tattooed arms. Muscles, too, straining against his short-sleeved tee-shirt. Hotter than hot. Doubtless, he spent hours at the gym, unlike me. He gave me a wave. *Moi?*

I wound the window down. Normally I wouldn't

let a guy chat me up on the street like this, but did I mention he was hot? No harm in just talking to him. Right?

"Hi." My voice came out loud and my cheeks blushed warmly.

Mr. Hot Guy bent forward to give me a closer look. Okay, I preened a little, glad I'd let my hair out of the braid before going to the Ale House. In the plait, I appeared to be about twelve. Released from the clasp, my naturally wavy red hair fell in corkscrews to the middle of my back. Kristen insisted my Irish hair was my best feature, although I longed for her straight brown hair and the dark eyebrows that complemented her steel-gray eyes. My eyes were hazel, neither green nor brown nor gray, and my brows were pale, darn it. And, worst of all, I hadn't taken a shower because I'd been drawn into the *YouTube* video. Did I stink like coffee? *Please, no.*

"Delaney?"

I tossed my curls over my shoulder and shot a pale eyebrow skyward. "How'd you know my name?" I'd never met him before. I'd remember if I had.

"I'm going to show you how to operate this rig you're driving." He wrenched open the driver's side door. "I'm Tanner."

"Oh—" I began to say, dropping my feet to the pavement.

"You're wearing high heels?" He laughed, taking in my skinny jeans and soft green, fitted shirt along with my shoes. "You'll never make it in the business dressed like this." His smile changed his face from serious to playful, with a hint of sexy.

My breath lodged in my throat and my cheeks

pinked up even more.

A police cruiser turned into the alley. The officer spoke into his cop-mic as he exited the patrol car. Another handsome dude, in his thirties with a handlebar mustache, strong chin, and short, prematurely salt-and-pepper hair. *Wow.* What were the chances of meeting two hunks in one night? Especially when I was single again. My jerk of an ex-boyfriend broke up with me just in time. *Heh, heh.*

Tanner rapped his knuckles on the truck roof. “Well, come on. Don’t want to keep the officer waiting.”

“What’s the cop doing here?”

“I’m going to repossess the car in that garage.” Tanner swung his left hand in the direction of the building. No ring. Not married. “To do that, I need the police to break the lock. I have the signed court order right here. I’d better give these papers to him. Go ahead and turn the truck around and back it into the alley.”

He made long strides over to the officer in the tan uniform and handed him a thin, manila envelope, while I pulled myself back up into the cab and readjusted the mirrors.

Note to self—bring along work shoes next time.

Executing a three-point turn around was not easy on this narrow, tree-lined street with this bulky tow truck, let me tell you. When I crunched the back end into a telephone pole, the cop’s head shot up, and when I scraped the same pole again with a small shriek of metal, both handsome men stared at me. I gripped the wheel tighter and gazed straight ahead, trying not to shake. This was going to take some practice. After one more attempt, I had the truck in position.

Officer Mustache nodded at Mr. Hot Tow Guy, then pulled a crowbar out of his backseat. Tanner hurried to my driver's door and motioned for me to move over. "I'll load the car this time and you can watch."

I scooted across the bench and Tanner got in. When the cop approached the garage, I leaned in toward Tanner for a better view. I swear that's the reason our heads were close together. Heat radiated off his body and I could smell his aftershave. I hoped he didn't get a whiff of the beer on my breath or the coffee aroma that followed me everywhere. I only had a sip or two of my IPA, but I swallowed convulsively and wished I had some peppermint gum.

Tanner took his gaze off the officer and turned in my direction. "Working around heavy equipment with long hair can be dangerous. You might want to pull it back." His voice sounded husky, a low whisper. I ran my fingers through my hair self-consciously.

The loud snap of the crowbar drew our eyes back to the mustached policeman. The overhead door furled upward with a grinding sound, revealing an indigo blue sedan. Pretty color. My ex-boyfriend had a car in that same color.

"Stay here, I'll be right back."

I peered out the rear window while he and the officer shined a flashlight through the car's windshield onto the dash. The cop consulted the paperwork from the envelope and they appeared to agree about something. Then the policeman returned to his patrol car, exited the alley, and drove off.

Tanner sprang back into my dad's truck. He pushed some buttons on a yellow box I hadn't noticed hanging out from under the dashboard. The truck gave an almost imperceptible sway and another of its moans and tings, and the rear of the car rose into the air.

How in the world did that happen by a push of a button?

Tanner said, "Turn around and put your seat belt on. We gotta get outta here."

I clamped on the belt faster than pulling a shot of espresso, and we flew down the road, tugging the indigo blue vehicle behind us. "I didn't see how you did that. And why are we in such a hurry?"

"If you're going to do any repos or snatches from towaway zones, which I presume you are with a self-loader, you need to be fast. Drive it like you stole it because that's what we do in the repo business." He shot me a glance. "Are you sure you want to do this? Some people can be real hotheads. Can you protect yourself?"

"Sure." *Uh, no. Not really.*

"Do you have pepper spray?"

"Do I need that?" I did have a tiny canister of mace somewhere, but it was old, and chances are, expired. "Can't I just call the police? You had the cops here."

"I only involve the cops when I need to break into a garage. If you want the respect of law enforcement you need to rely on yourself for protection. You won't get any city contracts or calls for accidents if you can't take care of yourself." He slowed down after turning onto Fifth Street. "I'll show you how it's done when we get to the yard."

I sat forward but darted a glance his way. What did he mean by "showing me how it's done?" Was that flirtatious? Does he think I'm cute? Or is he just helping me as a favor to Byron Oberly?

Tanner's lot was only a few blocks from my dad's autobody shop. We entered through a motorized gate cut into a six-foot chain-link fence capped with razor wire. After the barrier shut behind us, we both thrust open our doors and got out. I was glad he couldn't see my heels sinking into the gravel. This outfit seemed fabulous at the Ale House, but the green stilettos started to worry me now. I didn't want to break a heel.

I joined Mr. Hot Tow Guy at the back of the truck. The giant metal crossbar extended out from the truck bed all the way under the car, lifting the back tires high in the air. The front tires rested on the ground. A tow rig without a hook. *Amazing!*

Tanner explained, "This here is the recovery boom assembly. The arm is hydraulically powered and operates the wheel cradles, that is, the claws."

"Claws?" That was the only word I picked up on.

"See the arms on the wheel lift? The lifting pad? Those are called claws."

I stared hard at the machinery, determined to take it all in. "The curved rods wrapped around the car's tires?"

"Correct."

I got something right. He operated the remote to lower what I think was the boom, and the metal whined with the effort. The rear tires hit the ground with a soft *pumpf*, the claw-like things retracted, and the crossbar folded back onto the truck bed with a final squeak.

I grabbed Tanner's hard, muscled arm. "Oh, my God."

"What is it? Are you okay?" He steadied my elbow and a shiver went up my back.

"It's like a giant robot. Something out of the future." My nose bloomed bright red, I know, and my voice sounded excited. "That is *soooo* cool." And it seemed *soooo* easy.

His head tilted and his jaw set sideways. "I've got to leave for another job, so I don't have time to show you more tonight."

"Can we get together tomorrow?" I hoped I didn't sound like I was trying to arrange an actual date or something, although if he wanted to take it that way, fine by me.

He paused before answering, "Sure. I'll give you a call."

Having this easy-on-the-eyes man showing me the ropes was going to make the towing business more fun than I'd imagined. I swear I saw some interest in his eyes, but something was confusing…and hard to read. Not all married men wore wedding rings, especially those who worked with heavy equipment, so maybe he was married after all.

I levered myself up into the truck cab and managed to drive out of Tanner's lot without hitting the chain-link fence. Clutching the wheel in a death grip, I somehow made it to my apartment. Kristen wouldn't want me to leave this heavy work truck behind the coffee shop, but this once wouldn't hurt.

It had been a long day, so I scrubbed my face and changed into sweats. I poured myself a Belgium IPA because it was time to celebrate—I had no more than two sips of my ale earlier, okay?—and I'm a tow truck driver now. I'd already towed a car. *Yippee!* This was totally going to work out for me. Watch out world, here I come…Delaney, badass tow truck driver.

I'd just danced over to the couch to plop myself down when the doorbell rang.

The handsome cop with the big chin and handlebar mustache stood at the door. He was the one who'd helped Tanner break into the garage. "Delaney Morran?"

"Yes?"

"Remember me? Officer Bowers."

"Yes. What can I do for you?"

"A body was discovered in the trunk of that Dodge Challenger you towed."

You weren't expecting that were you? Neither was I.

Chapter 2

The ground had been snatched out from under me, and I had an up-side-down, light-headed moment. I steadied myself with one hand on the door frame.

"Do you know Jeremy Winslow?" The officer examined my face.

I glanced up from his handlebar mustache. "He was my boyfriend."

"When did you see him last?"

"Why are you asking me about Jeremy?" My eyes went to the trash can under the sink where I'd tossed the pictures of the person in question. The dead guy couldn't be my ex. *No. No, no!* I refused to believe it.

"The body's been identified. It's Winslow."

"What? Are you positive it's him?" I know that was a stupid question, but my thoughts whirled around like the whisk in a milk frother.

Officer Bowers said, "It's him."

Tears burned behind my eyes and a sob materialized in my chest and surged up my throat. Jeremy was dead.

"I need to take you to the police station for questioning." Officer Bowers rested one hand on his belt near his gun and handcuffs. "And we need your permission to search the truck and your apartment. If you'd like to wait for the search warrant, it's on its way now."

Words failed me, so I shook my head and handed over the keys. I descended the steps on shaky legs. Two patrol cars with flashing lights blocked the tow truck and uniformed officers clustered around the parking lot. Officer Bowers gave a nod to one of the cops who escorted me into the back of a police cruiser. As the cruiser turned onto the street, a shadow at the window of Kristen's apartment told me she was as perplexed as I was.

Once I was seated in the interrogation room, a different officer gave me a stern glare and took the opposite chair. The air filled with power and control, all on his side of the table.

He introduced himself, Officer York, and asked, "When was the last time you saw Jeremy Winslow?"

The last time was easy to remember, as was the first. Jeremy and I met at the coffee shop. Good-looking, not tall at five-ten but wiry and athletic, he wore a shaggy haircut and the stubble type of beard that's in style. He'd flirted with me for a long time before asking me out. He loved to take me dancing, and he didn't mind tagging along for shoe shopping, but then we were still in the throes of a new relationship. He seemed a decent guy, that is until he gave me the "we need to talk" talk. Now I thought him a coward. He'd broken up with me at the coffee shop, a public place guaranteeing I wouldn't make a scene. *As if*. He didn't know me well because I would *never*. That was the last time I saw him, one I wouldn't soon forget.

Officer York said, "Hey, I'm talking to you. When did you see him last?"

"We broke up two weeks ago." Somewhere in the back of my mind, I questioned whether I needed a lawyer. I knew an attorney I could call, but should I? *Nah.* The police would quickly decide I had nothing to do with this, and I'd be out of here.

"How long did you know Winslow?"

"We dated a little over two months. I'd met him a few weeks before that, so three months?" I ended on a high note. "Can you tell me how Jeremy died?"

"A blow to the head." Officer York's eyes bored into mine without breaking contact.

Pain fisted my stomach into a knot. "So, it was deliberate." Of course, it was murder. The fact that someone had hidden his body in the trunk confirmed that. I swallowed hard and rubbed a palm across my belly, and that's when I noticed my hands shaking.

The officer asked, "Is anything missing from your tow truck?"

"How would I know? I just got it today."

Note to self—go through the stuff in the tow truck.

"Are you left or righthanded?"

"Righthanded. Why?"

"Wait here. I'll be back in a few minutes."

The interrogation room held a scratched iron table, cold metal chairs, and ugly gray walls. No windows. The place smelled stale and sweaty, and I covered my nose. My breath felt trapped and my chest heaved as I started to cry. I couldn't help it. I didn't love Jeremy. I was even mad at the jerk, but no one deserved having his head bashed in and being thrown into the trunk of a car.

Officer York returned and stood looming over me. I dabbed a sleeve to my cheek to hide my tears, but I'm certain he noticed. "Did you and Mr. Utley have the body stashed in the tow truck, then move it to

Winslow's car after Officer Bowers left the scene?"

I drew in a ragged breath. "That was Jeremy's car?" *I know, I know*, I should've recognized the car.

"Yes." He glanced at me as if to say, *what a dummy*. "You wanted to get rid of your boyfriend to make way for Tanner Utley, was that it?"

I threw my hands in the air. "Jeremy and I had broken up. And besides, I just met Tanner tonight."

He tapped his forefinger on the metal table. "Officer Bowers didn't think it appeared that way." His voice had an accusatory tone. "You and Mr. Utley thought the body wouldn't be found for months, not until the car sold at auction."

Fear fueled me now. "I have no idea how Jeremy ended up in the trunk of his own car. I had nothing to do with his death. I want an attorney." Yep, time to call Will.

The officer kept his expression stony, but his hands clenched and unclenched. I'd played the *right-to-remain-silent* card. He said, "No need for that. I don't have any more questions at present. You can leave after providing your fingerprints."

I may know less than nothing about cars or trucks, but I knew that being allowed to leave meant the police didn't have enough evidence to hold me, and I couldn't get out of there fast enough. He led me out of the interrogation room and handed me off to a polite clerk who explained the digital fingerprinting process and settled me down with small talk.

When that was done and my keys returned, I spotted Tanner in the hall. We eyeballed each other. I didn't give him the sweet eye this time, and he definitely gave me the stink eye.

A police car had taken me to the station, but no one offered to drive me home. I was stranded at two in the morning. *Shit, it was late*. And I had to be at work at five.

Should I get a cab? Before now, I'd never had to phone for a taxi in this poky little town. Even if I could find a cab company, how long would it take for one to show up? Or, should I call Kristen? It sucked, but wouldn't be the first time I'd called my friend in the small hours of the night to come and get me—once before when I'd been caught drinking underage in high school. Another story for another time. I could count on Kristen, the dependable and mature one. So, I punched in her number, then watched from the front steps of the old precinct building until her Prius pulled up to the curb. She yanked open her door, put one foot out and half stood, gazing at me with rounded eyes over the roof of her car. I ran over and jerked the passenger door open.

She eased back into the driver's seat. "What in the world is going on, Delaney? The cops were all over your dad's tow truck."

I told her the awful truth. Jeremy, a murder victim. Me, a suspect.

There were now two deaths in a couple of weeks to come to terms with. Dad and now Jeremy. The double blow gripped me in the gut, and it was hard to take in. Bad things came in threes. What would surface next? I know, my arrest.

Suddenly, everything closed in on me and I sobbed in earnest. My friend patted my hand and let me get my cry on.

After I took one last gulp of brisk air, Kristen

started up the car. "Let's get you home." She steered south onto Pine Street. "I know you're hurting now, but God allows these things to happen for a reason."

I asked, "And what would that be?"

"To draw you nearer to Him."

Ha. Fat chance of that. I was a little miffed at God. *Lightning please don't strike me down.* I knew my friend would pray about the situation, and hypocrite that I am, I felt comforted.

By the time we got home, Dad's tow truck was the lone vehicle behind the coffee shop. The police were gone. The night had taken over. Kristen parked and we both got out. She reached the stairs first, and I almost stepped on the backs of her shoes I was so frantic to keep up. The idea that there was a killer on the loose in Spruce Ridge made prickles of alarm run up my spine.

I fumbled with my apartment key, got the door open, and pulled my friend inside with me. Together we turned on all the lights and inspected the closets and under the bed. The police had rifled through my clothes and tossed the sofa pillows into a pile. I offered to go with Kristen into her apartment across the landing from mine, but she wasn't the scared one. No, she flung open her door and boldly entered in. As for me, only after every light blazed was I able to sleep, the electric bill be damned.

I was always afraid of the dark.

****

Kristen banged on my door before sunrise the next morning on her way down the stairs. Five a.m., time to get to work.

The English Lit major, who was the new guy, had come in for training, and his name was actually Guy, easy to remember. Six years younger than us, he thought we were the old gals. Kristen had listed the opening tasks on laminated sheets, which hung in the back room, but I had the chores memorized the same as my boss did. Kristen assigned Guy the duty of refilling the cups, lids, napkins, straws, raw cane sugars, and organic creamers since we didn't bother to stock at night. That was always a job for opening, along with counting inventory to place more orders for product. So, after Kristen took inventory, she started roasting the beans and I began brewing the large urns of coffee.

I had trouble concentrating and kept glancing at the door, afraid the police would show up with more questions or a warrant for my arrest.

Once the bakery down the street delivered muffins and croissants, we arranged them in the display case. Two colossal steel pots simmered with hot coffee. Flavorings and cups waited next to the cash register. Ready for business, we had extra time to spare before opening. Guy studied for school in the backroom, while Kristen and I took a break out front to eat chocolate chip muffins and drink vanilla lattes. Once we opened there would be no time for breaks for a while.

"How'd you sleep last night?" she asked me.

"I didn't." I yawned, my chin practically hitting my chest.

"Me either, not much anyway, after we got home from the police station."

"Yeah, thanks again for picking me up." My eyes skimmed the parking lot out the window over Kristen's shoulder, but the lot was empty. What a relief, no cop cars.

Sierra swept in through the back door. Her bright

pink hair hurt my eyes at this early hour. She waved at us with her usual happy smile, donned her apron, and went over to interrupt Guy's studies. Good, they were both occupied. Kristen and I could discuss the *police-showing-up slash dead-body-found* dilemma without an audience.

She said in her quiet, calm voice, "The police will get to the bottom of this. They'll find the killer." I just nodded. She mentioned a few Bible verses she knew by heart, and some other uplifting kinds of things, then asked, "Are you feeling a little bit better now?"

I picked at my muffin. "Sure." *When pigs fly.*

Guy pivoted the "Closed" sign to "Open" and the first customers arrived, so we rose from the table. It was April, mud season, the rainy time between the end of winter sports and the beginning of summer tourism, and people were on their way to the ski slopes for a final spring run. We always brushed up on the snow report and slope conditions so we could chat with them, but I couldn't work up much enthusiasm this morning.

At noon, Kristen said to me, "Go on home. You seem beat."

My comfortable bed called to me, but I said, "You sure? You're tired too."

"No, go on. I'm going to train Guy on closing."

"All right." I didn't have to be told twice. When I got upstairs, I crawled under the covers, fully clothed and all. To heck with brushing my teeth.

At three in the afternoon, I woke up to my cell buzzing with a text message from Tanner.

—We need to meet.—

I'd been so busy dreading the police showing up, I hadn't given a thought to Mr. Hot Tow Guy. Awkward would not begin to describe the situation, but I texted him my address and dove into the shower.

One thing about curly hair, you can't brush it when it's dry or the curls turn to frizz. It needs to be combed when wet, so while under the water, I applied a palmful of conditioner and ran a wide-tooth comb down its length. After rinsing, I stepped out and pressed a towel against the dripping strands. I can't braid it when it's damp, either, or it gets big and clown-like, but if it's dry when braided, the corkscrews turn into soft waves. So, while I let my curls air-dry, I scrambled into a pair of skinny jeans, a tee-shirt, and black high-top tennis shoes with white shoelaces. I felt marginally better.

By the time Tanner rang my doorbell, I'd swiped on some mascara, but my hair was not yet in the braid. Oh, well, nothing I could do about it. After I opened the door, he motioned for me to follow. He clattered down the stairs and I took off after him. When we got to the parking lot, we both examined each other with narrowed eyes and hands on hips.

He said, "What the hell, Delaney?" His voice came out full of anger. "Did you and Byron set me up to take the fall for that dead guy?"

I expected more of a kindred spirit, but this *godawful* experience we'd shared had not brought us together. I'm sure my freckles blazed darker and my cheeks glowed red as they always did when I was put on the spot. "Of course not. Besides, I just met Byron. He didn't even know Jeremy was my boyfriend. My ex-boyfriend, I mean, and that's not because he's dead. My question to you is, did you and Byron set me up?"

His shoulders slumped. "No. I had no idea Jeremy was your boyfriend."

I swatted the air and said, "Ex. Ex, ex, ex," then I pinned him with a scowl. "Did you know Jeremy?"

"Yeah. But last night he was only a name on a court order to me." Tanner shook his blond head in an irritated way. "I didn't remember him until the police questioned me."

"It's a bizarre coincidence that you towed Jeremy's vehicle."

He leveled a finger in my direction. "You were the one who towed his vehicle, it was your tow truck. You had to recognize his Challenger with the spoiler on the back in that blue color."

"I didn't know it was his. I thought it was a car like his. All those muscle cars look the same." I started to tear up, so I glanced away. "I never even heard of a Challenger. Is that like a Camaro? That's what I thought he drove."

His hard expression softened a little. "A Challenger is a Dodge and a Camaro is a Chevy. You don't even have the right manufacturer."

Huffing out a deep breath of air, I said, "I knew the name of the color, indigo. Bet you didn't know that." I tugged my still damp hair into three sections and whisked the bunches over and under, twisting the strands into a single plait. Damn the curly hair rules. My restless hands needed something to do. Tanner gave me a wide-eyed stare while I secured the end of the braid with the band I had on my wrist.

We weren't getting anywhere, so I said, "I thought you came by to give me some pointers. Can you at least show me how to hook up the robot thing?"

He seemed to be considering me and I scrutinized him, too. Incredibly fit, his muscled arms and shoulders were likely the result of hard physical labor. He appeared the competent, self-assured type, serious about his job. I could tell his brain was working, peering through me right down to the soles of my shoes, while he tried to make a decision.

I probably needed more training than he was willing to give. He wouldn't want to waste time on someone like me.

Plus, to him I was a murder suspect.

He stared off while I held my breath, then he said, "All right, let's do this."

I made my fingers stop fidgeting. "That'd be great, Tanner."

He trudged over to the truck cab and returned with the yellow controller. "Here are the basics."

I stepped closer to take it all in.

He explained, "This Fulcan self-loader has an integrated lift. That's a wheel-lift system controlled hydraulically from inside so there's no need to get out of the cab. But you can get out because this device is wireless. It operates the tow boom, which lifts the drive wheels off the ground, and allows the tow truck to pull the target vehicle." He tapped the controller, and the T-bar lowered to the pavement. "See how that long arm extends out?"

"I do."

He hit a button and the T-bar released two curved, metal rods like pinchers on a gigantic bug. "The claws slide under the car and capture the tires."

I nodded as if I understood completely. "I remember the claws."

"Now, once the claws are around the tires, you engage the hydraulics to raise the car. If you're towing a front-wheel drive, load from the front, if it's a back-wheel, load from the rear. If all-wheel or four-wheel, you need to use tow dollies on the set of tires not captured in the claws so all four tires are raised. A lot of cars and SUVs are all-wheel drive. You'll be using the dollies all the time. Got that?"

"Yes." *Oh my God, I hope I remember even half of this*. "Can you show me with my car? It's the little silver Fiat."

"That's front-wheel." He started toward the tow truck, then turned back to face me. "How do you get around in that subcompact during the winter?"

"Piece of cake." Spruce Ridge did get snow, but not as much as the ski resorts at the higher elevations. However, I'd just bought the used Fiat 500, a cute Italian job similar in size to a Smart Car, and didn't know how it might perform in winter conditions. Why think about that in April?

Tanner piled into the truck cab while I got out of the way. He reversed in front of my Fiat, and I watched from the side as the self-loader performed its magic and raised the toy-like car with no effort. He spoke through the open window, "Did you see how the tow boom lifted the car and the front wheels came off the ground? You did see that, right?"

"Yeah, I got that."

He threw a glance at me like he wasn't sure I did.

I asked, "How do you know if it's front or back-wheel or four-wheel or whatever?"

His eyebrows shot up, I assumed at my lack of vehicular knowledge, and I cringed a little. He said, "If you know your makes and models, you'll know. But if it's a car you're not familiar with, then the VIN will indicate FW, RW, 4W."

I gazed up at him from the other side of the truck door. "Vehicle Identification Number?"

"Right."

Since I wasn't too knowledgeable about makes and models, I'd better learn what I could about VINs. "Where do I find the VIN?"

Tanner lowered the Fiat to the pavement, got out of the truck, and walked me back. He pointed through the Fiat's front windshield to a metal strip with a string of numbers and letters. "See that?"

I stood on my tip-toes. "Huh. I never noticed that before."

"Well, the VIN can be under the hood, inside the driver's door, in the rear wheel well. But, you should be able to find it on the dash. Always make a note of the number for your records. And if you're doing a repo, you'll have the paperwork from the finance company with the VIN. You need to verify that the VIN in the vehicle is the same as what's on the form. Be sure to do that. You don't want to snatch the wrong car." He chuckled, presumably at the thought of such an incompetent tower.

That would be me, but I barked out a laugh as if I agreed. I hadn't even thought of doing repo work before now. I'd pictured a stranded motorist on the side of the road, anxious and happy to see me arrive to save the day.

Not breaking into garages and stealing cars. What was I getting into?

Chapter 3

Tanner slapped the back of one hand against the palm of his other in a listen-up gesture.

I had no idea what he'd just said, something about bypassing brakes and locks.

Why wasn't I taking notes? Would he make fun of me if I ran upstairs to get a notebook and asked him to repeat all of that so I could write it down?

"Another tip. If the police aren't involved in the recovery, call them and let them know you've taken the vehicle, otherwise the owner could report it stolen and waste a lot of police time."

"Of course I'd do that." Now that I knew to do that. "Tell me again why you pull the car from the front?"

"With the vehicle in park on a front-wheel drive, the drive shaft locks the front wheels so they can't move. When you begin your tow the tires won't roll, they will skid along the ground and the transmission can suffer damage. If you lift the front wheels in the claws, the back wheels will roll. Just the opposite with rear-wheel drive. With all-wheel and four-wheel drive, all the wheels are locked so all the tires must be lifted, and that's when you need to use the dolly wheels."

I dare say my eyes were as glazed over as a Creamy Deluxe donut. This was getting boring now. "Can't I ask the driver to let off the parking brake and put the car in neutral?"

"Never count on being able to get inside the vehicle."

"You're talking about towing without the owner present?"

"Right. Vehicle recovery, like repo." He nudged the controller into my hands. "Now you do it."

We packed ourselves into the truck, me in the driver's seat this time, then Tanner pointed out which buttons to push on the wireless device. I hit the button…*presto, changeo*…the miracle claws swooped down with that metallic groan and lifted my silver compact into the air once more. I shifted into drive and pressed the gas. We towed my car around the parking lot, the car's front end raised, the back end rolling along behind us like a suitcase on wheels. Tanner explained how to back up with the car in-tow, how to use the side mirrors, and how to release the car, and then he watched as I maneuvered around a few times. I only jackknifed the Fiat twice before Tanner gave up on me.

"I'll practice backing up," I promised.

Tanner opened the cab door. "One more thing. Yours is a lightweight self-loader. You can haul up to seventy-five hundred pounds. That's just about every sedan, SUV, and light pickup. Some heavy-duty pickups are too large for you to haul. No commercial vehicles, semis, work trucks, school buses, RVs, stuff like that. But, you know, ninety-five percent of tows are lightweight. Don't forget to attach the tow lights to the target vehicle and use your LED bar whenever you're working on the side of the road. And wear a safety vest. There's one in your rig somewhere."

"Oh, sure." That was a lot to remember. Drive wheels, side mirrors, weights, limits, lights…

He glanced at his phone. “I have to get back to work, so I’ll catch you later.”

“Thanks, Tanner. I really, really appreciate all this.”

“Glad to do it.” He extracted his keys from his pocket but didn’t make a move toward his car. He didn’t seem in a big hurry to get away from me, a wacko murder suspect. He might even be reluctant to leave. I wish he wasn’t so hard to read.

“Could I ask, uh, for one more thing?” My face, I’m sure, betrayed me by turning red. “Could I do a ride-along? You know, to get more experience. Byron said you’d help me out,” I reminded him.

He shifted from foot to foot. “That’s not a bad idea.”

Relieved, I slumped against the truck. “Tanner, I didn’t have anything to do with Jeremy’s death. Honestly. It was just a coincidence we both knew the guy.” I put on my brightest smile. “Something for the weird files, right?”

“I don’t think cops believe in coincidences, and I’m sure we haven’t heard the end of it.” He stared down at me from his six-foot-plus height. “Call me to arrange the ride-along. Good luck, Delaney. You’re going to need it.” He angled himself into his black sedan, I had no idea what make or model, and drove off.

Note to self—pay attention to the types of cars on the road. To me, that would be like following football scores, but I had to do it if I was going to learn the towing business.

I struggled to keep my hopes up. As he’d said, I needed luck. That, and somebody who knew what they were doing, someone like Tanner, to tell me where to go from here. And the police to find the killer so I could learn the business without an unsolved murder hanging over me.

I hooked my car up once more using the controller and the claws. Clenching the steering wheel with white knuckles, casting glances at the rearview mirror, I towed the Fiat to Dad's old autobody shop, now Byron's. I wanted to get comfortable driving the truck on city streets with a tow on the back, and I had a long way to go with that.

When I turned into the lot, Byron came outside, wiping his hands on a faded red rag, so I powered down my window. He asked in his deep, rich voice, "You already have a tow?"

"Nah, this is my car." After shifting the gear into park, I took my toes off the brake.

"You forgot to turn on the light bar. Ya' need to do that to be street legal."

"Oops. Okay, I'll remember next time. I have a favor to ask." I squirmed in my seat. Another favor. Soon, I would run out of people to ask for help. "Can I leave the truck here when I'm not out on any jobs? I can't keep it at my apartment."

"You can use the back lot. Park facing Fifth Avenue and folks will see your truck when they drive by. Good advertisement for ya'."

"Thanks, Byron. I met with Tanner Utley last night for my first towing lesson. And this afternoon, too."

Byron jammed his red rag into his overall's pocket. "What? You were with Tanner when that went down?"

"You heard what happened?" Probably everyone in town was aware.

"Yeah. Poor Winslow got himself killed."

I turned off the engine and alighted from the truck. "It was awful. The police questioned me for hours, but I had no idea I'd towed his car. It was just a freakin' coincidence." I believed it, even if the cops didn't.

His lips turned down in a grimace. "That's a real shame. I feel bad you got caught up in that."

"Not your fault. I'm glad Tanner is helping me."

"He treatin' you okay?"

"He's been great."

A young girl in her teens pulled up in a yellow VW Beetle, a newer model with the original round design, and got out. She completed the vintage effect with oversized cat-eye sunglasses in green to match her sweater. Her layered light brown hair framed her face, and black running shoes peeped out from under her flared jeans. "Hey, Old Man," she yelled at Byron.

His face lit up. He waved her over and said to me, "This is my niece, Shannon."

I said, "Nice to meet you. I'm Delaney."

"The Old Man told me about you." Shannon gave Byron a one-armed hug around his thick waist.

"Old Man?" I asked her.

"That's what me and my cousins call him." She glanced up at her uncle. "My car's making funny noises."

"Let's take a look."

I said, "I'll talk to you later," and clambered back into the truck cab. The two walked over to the yellow Beetle, so I steered the self-loader behind the autobody shop. In an empty corner, I lowered my Fiat from the claws, the metal bars squealing, and blew out a sigh of relief that my car had arrived in one piece. I locked the truck and got into the Fiat, which started up with a turn of the key. I sped out of the lot because I wanted to see my stepdad at his office before the end of the day and Denver was an hour's drive east.

Once on the highway, it hit me that both Tanner and Byron had known Jeremy. I wasn't the only one. But, after all, Spruce Ridge is a small town.

****

Will Sharpton was average in every way, a capable lawyer who'd made partner, and a passable stepdad, who made my mother happy. He worked at a mediocre firm that handled family law, bankruptcy, traffic violations, and worker's compensation cases. I was often a tad cool toward my stepdad, a stubborn childhood habit, but it was the best I could do.

Will made rapid strides out to the reception area, then led me to his office, a small room with an unexceptional view. "So, you picked up the tow truck." He gestured for me to take a seat.

It was nice to have an attorney in the family, I had to concede. I would've called Will last night if the police hadn't released me. Thank God they did, and I avoided that phone call. I wondered if Will had ever handled a criminal case. At least he knew about estates and stuff like that. He'd helped me read through the documents with the news of my inheritance. He had enlightened me by spelling out the probate process; now I needed to enlighten him by explaining how I was linked to a murder investigation. I got away with it the first time, but I might need Will if, or rather when, the police questioned me a second time.

"During a training exercise, I towed a vehicle that had a dead body in the trunk," I blurted out. "The dead guy was Jeremy and the police think I'm involved."

Will stared at me in open-mouthed astonishment. "Whoa. Start over." He picked up a pen to take notes, and his eyebrows shot up several times as I told the story. I left out the part about Tanner being so good-looking and I may have exaggerated about the police being so mean. After I finished talking Will kept scribbling on his notepad, then he finally put the pen down. He shoved his chin onto his hand and gave me a penetrating gaze.

I sat forward. "What were you writing?"

"A list of things to do. I'll contact the Spruce Ridge police and try to get more information. I always thought Jeremy was no good." My mom hadn't liked my ex-boyfriend, so Will didn't either. That they happened to be proven right didn't make me feel any better. Will said, "Tell me everything you know about him."

"It's not much. We didn't go out for all that long." Which was quite possibly a good thing. Jeremy hurt my feelings, tossing me aside like an empty to-go cup, but worse than that, he was wrapped up in something that had gotten him killed. I gave Will the little information I knew—Jeremy's address, his birthdate, and his workplace.

"What are the names of his friends?" Will gripped his pen.

"I can't remember." I hadn't met any of his buddies. Strange that, now I'd thought about it.

"Did you recognize the place where you picked up his car?"

"No. I'd never been there before. And, no, I didn't know it was his car, either."

"Call me if the police show up again. Don't let

them question you without me." He frowned. "You know I'll have to tell your mother."

My lips drew back of their own accord. "I know."

"Come over for dinner tonight."

Might as well get it over with. I tried to keep my voice enthused. "Sure, I'd love to." Mom would throw a hissy fit about my involvement in my former boyfriend's death, but would be distracted from her usual drill. *Are you dating anyone new? When are you moving back to Denver? Why aren't you using your degree?* Her questions always caused me to put on a vacant stare.

"Now about this venture." He opened a file folder with my name written across the top.

"What do I need to do?" I urged my chair in and leaned my elbows on the edge of his desk. "I tried searching the internet for how to manage a towing company, but I'd rather have you explain it."

"Running your own business is complicated. Are you sure you're up for it?"

"That would be a yes." I made a forward motion with my hand. "Go ahead."

He held a sheet of paper against his chest like he wasn't sure he should give it to me.

I tore it out of his hands and read, "Number one, a towing carrier license. Number two, a commercial driving license." I glanced at Will. "What's with all this licensing?"

"A carrier license is required by the state." His mouth worked as if he was debating with himself. After a long pause, he said, "But you can take over Del's."

"How do I do that?"

"Phone the estate administrator and ask for the

transfer. I guess I can make that call." Then he perked up and added, "It's almost two-hundred dollars to convey the carrier license over to you," like that would decide the matter.

I clicked my tongue in a *tsk*. "That's not too expensive. Is there a waiting period…or?"

"You can work under your dad's license until it's converted over." He brushed a hand across his forehead. "I suppose we can have the business phone reassigned and the calls forwarded to your cell, too."

"Great. That'd be perfect. And I need a commercial driver's license?"

"A CDL. You go to the DMV for that. It's not required here for your lighter truck like it is for the long, heavier flatbeds, but it might be a good idea. Up to you."

I ran a finger over the next item. "Insurance?"

"Liability insurance, and it'll be *priceeey*." He drew out the word.

"Can I work under Dad's insurance for a while, too?"

He gave a reluctant nod. "But you'll need to purchase a policy soon. And I'll set up a limited liability company for you, an LLC." His expression changed to hopeful. "Or, there is an alternative."

"What's that?" Anything to save expenses and make more money was fine by me.

"You can sell the truck. I found a half dozen for sale on the internet, a ten-year-old self-loader for twenty-five thousand and another for thirty thou. Those were in good shape. I haven't seen yours so I don't know if it's worth that much."

That was more than I made in a year as a barista.

"Delaney, as your attorney, I advise you to sell this truck."

Chapter 4

"Laney, sell the truck."

Mom stood at the back of my chair, massaging my shoulders, wearing her standard outfit of beige pants and a sweater set. Her blonde hair was styled in its usual short bob. I twisted around and noticed her expectant smile.

She said, "I don't know what Del was thinking about when he left you that vehicle. It makes no sense, but then he had no sense. Will agrees with me, don't you Will?" While Mom had plenty of negative things to say about my dad when he was alive, she never criticized Will.

My neck stiffened and I didn't respond. She was right about one thing, at least. Dad entrusting me with his self-loader didn't make sense. Del Morran had left me his name and his Irish red hair and now his tow truck, but no explanation. Not even any instructions. The man who fathered me was an enigma. My parents divorced when I was seven, and that's the last I'd seen of him. No weekend visitations, no summer breaks. He never taught me how to ride a bike or drive a car or any of that, as I imagined other dads did with their kids. Twenty-one years had passed with no contact until now. The letter I'd received about my inheritance from the estate attorney surprised me, too. Another surprise was the heavy feeling in my chest that I suspected was grief.

As I opened my mouth to retort, Mom dropped her hands from my shoulders and went to the kitchen, saving me the bother. She returned to the dining room with a steaming taco pie in a casserole dish. Hamburger, taco seasoning, refried beans, and crumbled tortilla chips, all smothered in melted cheese. *Yum.* I liked to cook, too, but never made the old-fashioned comfort food I allowed myself at Mother's.

Her transition to the next complaint was seamless. "And I knew that boyfriend of yours was trouble."

You would think the death of a boyfriend, an ex-boyfriend that is, would dampen my appetite, but no way. I spooned some casserole onto my plate. "We broke up already. I wasn't with him anymore." I didn't know why he ended our relationship; he'd never given me a reason.

Mom poured water into my glass. "He was mixed up in something. I just thank my lucky stars he didn't get you involved."

I couldn't agree more. I was caught up in Jeremy's death, though. When we were together, I hadn't a clue, but now I had to believe he'd been up to no good. Huh, I had the same opinion as Mom. Go figure.

Will said, "I can see about selling the truck, Delaney." He wanted to return to that subject. "A few of my clients are in the automotive business. I can call them, but we can't sell until we receive the clear title. I'll get busy on that."

Mom said, "It's about time you got back into social work. You're already off to a poor start with that tow truck."

My mother and stepdad were ganging up on me.

Same argument, different approach.

I sat back in my chair. If I sold the truck I could get a big chunk of change, but then I'd have to decide yet again what to do with my life.

Mom had reminded me many times that I was underemployed. Being a barista didn't require the college degree I'd earned in social work. *Yada, yada, yada*. But after working for the Department of Social Services for five years, I decided social work was not the career for me. The tender-hearted type, I teared up at every dire situation, of which there were too many. Those five years were hard ones, but I'd managed to stick with it long enough to build a savings account to live on while I helped Kristen open her coffee shop. My money was depleted now, and my barista job paid even less than social work.

My options seemed limited. I didn't want to use my degree anymore, I didn't want to work as a barista forever, and I didn't have any other ideas…until the tow truck fell into my lap. I'd made up my mind right away, I was going to make a living driving the truck even if I was the only female tow driver in town. The inheritance seemed like an omen, a clear sign pointing me in a new direction. I could be my own boss and help people who needed my services.

But it wasn't going how I expected. You know…the part where a body turned up on my first tow. My dead former boyfriend in the trunk.

I acknowledge I was off to a bad start. Yeah, it blows.

"Laney, are you listening?" Mom squeezed my elbow. "You have so much potential. Why drive a truck when you could be anything you want to be?"

I said, "I'm learning how to operate the rig already. I towed my car around today." Then I asked Will, "Once I get all that licensing stuff taken care of, can you help me set up the books? And I need to work out what to charge for a tow."

Will stopped chewing and took a drink of water. "There are state regulations that cap the charges for nonconsensual tows."

"Is there a website?" Hopefully, one that would explain what nonconsensual tows are.

"Yes. Everything is online now."

"Text me the link and I'll read the rules. And could you please ask that estate administrator if we can get Del's books? That way I can model mine after his."

He closed his eyes in obvious frustration. "All right, Delaney."

"Thanks, Will." I gave him a grateful smile and he let out a big sigh.

He said, "It'll take weeks to get the new title for the truck issued in your name. Maybe a month. You know how slow the State works. That'll give you time to think about selling, if that's what you decide."

Yeah, well, I had decided. I'm keeping the truck. I could do this. I would do this.

I was committed to seeing it through and I was anxious to get back to Spruce Ridge. I got up from the table and carried my dishes to the sink.

Mom made me promise to call her soon, to keep her in the loop, to make plans, and so forth and so on. Saying goodbye was always a long process with Mom. We embraced at the door, then again outside, on the front step of the house I grew up in, the beige and white two-story with low junipers under the bay window. The neighborhood had giant, gnarly cottonwoods, red maple trees, and green, long-needle pines. Snowball bushes held big, puffy white blooms, and lilacs displayed light purple flowers. At last, I pulled away from my childhood home in all its familiarity, and Mom watched me drive down the street.

I raced west on I-70, the mile posts ticking off the distance, until black skid marks flew under my car and I was past them. The moon lit up the white cross on the side of the road.

****

Just after noon the next day, Officer Bowers, with the salt-and-pepper hair and the handlebar mustache, walked through the door of the coffee shop. The cops! I went on the alert.

But he only said in a calm voice, “Hello, Delaney.” His hair was styled in a tall crew-cut on top and a short-buzz on the sides, and his strong chin jutted out.

“Hello, Officer Bowers.” I gave him an uncertain smile. What did the police want now? Was he here to arrest me?

Kristen came out from the backroom. “Zach, how are you? You want your usual?”

“Sure, Kris.” His smile was friendly and familiar.

I gazed between the two of them while they grinned at each other. I said, “I didn’t know you’re a regular customer, Officer.”

“I stop by just about every day. You don’t have to call me Officer. Call me Zach.” The name on his shirt read, Zachariah Bowers.

Kristen’s eyes darted to me. “Zach usually comes in at closing time.”

I inspected the ceiling. Oh. *Oh!* “I understand.” I

gave her a quick wink and she blushed guiltily. On most days I opened, not closed, so this interesting situation had evaded my detection before now. Relieved, I turned a full smile on him. "I didn't know you were a friend of Kristen's." Then I remembered how he'd searched my apartment and Dad's truck as if I were a common criminal. Plus, he'd told that mean policeman who'd questioned me, Officer York, that I was in a relationship with Tanner Utley. Which I wasn't. How did Zach decide that after seeing Tanner and me only once at the garage break-in, anyway?

He said, "I had no idea you and Kris knew each other, but when I showed up to search your place I figured you probably did, living above the coffee shop like you do."

"Kris and I are *good* friends. We've known each other for years." Longer than you have, I wanted to add, but he should be able to get that message all on his own.

He asked Kristen, "Do you have time for a quick break?"

She said, "Of course, let me check the bean roaster and I'll be right there."

"Can we talk?" I asked him. There were no customers in line at the moment and I had time for a break, too.

"That's fine." He cast a glance over his shoulder. "Maybe we could talk over there?"

I stopped to wash my hands at the sink and straighten my apron. As I came out from behind the checkout, I accidentally kicked the trash container, and the sound of reverberating metal blasted through the shop. Zach watched me from where he stood near the window, so I tried to calm my nerves as I made my way over.

He scraped back a chair for me to take a seat, then took his own. I leaned in, held my lips tight so that I couldn't be overheard, and asked. "Do you have news about Jeremy?"

"I can't talk about the investigation."

I ignored that. "Do the police have other suspects besides me?" I peered around to see if Guy was listening. He wasn't in sight, but the men at the next table gave me a curious inspection. They couldn't help notice the policeman wasn't here only for a free cup of java.

"Another thing I can't comment on. After today it will be out of the hands of the city police. The sheriff's office is taking control of the homicide investigation."

"Why's that?"

"The county is better equipped and we only have a small department. The county sheriffs always handle homicides."

This officer may not be in charge of the case, but he'd been part of the initial search and now was my chance to find out what he knew. "Officer York told me Jeremy died from a blow to the head?"

"That's right."

I waited but Zach didn't add anything. "York also asked me what was missing from the tow truck." I may not know much when it comes to cars, but I could put two-and-two together. *Hello!* My mind made the leap. "Was the murder weapon something from a tow truck?" I asked him.

Zach's eyes darted around the room, leading me to believe I was right. *Aha!* That wasn't hard to figure out.

But where did that leave me? Still the prime suspect since I owned a tow truck now. That thought made my heart skip, so I rubbed a place over my chest to get it to slow down. Maybe I should lay off the coffee.

"Come on, tell me. Do the police really think I did it?" I pressed for an answer.

The officer wet his lips and snapped his gaze away.

Kristen plopped a steaming cup in front of Zach. "Here you go." She took the chair next to him with her own drink. I gave my friend a wide-eyed look that said *yoo-hoo, I need some help here*. She asked, "Is everything okay?"

"Officer Zachariah Bowers, here, thinks I had something to do with Jeremy's death." Yes, I was whining, but my heart was still pounding.

"Zach, believe me, she's innocent." Kristen crossed her arms on the table and drew her dark eyebrows in.

"I never said that she wasn't." Zach's pleading eyes stared at Kristen. He finally glanced in my direction. "You know I didn't say that."

"You might as well admit it. I'm the primary suspect, right?" I asked. He looked down, not meeting my eyes. I bit my thumbnail. "So, what's on a tow rig that can be used to kill someone?"

Zach swallowed hard, as if caught in the headlights. "I told you I can't talk about an ongoing investigation."

I pointed out, "Even if it's not your investigation? It's in the sheriff's hands, you said."

Kristen added, "Come on, Zach, that's a pretty general question. Can't you help us? It's me asking."

Zach glanced at Kris. "Of course, there's dangerous equipment on a rig like that."

"Like tools?" I asked. Zach's mouth puckered as he looked around the café. What else could it be? Darn it, I should have looked in the truck. I brought a mental image of a tow truck to mind. "Okay, just nod if I'm right. How about chains?"

His eyes widened, then he set his cup down and stood. "I need to get back on the job. See you Sunday at church, Kris."

Kristen said, "See you then," and we both watched as he yanked open the door and almost ran into somebody entering as he tried to get out.

"You know him from church?" I asked.

"Yes. He's a good man." She gave me a tight smile. "The police can't really think you had anything to do with what happened. You'll see."

I had a bad feeling about this, so, no, I didn't see it that way. My thoughts raced like an engine in first gear. So, if I had to guess, I figure the murder weapon was some kind of chain, like one commonly found on a tow truck. What if…no, the chain couldn't actually be from my dad's self-loader. No. No, no, no. I chose my friend's way of denial and refused to consider that possibility.

Kris asked me, "Ready to get back to work?"

"Sure." I'd think more about this mess later. I walked Zach's empty cup to the kitchen and Kristen went for a rag to wipe the table.

When the afternoon lull arrived, I poked my head into Kristen's narrow workroom. "Do you need me anymore today?"

"No. Guy will help with closing." She pointed to the college student pushing around the mop bucket. He glanced up with a smug smile.

"How's he doing? Everything okay?" I raised one eyebrow as I slipped my feet into my black stilettos with bows. Black was for getting down to serious business. My tow business, next on my schedule for today.

Kristen gave Guy a thumbs up from across the room. "He told me he's been sober for forty-two days now. He even keeps track of the hours of his sobriety and says he hasn't missed one of his classes." My friend hired people who had trouble finding work. She's good like that.

I bumped my fist against Kristen's. "I'm glad. See you tomorrow."

I stabbed my apron into the laundry bin and left through the back door. Once outside, I breathed deeply of the dusty pine scent so prominent in the mountains and listened while birds chattered from the trees. Spruce Ridge was aptly named, a city nestled between thousands of pines, not only spruces, but bristlecones, lodgepoles, and piñons.

I slid behind the wheel of my car and read over Will's to-do list.

First up was the Department of Motor Vehicles, so I boogied across town to the county buildings. After standing in line for over an hour, I filled out paperwork, paid a fee, and sashayed out of there with a temporary commercial license good for six months. That was alarmingly easy. I questioned the safety of all the truck drivers on the road who only had a temporary license like mine, but likely their employers didn't allow them to drive unaccompanied on a temporary. I could drive solo because the CDL wasn't a requirement for my class of truck. I wanted the commercial license because that would give me the credentials to prove I could drive the rig. That way I hoped to feel a part of the male-dominated truck drivers club and not like the lone female tower in town. I had half a year to prepare for the test. Plenty of time.

Once I got home, I headed to my computer to locate the Public Utilities Commission's website for the tow carrier regulations. I scrolled to "Transportation" and opened "Rules and Laws" to a hundred-page document I would eventually need to read. One of the requirements jumped out at me. The license holder could not have a felony conviction. Murder was a felony. Did I need to worry about this? *No, just no*. The police would figure out who killed Jeremy.

Steady on, I told myself.

I studied the to-do list once more. The commercial driver's license was in the bag, so I ticked that off. The towing regulations I'd scanned online, another thing to cross off. Carrier license…that was pending. Insurance…Will would get back to me on that.

It would be so cool if I could get a tow job right off the bat. I'd tackled the list, now I'd love to find some work. I tapped my teeth with the pen, thinking hard, then hooked my purse over my shoulder and headed out. I drove five blocks to the finance company where I'd gotten the loan for my used Fiat 500.

The woman behind the desk in the stark office was a few years older than me, professional in a blue business suit and starched white button-down. Her short charcoal hair showcased her high cheekbones, eyes that tilted up at the corners, and lovely long eyelashes. Her mahogany skin was flawless.

"Hello, Hailey."

"Yes?" She gave me a vague frown. I remembered her, but she didn't recognize me.

"I own Del's Towing and I'm available for repo work. Do you need any help with that?" I wasn't sure I wanted repo work but had no idea where to get customers. This was my best, and so far, my only lead.

Her eyes gave me a sweep. "We've used the same driver for a long while now."

I took a wild guess. "Is it Tanner Utley?" This was a small community after all.

"Yes," she admitted. "Tanner is the top tow driver in town. He completes the capture faster than anyone."

Not above dropping names, I said, "He's a friend of mine. He took me with him on a job last night."

Her business-like smile slipped. "That recovery was one of ours. We found the body when we picked up the Challenger. We were the ones who called the police."

I sucked in my breath and a hot wave burned across my cheeks. I could see the tip of my nose turning red. This small town, where everybody knows your crap, was hard to escape for both of us. "Did you see the body?"

She sucked in her lips and shuddered. "Yes. I don't think I'll ever forget it. The back of his head was caked with blood and there was bruising on his face."

Tears welled behind my eyes, but I blinked them back. Bruises. Was that how the police identified the chain as the murder weapon? I had to at least ask her this, "Any idea how that body got in the trunk?"

She stared at me for a moment and tried, it seemed, to get her bearings. "No. No idea." We both fell silent for a few more seconds. She said, "So, since you're a friend of Tanner's, why don't you fill out a bond application?" Hailey opened a drawer and rummaged through some files, then handed me a form. "You need to complete this before we can give you any of the repo work."

I sat at the same table where I'd filled out the loan application for my car. The office smelled like an astringent lemon cleaner, and a radio played symphonic music at a low volume from somewhere behind Hailey's desk. I completed my employment history: seven months at Roasters on the Ridge, and before that, five years at Social Services, and before that, volunteer work at a mental health clinic. Cashiering at the ice cream parlor during high school hardly counted, so I left that off.

I handed her the form. "I have my car loan with Friendly. You have all this information already."

She glanced at her computer screen. "We do. I found you in the system. I found Del's Towing, too. We financed a used tow truck for Del Morran. You're related to him, am I right?"

"He was my dad."

"I shouldn't tell you this, but since you're related..."—Hailey ran her perfectly manicured thumbnail over the mouse.—"...he paid that loan off in twelve payments a few months before he died."

Had I heard that right? Will said the vehicle was worth twenty-five or thirty thou, so I did a little round-figure math in my head. He would've had to make some pretty steep payments, yet Dad's autobody business had been sold to reconcile outstanding debts. Will had told me the bank didn't expect full repayment after liquidating the assets. He'd explained with much *lawyerese* that it was a good thing the self-loader had belonged to a separate business entity from the autobody shop or it would've been sold, too.

"He paid the truck off early?"

"He certainly did. Hardly anyone does that. It must be a lucrative venture to drive a tow truck."

"Yes, yes, it is." I *so* wanted that to be true.

She pressed her lips together. "I remember your dad. I'm sorry about his accident."

I nodded and averted my eyes. His death was still very fresh.

Hailey said, "Here's the deal with repos, we'll phone you when we need you. You come by for the paperwork. If you have to break into a garage, I'll get the court order. Then you call us when the recovery is complete. You will get paid a flat rate by the number of recoveries. Oh, and I need you to fill out this W4 form." I signed the W4 and gave it back to her. She said, "I'll call if Tanner's not available."

"Thanks. I appreciate it." I went through the door and stepped out onto the sidewalk. Would she call me or was this all wasted effort?

A smoothie place, a vitamin mart, a temp agency, and a consignment shop with high-end clothing sat in a row on the other side of the loan office in the strip mall. Three teenaged girls came out of the smoothie place, talking and laughing. They climbed into a red Porsche and sped out of the lot. Rich kids. Unlike me. I'd had to take out a loan on a used subcompact and I wouldn't be paying it off early. I loved the Fiat, even if it was cheap. And dirty. The clear afternoon sun made the grime stand out on my windshield.

Note to self—find out how many auto finance

companies are in this town. Maybe others needed a tow driver.

I drove to the autobody shop to stare at my dad's self-loader. Yes, it had a few dents, some already added by me, but if I worked hard, I'd be able to afford a new paint job one day. Maybe I could have "Delaney's Towing" painted on the door. Change the color to red, get rid of the white. A different design, a new start.

****

I know it was only a few days later, but I was disappointed Friendly hadn't called with a repo assignment. I'd hoped to be breaking into garages left and right, but that was not happening. Too bad people were making their car payments. Which reminded me, mine was due.

It was late in the day after the coffee shop closed, and I was organizing the shoes in my closet when the phone rang. "Is this Del's Towing?" A man's deep voice.

I was so surprised, I said, "This is Delaney."

"Delaney? So, are you with the tow company?"

"Yes, that's me," I squeaked out.

"I need my car hauled over to the dealer's." So, a regular customer, not a call from Friendly Finance for a repo. *Yay*. The number for Del's Towing must've been forwarded to my cell.

"Where are you?" I asked.

The man gave me his location. I threw down the shoe in my hand and said, "I'll be right there."

I hauled ass over to Byron's. As soon as I turned the tow truck's ignition switch, my hands shook and my heart thumped. I tried to convince myself there was nothing to worry about. Following the GPS directions, I steered the truck to a car on the side of the road with the hood up. Car silvery-green. Make and model unknown. I backed up to the front end and swept out of the truck, my black, peep-toed, high heels hitting the pavement. Then, I slapped myself on the forehead. I'd forgotten to change into sneakers.

"How nice. A young lady tow driver." The man, middle-aged in a business suit, smiled, his eyes kind.

I wanted to give him a hug—my first haul, not counting my dead ex-boyfriend—but didn't of course. Even though I felt like an imposter, I was trying hard to look like a professional, like I knew what I was doing. Would he guess he was my first customer? I marched up to him like a woman in charge and introduced myself.

He extracted a credit card out of his wallet. "I don't belong to a motor club and I don't have roadside assistance, either."

I had no way to take a credit card payment. All the information I'd gathered on licensing and insurance, the demos Tanner had given me, the business I'd tried to drum up…and I'd never thought about how to collect. "I'm not contracted with a motor club. If you pay in cash, I'll give you a discount."

"That'd be great. How much?"

"Where do you want the car towed?"

"The dealership. It's five miles from here."

I counted on my fingers and moved my lips, pretending to calculate a rate, and came up with an amount out of thin air. "How's seventy dollars sound?" Would he agree to that?

"Reasonable." He put his credit card back and pulled out cash. I hoped he didn't catch a look of relief on my face. Fortunately, he didn't ask for a receipt or I would've had to write one on the back of the Ale House napkin in my purse.

Note to self: figure out the price of gas per mile, factor in all the other expenses—who knew what those were—and come up with fair pricing. Do the math like a real pro.

Just to show myself I wasn't completely incompetent, I studied the VIN, but didn't spot FW, RW, or 4W in the confusing jumble of numbers and letters. I took a picture with my phone of the VIN for my records, then asked my customer, "Is this front wheel or rear wheel?"

"Rear."

"Stand to the side, please." I returned to Dad's truck and repositioned it behind the green car, pushed the buttons, held my breath, and watched with fingers crossed as the claws did their job. The vehicle rose into the air with a squeak and swoosh.

I stepped out of the cab like I did this every day.

The man said, "Don't you have to secure my car with chains? Lock it down?"

Did I? Tanner didn't do that. I wobbled around the self-loader, my heels sinking into the soft shoulder. I combed through the compartment under the truck bed but didn't find any chains. Did the police take my chains? What if I needed them? Like I knew the answer to that. Was it obvious I didn't know what I was doing?

I told the man, "This kind of self-loader provides a secure delivery without the need to lock down the load." Now, where did I come up with that? It sounded good to me, and he seemed to buy it. I opened the passenger door for him. "Go ahead and get in."

He eased into my dad's truck and directed me to the dealership where I unloaded his car. Even though my fingers ached from gripping the steering wheel so tight I could've busted my fingernails off, I shook his hand and thanked him for the job. "I'm growing my business, so please tell your friends about me."

He promised he would.

I projected calm, cool, professionalism, but once he was out of sight I jumped up and down and pumped my fist. *Yes! Yes*! The job went great if I could say so myself. I don't think he noticed how clumsily I handled it all. No way to take a credit card. No idea what to charge. No clue as to front or rear wheel. No idea about chains and lock-downs.

He didn't appear to pick up on any of those things. And I was so glad he'd already left when I exited the dealership, because I got a slight scrape on the truck's front bumper. That metal pole came at me out of nowhere. They shouldn't have a pole right next to the exit.

Any-hoo, in spite of all that, I was a darn good tow operator. Or a good faker.

I pulled into an electronics store and ran inside. Quick as a fox, I came back out with a credit card reader. I started up the motor and got ready to pull away when a huge black truck with "Tanner Towing" on the side stopped next to me. The door cracked ajar and the hot tow operator unpacked himself out from behind the wheel. "How are you doing?"

I ground the gears as I shifted the self-loader into park. "I had my first customer." My voice sounded high and excited.

"Hang on, I want to hear about it." Tanner flung

open the passenger door and sat himself inside, his tall frame taking up most of the space. He wore black jeans, a tee-shirt, and work boots. His sleeves did not cover the tattoos down his muscled arms, and I got an eyeful of a geometric pattern, a bald eagle, and another that could've been song lyrics.

Oooh. Sexy. I didn't actually say that out loud.

He asked, "Did you have any trouble?"

"Erm, none at all." *Ha.* A tiny fib, okay? "And see here, I got a card reader." The sales clerk had explained that I needed to download an app on my smartphone and sync the reader to my business account. Simple. Well, once I opened the business account, that is. Something to add to the to-do list. "I might have some more questions."

"Ask away." His bright blue eyes contrasted well with his dark eyebrows and blond hair. He had a light brown five o'clock shadow. His masculine scent, musky with a small hint of gasoline, brought to mind pleasant memories of speed boats and motorcycles. And summer. A warm summer, full of promise and possibilities. I was well aware of the man in the seat next to me. Can you tell?

"Do I need to use chains to secure the vehicle once it's in the scoopers, or I mean, the claws?" My voice was breathy.

He said, "With front-end loaders, what you use are tire straps. If you're doing quick recovery and drop off, don't bother. If you're towing more than a couple of miles, you'll want to strap the tires."

As per my usual, I nodded like I knew what he meant about the straps. "All right. So, how many miles can I tow with a self-loader?"

"Let's just say you're okay with a typical job around town, but if you're going any distance, you need a car carrier."

"Go the distance, huh? Just how far do I need to go?" That might have come out a little flirty. Did that sound like a come-on? Not my intention. Who was I kidding? Yes, it was. I was still flying high on my first success, feeling bold and gutsy. I asked him, "It's dinner time and I'm starved. Are you hungry? Would you like to grab something to eat?"

He chewed on his bottom lip.

I added, "I need to ask you more questions and we could talk over dinner. You're the towing expert, at least that's what Byron told me."

Tanner jostled around like he was uncomfortable. "Okay."

"Oh, good. There's so much more I need to know."

He stared out the windshield before popping open the passenger door. "Let's take my rig."

There were a lot of things I wanted to ask. Like, was he single? And, would he consider this a date?

I reminded myself once again that we were, the both of us, implicated in a murder. But, he couldn't be a killer. No way. And he must not believe I murdered my ex-boyfriend, either. That, or he liked to live dangerously.

Probably the latter.

Chapter 5

"How did you get into the towing business?" Sitting opposite Tanner at the Ale House, I sipped on a brown ale. The scent of hops filled my nose, and the arrhythmia-inducing beat of rock music bounced in my chest. The beer glass cooled my hands, but Tanner's blue eyes made me warm all over.

He said, "I got a job at a towing company when I turned eighteen. Got a business degree at night. After I graduated, I started my own operation. I not only handle repos, but also private property tows, and I monitor the police band for accidents. I'm on a rotation list with law enforcement."

"Police band? That's a radio, right?"

"Spruce Ridge still uses radios, although more police departments are getting away from them. But around here that's how you find out about accidents. Great tow opportunities."

"Good to know." I hadn't even thought about that. "You married?" I held my breath and my insides quaked.

His smile peeked out from behind his long-necked beer bottle. After taking a swallow, he said, "No."

Don't blush, don't blush. I tried to control myself. This subject was always cringeworthy. "I know this is a business dinner, but I want to know if I'm drinking with a married man."

"I get it." He propped his arms on the tabletop. "Go ahead and ask your questions."

"How old are you?"

"Thirty." He took another deep draw of his beer, holding the bottle with his left hand, trying to cover another smile. He saw through me. This wasn't about business…I mean, come on!

"You're a southpaw. I hadn't noticed before."

"Yeah. You know what they say about lefties."

Oh, Lord, where was this conversation going? Was he finally flirting back? Well, I brought it on myself. "No, what's that?"

He smiled at me. "We like to daydream."

Whew. Not what I expected. "What do you dream about?"

"I have two trucks, a front-loader and a flatbed, and I'd like to add to my fleet. I don't employ anyone else, but someday I'd like to."

Me, too. Heck, why not? But I felt silly admitting that right now. "Is front-loader the same as self-loader?"

"Yeah. I've heard them called auto-loaders, too."

"I can see why. That's great that you own your own business."

"So do you."

"Only because of my dad, Del Morran."

"I heard what happened to him. I'm sorry about that."

"Thanks." I gazed down at my lap while the server brought our burgers topped with green chili. Everything in Colorado comes with green chili. Having lived here all my life, I loved the spicy hot topping.

We went on to talk about how many tows to expect

on a good day, how much to charge, and which accountant to use for taxes, Spruce Ridge Accounting. Tanner warned me that tow truck drivers were busiest during the blizzard months and also in the summer when tourism brought more traffic. All helpful info.

He tossed his paper napkin on top of his plate like he was preparing to leave. "Hey, don't tell Byron we had dinner together. I mean, you can tell him we had a *business* dinner, that's okay to tell him."

That came out of nowhere. Would Byron care? I asked, "Why can't I tell him?"

Tanner's head bobbed back a fraction and his eyes half-closed, almost like he flinched. "I don't want him to get the wrong idea."

"What do you mean?"

He shrugged. "Nothing. You ready to go?" He snagged the bill from the table before I could grab it.

"I'll pay my share." I stood and reached for my purse at the back of the booth.

"Nah, you can get it next time."

So, Tanner paid for my meal. Had tonight been a *date* and not just a *business* dinner? And, he said there'd be a next time.

We walked out the door into a stiff breeze. Head down into the wind, I hurried to Tanner's truck. After I buckled in, I asked, "You were going to take me along on some tows, remember?"

"I didn't forget, though it sounds like you're not doing too bad on your own."

"I've only had one tow." I almost said again that he could teach me a few things, but didn't. *Nuh-huh.* It was a struggle, but I didn't allow myself to go there.

"If you have time on Thursday night, I can take

you along with me then. I'll text you where to meet."

"Sounds good."

Tanner dropped me at my dad's truck, and I watched him drive away until his taillights disappeared.

Once back inside my apartment, I put the cash from my first tow in a zippered pouch I emptied of makeup and wrote the date and VIN for the towed vehicle in a notebook.

Note to self: buy a police band radio, find out what private property tows are, and charge more money.

Seventy seemed a lot to me, but Tanner told me how much he charged, and I had underestimated myself. I'd price the amount higher from now on. Perhaps that's how Del Morran paid off his truck so quickly.

With fingers crossed there would be more tows and another date, I sank onto one of my two loveseats and daydreamed about Tanner. You didn't have to be a leftie to dream. What would it be like if he kissed me? Put his arms around me? *Oh, boy*. I fanned myself. I was behaving like a hormone-driven teenager.

I rapped my knuckles on my head. I've only been relationship-free for a few weeks now. I told myself, *don't rush*. Give yourself some time. Plus, I'd need to make sure Tanner wasn't a rebound.

I glanced around and did a mental check-in. The word art above my sofa spelled out, "family," and the mismatched floral pillows on the two facing loveseats shouted out "shabby chic," the style I loved. Kristen had given me the family plaque because she and I were like sisters and I didn't have much of a family of my own. No siblings. Just me and Mom. Oh yeah, and Will. I was in a borrowed apartment with a borrowed family—all thanks to Kris. I owed a lot to my best friend.

I got up and went into the kitchen. Just when I'd popped open a light beer, a knock sounded on my door.

A man in his late thirties or early forties, in military-fit shape and a pressed, light blue uniform, offered his badge and identified himself. "I'm Sheriff Ephraim Lopez. May I come in?"

I held onto the door. "You're the homicide detective? Officer Bowers told me the county took over the investigation."

"That's right."

"And my stepdad told me not to answer any questions without him present. He's an attorney." This is what I'd been expecting. In the back of my mind I knew I hadn't seen the last of the police.

Sheriff Lopez crossed his arms. "Is there a reason why you need a lawyer?"

"No, I didn't do anything wrong." What would it hurt to talk to the sheriff? Get it over with. Rip off the bandage. If he accused me of anything, I'd stop and call Will.

"I just have a few questions." The sheriff had a darkly tanned complexion, chocolate brown eyes, long, black eyelashes, and thick black hair. He smelled like jasmine. Not threatening, but clean and fresh. Appealing. Maybe this wouldn't be painful at all.

Jeez, I must need a new man in my life. I should slap myself. Hadn't I just warned myself about not rushing?

I let him in and walked stiff-legged to the kitchen, sensing his eyes on my back. "What did you want to ask me?"

"We found Winslow's fingerprints inside your tow truck."

"Get out!" I'm sure I had on a shocked expression and my heart began to thump like a race car engine, rocketing up to peak level. "*Inside* the truck?"

"I'm sorry, but it's a fact. We did find his prints inside."

"Not possible."

"We matched his prints quickly because he's in the criminal database."

What the hey? Does the criminal database mean what I think it means? Oh, Jeremy, what were you up to?

He asked, "Do you want to change your statement?"

"You mean my sworn-under-oath statement?" My voice came out high. "No."

"Are you sure? Your fingerprints were in his vehicle, too."

"So what? We dated. I rode in his car. The last time was a little over two weeks ago."

"We'd like to take your toe prints." He glanced down at my black heels.

Dizzy and slightly sick, I dropped onto the counter stool. "Toe prints? I didn't know you could get impressions from toes. I've never heard of that before. And why would you need mine?"

"We discovered toe prints in the Challenger. On the dash. If they aren't yours, we need to keep searching and find out who else has been in his car recently." He uncrossed his arms and relaxed out of his cop-stance.

"So, I'm not the only one who braces their feet on

the dash?" One of my favorite things to do was slip off my shoes and prop up my toes. Jeremy had teased me about it.

"No, it's not that unusual."

If the prints belonged to someone else and pointed to another suspect, I had no problem providing mine for elimination.

The sheriff said, "Last question. Where were you between March 31 and April 1?"

"I suppose that's the estimated time of death? Can't you narrow it down better than a two day period?"

"Not really. The victim had been dead about forty-eight hours before he was found."

I wrinkled my nose, feeling faint. "Wouldn't his body have smelled or something?" A fox had died in the woods behind the coffee shop last fall, and I would never forget that stink.

"We had a frost every night last week. The temperature kept the body cool."

"Oh." Spring was like that in Colorado. Some of the ski resorts were still open with plenty of snow.

"So, please answer my question. Where were you during that time period?"

I stumbled over to the mini calendar on my fridge. "That was a weekend." My mind rewound to that time. "I don't remember doing anything special, I don't think I had plans, other than working at the coffee shop on Saturday. You can verify the hours I worked with the owner, Kristen Guttenberg."

"Other than that, you weren't out with anyone? No one came over?"

"I went shopping Sunday, but I went by myself. I

could check my credit card bill for proof." I suspected I blushed red to my roots. He must think I'm a loser with no friends.

"Hang on to the bill, but that would only account for an hour or two of your time."

More like three or four, but what's the point? I grabbed my beer and took a swig. "You want one?"

"Can't drink on the job." His brown eyes turned even darker and his voice dropped abruptly. "Maybe I'll take you up on that some other time."

He gave me an appraisal, like a man gives a woman. Not like what a detective gives a presumed killer. Was he hitting on me? Or trying to figure out why I'm all alone on weekends? The appreciative gleam in his eye, and just after the date with Tanner—I'd convinced myself it was a date—made me blush hotter. *Wow*. This was good for a gal's ego. A gal who'd been dumped by the last guy in her life.

"Do you want to take my prints now?" I asked.

"Tomorrow's okay. Stop at the sheriff's office."

I'd have to take off my shoes and walk around barefoot on the same floor where the police brought common criminals through. That would be as disgusting as going barefoot through security at the airport. *Ugh*. Maybe it wouldn't be so bad if I got a pedicure first. Maybe candy-crush pink. "Okay. So, I'll see you tomorrow?"

"Ask for the intake clerk."

I nodded and escorted Sheriff Lopez to the door. As soon as the sheriff disappeared from view, I phoned my stepdad.

Will was as amazed as I was after I told him about the sheriff's visit. He said, "Jeremy's fingerprints in the truck? How in the world did those get in there?"

"Maybe Dad gave Jeremy a tow? That's possible, right?" I asked Will. If Dad had given Jeremy a ride before his car accident, that would explain how Jeremy's fingerprints were found in the truck. I wish I'd thought of that possible scenario when talking to the sheriff. Dealing with two deaths at once must have muddled my brain.

"Maybe. And what's this about toe prints? That's a new one on me. But you don't have a choice, law enforcement can require you to give prints. Do you want me to drive over and meet you at the station?"

"No. I'm only going to see the intake clerk. The sheriff didn't ask me to give another statement or anything."

"Okay, let me know if you need me. Keep me in the loop. If the sheriff questions you again or comes by for any reason, I need to know. Understand?"

"Got it."

"By the way, I have your dad's books for the last few years. The estate liquidator gave me some business cards, tow slips, and other stuff you might want. I'll send an overnight box to you. And I have the paperwork I filed for the LLC. You're good to go."

"Thanks, Will. I had a tow today. I got a phone call for Del's Towing."

"So, the number's been transferred to you then." He didn't ask how the job went or how I got paid, thank goodness. And he didn't badger me about selling.

****

The FedEx driver brought the package into the coffee shop first thing the following morning.

Inside were ledgers, a small carton of simple, white

business cards, a stack of receipt books with yellow carbons, and a gas and mileage record book. A separate envelope contained the LLC documents, plus insurance proposals and estimates. I chose the coverage with the highest deductible and lowest premium, but it'd still be a struggle to pay the bill. I filled out the application, scanned it in Kristen's office, and emailed it to Will to submit to the insurance company, then I ran to the bank across the street and opened a business account in the name of the LLC. After I returned, I sat at Kristen's desk to sync the account to my credit card reader.

I pulled out the list of tasks. Bank account—check. Business supplies—check. Insurance app—check. I was really and truly in operation now. If only I'd get another call for a tow.

The mid-morning lull turned into a late-morning rush. Kristen started up the bean roaster and the smell and sounds of the coffee beans popping under the high temperature filled the shop. I got busy preparing drinks, but Guy arrived to take over. He nudged me away from the espresso machine with an *I've got this* attitude, so after I checked with Kristen, I left. It was only noon.

I went to the nail salon for a pedicure. Instead of pink polish, I chose "Innocent Orange." I couldn't resist the name. Then I made a quick run to the shoe store to see if there was anything new. I tried on a pair of tall, denim wedges that were adorable with my above-the-ankle skinny jeans. Blue was a nice calming color, so irresistible, and I had a coupon, okay? And the shoes were from the sale rack.

And, yes, I'd put off giving my toe prints.

I finally dragged myself into the sheriff's office.

Contrasting with Spruce Ridge's police station

located on the corner of Main Street in an old, brick one-story, the Clear Creek County Sheriff's office was situated on the highway leading out of town in a modern building with big windows and lots of natural light. Pristine and quiet and new.

The clerk recorded my toe prints digitally like my fingerprints had been taken.

That done and out of the way, I drove to Byron's so I could put the business cards and the receipt book in the truck. When I coasted up, Byron's new eponymous sign was in place, "Oberly Motors." Del Morran's name had disappeared, leaving no evidence that he'd ever owned the place. A customer walked in the door as another exited. Byron appeared busy.

I opened up the truck, sat myself down in the front seat, and breathed in the faint smell of motor oil combined with a woodsy scent that clung to the upholstery. I rubbed my hand along the dash and over the top of the steering wheel. I was about to let my mind wander to the question of what Dad was thinking when he left me his truck, when my cell jingled from my purse and I answered, "This is Delaney."

"Are you Del? The tow driver who wears high heels?" A woman's voice.

"Well, yes." I'd forgotten to change out of my stilettos by mistake on my one and only single-handed tow. "How'd you know?"

The woman on the other end chuckled. "Read your reviews. I don't need a tow, but I'm out of gas. Do you do roadside service?"

I wasn't about to turn anything down. "I can bring you a gallon. Where are you now?" I punched her location into the GPS and told her I'd be there shortly.

I'd stowed a pair of old sneakers in the truck to change into, just in case I did get a call—which I did!—but this time I'd keep my new denim wedges on my feet since the caller mentioned the heels. I got out to explore the storage compartment under the bed. An empty tin can and a spout were in the bin, so I stopped at a filling station on the way. I kept the receipt—the businesswoman that I am—and made it to the customer's vehicle in ten minutes.

She stood to the side as I lugged out the heavy container. "Hello, Del," she said. "Your shoes are super cute. Where did you get them? I could use a pair like those."

"The discount shoe store next to the nail salon." I angled the spout to pour the gasoline into her tank. This I knew how to do since I'd run out of petrol myself a time or two. "Do you get their coupons?"

"I do." She handed me her credit card. I had the card reader already attached to my phone, so I ran it through. She thanked me and I gave her one of Del Morran's business cards with the phone number that had been forwarded to my cell. Didn't I say I had a head for business? And she even gave me a tip.

I felt good after she drove off. My second customer, seemingly satisfied like the first, without a clue that I had no idea what I was doing. I recorded the transaction and mileage in Del's Towing account book and crushed the pages to my chest for a glorious moment.

Then, I searched online for a review. Found it on the internet: *driver arrived quickly and best of all showed up in high heels. Most of us think tow truck drivers are goons out to rip us off, but Del was pleasant and reasonably priced. Would use her again.*

Aw, how sweet. Except for the insulting "goon" part. Tanner Utley wasn't a goon. And neither was Del Morran, I'm almost positive.

Should I continue wearing the high heels for tows? I swirled my right ankle around to admire my wedges, more suited to my former life in Denver than in Spruce Ridge. I could always arrive in heels, then switch over to sneakers if I needed to, or better yet, work boots like Tanner's. I'd have to buy a pair of safety boots, and I'd forgotten all about wearing my dad's safety vest.

Once more, I scoured the bin under the truck, this time looking for the vest. Crammed inside were LED lights, flashlights, road cones, flares, and a first aid kit. Other stuff, too, that I didn't know about. I took pictures of the unknown odds and ends to ask Byron or Tanner about later.

A yellow slip of paper held fast, jammed in the corner of the compartment, so I nicked it out with my fingernails. A receipt signed by Jeremy Winslow.

I clapped a hand to my mouth. *What the hell?* Jeremy's signature scratched on a Del's Towing receipt? And, even weirder, the ticket was dated the day Jeremy broke up with me, March 15. I flipped the paper over and studied it from top to bottom. The ticket was for a late model Mustang delivered to L&B Garage and Services.

All right then, I knew Jeremy had worked at L&B. This was starting to make sense. Jeremy had signed on the line for the tow driver by mistake. What other explanation was there? *Yeah,* he'd written his name in the wrong place.

That was it. Had to be.

Chapter 6

I'd talked myself into solving the Mystery of the Tow Receipt. I couldn't help it. I needed to know. Whatever the situation, Jeremy and Del Morran had crossed paths, and the ticket could be a clue of some kind, explaining how Jeremy's fingerprints ended up in the truck.

I steered toward L&B Garage on Industrial Lane. The narrow road wound a short way up a tree-lined canyon posted with warnings of wildlife crossing the highway. Small herds of antelope and a few deer grazed in the fields, and hawks cast swooping shadows on the pavement. I continued past stark, brown pines, dead from beetle-kill. This wet time of year would soon give way to the dry months of forest fire season.

An industrial park came into sight, tin-roofed buildings all bustling with activity. The closest housed a row of six large-scale auto bays. Not particularly pretty, with vehicles parked haphazardly over a cracked cement lot with no landscaping. The sound of air pressure meeting concrete was an indication of work inside. This was a rough business operated by rough men, like that was going to stop me. I was sure the police checked out the garage already because they'd have been certain to discover Jeremy worked there, so what could it hurt for me to ask a few questions myself? I shouldered my purse and stepped past oil stains and carelessly tossed cigarette butts.

A teenager stood behind the service counter in a knit cap and a blue work shirt with the cuffs rolled up. A cell phone wired to earbuds occupied his attention. His name tag read, Axle Guttenberg.

I couldn't help but ask, "Is that your real name? Axle?"

"Yeah." He didn't bother to look up from his device.

"Sorry, you probably get that a lot." He didn't answer me, so I asked in a louder voice, "Are you related to Kristen Guttenberg?"

He bounced a glance in my direction. "We're cousins. Why? You know her?"

"She's a friend of mine. I work for her at Roasters Coffee Shop. I didn't know she had a cousin in town."

He just tapped on his screen. *Jeez.* I was accustomed to guys being more sociable, even the teenagers because I didn't appear my age. I wasn't used to this.

"What's the matter? Do you have an ax to grind or something?"

He glanced up, his grip tightening on his phone. "Like I haven't heard that one before, carrot top."

The tip of my nose shone red and I could feel the rest of the blush spreading across my cheeks. My hair *was* more orange than red. Darn it.

He yanked the buds from his ears. "Did you come in for a reason?"

"Do you know Jeremy Winslow? He used to work here."

He snickered. "Not anymore, he doesn't." Alarm bells went off in my mind. Does this kid know something? Was he involved in Jeremy's death? Am I in danger here? Or, is he simply showing a cocky-teen attitude? Probably that.

I handed him the receipt. "See this? I wondered if you could explain the transaction."

Axle took the yellow slip from my hand. "He delivered a Mustang here." The teenager gave it back to me.

"Good answer, Sherlock." I sighed out a big breath of air.

"Thanks."

An older man, barrel-chested, work shirt dirty with grime, came through a door into the lobby. The ear-splitting sound of an air winch blasted in with him, then retreated as the door shut. The mechanic crossed over, his eyebrows drawn in and the corners of his mouth turned down. The lingering scent of stale cigarette smoke made me want to pinch my nose. His name tag read, "Freddie Haag."

"Excuse me, Mr. Haag, can you help me with this receipt?" I thrust the paper across the counter.

"What do you want to know?"

"Why Jeremy Winslow signed it?"

His gaze landed on my dad's tow truck parked on the other side of the window, then darted back to me. "Did you work with Jeremy?"

"He was my boyfriend."

Freddie Haag shrugged and shook his head. "Don't know anything about it."

The surly teenager said in a suspiciously friendly tone, "Is there anything else we can help you with?"

"No, thanks. Keep it real." *Yeah, right*. I backed out the door and climbed into Dad's truck. Both Axle

Guttenberg and Freddie Haag watched me leave.

Hmmm, very suspicious…I didn't trust these two. My antenna buzzed, telling me someone was lying, covering something up. But what? What did the tow receipt have to do with anything? Maybe they were just being jerks.

The most obvious explanation was probably the correct one—Jeremy signed for the Mustang and didn't tow it here. So, mystery solved, I guessed.

I reversed from my parking place at the same time a gold Corvette driven by a blonde woman pulled in to the lot. Yes, I knew the car was a Corvette. It was one car even I could recognize. Mostly I paid attention to the colors, not the makes and models, but I was trying to notice all the cars on the road now.

Thank God I managed not to hit anything when I turned this big tow truck onto the street.

Was I a car snob? Recognizing Corvettes, but knowing nothing about Fords or Toyotas? It was time to do something about my automotive illiteracy, so I stashed the truck at Byron's shop and drove my Fiat to the giant book retailer near the mall.

There I found a book on the history of motor vehicles, a heavy encyclopedia with makes, models, and features, including front or rear or all-wheel drive. I studied the pages for a while. An added bonus was information about a VIN decoder app available for smartphones. The price of the encyclopedia was steep, but how else was I going to learn about cars? Forget the library. Whatever I borrowed I'd have to return, and I needed the book for more than a few weeks. I'd better bite the bullet and purchase the heavy handbook.

After paying at the register, I circled through the

in-store coffee shop to size up the competition, then returned to my apartment to file the sales slip, a proper business expense.

I turned on my electric kettle, got a tea bag out of the cabinet, and settled myself in front of my dad's account books. This was my first opportunity to look them over so I could organize my transactions the same way.

Bank statements. *Boring.* Computer printouts with columns of figures. *Boring.* Shoebox-sized carton of yellow tow receipts. Not exciting, but more promising. I made a note of the amounts Dad charged for various tows. Wanting to be thorough, I found the tickets for March so I could file the confusing L&B receipt signed by Jeremy. My fingers walked through the dates and stopped when I spotted Jeremy's name. Then I saw his name again, then again, then again.

Get the heck out! Were my eyes playing tricks on me? I shook my head to clear my vision while I shakily thumbed through another section. My ex-boyfriend's name showed up on quite a few more tow tickets. *Ah, man…*Jeremy worked for Dad. The Mustang receipt was not a one-time mistake.

I pushed the box of tickets away. What did this mean? I tried to think of an explanation, any other excuse for this obvious fact. Why hadn't Jeremy told me? He had to have realized Del Morran was my father, no mistaking the same name and red hair.

The sharp *beep-beep-beep* signaling the water had boiled startled me and I got up to pour a mug, then plopped a tea bag in to steep.

Now, it's not a surprise Dad never mentioned this, because as you know Del Morran and I did not meet up, not even once for any chit-chat, but my ex was another story. Jeremy told me about his employment at L&B Garage, but not about his job at Del's Towing. He'd kept that from me. Why? Jeremy was a rat fink for breaking up, but he must've been an even bigger rat fink, a lying, creepy, sneaky sort of a rat. And—this stank worse than burnt espresso beans—the detective had to have known Jeremy worked for Del's Towing and that's why his fingerprints were in the truck.

Those bullies in their Crown Vics. Yes, I now knew that's the kind of vehicle the cops drove.

Was this the reason I was the prime suspect? You could answer that in the affirmative. My ex-boyfriend worked for my dad. His prints were in the truck. The murder weapon was a chain, I'm guessing, like one from a tow truck. In an ugly coincidence, I'd towed Jeremy's car with him in it.

The police would search no further than me. The killer was out there somewhere, getting away with…murder, while I was sure to be an easy target. Just as I needed to solve the Mystery of the Tow Receipt, I needed to figure out the Mystery of the Dead Boyfriend, too.

Before I became a blubbering wreck, I gave my mom a call. I didn't tell her about this hot mess, but I didn't need to. Her voice alone comforted me. I sipped my hot tea while she shared some gossip about the neighbors and we made plans to go shopping over the next week or so. I may have my dad's red hair and his name, but I had my mom's love for shopping. A little browsing, maybe even a little buying…doing something fun would help settle me down.

****

The morning aroma in the coffee café was always a wake-up call.

At five a.m. I arrived half asleep, but after Kristen started the brew and the smell of beans permeated the air I was fully alert. Guy joined us to open the store. He proved to be a fast learner and had the list of chores on the laminated card down pat…as he made sure to let me know. Soon Kris wouldn't need me anymore.

When we took our break for a muffin and coffee, I asked my friend why she hadn't mentioned she had a cousin named Axle.

"He's ten years younger than us. I don't know him well. Besides, he hangs with a rough crowd, so he and I don't cross paths much except on holidays." Kristen fell silent while the bean grinder shrieked with a deafening, pulverizing sound. Once quiet resumed, she added, "My mom told me Axle has always been a handful, always in trouble, so I avoid him."

I gobbled down a mouthful of muffin. "Wow, Kris, you never have anything bad to say about anyone."

My friend's face fell. "You're right. I need to hate the sin and love the sinner."

"You of all people don't have a problem with that." I couldn't criticize, because Kristen lived her faith. Always willing to believe the best about everybody, she took some risks. I glanced over at Guy washing the dishes and Sierra sweeping the sidewalk. Both acted like they were doing better and living a healthier lifestyle since coming to work at Roasters. Maybe with her paycheck, Sierra, the punkette, had been able to afford a place to live and move away from the homeless shelter. And Guy, a former alcoholic, appeared to have turned his life around, studying English Lit at the community college.

I asked Kristen, "So, you have any more relatives in town?"

"I do. You're not the only reason I opened the coffee shop here." She nudged my elbow. "I have an uncle, an aunt, and a few cousins in Spruce Ridge. Axle has a sister, Annalise."

"Where'd they get those names?"

"Good German names."

"Well, Axle's name won't be easy to forget." The little twerp. "You should've told me about him before this." I slapped her shoulder.

Kristen made a spiraling motion with one hand. "You know I come from a big family. Remember Sarah?"

"Yes." I'd known Kristen from grammar school days and I'd met a few of her relatives.

"Cousin." She ticked off a finger. "Ben?"

"Yes."

She ticked off another finger. "Cousin. I could go on. Anyhow, where did you run into Axle?"

"At L&B Garage. Did you know he's employed at the same place Jeremy worked?"

"No, I didn't. And Axle's name is prophetic, don't you think?" She laughed. "I suppose his parents didn't know he'd become a mechanic."

"I have even bigger news. Get this, I just found out Jeremy not only worked at L&B, he worked for my dad, too. He'd forgotten to mention it to me! How absurd is that?" I let out a *can-you-believe-it?* snort.

"Good Heavens." Her gray eyes grew round under her black eyebrows, and she flipped a lock of her straight brown hair over her shoulder. "Unbelievable."

"There's something peculiar about the garage, too. They were extremely rude and had no customer service." Or maybe it was just Axle who had pushed the boundaries of rudeness. "I think there's a clue there."

A woman in a ski jacket and stocking cap burst into the café and skidded to a halt at the checkout, so Kristen said, "Speaking of customer service," and rose to greet her. I followed Kris behind the counter.

My friend and I would have to mull over this astonishing clue in detail later. My cell vibrated from my pocket, so I hit the answer button. It was my stepdad. "I know someone in Spruce Ridge who owns a car dealership. He also provides the financing and he wants to give repo work to Del's Towing."

I sucked in my breath. "O-kay." This was too good to be true.

"Surprise, right? I think he was simply tracking down a car-hauling company and because of our connection he thought of you."

"Thanks, Will. So, who do I call?"

Will gave me the information, and I told him I'd contact Abington Auto Store as soon as my shift ended.

****

Armed with all the confidence I could muster, I breathed in a deep intake of air, whispered under my breath, *you can do this, you can do this*, and pushed through the door.

The enormous, glass-enclosed showroom displayed shiny new cars, and the sales staff in pod-like offices looked busy. A pretty receptionist not long out of her teens, with short blonde hair and red painted nails, sat behind the counter. After I explained why I was there, she ushered me into a more lavish office behind a glass door with leather furniture and what appeared to be original art.

The man at the walnut desk stood to offer me a firm grip. "I'm Rob Abington. So, I hear you're going to be working for me." Thick white hair covered his head and wire-rimmed glasses perched above round, rosy cheeks. A gold ring squeezed the flesh on his left finger and a gold watch with diamonds rode on his right wrist. He wore a dark gray suit while everyone else wore business-casual. His shoes were tasseled and highly polished.

I returned the handshake. "Delaney Morran." I hoped he didn't spot the blush migrating from my neck to my cheeks. "You know my stepdad, Will Sharpton. I guess his firm does your legal work?"

"Right. Please sit down." He went on to describe how he financed the vehicles sold on the car lot. While he talked, I studied the ledge behind his desk. A picture of a fifty-something woman with an expensive color job and hairstyle, professional make-up, and diamond earrings smiled from a silver frame. His wife, most likely. The rest of the shelf held awards from the Chamber of Commerce and Better Business Bureau engraved with his name, Robert C. Abington. He folded his hands together on his desktop. "So, about this repo operation, sometimes buyers get behind on their payments."

"I understand." All too well. He didn't need to explain that part to me.

"After sending two certified letters, we initiate the repo process. I've got an agent, Patrick Crump, who does the locates. Crump will call to tell you where to show up, then you tow the car to the dealership."

With Abington Autos I didn't have to worry about paperwork or VINs. Just show up. Tow. That's it. Mr. Abington hadn't asked me to complete a bond application or anything.

"I also work for Friendly Finance Company." Not technically true, but kinda. I was embellishing, okay? Abington didn't need to know I hadn't done any repos for Friendly yet. "Your procedures are different from theirs."

"Well, every business does it their own way." He walked me to the door.

I said, "I'm looking forward to working with you. Thanks for the opportunity." We shook hands.

What I thought would take all afternoon only took an hour and I was home by three. I'd just recorded information into my dad's books for the roadside service the day before—daring to hope for a future where I would be entering more than one job at a time—when I got my first phone call from Mr. Abington's repo agent, Patrick Crump. With an assignment. Already!

Someone other than me was having a hard time making their payments.

Within fifteen minutes, I'd picked up the tow truck and made it over to the local grocery store where Patrick Crump said to meet. Was I ready? *Yes. All right, here goes…*

The repo guy stepped out of a pearl-gray sedan and flagged me down. Crump was about my age, on the small side, around five-foot-eight and slightly built, in jeans and an untucked dress shirt and tie. "Tow that Jeep Wrangler over to Abington's. You'd better be quick about it." He pointed to a brand-new Jeep, a sporty hard-top in that cool, army green color, then he vaulted back into his car and took off.

Rifling through my encyclopedia, I happened to spot Crump's car—a Ford Taurus—then searched for the Jeep Wrangler. *Found it.* A four-wheel drive. So, I would need to use the dolly wheels Tanner told me about. I'd watched an instructional video on *YouTube,* so I had an idea of how to attach them to the Jeep. You can find anything on *YouTube*.

First, I positioned the self-loader near the front bumper of the Wrangler and used the T-bar to raise the front end with the claws. The squeaky metal rods didn't seem to make such a loud noise in the crowded parking lot next to a busy street. *So far so good. I'm such a badass.*

The dolly wheels sat on top of the truck bed, so I had to get out of the cab. I kept darting glances all around while I wrestled with the first dolly wheel, but it weighed a ton, too heavy for me to lift down to the ground. I pushed both dollies over the edge of the truck bed. The first one slammed onto the blacktop, then the other, bouncing with several loud booms. I cast an eye around but everyone bustled into the store, not paying me any attention. As fast as I could, I rolled the first set of dollies to the back of the Jeep, where I spotted a metal plate that read, "Wrangler 4X4."

Note to self—walk the length of the vehicle before wasting time looking in the encyclopedia.

Once I'd positioned both dollies under the knobby rear tires, I jacked up the foot pedals, my foot pumping up and down, elevating the rear wheels off the ground. Back in the truck, I pulled forward, but a terrible scraping sound made me hit the brakes.

The dolly wheels hadn't stayed with the tires, they'd been left behind. *It's okay*, I patted my chest. I lowered the Jeep and released the claws, ready to start over.

A heavy-set, bald man rushed up, ape-like, running with his grocery cart at full speed, not stopping. He banged into the side of Dad's truck. *Bam!* His face was purple with rage, his cheeks puffed out, and his mouth snarled, "Get away from my Jeep. Get the hell outta here!"

Shit. The owner. This was the kind of hot head Tanner warned me about.

I sat shaking in the driver's seat while he tossed his shopping bags into the back of the Wrangler and sped out of the parking lot, throwing me one last dirty glance and a rude hand gesture. I waited for several minutes to make sure he wasn't coming back, then swung down from the cab to determine the damage. A deep dent on the driver's door was scraped down to the metal. The dolly wheels were abandoned on the pavement like shoes kicked off at the door.

No way could I lift those heavy contraptions onto Dad's truck, so I trundled them to the edge of the blacktop under some tall blue spruce trees. I texted Crump that the owner had returned before I made the recovery and to please contact me again when he relocated the vehicle. I hoped he wouldn't pick up the phone and call me since I did not want to give him the embarrassing details.

Great job, I told myself as I pulled away. I still shook and my feet skated around on the pedals. My first repo assignment. I lost the Jeep and had to leave the dolly wheels behind.

What had I called myself? The big, badass tow truck driver?

Bad and *ass* were all too true. I was getting good at this one thing—beating myself up.

Chapter 7

Tanner's black tow truck caught my eye as I sped along Main Street. This time I waved him over and hauled myself up into his passenger seat.

"I got the Abington Auto Store repo work. Turns out my stepdad knows the owner."

He leaned one elbow against his steering wheel and faced me. "Nice. I heard they provide their own financing. Do you know who was doing the repo work before?"

"I don't." Should I tell him about the abandoned dolly wheels? I felt foolish and worried someone would take them. Until I went back for the dollies and had this all figured out, I wouldn't be able to make another attempt. I asked, "What do you do if the owner shows up before you can tow their car?"

"You need to be smarter than they are. You need to be fast."

"I'm not sure I'm fast enough." I scrunched my eyes closed and pinched the bridge of my nose. Admittedly, I hadn't thought this through. Did I want the repo work? Maybe that owner was over-the-top angry because he needed to rush milk and bread home to his hungry children. Maybe he was late for his job at the hospital where sick people waited for him to discover a cure for cancer. Hot Head didn't seem to me like he was busy doing any of those things, but still, I didn't know. This seemed like a moral gray area.

I asked Tanner, "What if the person needs their car for something important?"

"Delaney, you have to understand they're not paying their bills. They are in default on their loans. Do you know what the most repo'ed car is?"

"No. What kind?"

"The most expensive kind. A lot of repos are forty to fifty-thousand-dollar cars or more."

Like Wranglers, not in my budget. Because I was having trouble paying bills myself, was I actually identifying with Hot Head? Don't put that out in the universe.

Tanner presented that smile of his. Did he think I was amusing? "You're all concerned about people you don't even know."

"I feel bad for those going through a hard time, Tanner." I tossed my red plait over my shoulder. I could be one of them. A glib statement, but all too true. Repossessing cars felt mean.

"There are some buyers who don't even make their first payment. Pretty lame since the loan company has their contact info and knows where they live. But then they hide the vehicle and wait for the repo agent to get tired of searching for it."

"Does that work? Do the finance companies just give up?"

"It takes a while, but sometimes, yes. Buyers in arrears are always given a chance to voluntarily return the car, so when they keep the vehicle anyway, that's stealing. Repo basically means you're recovering a stolen vehicle for the lienholder. And, if you don't do the work, someone else will."

"Okay." That made sense, but maybe after I got established I could quit the repos. I hadn't even completed my first job, and I was already thinking of packing it in. "I need a favor, Tanner."

"Yes?" He didn't seem to mind that I asked.

"Can you help me lift my tow dollies onto the truck?" I swallowed my pride and told him where I'd left them.

"Of course. Let's go." He followed me to the grocery store. We both rolled the dollies out from under the trees, then I watched while he boosted them into place. I tried not to stare at his muscles. And his backside wasn't a bad view, either.

I smiled for the first time that day and asked him, "Are all tow truck drivers this awesome?"

He stopped locking down the dollies to eyeball me over his shoulder. "Maybe you shouldn't haul anything that requires dolly wheels."

"But you told me most tows require them." See, I did retain some of the important stuff.

"That's right."

Not strong physically, I couldn't do one single pull-up on the exercise bar. Did I have to be in tip-top shape to do this job? Did I need a gym membership? Would I be able to hold my own? I traced my finger over Tanner's name on the door of his cab. "Don't forget, it's Thursday and you're taking me out on some tows tonight, remember?"

I stepped away as he scraped open his door. "I didn't forget."

"I can't wait. I want to see more of this amazing machine." I meant his truck, but Tanner was welcome to take that any way he wanted. "You have time to grab something to eat?" Yes, I was the one to ask—again. "Then do the ride-along after?"

He rubbed his eyes with the heels of his hands. "Sure. I'm working PPI tonight. It'll be good practice for you."

"What's PPI?"

"Private property impounds. Towaway zones." He got in behind the wheel. "Meet me in half an hour at that Mexican place on Rio Grande Ave."

"Okay, see you in a bit."

I rushed home as fast as I could. I finger-combed my hair into waves down my back and stepped into skinny jeans, a lemon yellow top, and flat, yellow ankle boots. Yellow for happiness. Plus, they were the closest thing I had to work boots. Was the outfit date worthy?

Maybe it wasn't really a date. Maybe it was just dinner because we had to eat. No, I told myself, it's a date. Even if I was the one—again—to ask.

So, now I had a second date with a hot guy in a tow truck. How many girls would die for the chance?

Okay, maybe not the tow truck part. Except for this girl.

Forty-five minutes later, we were eating chicken chimichangas with green chili and washing the food down with *cervezas*. Tanner was depressingly quiet, and I had to search for something to say to keep the conversation going. There were only so many towing questions I knew to ask. He seemed to concentrate on his plate, preoccupied, and that added an extra layer of disappointment.

After we stuffed ourselves, Tanner drove us downtown to the touristy, but quaint, Main Street with expensive boutiques, stores selling outer winter wear, and several breweries, plus a coffee shop that rivaled Kristen's.

He turned down the alley with "no parking" signs posted on the backs of the old brick buildings. A Hyundai Santa Fe was reversed in, blocking a loading dock made of crumbling cement and covered in graffiti. Tanner noted the time on his watch and we rode around for a few minutes, then circled back. The driver had not moved the Santa Fe, front-wheel drive, so we scooped it up and hauled it out of there, fast, because once you made the capture you didn't want to get caught. We stowed the car in Tanner's lot behind the locked chain-link fence topped with circles of razor wire.

"You want to see how to strap the tires?" he asked.

"Sure."

Tanner returned the Santa Fe to the lifted position, then got out and rummaged in the hold of his truck. He brought out some sturdy black tie-downs and did a quick demo for me. "This is for added safety, but unnecessary if you're not towing very far."

"Okay." I'd have to look for some of those straps in Dad's truck.

He lowered the vehicle once more and stored the straps under his truck bed. As we drove away, I asked, "How do people get their cars after you tow them away?"

"I'll show you that, too."

When we returned to the alley, Tanner pointed to the towaway warning sign with his phone number painted in large numbers. Beneath Tanner's number, the name of a different towing company tried to bleed through.

"Who had this lot before you?"

"Del's Towing. You didn't know?"

I pivoted in my seat to face him. "When did you take over?"

"Recently. I got his lots after your dad died."

Blood rushed to my face and I ducked my head. "Oh."

"Sorry, Delaney." Tanner asked, "Were you close?"

"No. My parents divorced when I was a little kid. I moved to Denver with my mom and my dad stayed in Spruce Ridge." The reason that I didn't know Del at all wasn't a fun fact I trotted out for small talk or first dates. Only Kristen knew how I felt about my absent dad.

When Kristen scouted locations for her business, I was the one who suggested the city where I was born, and when my friend asked for my help, I agreed thinking I'd bump into Del Morran. This is a small town and there was a good chance I'd run into him. I'd believed I had all the time in the world to satisfy my curiosity, but Del had been killed in a hit-and-run accident three short weeks ago, leaving me with his truck and a lot of questions. Jeremy's death following so closely after Dad's was not cool, either.

"Someone had to manage the towaway zones, Delaney." There was an apologetic tone in Tanner's voice.

I lifted my head back up. "It's okay."

Tanner's eyes studied mine, but I blushed under his gaze and broke the connection. He asked, "Would you like some of this work? We could divide the time. What do you say?"

This was a chance to earn money, so there was no

way I could turn it down. "Explain this business to me again."

"A lot of drivers don't understand they're on private property and that the owners have the right to decide which vehicles can park here. They don't get that they've broken the law and parked against regulations. I only work for a few select customers, but it amounts to about two to three tows a day, more on Friday nights when people go to the bars."

"So, you cruise around to find these illegally parked cars?"

"Parking is restricted from nine to nine when the businesses need their loading docks for deliveries. During the day the business owner calls if someone is blocking their drive, but after hours I make a few rounds like we did tonight. I try to give the drivers a little time to move their cars, but I don't wait too long. When the drivers realize their transportation has disappeared, they call my number." He pointed to the painted-over sign. "And they meet me at my yard, pay me, and I release their vehicles back to them."

I asked him, "Do you get to keep the whole amount? Or do you kickback a percent to the business owners?"

"No. I keep the fee, plus the businesses compensate me to make sure their private lots are cleared. It's a good gig."

"Two or three a day?" The mini downtown did not have enough parking spots, and I'd even thought about leaving my car in the alley myself a time or two. I'm glad I hadn't. "All right. I'll take whatever hours you don't want."

Tanner said, "How about you take Tuesdays and

Thursdays? What I need is someone to cover the daytime hours, but you can have the evenings, too."

"Sounds good."

He gave me his hand and we shook on it.

"I'll arrange for the businesses to call you during the day, but you'll need to drive around from five until nine in the evening like we're doing tonight. Go ahead and tow the vehicles to my lot. During your shifts I'll forward my number to your cell so the drivers can get a hold of you to get their cars back." He wrote his gate code on a slip of paper.

"Thanks." No one had called me on Del's Towing line this whole evening, so a share in Tanner's private property business would be a good thing. "Did you know Jeremy worked for Del's Towing?"

"Yeah. I saw him in Del's tow truck a couple of times." Tanner's phone rang and he picked up. He mouthed at me, "The call for the Santa Fe," and I bobbed my head up and down.

He started his rig back up and we took off for his lot. After a few grumbling complaints, the driver paid the fee and Tanner released his vehicle to him. During the next hour, we captured another violator. Tanner let me operate the controls; I drove to his lot and disengaged the car. Easy enough. At least with this hot tow operator right there by my side.

When he dropped me off at the Mexican place where I'd left my Fiat, I asked, "One more thing. Can you explain these?" I unlocked my phone and showed him the photos I'd taken of the gear in Dad's truck. Finding Jeremy's tow ticket had erased all thoughts of the equipment until now.

"That box with the handle on it is a jump starter.

You don't use jumper cables to connect one car battery to another like in the past. That's outdated." He named the other pieces of equipment—wheel ties, wireless tow lights, and jack stands. The small plastic box that held various wires and hooks was an "unlock kit." He said, "People will phone you when they have a dead battery or when they lock their keys in their car. You'll be using this stuff a lot."

I'd already taken a call for gasoline, so I knew calls weren't always for tows. Rather than ask yet another question, I thought I'd search *YouTube* for pointers on jump boxes and slim jims. I did ask, "What kinds of chains are in tow trucks?"

"There's a lot of different ones. There's couplers, recovery chains, tie-down chains, tailboard chains, v-bridles." He scrolled through my pictures. "I don't see any in these photos, but I have a few on my flatbed if you want to see what the chains look like."

"Okay, thanks. Maybe I will another time." I put my phone away, we sat in silence for a bit, then I gripped the door handle. "Well, I appreciate your help, Tanner. You're a great teacher."

"One of my charms."

"One of many, I suppose?" I gave him a flirty smile, laying it on. "I don't want to know about your other charms, or do I?"

But he only said, "See you later," so I scrambled down out of his rig.

He didn't try to flirt or anything. Not a date. Just a regular work night with a colleague. Was there something going on between Tanner and me besides wishful thinking on my part? Probably not. Nothing resembled an attempt to hook up. I guess he wasn't looking to get lucky. Not that he would have, even if he did have dreamy eyes and a hot bod.

****

I was the one who got lucky.

A call came in on Del's Towing line early the next morning. Thankfully, today was Friday and I had the day off from the coffee shop. Once I showed up, I threw my shoulders back and advanced to the stalled vehicle like I belonged there.

The older Toyota Corolla was front-wheel drive, so I scooped up the front end. I felt confident as we sailed along, brown, stacked heels on my feet, paying customer on the passenger seat. That feeling was short-lived when we arrived at our destination—his house—and I jackknifed reversing into the driveway.

I pulled forward and tried backing up again. Jackknifed again.

The man white-knuckled the door handle and shot glances at me from the corner of his eyes. Finally, I got everything straightened and released his Corolla, and once the tires hit the ground, he just about fell out of the truck.

Note to self—quit scaring the customers. Practice backing up.

He wiped his brow. "The last time I needed a tow, a man came out."

A man. Go figure he'd bring that up. "I appreciate you calling me."

"I always use Del's Towing."

"The man who responded, was he young or old…er, I mean…middle aged?" My dad had been about the same age as this guy.

"Younger. His name was Jeremy."

I stared at him, my eyes wide. “Oh, you knew Jeremy?”

“Not really, but I remember his name. Remember everything about that day, because that very night my car was stolen, right here off my driveway. I’d just paid to have my Mustang towed here, and before the check even hit the bank, the damn car was gone. Sorry for the language.”

“Shit.” I bit my lip. “Oh, excuse me, but that sucks.”

“You’re right.” He asked, “How much do I owe you?”

I told him and he handed me his credit card. “I appreciate your call. Contact me whenever you need a tow.”

His gaze travelled down to my brown heels and back up to my red curls like he didn’t think that was a good idea.

****

Saturdays always rushed by with a constant stream of customers wanting their lattes and iced coffees super quick. I checked my phone constantly for missed calls for tows and watched the doorway just as incessantly for the police to walk in. I was certain I hadn’t seen the last of the cops. When my shift ended, I hightailed it out of there. After showering the caffeine out of my pores, I ate pizza in front of the shopping channel. All by my lonesome. Tanner was either covering his private property lots or on a real date with a real girlfriend.

Sunday was the only day the coffee shop closed, so I did some chores wishing all the while for people to phone for a tow, wondering why my cell stayed silent…when *finally* the stupid thing rang.

"Are you trying to take over my business? Friendly Finance told me you asked for repo work, that you said you're a friend of mine." Tanner's voice had an edge.

"Uh…it's not like that." *Jeez.* Was he going to share his private property work, but get angry that I made a simple sales pitch to Friendly? Another call was coming through. "Sorry, I'll have to phone you back."

A customer on the Del Towing line. *Yes!* A breakdown on the side of the road. *Yes!* Well, bad for them, good for me. I raced over to pick up the tow truck and then sped as fast as I could to the address I was given, but when I arrived I found the car, a front-wheel drive Saab, angled in a ditch. I tried but couldn't get the claws to go under the tires. Vehicles had to be flat on their wheels for the self-loader to work effectively.

Hiding behind Dad's truck in my three-inch, black and white pumps, my elegant dress-for-success shoes, I called Tanner. "Are you available right now? I have a Saab down an incline. A fairly steep angle."

"It needs a flatbed." He blew out a sigh. "Where are you?"

"Off County Road 10 near the cut off to the ski resorts."

I returned my phone to my pocket and approached the customer. "You need a flatbed to pull your car out of that gulley. One's on the way."

"Why didn't you bring one with you?"

I used my polite voice. "I'm sorry, I should've asked if your vehicle was on all four wheels or in a ditch." I would next time. We both stood around, putzing on our phones, not speaking to one another for ten minutes.

At last, Tanner arrived in worn-out boots and well-toned muscles. I'll admit watching him at work took my breath away and made my heart skip. He put the car in neutral, attached a winch to the Saab's undercarriage—I'm learning the terms—and hauled the car onto the flatbed in no time at all. He tied down all four wheels and tightened the straps.

He was heading toward his truck when I stopped him. "Collect the payment from the customer." I jiggled a thumb toward the man.

"No, you collect."

I didn't want to argue with the guy standing right there. "Thanks for your help."

Tanner dove behind his wheel and whirred down the window. "The police stopped by my house to ask me more questions about Jeremy Winslow." He slanted his eyes at me and shook his head like I was a real pain in the you-know-what.

Well, excuse me. I was about to tell him to go play in traffic, but he'd already left the scene. I opened the truck door and swiveled up behind the wheel. All my feelings of accomplishment were blown to bits and scattered on the Colorado wind. I wanted to launch my phone out the window, but I took a few seconds to compose myself and just turned the dang thing off.

Earlier today I couldn't wait for the phone to ring.

But now I didn't want to talk to any customers. I didn't want to talk to Tanner. And I didn't want to speak to the police.

Chapter 8

What could I buy for twenty or thirty thousand dollars?

Just think about it.

I was back in my apartment in front of my laptop, so I queried self-loaders for sale. Yes, they went for thirty thousand crisp ones, as Will had told me. After a few minutes imagining how I would spend the money, reality returned, and I switched my phone ringer back on.

I couldn't sell the truck because I didn't have the title yet.

Plus no matter what, I still needed to make a living and driving the truck seemed the best option. Del Morran had made so much money with this truck he'd paid it off early. And it appeared to me Tanner brought in a good income on private property lots, plus what he made in repo work, and if he could do it, so could I.

I was turning into such a good con artist, I was even conning myself.

Besides, the thought of telling Mom and Will they were right, that I couldn't handle the business, didn't sit well.

Now I was impatient for more customers to call.

Del's Towing company cards spilled out of the box onto the counter. Too plain. With a black, felt tip pen, I doodled an outline of a stiletto around the phone number. *Nice.* That's when I noticed a website was printed on the card, so I brought it up on my computer.

Mostly the webpage described Del Morran's autobody services, but towing was mentioned, too, along with the job description I now planned to adopt, "vehicle recovery specialist." Recovery specialist sounded way-cooler than tow truck operator. A picture of Dad dominated the *About Us* page. I hadn't seen many pictures of my father, and those I'd seen were old, but this one appeared recent. Funny, I hadn't thought of searching the internet for him before, but there he was.

His thick, carroty-red hair, dark freckles, pale complexion, and heart-shaped face he'd handed down to me. I was a softened, female version, mini-me, of Dad. All I got from Mom was my height and petite frame. And the love of shoes.

I queried other towing websites, just for comparison, and discovered one where customers could click on a button and a call was put through to the service. *Nifty*. I returned to the query screen where a news post appeared at the top of the page—"Owner of Del's Towing Questioned in Murder Investigation. Charges to be Filed Soon."

My eyes skimmed the short article at record speed. It simply reported that Del's Towing hauled a vehicle with a body found in the trunk. The writer didn't say charges would be levied against me. There was nothing except the truth, but what would people think? I didn't appreciate that incriminating kind of headline showing up on the internet. I'd call that journalist and give him a piece of my mind, but there was no phone number on the site, only a place to leave a comment.

Frustrated, much?

If I could find another suspect beside myself, maybe I could do something about that article. Like, provide the newshound a tip to send him in another direction. And I couldn't help wondering why the police contacted Tanner. Was the detective going to appear at my place as well? Did the forensic team find my toe prints? I wanted answers, too.

My doorbell rang so I went to get it. When I threw open the door, Kristen said, "I'm bored. Let's do something tonight. You have any ideas?"

I motioned her inside. "Boy, do I. Are you up for a little investigating?"

Her dark eyebrows shot skyward. "I'm up for pizza."

"I just had that last night." Kristen gave me a pouty face, so I said, "We can stop at the pizza-by-the-slice place first, how's that?"

She hesitated. "What do you mean, investigate?"

"Did you see the article that said I was questioned about Jeremy's murder? It made me look bad." *Really bad*.

"No. Let's see it."

I showed it to her.

Always my champion, Kristen said, "I'm going to call them and demand a retraction."

"I tried to locate a number, but couldn't find one." I shoved my fists on my hips. "The police have been talking to Tanner again and I want to know why."

She leaned against the kitchen counter. "How are you going to find that out?"

Having no idea, I said, "Give your friend Zach a call. See if he knows what's going on."

"I asked him at church this morning. He says he can't tell me anything. Let's head out for that pizza. I'll grab my purse and meet you downstairs." Kristen went back to her apartment while I locked up mine.

Once at the pizza parlor, we ordered a couple of slices with sausage, pepperoni, and jalapenos. I glided one of them onto my plate. "I want to know why Jeremy's car was in that garage over on Third. I wonder what trouble that rat fink, Jeremy, could've gotten into."

My friend reminded me, "You need to cut him some slack. He's dead, after all."

I rolled my eyes and stuffed a bite of pizza in my mouth. After I swallowed, I said, "I sort of went on a date, or maybe two, with Tanner Utley. Well, I'm not sure either was a date. I'm getting a weird vibe that I can't put my finger on."

"What do you mean?"

"I thought he might be interested in me, but I guess I was wrong."

"Is he married? Is that it?"

"He said he isn't."

"Hmm. Something else, then. What could he be hiding?" The corner of Kristen's mouth hinted at a smile. "You've always had a soft spot for the bad-boy types."

I laughed. "You're the one who's the bleeding heart, but you manage to avoid dating the dangerous ones." My friend tended to go out with the pastor's son or the seminary student. "The sheriff mentioned Jeremy was in the criminal database. Doesn't that mean he had an arrest record?"

Kristen bowed her head. "Wow. He was on the

wrong side of the law."

"Do ya' think?" I fluttered my lips, making a sound like the air let out of a tire. "I sure know how to pick them."

We chewed on the gooey slices in slow silence, while my mind sped along. Maybe Tanner was holding back because he thought I killed Jeremy. Who could blame him? That headline implied I was the murderer.

When the last of the pizza disappeared, I asked, "You want another piece? I can get another slice."

"Nah, I'm good. What now?" Kristen stood up and slung her bag over her shoulder.

I told her, "I've got an idea."

We motored over to the place where it all started, 913 Third Street, in the old part of town. This is where the working class lived, the people who cleaned houses and served in restaurants, the ones who took care of all the rich and famous in Spruce Ridge. I circled to the front of the house and killed the engine.

"Here's some pepper spray." I handed the tiny canister to my friend.

"What's this for?"

"You stay in the car. I'm going to see if someone's home. If anything happens, you're armed." If the spray still worked, that is.

She clutched the pocket-sized can to her chest and nodded with wide gray eyes. The mace was an afterthought because I didn't really think Kristen was in danger. The sheriff would've questioned the occupants and searched the house already. All I planned to do was knock on the door and find out who lived here.

Dirt fought with weeds and yellow stubs of grass along the walkway to the porch. I ascended the steps and rang the bell. No one answered after a few more rings, so I returned to the car. See, nothing happened, nothing to worry about.

Kristen gave the pepper spray back to me. "What next?"

I shook the canister to see if it was active. It was not. *Oops*. "We can try Jeremy's apartment."

"Okay. Let's go."

We rambled over to a new complex of four-story brick buildings surrounded by tall fir trees with well-maintained landscaping. I parked on the other side of a wrought iron fence surrounding a heated pool and volleyball court. As we took to the sidewalk and mounted the outside staircase to the third floor, the mulch gave off a strong scent of pine bark and decay.

I felt more confident at this familiar place, expecting the apartment to be empty and hoping to look through uncovered windows, but after I knocked a stranger answered the door. A woman I'd never met before, somewhere near forty in sweatpants and a hoody.

I introduced myself and said, "Do you know Jeremy Winslow? He lived here."

"He was the renter before me. I moved in two weeks ago. Never met him, but I saw in the news that he died. I only know this was his apartment because I get some of his mail. Why?"

"I'm a friend of his. Do you still have his mail?" I had no idea he'd moved out.

"I put it back in the mailbox to return to the post office."

"Did you notice who the letters were from?" How this would help I had no idea.

"A few from Friendly Finance, that's all I remember."

Well, it was obvious what that was about, collection letters for the repo'd Challenger. I thanked her, and Kristen followed me back to the Fiat. When she cracked the car door open, Kristen said, "What are you trying to accomplish, Delaney?"

"I told you, I'd like to know why his car was in that garage on Third."

"Have you talked to any of Jeremy's friends? Maybe one of them knows."

"I never met any. Strange, isn't it? We went out long enough for him to introduce me to his peeps."

"Maybe he didn't want them to meet you."

"Not very flattering. Or…he didn't want me to meet them. There is a difference." When Kristen only shrugged her shoulders, I said, "Let's try where Jeremy worked, L&B Garage."

Kristen fastened her seat belt. "On a Sunday night? It's closed."

The garage was my last lead. "Let's get ice cream, then drive by. My treat."

"Sounds good to me." She held out a palm for a high five.

We went through the ice cream parlor drive-up window for milkshakes blended with toppings. Both of us got butterscotch. Great minds think alike.

Industrial Lane was deserted with closed businesses and nothing much happening, but I turned into the office complex across the street and edged the Fiat alongside a Ford Excursion, one of those monstrous four-wheel drives. The strong breeze kicked up and an empty plastic bag scudded over the concrete to become tangled in a prickly shrub. It felt gloomy after hours in front of these empty offices opposite the shuttered mechanic's workshop.

Feeling like a PI, I said, "Let's stake out the joint." I unwound my window and a draft blew in. The April air had a bite. "Nobody can see us over here, right?" The ginormous vehicle next to us cast a huge shadow over my tiny car.

Kristen jabbed her plastic spoon in her ice cream and set the cup in the holder. "They can't see us, but we can't see them either. We should get out."

We both opened our doors without making a sound and darted around the corner of the one-story brick office building. Creeping along the back wall, we came out the other side near the mechanic's garage. I ducked low behind two potentilla bushes and manhandled Kris down next to me. Several vehicles swept past on the street. A few moments later, a copper-colored truck turned in to the garage—I didn't know what make or model, although the color was eye-catching. The door to the auto bay rolled up, the vehicle entered, and a similar truck could be seen up on the rack. The door unfolded back down.

I whispered, "Someone's working tonight after all."

A few minutes later, two more identical-looking trucks arrived and disappeared around the back. A barrel-chested man in work boots, dirty blue jeans, and a floppy baseball cap popped out a side door and cast a brief look our way. He lit a cigarette and took a deep drag. Freddie Haag.

The sound of his cell chirping carried over in this quiet time of the night. He bellowed into the phone,

“No…I said Ford Ranger,” and hung up, shaking his head. The phone rang again and he answered, “Oh, hello, R.C. Yup, I’m working on it. Waiting on the last one now.” He mumbled a few more words before sliding the phone back into a pocket.

I asked Kristen, “What’s going on? It’s like they sent out a request for those particular trucks. I wish I could see what they’re doing inside there.”

Note to self—buy some binoculars.

The mechanic loitered around the door staring every which way, flicking the ash off his cigarette.

I told Kristen, “I talked to that man the day I met Axle. He was downright hostile.”

Haag stared hard in our direction and goosebumps sped up my arms. He tossed his spent butt and stomped inside with one last glance our way. Kristen and I gave each other wide-eyed looks.

A light bulb went off in my brain. “Kris, I think this is a chop shop.” I pulled her with me out of sight and leaned against the back of the building. I opened the search engine on my cellphone and made a query. “It says, ‘Chop shops are illegal garages that buy stolen cars, dismantle them, and sell their individual parts for profit. They often target specific makes and models.’ ” I faced the screen in her direction so she could see for herself. “I don’t know the makes of those trucks, but they look all the same. Ford Rangers?”

“I’ve heard of some cars being stolen around here, but a chop shop in Spruce Ridge?” She stared at me in disbelief. “Maybe there’s a recall on those Rangers.”

I flattened my lips in a *get-real* expression.

The sound of a powerful engine made us poke our heads back out. A wrecker lumbered past with a truck on the back. We both got a glimpse of the decal before it pulled into the garage. A Ford Ranger.

I pointed to her phone. "Text your friend at the police department and let him know L&B is operating a chop shop."

"All right."

"So, you believe me now?"

"I guess so," she admitted. After her text went through, her phone vibrated. She said to me, "It's Zach," then into the phone, her voice low, "Zach, I have a tip for you. Delaney and I are out on Industrial Lane and saw some…er…suspicious activity at L&B Garage." She paused to listen, then answered his questions. "Uh-huh…uh-huh. A whole bunch of the same kind of truck kept showing up…yeah, uh-huh." Once she hung up, she said, "Zach is going to report our tip and a patrolman is going to check it out."

I talked in a quiet voice to match Kristen's, careful the sound didn't carry. "Don't you think the police would've already examined that garage since Jeremy worked there?"

"Maybe they only do the illegal stuff when no one's around. Like tonight. Didn't you go there when they were open and you didn't see anything strange?"

"I did think there was something dodgy about the place, but I don't know what's normal. Or what's fishy."

"You're the one who got the idea they're a chop shop. Do you think we should leave now?"

"I want to see what happens when the police turn up."

Kristen said, "Okay, I guess we'll be safe enough."

We stole back to the Fiat to wait. I took a long,

tight draw of my thick milkshake to settle in for the show. Kristen picked hers up, too, and we both slid down low in our seats.

"We should be okay once the cops arrive unless bullets start to fly, don't ya' think?" I laughed.

A sound like a shot going off exploded in our ears. We both screamed and my frozen drink flew out of my hands. I was right about the bullets. We were in the middle of a police raid. Oh, why did I drag Kristen into this?

A loud rap on Kristen's window sounded like another gunshot, then a man ripped open the passenger side door. A scream rang out again, breathless and hoarse. It was me. I was the one screaming.

Kristen yelled, "Axle!"

He put one foot on the door frame and leaned in. "What are you doing here?"

I patted the place over my racing heart and took a deep breath. There weren't any bullets, only Axle knocking on the glass. I picked my milkshake up off the floor, the lid still intact, and stuck it in the cupholder, then stuck my head out of the car and strained to see around the hulking teenager. The police were nowhere in sight.

Kristen said, "The cops are on the way here to bust the chop shop. We called them." I gouged her with my elbow and tried to silence her with a super-laser glare.

Axle cast a glance over his shoulder. "What did you call them for? You don't know who you're dealing with."

"How did you find us?" I asked him.

"I was over at the garage and saw the Fiat parked here, then I recognized you two inside."

Eek. I thought the car well hidden. If Axle spotted us, so could the car thieves at L&B. Where were the police? What was taking them so long? I felt exposed now and started shivering like I was caught in a snowstorm without a warm, puffy coat.

Kristen's gray eyes widened and her skin turned pale. She must be feeling vulnerable, too. "We need to get out of here."

"I agree. Let's go." I stabbed the key in the ignition.

"Step back." Kristen shoved her cousin out of the way and slammed the door shut. "Go, go, go!" She rocked back and forth in her seat to make the Fiat move faster.

Axle snapped the door back open. "Hey, wait. Can I bum a ride with you? I was dropped off and I don't have a way home."

Kristen said, her voice excited, "Sure. We can do that, can't we, Delaney?"

I wondered if he was dropped off, or if he was the one doing the dropping off, like delivering stolen Fords? Although he was a stranger to me, he was Kristen's cousin and he needed our help to escape, so I said, "Of course."

I leaned over and thrashed around the pint-sized back seat, a crowded mess of old sweatshirts, jackets, and shoeboxes. "I'm not sure there's room in my car, Axle. What should we do? What should we do?" My voice wobbled.

He glanced around inside. "What's with this itty bitty car?"

"It's mine."

"Yours?"

"Well, I guess so, I'm the one driving it." My voice came out shrill and my eyes darted past the Excursion. Was someone at L&B watching us?

"I won't fit back there."

Kristen said, "Hold on, you can take my seat." She sprang into the back, jamming herself into the tight compartment. Axle shoehorned himself into the spot she'd just vacated and banged the door shut. Squashed, Kristen spilled over the seatback, her chin close to Axle's shoulder. Both of the cousins' eyes were that unusual gray.

I floored the gas and we took off, laying down a few inches of rubber, my eyes glued to the rearview mirror. What if we'd been seen? Axle had sighted us; Freddie Haag must have as well. I didn't know what he would do about it, but the man gave me the willies. We hurtled down Industrial Lane, my Fiat's motor humming under the strain. Only after we were well away from the garage did I ease off the accelerator and slow down to match other traffic.

Axle shifted in his seat and gripped his cellphone. "Keep heading toward downtown and make a right on Main then left on Columbine."

"Roger that." I didn't complain about the stagnant traffic on Main Street. The crowded road felt safe.

After turning onto Columbine Court and entering a run-down trailer park with overflowing garbage bins and rusty cars, I crept the Fiat past three, no four, scary men sitting on top of a picnic table. They quit talking to watch us the whole length of the street. I shut off the engine in front of a dingy white mobile home with a flimsy-appearing awning over the door. A car from the other side of the park backfired. My dry throat sucked in air and I screamed, loud. *Again.* Okay, so I was still a little wigged out.

"You're such a weenie." Axle launched himself from the car and Kristen tumbled out after him.

I exited from the driver's side and skirted around the back bumper. I said, "Am not."

"Are, too."

"Am not!"

Kristen said, "You're bickering like brother and sister. You guys act like you're the ones who are related." My friend asked her cousin, "Well, what do you say?"

Axle leaned against the car door with his arms crossed. "Thanks for the ride home. I owe you one. Bring your tow truck by and I'll give you an oil change." He sounded like he meant it.

I said, "I don't need any service, my dad kept the truck in top shape." Kristen gave me the eye, so I added, "But I appreciate the offer. Do you know what tow dollies are?"

"Of course I do, I'm not stupid."

"I didn't call you stupid."

"Sure you did."

Kristen interrupted us with, "Kids, kids, play nice."

"Here's the problem." I explained my dilemma with the heavy tow dollies while he nodded a couple of times.

He said, "Those old dolly wheels weigh about sixty pounds each. They make ultra-light ones now."

"I'd rather not have to buy any new equipment."

"Okay. I can add wheel mounts under the truck bed. Pick me up in the morning and we'll take your rig over to the garage."

“What are mounts?”

“I’ll show you tomorrow.”

I asked, “But won’t the shop be shut down by the police?”

“Nah, I texted them on the way over here. They’ll be open.”

Kristen’s hands flew to her mouth. “Oh no, nobody tell Zach we alerted the chop shop.”

I felt a moment of irritation. “You mean, the garage can cover up the operation that fast?”

“What operation?”

I glared at Axle. “Keep up here. A chop shop.”

“I don’t know what you’re talking about.” Axle strolled toward the mobile home and threw his words over his shoulder, “Pick me up in the morning.” He disappeared inside and the door slammed behind him.

I turned to Kristen. “I guess I’ll be late for work tomorrow, boss.”

Chapter 9

The next morning, Axle was his usual grumpy self. His brown hair poked out from under a knit cap, the familiar earbuds hung around his neck, and he only grunted a hello.

First, I had to take him to the fast food burger joint for breakfast, then we traversed the length of Main Street, with the quaint tourist stores lining the sidewalks and red hummingbird feeders and flowering baskets hanging from light poles. We drove past several women in fur-collared jackets and high-end boots carrying humongous shopping bags, and I had to dodge a couple of athletic-looking men in biker shirts on racing bikes in the middle of the street. That made the sweat pop out on my forehead since the truck was wide and the side mirrors stuck out. I hoped Axle didn't notice my feet could barely reach the pedals because I was not wearing my heels and I wasn't in the mood for his insults.

"Turn left at the next light," Axle said around a full mouth of breakfast sandwich.

"I know where I'm going. Remember we were there last night." I needed a latte this morning, bad, *real bad.* As bad as a dead-tired girl on a caffeine-deprived rampage. The boiling-hot coffee from the burger place didn't hit the spot. And Axle annoyed me, pawing through the glove compartment. I asked him, "What are you searching for?"

"Napkins. You didn't get enough." He pulled out a small, white carton. "What's this?" He extracted the top card with my drawing of the high-heeled shoe.

"My business cards. What do you think of the logo?"

"It looks dumb, but it goes with your name, Delaney Moron."

"It's not moron. It's pronounced, 'more-ann,' you moron."

"No, it's like moron, moron," he chanted.

Not to be topped, I said, "Axle, like ax-murderer."

He threw a balled-up napkin into the take-out bag.

I tried again, "Axle, like not all your engines are sparking."

The window absorbed his attention.

I turned off on Industrial Lane. "Axle, like a wheel is loose." Nothing. "Axle, like Paxil."

His eyes flashed and his eyebrows formed a "V" over his nose. "What's a Paxil?"

"A tranquilizer. I need a chill pill when I'm around you."

He laughed that time.

We arrived at the garage, and sure enough L&B was open for business. Was Axle going to fabricate the wheel mounts from chopped-up car parts? Don't ask, don't tell.

He said, "Where do you want me to bring the truck when I'm done?"

"I have to work at the coffee shop, so why don't you meet me there?"

"Roosters?"

"It's Roasters on the Ridge. Roasters. Like roasting coffee beans."

Axle lifted his nose in the air and sang, "Cock-a-doodle-do."

I just shook my head and shoved out of my seat. Kristen waited for me in her Prius, so we sped back to the coffee shop in time for a much-needed caffeine infusion for me, and—oh, yeah—to work the morning rush.

My shift ended at noon, but Axle hadn't called yet, so I went upstairs to my apartment to study my auto encyclopedia. While I flipped the pages, a call came in for Del's Towing.

"I'm sorry, the truck is in the shop, but I have the number for another tow driver who's good." I gave them Tanner's contact info.

"Is he the one that has the driver in the high heels?"

"Uh, doubtful, but you can hope." I texted Tanner a heads-up, but he didn't reply. *Cripes*…was he still miffed with me about Friendly Finance?

What was I waiting around for? Time to get busy. Axle might think my business cards stupid, but callers asked for the high-heeled driver and that set me apart. I opened my laptop and searched for a logo maker. I found a stock image of a stiletto and used it to design new cards for Del's Towing, recovery specialist. The price of the merchandise was discounted for first time customers—a bargain—so after thinking about it for half a second, I hit the "buy" button. I ordered 100 cards and 20 key chains, each with a black stiletto charm stamped with the name, "Del's Towing." *Swag.* The businesswoman I am.

A horn sounded outside my apartment window and I scurried over to look out the curtain. Two guys stood with Axle next to Dad's truck. One handed the keys to

Axle, then the two men got into a pickup idling on the street, took off, and left the teenager behind.

I ran down the stairs. I'd missed that self-loader, that big ole hunk of metal.

"Here you go." The keys made a ringing sound as Axle dangled them in front of my nose.

I swiped the jingling keys out of his hand. "How's it work?"

"See that?" He pointed under the truck bed.

I crouched down and caught sight of the dolly wheels held in place by metal racks. He showed me how to unlock the latch, and once I released the clip, the wheels rolled out onto the ground. To return them, all I had to do was push the dollies back up into the mounting brackets. Snug them into place. Shut the latch. Done.

"Wow. Did you invent this, Axle?"

"No. Well, I fabricated the mounts, but there are systems you can buy to retrofit these trucks."

"I owe you one. I appreciate it." I couldn't help but add, "little cousin," and punched his arm, hard.

Axle rubbed his skin. "A couple of things. There are weight limits with these dollies. No more than three thousand pounds on each one. The large tires on the heavier vehicles won't fit in the dollies, so you can tell. And keep your speed under fifty."

"Thanks. I mean it. I didn't know about all that." I didn't mind admitting this to Axle. He saw through me anyway. "So, nothing went on at the garage last night?"

"Police drove by, but it was shut tight, no one there." He stared down at his feet.

"You need to get another job."

He just shrugged and found something interesting

to stare at on the ground.

"Do you know what happened to Jeremy?"

"I don't, Delaney. Honest. I only started working at L&B a little while ago. I didn't know him." I inspected his face, but he turned away and wouldn't look at me. He muttered, "Can you drive me back home?" His ride hadn't stuck around.

"Sure."

We hoisted ourselves up into the truck. I nudged the seat forward and all the mirrors back into place, then pressed my toe on the accelerator. I repeated, "So, Axle, you should get another job, a better one. That garage seems like a dangerous place to work."

"It's not. Nothing is going on there. You're wrong, Delaney."

I threw him a look as if to say, *no, you're wrong.*

He matched my gaze with a pout.

As I turned the steering wheel to take a right on 12th, I said, "You're so gifted mechanically. You made these mounts and everything. You wouldn't have any trouble getting on somewhere else."

He only grunted and repositioned his earbuds. I drove the rest of the way without saying another word. After I stopped in front of his trailer, he flapped a hand goodbye and went inside. He hadn't heard the last of it, though.

Sailing along with the windows down, I cranked the radio up and let in a brisk breeze.

Mid-April in Colorado. Spring snow on the mountains giving way to greening aspens across the Front Range. Clear blue sky with a blinding sun. A postcard-perfect town with visitors from all over the world, people shopping, jogging, and bike riding, all outside and enjoying the awesomeness of the west.

Skiers were often fooled by the spring temperatures. Many times, I'd seen out-of-towners come into the coffee shop with sunburns, not realizing they risked sunstroke or hypoxemia in the thin atmosphere and oxygen-deficient air. My town even boasted an oxygen bar, a gimmick, since only the tourists ever went there. Soon, spring would morph into a hot, dry summer with different kinds of visitors, those who wanted to camp and hike. Would I still be taking shifts at the coffee shop in June or would I be hauling vehicles full time?

A cherry red sportscar drove by. I now knew the convertible was a Lexus LC with a variable transmission. See, I was better at this. The woman driving appeared familiar, the same one I'd seen in a yellow Corvette. Her cars were so distinctive and easy to remember. If only all vehicles were that simple to tell apart.

While I was on the road, my cell sounded with Mom's ringtone. I thought about letting the call go to voice mail, but I hit the speaker button and balanced the phone on the console.

"Hi, Mom."

"How's the new job going?" She pronounced "new," *n-ewwww*, as in yucky.

"It's going. I'd been on a few tows."

"Don't forget we're shopping Friday."

"I won't."

"Okay, hon." Mom shared some gossip about Will's sister's kids. She knew the latest about her husband's family, the other lawyers at his office, and her neighbors. She asked me, "So, anything up with you?"

"Not really. I just pulled into Byron's auto shop. Gotta go." We exchanged *I-love-you* goodbyes and disconnected. I'd rather break a heel than tell Mom the truth about the Jeep repo attempt. And no need to mention my excitement last night at L&B Garage. Or that I was on a mission to expose a killer. Well, sort of.

Before I could give my little investigation any more thought, another call came through for Del's Towing, a woman who said, "Del, I need a tow. Can you come right now?"

Yeah-ez!

I asked all the questions, the address, make and model—Toyota Camry, front-wheel drive. On the side of Pine Street in the five-hundred block. On all wheels. Not upside down. Not in a ditch. All good. The perfect customer for me. Time to make some *moola.*

When I pulled the truck up to the stalled Camry, the woman was holding the hands of two elfin-looking girls, aged four or five, in matching pink dresses. She said, "Thanks for coming out so quickly. I don't have tow insurance or a credit card." The little ones held on tightly to their mom with an anxious appearance.

"No problem. I'll mail the bill."

I hauled the vehicle to her house, the two kiddos buckled in the truck's narrow backseat, not saying a word. Their wood framed ranch sat at the end of a dirt road in an unincorporated part of town. A pair of purple tricycles crowded the front door and a tire swing hung from a gnarly old cottonwood.

The young mother extracted my solemn promise that I would mail an invoice. I noted her address in my cell's directory, but I knew I wouldn't be able to send the bill.

****

Tuesday arrived. My first day to work the PPIs—Tanner's private property impound lots—so I kept an eye on my phone for calls. One came through from the antique store. "There's a car blocking my loading dock. It's been there a while. Can you move it?"

"I'll be right there." I ran into the stockroom and asked Kristen, "Can I leave now? I got a call for a tow." Today I was scheduled until the coffee shop closed and it was still early yet.

Kristen's gaze took in the group coming through the door, and though it was the end of ski season, it was an opening day sized crowd. In spite of the influx of business, she said, "Sure, but can you come back after?"

"Of course, as fast as I can." Feeling guilty, I unwound the apron from my hips. Kristen had just finished roasting the beans, so she joined Guy behind the coffee bar. He mumbled something under his breath as I swished past. I said, "Excuse me? Did you say something?"

"No." He snorted.

Determined to get back as quickly as possible, I tore out of there and went for my dad's tow truck, then zipped over to the antique store in record time. I snatched the black Honda Accord, front-wheel drive, without any trouble and towed the car to Tanner's lot. I keyed in the code, the gate swooshed to the side, and I deposited the car behind the fence.

Easy, peasy. Boy, oh boy, this was going to be great.

I struck back out for the coffee shop, but before I'd

even hit Pine Street, my phone rang. "Did you just tow my Honda?"

I screeched to a halt. "Yes."

"I want it back."

I gave him the address for Tanner's lot, and added with as much confidence as I could muster, "It'll cost $160." The amount Tanner charged and the fee we were allowed for nonconsensual tows.

He shouted into my ear, "That's crazy! Unbelievable!"

I pulled the phone away. "I'm sorry, but you parked on private property."

"I got an Uber coming, I'll be there in a few minutes."

I spun the truck around and raced back to the lot, my heart kicking up to match my speed. I waited outside the gate, thinking wistfully about police protection, but Tanner told me I couldn't call the cops. I had to do this on my own.

A Saturn drove up and a man got out. He paid the Uber driver and stalked over. He said, "I only left my car for five minutes. Did you have to tow me?"

"Sorry, but yes." I punched in the code to open Tanner's gate, knowing the man had to have left his car longer than five minutes for the antique store to have called me. Plus, it took longer than that for me to arrive and tow his car.

The man plowed right over me, pushing me to the side. "You'd better not come near my car again."

"Wait! You need to pay me." I waved my phone with the card reader sticking out the top, while he unlocked his car door and started up the engine. He called me a few choice words as he sped off. I stomped around, wanting to smash something. Making money was proving next to impossible between the sweet mother with the little girls and the mad driver who did a runner. Talk about extremes.

Note to self—don't open the gate until the hard cash is in hand.

I cursed all the way to the coffee shop, where a long line wove through the tables. I stepped behind the espresso machine and got busy. I banged the cups and saucers around, not chatting with the customers as usual. Not only Guy seemed relieved when I left at closing time, but Kristen did, too. I was not looking forward to spending the next four hours working the towaway zones if the drivers of the towed cars were going to be nasty like that.

Now in mean-mode, I returned to the alley behind the antique store and kept gunning the truck's engine, daring anyone to try to get away with parking illegally. *Bring it on, baby, bring it on.*

Nothing was happening there, so I weaved around the corner over to the back of the brewery and skated to a stop behind a Toyota Yaris, front-wheel drive. I slammed the truck door when I got out to photograph the VIN for my logbook. The capture went quickly.

The Yaris owner, a middle-aged man in a business suit, showed up at Tanner's yard in a matter of minutes. I kept the gate locked tight while he gave me the full hate-rant. "Who do you think you are? I'm not paying you a thing."

I said, "Oh, yes, you are. Yes, you are, Yes, You Are," my voice reaching shriek levels, "if you want your car back." *Ha.* No way he could get to his car since I hadn't opened the gate.

He said with clenched teeth. "Is that right?"

All my resolve blew out in a blue funk and evaporated like black exhaust from a diesel. A tear escaped my eye. I couldn't help myself…that day had been a long haul, my first day working the impound lots.

He stopped yelling and seemed to notice me for the first time, taking me in from the tips of my pink-beaded heels to the top of my carrot-red hair. Then he patted me on the back. "Now, now, young lady." He got out his wallet and handed me his credit card without another complaint.

Being a red-headed girl in pink high heels was a plus after all.

I could do this job. Yes! I did a happy dance in my mind.

I just needed to be more assertive. Stick up for myself. Toughen up. Insist on payment. I enjoyed helping people, but I needed to balance the free hauls with the paying tows.

Just as the Yaris pulled away, the repo agent, Patrick Crump, called. "I spotted the Jeep Wrangler." He gave me directions and told me to get over there fast. This was my chance to repo that Jeep and prove I could do the job. Mr. Hot Head, here I come.

Since it was close to nine and I didn't need to remain on Main Street any longer, I met Crump in an alley behind a brick building in the seedier section of downtown. But before I even came to a stop, the agent yelled out his window, "Don't mess up this time." He zoomed off, his tires kicking up mud.

I inched down from the truck cab until my high heels hit the wet dirt.

The sun had set so the light was dim. The backstreet was narrow and damp from recent rain. A fly-covered dumpster reeked like a pit toilet. Across the lane, a tall chain-link fence enclosed old cars and scrap metal, and litter banked against the building, stirring with rodent-type, scratching noises. A creepy-crawly feeling ran up my arms and down my back, but at least I didn't need to worry about lifting the tow dollies off the rig. I could just roll them out from underneath. Thanks to Axle.

Everything's okay, I told myself, as I bent over to unlock the dollies. Perspiration dampened my armpits and the skin under my braid.

The metal door on the back of the building clanged and a man dashed out. The hot-headed Jeep owner. I jumped a mile and banged my funny bone against the cab door.

He stomped up to me and yelled, "Not you again."

Sweat broke out over my face and chest now, too.

"Whaddya think you're doin?" Hands on his hips. Whiskey on his breath. Body odor on the brink of putrid. His, not mine.

"I'm repossessing your Jeep." My voice came out in a squeak. Mr. Hot Head didn't think my pink-beaded shoes cute or my red-headed self adorable. No pat on the back. No handing me the keys.

"Jesus. Do you get off on making people miserable?" Taller than me by a good six-inches, he lowered his face to mine, and I got a close-up view of his yellow teeth and bloodshot eyes. A vein throbbed in his forehead.

He swung one of his beefy arms, I ducked, and his fist rammed into the metal fence with a loud, ringing *twa-a-a-n-n-ng!*

My heart tightened like a French press bearing down on packed coffee. Was it time for the pepper spray? Absolutely. If only the canister wasn't in my purse in the truck, quite possibly empty. I pried off my left heel and held the stiletto out in front of me like a weapon. I could do some damage here.

Note to self—buy new mace, a big can, and keep it in my hand, not in my bag.

I said, "You need to back off." Strong words, right? But my voice still came out squeaky, high and tight.

He ground a fist in his palm. "You're the one who needs to back off. You should leave."

"Are you going to take another swing at me?"

"Yeah, I think I will." He edged closer.

I yanked open the truck door and leaped inside, hitting the locks before my butt hit the seat.

Mr. Hot Head gave me a sneer through the closed window. "You piece of crap, chickenshit."

I muscled the stick shift into reverse. The rear bumper slammed into the dumpster, grinding metal-on-metal, knocking the giant trash receptacle back an inch. No way was I going to leave a note for the building owner with my, or rather my dad's, insurance information. No…I dropped into first gear and shot out of there, careening down the busy street. A couple of drivers honked at me, I drove so fast and crazy, my hands shaking on the wheel. After rounding the corner, I cut down Columbine Court to Fifth, past Friendly Finance, back to Byron's autobody shop.

I turned off the ignition and sat there until my heart returned to a regular beat and my hands stopped trembling. I called Crump. "What's up with this guy? I was no more out of the truck and he was on me. It's like he knew I was there. And he took a swing at me."

"You didn't recover the Wrangler?"

"No, I did not." I flung the truck door shut behind me. It was then I realized I only had on my right shoe. The left one was in the alley with the other rubbish. I hobbled over to the rear bumper to see the damage from hitting the dumpster. It looked as if someone had taken a baseball bat to the chrome. "Next time you should stick around, see what this guy's like for yourself."

"That's your job."

I felt my mouth drop open. Crump was just as scared of the hot-headed bully as I was. "So, I'm on my own?"

"If you can't handle the work, get out of the business." He hung up.

I moved my dad's tow truck to the back of Byron's lot and crawled into the Fiat. I dialed up Kristen. "I can't do this anymore." A tear spilled down my cheek. Between the no-parking zones and the repo business, work sucked, wouldn't you agree?

"Where are you?"

"On my way home."

"See you in a few."

I cranked the Fiat's engine and hit the gas. Five minutes later I was in the parking lot behind the coffee shop.

My friend was waiting at the door of my apartment. "Did you lose a shoe?"

I glanced down the length of my frayed, skinny jeans to one pink-beaded high heel and one pink bare foot. "Yup." I burst into tears. Losing that high heel, one of my *favs*, on top of losing the repo, was the absolute last straw.

Kristen followed me inside, went to the kitchen, and plugged in my teakettle. "Okay. What happened?"

I told her the whole, pitiful story of the failed capture.

"You should inform the police."

"I can't. I need to do the job on my own."

"He threw a punch at you. He drove away drunk, most likely. Those are both crimes and I don't think reporting a crime is a bad idea."

"No. No, no, no. If I call the cops I might as well quit."

Kristen shook her head. She sorted out the teabags while I found the mugs. When she poured the water, she didn't tell me to give up, but she did tell me she'd pray for the angry man. She circled a palm along my back. "It's going to work out. Everything has a way of working out, you know."

"You think so?"

"I know so. You'll feel better tomorrow. You have the day off, so go do something fun."

****

Since I didn't have a shift at Roasters, I slept in a little. A new dawn, a new day, and I felt good just as Kristen had said, ready to put Hot Head behind me. Forget about that *asshat*.

After getting ready for the day, I stopped downstairs for two lattes, then drove over to the autobody shop. Byron was outside with a customer, so I sipped my double-shot latte and waited. The grounds now had a cared-for look, swept and clean, with a patch of fresh-turned dirt dotted with green sprouts on either side of the entryway.

A few minutes later Byron's customer took off, so I got out of my Fiat and carried a steaming latte over to him along with my own. "Good morning."

"Thanks. You didn't have ta' bring me anythin'." He gave me his gap-toothed smile and I gave him his coffee. "But I appreciate it. Come on inside."

I studied the interior with a comfy-looking, tan sofa and matching chairs. Car magazines covered a low, black table. A coffee machine with single-serve pods sat on a corner shelf. Crisp, green plants hung in baskets in front of the window. The mocha color on the walls was calming, more like a living room than the typical autobody shop owned by a grease monkey.

"Did you change anything in here, or was this the way it was when you bought the shop?" I asked.

"Oh, I've been sprucin' the place up." He chuckled.

I sank onto the couch. "Do you have a minute?"

"Sure." He perched on a stool, took the lid off his coffee, and blew over the rim of the steaming cup. "Tell me how it's going, after your rough start an' all."

I didn't intend to say much, but it all poured out. Towing a dead body. Being questioned by the police. He knew all that, but he hadn't yet heard about Hot Head. "The first time I tried to repo the Jeep Wrangler I had to leave my tow dollies behind. The second time the guy almost punched me out and I lost a shoe." My cute pink beaded high heel.

"Did he hit you?" Byron appeared to swell up, supersizing, making him seem scary and dangerous.

I threw my hands into the air. "No. I got away. I'm fine, just fine." I held my breath, then let it out when he seemed to settle back down and look more his normal self.

He asked, "What happened to the tow dollies?"

"Tanner helped me lift them onto the truck. But I think he's mad at me now, too."

"Tanner? You let me know if he's not treating you right." Another dark expression passed over his face, like an oil spill spreading across the driveway, and he puffed up again. "I told him he had to watch himself around Del's daughter. He hasn't made any unwanted advances, has he?"

I blushed as crimson as my red leather shoes. "Gack, no." *Jeez*, this was like talking to my mom about the birds and the bees. Time to change the subject. "A friend of mine installed mounts under the truck for the dollies."

"Really? Can I see them?"

"Follow me."

We went outside. He knelt on the ground and scanned underneath the self-loader, then stood up and his joints cracked. "My old bones can't bend anymore." He brushed the dirt off his pants. "This mechanic did good work for ya', Delaney. Who put these on?"

"Axle Guttenberg. He works at L&B Garage."

"That place?"

"Yep." I took a sip of my latte. "Did you know Jeremy Winslow worked there? And that he hauled cars for my dad, too?"

He gave me a curt nod. "Del let him go."

I drew my head back. "Why?"

"Don't know." Byron scratched his scalp. "Funny thing, he fired Jeremy, gosh, the day before his wreck."

I took a moment to process that. A lot of bad things

happened at once. My boyfriend dumped me the same day he was fired, and my dad was killed in a car accident the very next day. The break-up felt crummy, and Jeremy's murder was creepy and sad, but Del Morran's death left me with a heavy disappointment. I didn't feel a crippling loss at Dad's death, but that only added to the grief. His accident robbed me of the chance to know him, and I felt sorry for what might have been.

"Jeremy never told me he worked for Dad."

The overall-clad mechanic slid a glance my way. "That's odd, neither of 'em saying anything."

"Yeah, well." No argument there. What else had Jeremy, the jerk, been hiding? The police mentioned a criminal history. I shuddered at the thought and wondered again what my ex had gotten mixed up in. "Who could have killed Jeremy? Why was he put in the trunk of his car?"

Byron shook his head in a slow, solemn way, his voice deep and thick. "It's bad business."

We both stared past the brick outbuildings behind the auto bays, taking in the blue sky with soft white clouds over the snowcapped mountains.

"How's your niece?" I asked.

He beamed and his eyes lit up. "Shannon? She's doin' good. A fine girl."

"You two seem close." I pulled on my braid. "You don't mind that she calls you 'Old Man?' "

"I don't have any kids a' my own, ya' know, so I like it when the nieces and nephews call me their Old Man." His gaze drifted over to me. "You can call me 'Old Man' if you want. You must be missin' your father, and all."

I addressed my stepdad as "Will," not "Dad." I thought of Del Morran as my dad, sure, but in name only since he'd never been around. I patted Byron's arm. "You'd make a good dad, you know."

He gave me a sad smile. "I need to get back ta' work. You want to come with me? You can watch me finish a job."

I laughed. "Gosh, just like *bring-your-daughter-to-work* day. But I need to get going, too, so I'll see you later." I took Byron's empty cup and threw it in the trash with mine, then made my exit.

Maybe the bad things that came in threes had all happened already. The breakup. Dad's accident. Jeremy's murder. Except, Jeremy dumping me wasn't on the same scale. The breakup was a small thing and probably even a good thing. That Del Morran fired Jeremy made me all the more uneasy.

I was glad I hadn't had anything more to do with Jeremy. Seemed like my dad may have felt the same way.

Chapter 10

My cell rang in the middle of the night.

I shot up in bed and fumbled with the phone. “Hello, Del’s Towing.”

“Del, are you the one that towed the dead body in the trunk?” A male voice. Before my sleepy mind could think of an answer to that one, the man said, “I need a tow. Come out to County Road 6 and Pioneer Parkway,” and hung up.

The clock glowed three a.m.

I debated rolling over and going back to sleep…but I couldn’t turn down a customer. Someone needed me. Plus, what if I didn’t show up and he left me a bad review? I didn’t get a chance to ask him what kind of car he drove or if he’d been in an accident, but at least he wouldn’t be hard to find at this hour.

The jeans I wore that day were tossed over a chair so I shimmied back into them. Forget the heels. I jammed my feet into black chucks and zipped myself into a sweatshirt. My hair went into a ponytail and I went out the door.

The sky had darkened to a coffee-with-no-cream kind of black, reduced from its usual daytime robin-egg blue. No moon, no stars. The shallow wind stirred strands of loose hair across my face, and I tucked a lock behind my ear. The obsidian darkness was deep and scary.

I took the Fiat to the tow truck and the tow truck to Axle's trailer and called him from his driveway.

I know. I'm a wimp. I guess I was still rattled by Mr. Hot Head, and of course I'd left my pepper spray at home. Axle's place was closer than going back to the apartment for it, I told myself. For all I knew, the mace didn't work, and the extra-strong flashlight I'd shoved into the glove compartment was not going to send the black shadows packing either.

"Hello?" Axle sounded like he was awake.

"Can you come with me on a tow? It's out in the country."

He stayed silent for a moment. "Are you crazy? I'm getting my beauty sleep."

"Nothing can help your looks. Get out here. I'm parked out front."

A curtain twitched at the window. "I thought you were pranking me."

"Why would I do that?"

"Just to give me grief." He stepped outside, the phone at his ear, then hung up and snaked it into his pocket.

I cracked open the passenger door from the inside. "You're dressed."

"This is what I slept in." He hitched up his baggy jeans and stretched the bottom of a gray hoody down over the top of his waistband. A skull and crossbones and the name of an indie band, "Badflower," adorned the front. His head sat back deep in his hood with only his nose poking out. "Why didn't you ask Kristen to come with you?"

"Right. Two girls against a serial killer. A two-for-one killing opportunity."

He stopped in mid-click of the seatbelt. “Where are we going?”

I hit the gas before he could change his mind. He may be young, but he was sturdy and slightly intimidating in his baggy pants with the skull and crossbones sweatshirt. “I got a call for a tow. I’m just kidding about the serial killer.” *I hoped.* But what kind of maniac asks if you towed a dead body?

The ten-minute drive to the county road should have been tranquil with no traffic, no one about, the sleepy houses and closed businesses quiet. I should have been soothed by the stillness, but I was not a night person. I was an early morning person. A sunshiny day kind of a gal. The dark appeared dangerous and unnerving, making me go on high alert, although I considered myself safer having Axle with me.

The caller stood next to his Chevy Impala with the hood up. He was about eighty, not much over five-foot and with a feeble look about him, not exactly built for killing, serial or otherwise. He wore a black suit that hung on his thin frame as if he were dressed for his own funeral. He did appear ready to keel over at any minute.

I asked the elderly customer to stand back.

“Of course, young lady.” A polite gentleman. What had I been worried about?

The Impala was front-wheel drive, so Axle did not get to see his dolly mounts in action. I scooped up the front wheels with a metal grating sound. After the Impala was lifted, the gentleman handed me his gold credit card, and I charged him top dollar, even though I was only towing his car a couple of miles. Night shift paid better than day shift, right? Another old guy pulled up in a Cadillac to pick up my customer, and we all left at the same time.

When I dropped Axle off, I said, "Thanks for going with me. False alarm, I guess. But I appreciate you coming along."

"Call me whenever you have a night tow. You shouldn't go alone." Axle gave me an understanding glance.

A turd, yes, but also a good wingman.

****

The next morning, I had a little time before I needed to be at the coffee shop, so I retrieved my dad's ledgers, sat down on the couch, and puzzled over the accounts. What could I learn from the books?

Seeing Dad's handwritten notes on his computer printouts was uncanny. For a moment, it felt like Del Morran was sitting next to me, showing me how business was done, but the surprising feeling vanished as fast as it had come.

Some of the customer names seemed to repeat, and it occurred to me to take inventory. I started a spreadsheet of his clients, then searched the internet for other automotive shops that might need a tow truck driver, and sent my compiled list to the printer. Cold calling wouldn't be fun, but my business wasn't going to market itself.

I dialed up one of Del's customers, Spruce Ridge Limos. "My name is Delaney Morran. I've taken over Del's Towing, and I would love to be of service if you ever need vehicles moved." They politely took down the information. I went through the same spiel for the car rental place on Eagle Ave. and several others. Same response.

Well, I tried. It was time to head downstairs to

Roasters, so that was a good excuse to quit. I wasn't slacking, just postponing, I swear.

Sheriff Ephraim Lopez rambled into the coffee shop soon after I arrived. His light blue pressed uniform stood out in the crowd. On his belt was a walkie talkie and flashlight. On his hip, a gun. He waited in line behind everyone else, and when his turn came up, he said, "I need you to accompany me back to the sheriff's station. Just a few routine questions. Nothing to worry about."

My breath stuck in my throat but I said, "All right." I started to shuck off my apron, then paused. "Do I need an attorney?"

"Up to you."

The thought of calling Will made me want to scream. He'd tell Mom and I wouldn't hear the end of it. If I answered the sheriff's questions, I could clear up any suspicion surrounding Del's Towing, handle this on my own, and be the mature adult I pretended to be. It would be a great relief if I could get my name crossed off the suspect list. "You want a coffee to go?"

"Sure." He gave me his order and paid for it. His smile showcased his dimples and I thought that smile was a good sign.

I made myself a double shot latte, too, and told Kristen I'd be right back. Guy elbowed me out of the way to take over the counter.

The sheriff and I carried our coffees to a white four-door Chevy Silverado pickup with *Sheriff - Clear Creek County* painted black on white. Chevy trucks came in both rear-wheel and all-wheel, I now knew. I rode in the front passenger seat, not in the back, another good sign.

After we set our drinks on the conference table, Lopez said, "We found your toe prints on the dashboard of Jeremy Winslow's Challenger." His expression was unreadable, all cop-face, as blank as my bank account.

But there was no bombshell here. I always propped my feet up in my boyfriend's car. "The only ones?" I adjusted myself in the chair.

He stared straight in my eyes. "Yes. You were the last person with your toes on the dash. Or maybe the only one. We did not discover other prints."

I shrugged a *what can you do?* But my stomach churned at the thought I remained the prime suspect. Exactly what I was afraid of. Was now the time to ask for my phone call and hit speed dial for Will? My freak-out was interrupted when an officer walked into the room and plonked a folder on the table. Neither of us said a word until the officer left, then I gripped my coffee and asked, "Did you expect to find anyone else's?"

"Winslow's wife's."

My to-go cup slipped out of my fingers and landed upright on the table with a bang. "Jeremy was married?"

"Separated, in the process of a divorce. I guess you didn't know about the wife."

We studied each other. He with his neutral expression; me with shock and dismay.

"You guessed right." Here I'd suspected Tanner of being married, and I never, ever, even considered that Jeremy might've been. I parked my elbows on the table, steadying myself. "Did the wife have a motive?"

He sat stony faced without answering.

I could be stony faced, too. "Was she fighting the

divorce?" No comment. "Did the wife stand to inherit anything?" No comment. "Was there an insurance policy with her name on it?" His brown eyes narrowed. I raised a palm. "That's it. She has a motive."

But his cop demeanor did not give anything else away. He said, "Your prints are all over his car and his are all over your tow truck."

"This again? He worked for my dad. Come on, you knew that. You were bound to find his prints in the truck." My voice sounded an octave higher than usual.

"That was in March. This is April. Fingerprints do not last that long." The sheriff drew his lips into a straight line. "It's not like on television when the police lift prints from old evidence."

I cleared my throat and tried to lower my voice. "March wasn't so long ago."

"It is in Colorado. It's too dry here for impressions to remain viable for very long." He looked like he hoped I had a good explanation.

I attempted to come up with one. "We had a lot of moisture. It's been chilly and wet."

"I'm not saying it's impossible." He leaned forward on crossed arms. "When your apartment was searched, pictures of the two of you were found in your kitchen trashcan. If you broke up weeks ago, why did you wait until recently to throw the photos away?"

"I don't know. I just didn't get around to it earlier."

"Why didn't you tell us your father employed Winslow?" His brown eyes had an almost hurt expression.

"I only just found out when I saw Jeremy's name on some tow receipts." I felt the blood rising in my cheeks and blushed up to my ears.

"You didn't know your boyfriend worked for your dad?"

I blurted out, "He never said a word. Neither of them told me. My dad, of course, wouldn't have, but my boyfriend should have."

"Why wouldn't your dad have told you?"

"Let's just say we weren't close." Indeed, Del Morran might not have even known I was in town. But Dad and Jeremy knew each other. And now they both were dead. *Coinkydink?* How could it be otherwise? I asked, "Are their deaths related?"

"There's no evidence of a connection."

"Did you find Jeremy's murder weapon? It was a chain, right? A heavy chain like one from a tow truck?"

"I can't tell you that."

"Well, you don't have enough evidence to arrest me, so that chain you're searching for wasn't in my dad's truck."

Sheriff Lopez bumped a fist against his lips. "Maybe you ditched the chain."

I clamped my mouth shut. But now I knew for certain the murder weapon *was* a chain. "How did you determine the weapon?"

He paused as if considering what to reveal, then his eyes sharpened on me. "The evidence on the body, the impression on his skull."

"Is that right?" I forced down the venti-sized lump in my throat.

The sheriff opened the folder in front of him and shifted a photograph across the table. "Do you recognize this man? Have you seen him before?"

I took in the mug shot of a man with dead eyes, defiant, full of contempt. His face was thin and long with a dusting of whiskers. His nose had been broken at one time. His dull brown hair stood up on one side like he'd slept on it wrong, a classic sign of intoxication.

He must be a suspect, but who the hell was he?

I answered, "I don't recognize him at all."

Sheriff Lopez continued to thumb through the file.

My cell phone rang, so I extracted it from my purse. "Can I take this call? It might be someone needing a tow." He nodded, his eyes on the papers in front of him.

I punched the button to disconnect—the caller could leave a message—then I hit the camera app and fake-answered, "Hello, this is Del's Towing." I turned my head, as if to have a private conversation, and pointed the lens at the mug shot on the table between me and the sheriff. I flipped the button to turn the sound off and silently took a couple of pictures, hoping one would capture the image. I added, in case the lawman was listening, "Uh-huh, uh-huh, I'll call you back in a few minutes," and then acted like I hung up.

Lopez started to stand. "We're done here."

"Can I have a ride back to the coffee shop?" I gave him a hopeful smile. I felt lucky getting the picture. Maybe my luck would continue and I could wiggle more information out of him.

He smiled back, turning his stern expression into an attractive one. "Sure, come with me." He crammed the photograph into the folder and picked up his cup. I grabbed my coffee, too, cold now, and he motioned for me to walk ahead of him. He placed the file on a desk outside the conference room, then directed me through the lobby.

He pulled open the passenger door of his pickup.

As I fastened my seatbelt, I asked, "Are you close to an arrest?"

"Yes."

"Who?"

His features resumed the cop mask as he went around to the driver's side.

I crossed my fingers. "Not me, right? I'm off the hook because the weapon was not in my dad's truck."

He paused with the keys in the ignition, chin down, and gave me a sideways glance. "I'll tell you this much, Delaney, the coroner thinks the perpetrator was left handed based on Winslow's injuries. That doesn't eliminate you, though. That's just one piece of circumstantial evidence. We're still considering everyone. I'm sorry, but we'll need to talk to you again."

This annoyed me to no end. I was still on the suspect list, but at least I wasn't the only one. I was one of three. Me. The man in the picture. The wife.

I knew my ex came from money. His dad was a petroleum engineer for one of the big oil and gas companies. I'm sure his parents were respectable folks. Jeremy drove a nice car, lived in a fancy apartment. Evidently had a generous life insurance policy. All top notch.

But perhaps his wife was not so nice.

And the man in the mug shot wasn't pleasant.

Lopez had been watching me while my brain spun. "What are you thinking about, Delaney? You got a problem? Maybe I can help you."

I ran my hands through my hair, loosening my braid. "Sheriff, I'm still stunned that Jeremy's dead, and I want to know who killed him."

"You can call me Ephraim."

I stared into his eyes and he gazed back at me while my face radiated heat. I said, "Ephraim's an unusual name."

"Not where my parents are from, Mexico." He started up the engine and turned the steering wheel with his strong hands. "I was born here, but Spanish is my first language."

"I was born here, too, in Spruce Ridge."

"Good place. I love this town."

We fell quiet. He had to be in his late thirties, early forties, and in all likelihood, married. Likely had a couple of kids, too. Why did I wonder about him? No way this detective would be interested in me. Where did that idea come from? No one wanted me at the moment. Not Tanner. Not anybody. Pity party time.

He stopped his truck at the coffee shop and asked, "What are you thinking now?" *Eek.* He could guess. Handsome, eligible bachelors had a way of knowing, if he was single, that is.

"You don't need to open my door, I got it. Thanks, Ephraim." I waved him goodbye.

His gaze followed me as I hurried inside.

Kristen asked, "Everything all right?"

"Sure." I wanted to tell my friend about this new development, but we weren't alone for a minute, with Guy behind the checkout, dogging my every step.

We got busy with rushes, and soon it was time to close. I mixed up a bucket of hot vinegar water and grabbed a clean rag, then scrubbed all the tables and chairs. Guy squeegeed the windows behind me, then swept and mopped floors around me, never far away. Kristen ran lemon water through the coffee machines and cleaned the roaster. The kitchen had been scoured earlier during a lull. When Guy took care of garbage detail, I brought in the flower pots and gave them a drink of water.

We all walked out together, and I popped on my sunglasses against the blaze. After Guy took off on his motorcycle, finally, Kristen turned to me. "Guy's coming along, isn't he?" She smiled, that satisfied smile of having accomplished something.

"Uh-huh. He seems better, I guess." He'd lost the desperate appearance he had on his first day of work. "Now that we're by ourselves, I can tell you…"

She'd started across the parking lot, but came to a halt. "Tell me what?"

"Jeremy was married."

Her mouth fell open. "You're kidding! Is that what the sheriff wanted to talk to you about?"

"Yes. And my toe prints were on Jeremy's dashboard. You already know his fingerprints were in my dad's tow truck. The police are making a big deal out of it." I grabbed her arm. "There's another suspect besides me and the wife. Ephraim showed me a mug shot."

"Ephraim?"

"Sheriff Lopez."

"Ah…so who's in the mug shot?"

"Your guess is as good as mine." I produced my photo of the man; the image was in amazingly good focus. "I'd like to find out who this is and I need the wife's name, too."

"Why don't you call your stepdad? Attorneys have access to divorce records, don't they?"

I snapped my fingers. "Great idea. And another

thing, Jeremy had some kind of an arrest record, remember? Can you ask Zach about that?"

Kristen adjusted her bank deposit bag and extracted the Prius keys from her pocket. "Okay. You should check to see if Will can get a hold of criminal histories, too, and I'll ask Zach. But, Delaney, what are you going to do with the information? How is it going to help?"

Good questions. I lifted my sunglasses and drove a heel of one hand against my eye then dropped the glasses back down. There were so many reasons why I needed to know, but the most obvious would do. "What if the police arrest me? I don't want to go to jail for a crime I didn't commit."

"You won't." Kristen rubbed my shoulder. "Trust God. It's in His hands."

I gave her a stiff nod and watched as she sidled behind the wheel of her Prius. My friend was one of the good guys, always kind and helping others. Presumably God had many little helpers. It would be great to be one of them for a change, like Kristen, instead of the one causing all the problems.

I called Mom as soon as I got upstairs. The need for my mother outweighed my usual reluctance to share details, plus she would appreciate the gossip. "I just found out Jeremy was married, in the middle of a divorce."

She gasped out, "Really!" I could tell she was pissed off on my behalf, almost as much as I was.

I asked, "Can Will find out the name of the wife?"

"Of course he'll find out."

"Also, I'd like to know if Jeremy had a criminal history."

"You think he did?" Her voice hit a high note.

"Yes. And can you ask Will, please, to check out someone else for me? Tanner Utley."

"Who's he?"

"A person I'm doing business with. I want to make sure he's on the up-and-up." Why not? It felt like he'd discarded me after two dates—yes, they were dates!—and getting dumped was getting old. I wanted Will to search for a marriage record for Tanner, too, but couldn't bring myself to ask.

"Okay, honey. Nothing about Jeremy surprises me. I'll get the scoop on him and the other guy, too."

It was a start.

Chapter 11

I spotted a parked car in one of the towaway zones on Thursday night. *Yeah-ez!* A maroon Chevy van, front-wheel drive. Tanner may have ditched me, but at least he still allowed me to monitor the private property lots for impounds.

Once I had the Chevy ready to roll, a woman rounded the corner wearing yoga pants, carting a yoga mat. She screamed and rushed at the tow truck. "Where are you taking my van, bitch?" Her face turned crimson and her eyes shot out red beams. At least, it felt like that.

Four or five other women carrying mats came running over and surrounded the front of the self-loader. One yelled, "You can't do this," and another cried out, "You have no right."

Right.

I powered down my window. "Take a deep yoga breath." When they pounded my car with their mats, I yanked my head back inside the truck. I hit the button to close the window as bits of foam started bouncing off the hood in all directions. Red and blue and purple chunks of polyurethane soon covered the windshield. The LEDs on the light bar reflected off the rainbow of debris flying hither and yon.

Finally, nothing was left of the mats. Colorful flecks clogged my wipers when I hit the spray to clean the glass.

Except for repo cases, the carrier regulations required me to return vehicles to their owners if they showed up before I pulled away. I was allowed to demand a drop fee, or I could be nice and let the woman have the vehicle back without charge, but I didn't feel the Zen vibe. This had been work and now abuse.

The yoga women went into lunge positions with their arms raised over their heads, crescent moon poses. One woman's outstretched hand gave me the middle finger.

I slid down out of the tow truck with my cellphone in hand, ready for an argument, ready to dial 9-1-1—yes, I might have to, being outnumbered, figuring these women were in good fighting shape—but they hung back and appeared subdued.

"I'll unhook, but you owe me the drop fee."

The owner handed me her credit card without a word. She must have found her inner peace after all. When I returned her card, the yoga ladies crammed into the van and took off.

I picked bits of mat off the windshield and flicked them to the ground. Who cared what these women thought? I had a little money in the bank, and every little bit added up.

****

I talked Kristen into leaving Roasters early the next afternoon and letting Guy close the store on his own. She didn't need a lot of convincing and Guy was all too happy to do it.

The two of us met my mother at the mall in Lakewood. Mom zeroed in on the anchor department store for more sweater sets. I bought a couple of much-needed tops at a trendy boutique where Kristen picked up a beautiful scarf, we all lusted over the exclusive name brand purses, then we perused the shoe store. Shopping with Mom was not only fun, but she also purchased new shoes for both Kristen and me.

"You don't have to pay for these, Mom."

"I love to help out my girls. Besides, one day the shoe will be on the other foot—ha ha—and you'll be taking care of me."

Kristen and I exchanged glances. I chuckled. "Funny. And something to look forward to."

We stopped for a bite to eat at a Mexican fast food place. My friend and I split a plate-sized burrito and Mom got a salad.

After we took our trays to a table and Mom set her pocketbook on the chair next to her, she said, "The wife's name is Melissa, maiden name Crump. Will told me it appeared to be an amicable divorce. The ninety-day period hadn't ended yet for the judge to sign the decree. No kids."

"Ninety days? So, when did they file?"

"In January."

"What date exactly?"

"Will didn't say. I can ask him."

I unwrapped my half of the burrito and the aroma of spicy chicken and hot peppers hit my nose. "Jeremy started dating me in January, maybe even before they filed for divorce."

Kristen said, "Right. You'd only been going out a month or so before Valentine's Day. You asked me what you should get him since the relationship was new."

Mom unfurled her napkin. "Well, who knows how long they lived apart before commencing proceedings. You'd be surprised how many couples put it off." Mom would know because Will handled family law cases.

"It bothers me Jeremy never said a word about a wife." I didn't mention he hauled vehicles for Dad or my suspicions that he worked for a chop shop, too. Mom would worry in retrospect. "Did Will find out anything about the investigation? He planned to talk to the police."

"The police won't tell him anything. But Will found an arrest for armed robbery. Jeremy went to jail for it."

I choked on a lump of burrito that burned where it went down hard. I don't know what I expected, but it was not armed robbery. "What the *eff*? No way."

Mom said, "Delaney, language. He got a sentence of eighteen months, served twelve, and got off on probation last fall, in September."

"I wonder what went wrong in his life, pour soul." Kristen had been silently listening until now.

"Holy mother of…uh…holy moly." I made my fingers unclench. "A year in jail. I can't believe it. Jeremy didn't seem the type." Who knew what he'd been hiding? What else was I going to find out?

"Well, I'm not surprised." Mom arched her eyebrows and touched her napkin to her lips.

I could not shrug off the feeling there was more to the story. "So, last fall he gets out of jail. In January he files for divorce. Or…wait, who filed? Jeremy or Melissa?"

"Melissa."

"I recently met someone else named Crump. I

wonder if he's related to her. I'll bet he is."

Mom speared a tomato with her plastic fork. "No criminal history for that man, Tanner Utley. How do you know him, Laney?"

My friend glanced between us without saying a word, bless her.

"He took over Dad's impound lots and he's giving me some of the work." Ten to one, Tanner knew Del Morran, maybe even knew him well. Jeremy knew Del Morran. Everyone seemed to have a relationship with my dad but me. But I hadn't made an effort to contact Dad when I moved to Spruce Ridge, so what did I expect? And why hadn't I made the effort? To be honest, I wasn't sure what my reception would have been. Rejection? Or worse, indifference?

And why Del Morran left me his tow truck was another mystery.

Mom said, "I was hoping you'd get tired of driving that truck and go back to Social Services." Mom turned to Kristen to explain as if I wasn't sitting right there and as if Kristen didn't know all about me, "She's wasting her college diploma. I wanted more for Laney."

I ended up with a Bachelor's in Social Work, mostly because I was interested in the classes. The degree fit with the courses I enjoyed. The social worker job didn't fit, though.

Kristen said, "Eve, your daughter's doing what she wants, and she's been getting a lot of calls for tows."

I said, quite modestly, "I have some nice reviews on the internet. I'm called the 'high-heeled tow truck driver.' I'm using that as my brand. Maybe someday I can buy a flatbed, too, and hire another tower." I thought of Tanner's goals, and it seemed like he had a good business plan.

My mother pinched her lips together.

I lifted my shopping bag. "Thanks again, Mom, for the new shoes."

"Sure, honey." Mom gave me a knowing gaze. "I understand why you always wear heels, Laney. You have to be the prettiest girl in the room, drawing attention to yourself with that bright orange hair of yours. You should cut your hair. There are more flattering styles, maybe a shoulder-length bob…"

I tuned her out. Mom wore her hair in a bob. But was I the prettiest in the room? As I fingered my braid, I twisted my foot to study my heels—the denim wedges again, blue for peace and tranquility, which I needed when dealing with Mother. Glancing around the eat-in area, I meant to evaluate the competition, but there was no one other than the three of us. Mom in her perfect coif and pearls, and Kristen, well, she was just perfect. No outshining her, not that I wanted to.

The tail end of Mom's next words bore into my consciousness. "I'm glad you're rid of Jeremy. Well, not that he's dead, but you know what I mean."

So, she was back on that subject. This time I couldn't agree with her more, but why did he break up with me? I should've been the one to give that jailbird the heave-ho.

****

The next morning Officer Zach Bowers stopped by the coffee bar earlier than usual. His premature salt and pepper hair and thick handlebar mustache were becoming regular features in the shop at all times of the day.

Kristen said, "Let's take a break and talk to Zach."

I poured two shots to make his drink, then stepped over to their table.

"Do you know if that used equipment is ready for me to pick up?" Zach asked Kristen. He clenched his hands together with his arms outstretched and acted like he was swinging a bat.

"Yes. I think you'll have enough for your team. It's nice of you to volunteer this year, Zach." My friend gave him an approving glance. "Just go to the church office and ask for Suzanne."

My break would be over too soon, so I butted in with, "Do you know the county sheriffs very well, Zach?"

"Sure. We have to work together often enough."

"You know Ephraim Lopez?"

The Spruce Ridge officer nodded while sipping his hot drink.

"Is he married?" I told myself, *Do Not Blush*. Zach gave me an *are-you-serious* expression. I asked again, "Well, is he?" I couldn't help but be suspicious of every guy, now that I'd been surprised by Jeremy's marriage.

He gazed up at the ceiling with his big chin sticking out. "Divorced for a couple of years now."

Nice to know. Change of topic. "You told us Jeremy had a criminal record. He did time, right?"

"Kris already asked me about that, so I looked it up." His eyes darted to his girlfriend. "I haven't had a chance to tell you yet." His gaze jumped back to me. "But why do you need to know, Delaney?"

My turn to shell out some attitude. I gave him a crossed-eyed, *isn't-it-obvious* look. "I went out with the guy."

Presumedly, Zach thought I was a desperate

woman, curious about all the available men in town plus the dirt on the ex, because he answered, “He was arrested for armed robbery. Got eighteen months, served twelve.”

Neither Kristen nor I mentioned we’d already heard. Kristen shook her head. “It’s unbelievable. Armed robbery.”

I said, “I suppose I didn’t know Jeremy very well. I didn’t even know he owned a gun.”

Zach said, “He didn’t have possession of the weapon. And it was a knife, not a gun. A friend of his held up a convenience store, and Jeremy drove the getaway car. He claimed he didn’t know what his buddy was up to, that he didn’t know what happened.”

Kris asked, “Was he telling the truth?”

“Everyone says the same thing.”

My mind wanted to race through possible alternate scenarios. I kind of wanted to give Jeremy the benefit of the doubt because otherwise what did that say about my judgment, but a jury must not have seen it that way, since he’d served time.

A bunch of teenagers came through the door, boisterous, bouncing off one another, and Kristen said, “I’ll be right back.”

Zach seemed to notice I remained. He reached over and squeezed my hand. “I’m sorry about your boyfriend.” His voice had a sympathetic tone.

“Ex-boyfriend.” I remembered this police officer had once thought Tanner and I had something going on. Just as if my thinking about him could conjure him up, Tanner strolled in the door.

I whisked my hand away from Zach’s. “I need to help Kristen.” I rose from my chair and zigzagged around the tables to work my way behind the register.

Tanner crossed his tattooed arms over his chest. "Who's that?" He slitted his eyes and drew his dark brows in.

"Who? What?" I surveyed the room. The teenagers were loud at the other end of the pickup counter. The Spruce Ridge officer was the only other person in the place. "Zach?"

"The cop." Tanner glowered at the handsome policeman rubbing his handlebar mustache and poring over his phone.

"Officer Bowers is a regular. He comes in to see Kristen." I inclined my head toward my best buddy while she capped drinks and called out names. The coffee shop was a good place to meet people—it's where I'd met Jeremy, since he used to come in every day, too. Kris and Zach's budding romance was cute and I was happy for her. Plus, because Zach was smitten with Kristen, he was willing to share info, an added bonus for me. I asked, "So, what's up?"

"Not much. How's the repo business?" His fingers drummed on his elbows.

Better to address this head-on. "I haven't done any work for Friendly. *Nada*. They haven't called me and in all probability, they won't. Hailey thinks you're the best." Was I in competition with Tanner? Did I want to be the top tow truck driver in town? What can I say? Of course I did. But I had a long way to go. I poured some coffee into a large metal cup to blend with vanilla and ice for a frappé. He seemed like he needed a jolt of something sweet.

Kristen left for the stockroom. Tanner moved along the bar across from me.

I decided to be chatty. Act like there was nothing wrong. Ignore Tanner's bad mood.

"You remember the repo Abington Auto Store assigned me, the one I tried to recover at the supermarket? Well, I've attempted to tow that Jeep several times now, but the owner always catches me. I'm afraid I'm not good at this repo business." Along with the whole carrier operation. But hey, I should get points for effort. "I really, really appreciate you giving me the no-parking zones, Tanner. At least I sort of have that figured out."

"You're doing me a favor. I have a commitment on Tuesday and Thursday afternoons."

I poured the blended iced coffee into a large plastic cup and handed it to him. "What kind of commitment?"

He took the tall drink from me and examined the contents. "What's this?"

"Vanilla frappé. On the house." I gave him a straw.

He cast another glance at Zach, then leaned in close, resting his elbows on the counter, and gave me one of his sexy smiles. "Thanks for the drink."

I fiddled with my braid. I only had on a thin layer of mascara, I smelled like stale coffee, and dark spills dotted my shirt and my low-slung apron. So, I didn't look great today, okay? The shop had quieted once the teens had gone out the door, but another customer lined up at the cash register. I glanced at the clock on the wall. A little before noon and the rushes were over for the day.

I said to Tanner, "Hey, if you're not too busy, stick around for a minute. I can get off work once I wait on this lady."

He walked over to the window to peer out. I smiled

at the new customer and took her order. After I made the Americano, I unwound my apron and went to the stockroom to ask Kristen if she needed me the rest of the day. My friend shook her head, no, and waved me off as she made her way to Zach's table. Guy muscled up behind the checkout and busied himself, even though no one waited in line.

After changing into my Mary Jane platform heels and stowing away my high-top sneakers, I joined Tanner at the door and we went outside. He climbed into his tow truck and motioned for me to get in, too.

He rested his tattooed arms over the steering wheel. The bluish-black-inked bald eagle made his biceps stand out even more. I felt my face flush hot, painfully aware of his proximity, and wondered what it would feel like if he kissed me, then I went hot all over. I hadn't made-out in a car since high school. This was as awkward now as it was then.

I said, "So, I was hoping for another ride-along."

"Yeah?"

"You can take me for a ride anytime." I chuckled to myself.

He ignored me. Another brush off. My own fault because I'd flirted wildly, but it was innocent fun. This gorgeous tow man seemed safe since he never acted on anything.

We sat in silence for a couple of beats. I said, "So, funny thing, I talked to Byron, and he sort of warned me about you."

Tanner jumped in his seat and his face swiveled toward me. "What did he say?"

I laughed out loud this time. "He asked me if you'd made any unwanted advances. Ha, ha, old-fashioned, huh?"

His face blanched. "What did you tell him?"

I gave him a fake punch on the arm. "Uh, I may have said you did."

A muscle twitched in his cheek and I felt him stiffen in the seat beside me.

"Just kidding. That's the last thing I'd expect from you." I blushed up to my ears and wished I hadn't brought it up. "So, um, Tanner, about another ride along, you got time today?"

"I'm busy this afternoon."

My heart dropped. "Are you still mad about Friendly Finance? Cause I'm not trying to horn in on your business."

He relaxed his shoulders. "No, no. I really am busy."

Hunh. "Oh, now that I think about it, I'm busy, too."

"You're off work from the coffee shop. What else do you have to do?"

"Take care of some business." Sure, let's go with that.

He turned away from me and stared out the windshield. "Like what?"

"Like, what do you have to do on Tuesdays and Thursdays?"

His eyes darted back to me. "Do you have a date with the cop?"

"Of course not. I told you Zach likes Kristen." I smiled at the thought. My friend, gray-eyed, pretty as a peach, but shy with the fellas, only dated once in a blue moon. My hair escaped from the braid, so I pulled out the band and finger-combed the waves. "Why…do you have a date?" Maybe Tanner was in a relationship. That must be it. I was dreaming if I thought there could be anything between us.

His blue eyes went dark. "No."

"No girlfriend waiting for you to call?"

"No."

Why didn't the man just ask me out, then? It was Saturday. Tonight was date night. He didn't say a word, but perhaps he didn't want to admit he wasn't interested. Maybe I was too stinky from the bitter coffee smell that clung to my shirt. Or maybe he did have a girlfriend after all. *Whatever*. A date with Tanner wasn't in the stars for this girl.

I shoved open the door to his rig. I said, "I guess I'll see you around," and slammed the door shut.

Tanner kept his eyes on me until he turned his truck out of the lot and motored down Pine Street.

Note to self—find out what Tanner does on Tuesdays and Thursdays. I couldn't help but be skeptical, the way he acted, all mysterious like he was hiding something. I didn't need another person in my life with dark secrets.

As I went upstairs, I ran through my cell messages, then listened to a missed call from the repo agent: *Found the Jeep Wrangler again. It's in the alley behind the bar like last time.*

I reversed down the stairs and raced over to get my dad's tow truck. I recited the mantra, *Keep it together, keep it together,* and *you can do this.*

I nosed down the alley and spotted the Jeep, but continued on, circling the block, more cautious this time. I cruised past the front of the bar, Big Hal's, a strip joint. The only one in town. A sign on the entryway posted the hours, open 10:00 a.m. to 1:00 a.m., closed on Sunday.

So, this is where Hot Head went when he left his Jeep in the alley.

I parked in the next block and dashed back. Stopping with my hand on the door, I sneaked a peek left and right, worried someone I knew would recognize me, then I took a deep breath and stole inside. Need I explain? This is a small town.

My eyes took a moment to adjust to the dark. One girl wearing a thong—thank goodness she wasn't anyone I knew—was on stage. Mr. Hot Head sat at the bar with a tall beer, foam on top, glass full. Looked like he had just been served a fresh, cold one, and this early in the day, too. I backed out the door, ran for the tow truck, and zipped back to the alley as fast as I could.

I angled the truck in front of Hot Head's Jeep and muscled the dolly wheels over to the rear end, crouching low to the ground, getting a whiff of the rank dumpster. Hot Head couldn't see me from inside the building, but he had a sixth sense about me, and I was determined to keep under his radar. I jacked up the first dolly wheel and was on my way around the back bumper to jack up the second one, when *Bam!*

I stumbled right into Hot Head.

He had a tire iron in his meaty fist.

Chapter 12

I screamed like this was a frickin' horror movie.

All I could think was, *get outta here get outta here get outta here!* I tore open the metal door on the back of the building and sprinted with arms and legs pumping, down a narrow hall that stank of urine, past the restrooms—oh, that explained it—into a dead end crowded with tables and chairs and racks of clothes.

My breath blowing in and out and my heart pounding, I ducked down behind a garment rack. The skimpy costumes did not hide me very well. A naked girl, with big hair and bigger body parts, sat at one of the tables and stared at me with her mouth open.

I explained, breathlessly, "A bad man is chasing me. I just need a minute."

The dancer sneaked a look around the corner. "There's an ugly guy in front of the restrooms. Shaved head. Holding a tire iron."

"That's him." My knees shook. I sat back on my heels and tried not to fall over. I've been in many a weird spot in my life, but never before in a strip joint. Hiding from a guy with a tire iron.

The well-endowed girl snuggled a tight teddy over her head and down past her hips, then slid some of the hangers along the clothes rack. "That man is not budging, so I have an idea." She handed me a hanger holding a white shirt attached to a short, pleated skirt.

"Put this on. You can go on stage with me and sneak out the front. This outfit will go great with your Mary Jane shoes. Here, I'll turn around to give you some privacy, and I can keep watch, too."

She aimed her back toward me, and I wiggled out of my jeans and into the one-piece costume that had some complicated snaps. "Ready."

She said, "Perfect. That style goes with your freckles and braid. Too bad you're not in pigtails."

"What if that guy comes out front and recognizes me?" I flipped my distinctive red braid over my shoulder.

"He won't be studying your face. Trust me." She was calm about it, like this happened every day.

We both paused and cast a glance down the hallway. Mr. Hot Head still leaned against the wall next to the ladies' room. I followed close behind the dancer through a black curtain steeped in cigarette smoke and stale whiskey. Standing to the side, I watched while she strolled, hips swaying, across the stage and grabbed hold of a pole. Not knowing what to do, I remained frozen in a dark corner through two long rap songs and one brief teddy. Finally, I forced my feet to move toward the stairs leading off the platform and pretended I was invisible. Who would notice me? Not with the naked dancer on the stripper pole.

My shaky legs made jerky movements, like a wind-up toy on its last crank. I made it to the floor without incident, except for some tips stuffed into my waistband, and broke out the front door. Hot Head had not entered the bar area. I scanned the street, no Hot Head outside either, so I walked fast around the corner to the alley.

I guess that bully got tired of waiting because the Jeep Wrangler was gone…and so were my dolly wheels.

Here I'd tried to snatch his Jeep, but he stole my dollies.

And, the tow truck's windshield was splintered into a million cracks.

That knocked me back. This wasn't the way it was supposed to work. I hoisted myself into the driver's seat and slammed my palms into the steering wheel five or six times, my stomach churning in on itself. Look on the bright side. Better that he took the tire iron to the truck than to me. I turned over the engine and chugged past the dented dumpster. One of the dolly wheels protruded from the top of the metal bin, so I rocked to a stop and got out, then clambered onto the hood and stole a look over the edge. He'd thrown both dolly wheels inside with the garbage and there was no way I would be able to lift them out.

I extracted my phone and called Axle. "Hey, little cousin."

"What do you need now?"

"Remember you owe me a favor?"

"No, I don't. I paid that back."

"Hardly."

"Did so."

"Did not." I drew in a deep breath, getting ready for an argument, then coughed and gagged at the smell. *Pee-yew!* "I need help lifting my dolly wheels out of a dumpster. Someone got mad at me and threw them in there. I'm behind Big Hal's."

Axle gave out a belly laugh. "No way."

"Way."

"No!"

"Wish I was kidding."

"I'll be right there."

I texted Crump that I was not able to recover the Jeep. I thought about adding, and *thanks A LOT for your help*, but didn't. Nor did I bring up the broken windshield. I'm sure I was on my own for that, too.

Truck doors locked, I settled back to wait. While I was in the strip joint the sky had filled with dark purple clouds and the wind kicked up. Discarded fast food bags and cellophane wrappers—don't ask me to look and see what kind—tossed in whirlwinds along the gravel alley and up against the brick building.

Before long, Kristen's Prius turned in and her cousin got out. Kristen buzzed down her window, scrunched her nose in a stink face, and asked, "You okay?"

I stretched down out of the truck. "Yes. Just need a little help with the dolly wheels. I can drop off Axle afterward."

"That works. I need to get back to the coffee shop." She waved goodbye and left.

I asked her cousin, "Don't you drive?"

"Don't have a license."

"Why not?"

He spun me around. "Your ass is hanging out." I felt his fingers close a few of the snaps. "I swear this is something a stripper would wear. You moonlighting?"

"Very funny. Har. Har." Under the schoolgirl costume, I wore my white cotton briefs, which provided plenty of coverage, so I was safe from total exposure. "Why don't you have a driver's license?"

"Suspended. Too many speeding tickets." Axle

jacked himself onto the hood and checked out the dumpster. He leveraged the dollies over the side and down to the ground. Together we propelled them under the truck and latched them into place, and a couple more snaps burst open. Axle fixed my snaps and I gave him the cash from my stripper tips. I asked him to wait in the truck for a minute, then I went back through the metal door to retrieve my jeans. The dressing room was empty. The dancer must still be performing.

On her dresser was a picture of a pair of rosy-cheeked boys in tiny suits, aged three to five, maybe, and a crayon drawing, "to mommy." I left the costume on her chair with my business card and "thanks" written on the back.

When I returned outside, Axle was sitting in the passenger seat, his earbuds in, his knit cap on. I got behind the wheel and swiped my hand up the side of his head, knocking the buds out.

"What do you want now?" He flipped my braid and it flew up and hit me in the face.

"Hey." I smoothed my plait back in place. "I've been meaning to ask, why did you warn us about L&B Garage? You said something like, we didn't know who we were dealing with."

"When was that?"

"When we were in my Fiat, me and Kristen, waiting for the police raid."

"Oh, that. Just…repair shops send a lot of customers to tow companies. You don't want to piss them off if you need their business. If you're hunting for work, I could ask around for you." He inserted his earbud back in. I longed to keep pressing him, but he tapped his knees and bobbed his head to the music.

I ferried Axle over to L&B Garage. He pushed open the truck's door to get going, but paused one foot out and one foot in. "Did you see that article in the news?"

"Which one?"

He thumbed his phone and handed it to me. The headline, "Owner of Del's Towing questioned by police in murder investigation," now included the comments: "Is it safe to use this company?" and "Why hasn't Del been arrested?"

"Crap. I did see this, but the comments are new."

He got out the rest of the way and shut the door, then leaned in the window. "Well, be sure to cover your ass at all times."

"Aye, aye." I gave him a salute.

"And call me if you ever need assistance with snaps again."

"Not funny."

He dropped his arms from the window and went inside.

I let off the parking brake and drove back into town. A red light at Main and Pine caused me to halt at the intersection.

I stared in the rearview mirror at my pale, heart-shaped face, reminding me of my dad's in his website picture. No wonder I was curious about him, since I was a younger, feminine, longer-haired version of red-headed Del Morran. My hands tightened on the wheel where Dad's hands rested a month ago. Dad must have shifted the gears and hit the brakes and handled the controls many times, just like I did now. For a fleeting second it felt like he was here with me, like a déjà vu moment, a long-ago, vague recollection I couldn't quite grasp.

A car behind me beeped its horn and brought me back to the present. The light was green so I went through. As I cruised along Main, super-sized raindrops plopped onto the cracked windshield, then began to pound down harder and faster. The rain turned into freezing sleet, pinging off the windows and roof of the cab. Quick melting snow pellets skittered in rivulets down the hood and solid bits settled on the wiper blades. The ice crystals ripened into marble-sized hail, and the noise became so loud it sounded like bullets in a combat zone, ricocheting everywhere. The temperature had plunged enough to make a bear run for hibernation.

I pulled off on a side street and parked. No sense trying to drive out of this. I put my elbows on the steering wheel and my chin in my hands, prepared to wait it out, on edge that the cracked windshield might shatter. The hail didn't seem to be letting up.

After a minute my mind drifted back to the prior owner of this tow truck. Mom always said she was glad Dad wasn't in our lives. And she didn't like me asking questions about him. So, I made excuses to myself for an absent dad. I liked to envision him as a successful and upstanding part of the community, performing needed services, coming to the rescue of stranded motorists. Here I was, still covering up his truancy with daydreams, a leftover defensive mechanism from childhood.

And now, more than anything else, I wanted to step into that dream and make his towing business work for me. Maybe I'd find out what kind of a man he was by doing the work he did.

But I felt an imposter, like I felt on stage at the strip club. I didn't have the moves of an exotic dancer. Or a vehicle recovery specialist. Was I crazy thinking I could handle the job? It would've been sweet if Dad had showed me how to manage the tow business instead of leaving me on my own with the keys and nothing else. But, no. He'd simply abandoned me once again.

Why did he give me the truck? What was he thinking?

The hail came to an abrupt halt, and yellow, watery sunrays broke through an opening in the clouds. A typical spring day in the Rockies. I fought my way out of the truck cab to examine the destruction. At least the hail hadn't done any more harm to the cracked windshield, but half a dozen small, round pockmarks dented the hood and pooled with water. *What the heck.* I swear I can't catch a break.

I had no command of the weather, but there were some things within my control, like working hard and taking better care of this truck. I wasn't a quitter. I was determined more than ever to capture the Jeep, acquire new customers, and make the business profitable so I could pay for truck repairs and support myself.

There was the murder to get past, too. Solving the crime would help quash those negative posts linking me to murder. I wouldn't get calls for tows with those bad comments. Improving my reputation would put me in a better place, so I needed to clear the suspicion that surrounded me. The murder rose higher on my priority list. I could do both, figure out the killer, build up the business.

I struggled into the truck and started up the engine.

Instead of returning to Main Street, I proceeded to the golf course community, my tires cutting a swath through pools of water, and pulled up in front of a three-thousand square foot house with a white-pillared porch and an extra garage stall for a golf cart.

Home of Mr. and Mrs. Winslow.

I'd only met Jeremy's mom once, but I recognized her when she answered the door. A very different woman from the one Jeremy had introduced me to a month or so ago. At that time, her outfit was fashionable, a crisp blazer, tailored pants, and boots. Now, her tee-shirt and blue jeans were baggy, her eyes droopy, and her shoulders hunched in defeat. What you'd expect from a mother who lost a child.

"Remember me?" I placed my hand over my heart. "I'm sorry for your loss."

"Yes, Delaney, I certainly do remember you." Her lips trembled and she started to shut the door.

"Wait. What is it, Mrs. Winslow? Are you okay?" I considered the stupidity of my question and blushed to my roots.

The door halted in mid-swing and she gave me an accusatory look. "I heard you found my son's body. Did you hurt Jeremy? Was it you?" Her voice came out as hoarse as a whisper.

My mouth dropped open. Had I heard her right? Did she believe I committed murder? "It wasn't me. I really cared about him." I did once, no lie. I asked, "Please can we talk? I just need to talk to somebody about Jeremy."

She hesitated. "I don't know what to think." Water welled in her eyes while we considered each other with sad looks. Then she stumbled back from the threshold and held open the door. "I was brought up not to be rude, so come on in."

She kept casting worried glances over her shoulder at me as I followed her past a formal dining area and fancy gourmet kitchen. We entered a family room at the back of the house with floor-to-ceiling windows and a view of the golf course. Fresh flowers and enormous green plants in floral vases covered the sofa table and fireplace mantle. Condolences. A ceiling fan whisked the strong scent of lilies around, tickling my nose. She trundled the sliding glass door open and we stepped outside.

"Would you like something to drink? Coffee?" She was being a polite hostess, but I was imposing too much already.

"No, thank you."

We took seats at a wrought iron patio table facing the tee box. Short piles of white hail banked against tuffs of tall grass in the rough on the far side of her yard. A man and a woman were readying to tee off.

Mrs. Winslow said, "The golfers ran off the course when it started to hail, but they've resumed play now." Jeremy's mom probably felt safer outside in full view of the golfers since she suspected me of being a murderer.

"Yeah, that was some weather." This was tougher than I thought it would be, but I dug in. "You know Jeremy and I broke up."

Tears leaked out of her eyes and down her cheeks. "He told me." She held a tissue to her nose.

"But that doesn't mean I'm not heartbroken by his death. I am. This is all a shock to me, too." I blinked a few times to dry my own dampening eyes. "How are you managing?"

"It's hard. I keep thinking about JJ when he was a little boy." She choked up a bit more, her breathing shallow and uneven.

"You called him JJ?"

"Jeremy James. He was so sweet. Not one ounce of trouble." She glanced at me, as if expecting an argument.

"You're right. He was a great guy." I'd thought so at the time, anyway.

She nodded, breathing easier, seeming to relax a little. "I miss him."

"I know." I could feel the afternoon sun on my skin. The sun was warm but the breeze was balmy, left over from the hailstorm. "I heard he went to jail. I didn't know about that when we dated. He never told me."

"He didn't like to talk about it." She pursed her lips indicating she was unwilling to speak of it herself. "He went to DU. He was a good student," she added, some pride in her voice. Denver University is a private college.

"He didn't tell me he was married, either." I was still trying to get past what he'd conveniently forgotten to mention, along with the jail part. "But I understand he was getting divorced."

Mrs. Winslow dropped her head, clenching the tissue in her fist. "That's right."

How was I going to break into her reserve? "I'm trying to find out what happened to Jeremy."

"I want to know what happened, too."

"Can you please tell me about his wife?"

She twisted her tissue for a few more moments.

"He met Melissa while he was at school. She worked somewhere on campus. She married him because she thought he had money, but we're just average people, we're not millionaires."

I took in the view of the golf course and the mansions on the other side of the fairway, but didn't say anything. "Why did the marriage break up?"

"Melissa left him after he was arrested." She folded her arms around herself. "But he never should have gone to jail. JJ was just in the wrong place at the wrong time."

"Please tell me about it. I almost keeled over when I found out he had been in jail. That's not the Jeremy I knew."

"You're right. None of it was his fault."

"I heard he committed armed robbery, that he drove the getaway car." I let that hang out there.

She bristled. "That's not what happened."

"Then what did happen?"

She cast her eyes down and didn't speak for a long couple of moments, and when she did, her voice came out low, as if ashamed. "He met an old classmate at a concert. His friend asked him for a ride so JJ gave him a lift." Her voice hardened, like a dirt road that changes from soft clay to solid concrete. "Then the guy saw a convenience store and asked JJ to stop, said he needed to use the restroom. The guy went in, but seemed to be taking longer than usual. When he came back out, he gave JJ some gas money and they left. A few blocks later JJ was stopped by the police. Turns out his so-called friend pulled a knife on the clerk and demanded cash from the register. The clerk was an elderly man who called the police and gave a description of the car."

She sniffed like her nose was congested. “Then, the clerk died of a heart attack.”

“Oh, no.” I reached over to pat her hand, but she drew back like she still wasn’t sure about me. “What happened next?”

“JJ was charged with armed robbery under the felony murder statute. He took a plea, and they dropped the murder charge, thank God. He pled guilty to what the lawyer called ‘felony theft and accessory’ and got eighteen months in jail. At least there was some justice. The real criminal got ten years.” She crossed her arms and stared at the tee box where a new foursome now waited to tee off.

“You’re right, that wasn’t fair of the guy to involve Jeremy. What a terrible person.” I bit my lips and scrolled through my phone. “There’s a picture of somebody I want to show you.” I rotated the screen in her direction so she could view the mug shot. “Do you know this man?”

She shook her head, then froze and sucked in her lips. “Maybe. A man came by asking for JJ a couple weeks ago. Someone he knew from jail. That might be him.”

I took another glance at the photo myself and shivered before putting my phone away. “Did the man tell you his name?”

She pinched her eyes shut and bowed her head. A few more tears rolled down her cheeks. “He did, but I don’t remember it. My husband might know.”

“Did Jeremy have any enemies?” I felt terrible asking. Her red eyes met mine, assessing me. Was there something she was holding back? “I had nothing to do with his death. I wish I could make you believe me.”

My voice cracked.

She turned slightly and stared over to where a golf cart had parked on the path. "I guess I believe you."

I breathed a sigh of relief. "Was Jeremy having problems with anyone? Somebody from jail? Or another ex-girlfriend?"

"No."

Maybe the suspects would show up at the funeral, so I asked, "Are you going to have a service?"

"No. No ceremony." She shook her head.

"Why not? You could at least have a memorial or a celebration of life." It seemed to me like she could use something to plan.

"Maybe, but it's just so hard to face people." She dabbed the crumpled tissue to the corner of her eye. "I never told my friends about Jeremy's troubles. When he went to jail, I just said he had to work out of town for a while."

"You need someone to confide in." I gave her an encouraging nod when she turned back to face me.

"I can't believe I told you this much, but you're actually easy to talk to. Jeremy always said that about you."

We fell silent as we watched the foursome stuff their clubs back in their bags and head down the fairway.

She chewed the inside of her mouth, then said in a low voice, "If there was one person I thought could harm my son…"

I leaned forward, my elbows on the patio table. "Yes?"

"Well, I never liked his wife." Her face constricted with narrowed lips. "I always disliked her."

"Do you think Melissa killed Jeremy?"

She shrugged and went on to talk about how overwhelming everything was, how her friends had been calling, but she didn't feel like going out. This had to be the absolutely worst thing that could happen to any parent. Jeremy's death made my towing problems seem trivial. Everything's relative.

"Let me know if I can help in any way." I got up to leave. She led me back through the house the way we'd come in. As she closed the front door behind me, I noticed her face had a look of relief. Did she still think I was a threat? What could I do to ease her mind?

Note to self—ask Kristen how to help Jeremy's mom. My friend always knew the right words to say.

Walking back to Dad's truck, I tipped my head up to the sun. With the sudden rise in temperature, the hail had evaporated fast, disappearing into the atmosphere. I felt like escaping out of there, too. There had to be another reason for Jeremy's death other than him getting mixed up with the wrong person. Yes, his rotten friend was the bad guy, and I could see how a mother would want to blame someone else for her son's bad decisions, but Jeremy was an adult, not a teenager caving under peer pressure.

I drove over to the house on Third Street. I still had questions about this place. A few quick ones. Like, who lived here? How did they know Jeremy? Why was Jeremy's car left in this garage? Maybe someone at the house could explain how Jeremy got so messed up.

I parked the rig out front and walked up the broken sidewalk past the weedy bushes. This time somebody was home. A thin, blonde woman in her twenties responded to my knock. No makeup, but an attractive face. About my height. And I recognized her. I'd seen her driving the yellow Corvette and the red Lexus sportscar around town. Fancy, expensive cars for a person living in a working-class neighborhood.

I just came out and asked, "Did you know Jeremy Winslow?"

"Who wants to know?"

"Me. We used to go out."

She gave me an up-and-down sweep of the eyes, peered around me at my dad's tow truck, then said, "I don't know who you're talking about," and slammed the door.

Rude, much? And bizarre. How did Jeremy's Challenger end up in her garage? With him in it? Who was this person? No easy answer was here, after all.

I eased back into the driver's seat and fired up the self-loader. The rumble of the engine was comforting as I stared blankly out the cracked windshield. Here's an idea…what if his body was stowed in the trunk *after* the Friendly Finance repo agent opened it up at Tanner's lot? I wasn't the last one with the vehicle before the police showed up. *I mean, really, why should this all be on me?* Was Friendly a loan-shark kind of a place that would kill someone who couldn't pay? *Uh-oh*. I had my car loan through Friendly. But if the loan company got the car back, why would they murder Jeremy and toss him in the trunk, then call the cops?

Since it was Saturday, Friendly Finance was closed, but L&B was open, so I took a ride out to Industrial Lane.

With the sun out, the warming air caused the wind to whip up. Pine branches creaked at the sides of the highway from the strong Chinook winds rushing through the valley. I gripped the wheel tight while the truck jolted all over the road.

I brought the self-loader to a stop in L&B's lot and cut the motor. The garage sounded busy, with the shrill whine of machines and a boom of something heavy hitting the ground. Should I do this? Was I crazy? It's one thing, even normal, to talk to Jeremy's mom and check on his family, but to question the chop shop employees—that's taking a whole new direction. Steeling myself, I plunged through the door.

Axle was not in his usual spot behind the service counter, so I kept going, walking straight into the first bay.

A mechanic put down his tools and came over, a pervy smile on his face. "Hey, beautiful." He gave me a wink. He smelled of sweat and engine grease. Jeremy had worked here too, but he was always clean and well groomed. This guy's blue jeans and fingernails were dirty, and he stared at my boobs. *Yikes*. "What can I do for you?" he asked me.

My lip curled back, but I brought my phone up to show him. "I'm trying to find this person. Have you seen him?"

He stopped leering at me and said, "Let me get someone." He vanished behind a vehicle on a lift with its wheels off.

A few minutes passed, then Freddie Haag burst out of a side door. "What do you want?" He paused with his work boots a few inches away from the toes of my Mary Janes, enveloping me in a cloud of cigarette breath.

I took a step back and held up the mug shot. "Have you seen his man?"

“Nope. Never saw him before.” Haag didn’t even pretend to glance at the picture.

I felt a tug on my arm. “Delaney, what are you doing here?” Axle gave me a shove, and pushed me out of the bay. “You shouldn’t be back in the work area. Didn’t you see the sign, ‘no customers allowed?’ Why are you here?”

“There was no one in front. I’m just asking a few questions.” I peeled his hand off my arm as we strolled over to the side of Dad’s truck.

“Like what?”

I showed him the mug shot. “Have you seen this guy?”

“He’s been hanging around. Why? What’s he done to you?”

“He’s a suspect in Jeremy’s death.”

“Oh.” Axle squinted at me with a look of unbelief. “Haven’t you had enough trouble for one day? Getting your dolly wheels trashed in the dumpster, now this?”

“Axle, get back to work,” Haag called from the open bay.

“I need to get going.” Axle turned on his heel and trotted inside.

I yanked myself up into Dad’s truck cab and rubbed my eyes to rid myself of the creep-job that was Freddie Haag. The perv mechanic was also high on the scumbag-scale.

This whole encounter felt really off. Freddie was covering up something major and not just his lack of social skills. Maybe he hid a murderer.

Chapter 13

I was all by myself on a Saturday night with no plans. Again. I hate when that happens. I had texted Kristen only to discover she was on her way to her folks' house for dinner. She invited me to join them, but I told her maybe next time. So I had a lonely evening ahead of me. I'm sure even Hot Head had better prospects than I did, since he had a regular barstool at Big Hal's.

Well hello. I could take myself on my own damn date.

Choosing what to wear was the easiest decision of the day. A short, blue-jean, pencil skirt with a jade, scoop-neck, stretchy top, hoop earrings, wavy hair down, extra mascara layered on thick. I opted for one of my many pairs of gladiator sandals, this one in green with lace-ups to mid-calf. Toes painted a green shade, too, for nature and harmony.

I drove over to Rio Grande Ave. to the Mexican place with sunshine yellow walls, tangerine orange tables, and cheerful *Grupera* music. The aroma of melted cheese, sautéed onions, and cumin hit my nose when I walked in the door.

I'd just placed my order when Tanner ambled in.

There I was, totally exposed at a table in front.

His tight black jeans over work boots drew my attention, along with his tee-shirt, flat against hard abs, and his blond hair sticking up in a casual, *just-ran-my-fingers-through-it* kind of way. I tried to make up my mind whether he would be hotter in cowboy boots when he spotted me and sauntered over.

"You here by yourself?"

"Yes." I was too wiped out to be embarrassed. The day had been long and I was low on energy. "No towaway zones tonight?" I asked.

"The no-parking restrictions don't apply on the weekends."

"I guess I didn't realize that." So, when he'd given me two days, Tuesdays and Thursdays, that was almost half his workweek. I motioned for him to take a seat.

"You already order?" He pulled out a chair.

"Yes. Tacos *carne asada*."

"That sounds good."

The waiter hurried back, and while Tanner placed his request, one of the staff brought out my tacos with a basket of homemade tortilla chips and guacamole.

Tanner said, "Go ahead and eat."

"Have some chips." I nudged the basket in his direction. He took one and dipped it into the spicy, mashed avocado topping. I loaded up a chip, too. "So, here we are."

"I guess so." He studied his hands. "You come here a lot?"

"Why? Are you afraid you'll run into me again?"

He choked a little and took a sip of water. The waiter brought his taco plate to our table, and we both dug into our meals. After numerous bites and more than a few moments of uncomfortable silence, he asked me, "Do you miss Denver?"

I was grateful for the conversation starter. "Denver

has lots of cool restaurants, breweries, museums…concerts. But I love it here." I did love it, but didn't fit in, yet. I was used to the big city. I wore high heels when people here wore hiking boots. This outdoorsy town was a mountain paradise. That I caught views of the mountains every day never dulled my appreciation of the scenery in Spruce Ridge. And Denver was only an hour away, an easy drive back. I asked him, "How do you like living in a small town?"

"Not that small. Almost twelve thousand."

That included the mansions up the canyon and outlying area, but Spruce Ridge proper was rather minuscule. If you ran into somebody you didn't know, there was a good chance the two of you still knew someone in common.

"Is your family here in Spruce Ridge?" I asked.

He set down his fork and leaned forward. "Both my parents died within a few years of each other. One had cancer, the other lupus."

My throat closed up and I felt moisture at the back of my eyes. We'd had similar losses, but his was greater. "I'm so sorry. That's tragic."

"I'm the oldest of three. Got a younger brother and sister. We still live in our parents' house because it made it easier to keep them in the same schools. The house is paid for and secure, something solid for them."

I fiddled with my water glass. "I'll bet you're great with kids."

He shrugged, appearing calm, maybe resigned, not broken up or upset, so I stayed upbeat, too.

"You're amazing, like a superhero." I prodded his foot with my shoe when he didn't respond. "Come on, I'm teasing you like I always do." I put on my best and brightest smile. "But I really mean it."

His lips quivered. It took a moment but I finally realized he was laughing, and my cheeks burned hot. He didn't know how he affected me, how my heart beat faster.

"Seriously, that's a big responsibility. I'm impressed." I chided him some more, "Out of all the Tanners I know, I think you're my favorite."

"You're halfway decent, too." He flashed me that sexy grin.

This was more like it. "You know about my ex-boyfriend, but you haven't told me about any girlfriends. I suppose you've been in a serious relationship or two?"

"My last girlfriend dumped me." He tapped the ends of his fingers together. "My brother got very attached to her, so the breakup was even worse."

"Sorry, Tanner." Being ditched was something else we had in common. The waiter came to take away our plates and ask if we wanted dessert. Neither of us did.

Tanner paid the bill and walked me outside.

His sedan, a black Volvo S60, was parked next to my Fiat. His was a nice ride, and most importantly, front-wheel drive. *Ta-dah!* I knew this. We sagged against his Volvo, side by side, arms crossed. My shoes didn't have much of a lift, so I felt even shorter than usual next to this tall, attractive man.

He said, "You look nice tonight." His blue eyes turned smoky as they wandered down my top, then skirt, then all the way to my gladiator sandals.

A warm flush came over me. We hadn't talked about towing all through the meal. Definitely not a business dinner. Very date-like, playing the question game, getting to know each other, handing me a compliment on my appearance. Giving me *the look*. A date, even if we hadn't arranged it, right?

Well, it felt like a date to me. I could see his pulse thumping in his neck, smell his musky aftershave, and feel the heat coming off his body…I scooted nearer to him. He leaned away. I inched even closer. He stretched even farther away, spilling off the tail end of his car, stumbling to keep himself from falling to the ground.

He straightened up. "Well, so long." Then he banged his car door open and jumped inside. His Volvo careened out of the lot.

What the…? Jeez. I'd read him all wrong.

Was something the matter with me? Did I have cooties? *No*. He said I looked nice tonight, and I know I didn't reek of coffee this time.

Maybe he still thought I had something to do with Jeremy's death.

Ouch. This cut me deep. Tears threatened to appear and made me pinch the end of my nose.

This was my third time to make a move. Third strike. He was out. He had his turn up at bat and now the game was over.

****

I woke up late Sunday morning. Roasters on the Ridge closed. Kristen at church. Me at loose ends.

Might as well head over to the autobody shop for Dad's truck. It needed gas in case a miracle occurred and someone called for a tow.

Byron was working in one of the bays with the overhead door open. I hadn't expected him there on a Sunday. His back was to me, so I knocked on the workbench. "Morning, Old Man."

He looked up, his eyes hidden behind safety glasses. Gobs of blue splattered his overalls and paint fumes filled the bay. He gave me his gap-toothed smile. "Good mornin', Delaney."

"Why are you working today?"

He shoved the clear plastic glasses to the top of his head. "I'm finishing up a job, but I'm 'bout done here, so I'm glad you came by."

While he gathered his tools, I told him about my repo attempt and stage debut at Big Hal's. I attempted to make the story funny, not scary, but he wasn't fooled.

"You coulda' called me to get those tow dollies outta' that dumpster. I would've helped you, but Axle seems like a good person ta' know." He tucked a rachet wrench inside the red, chest-high cabinet.

"He is." I waited while Byron put away the last tool. "Do you replace windshields?"

"Sure. Actually, I hire a guy. It's his specialty and it can be tricky. Do ya' need a windshield?"

"Yeah. I got a crack." Or a hundred. "I'll let you know when I can afford to get it done."

"I'll get ya' a good deal."

"That'd be wonderful." I didn't have the money to fix the hail damage, either, so I didn't mention it. "Axle told me auto repair shops hire tow truck drivers. What about your business, Byron? Can you refer anyone my way?"

"You don't have to ask, I'll recommend ya', don't worry."

It'd be great to work with the Old Man. I gave him a big smile. "I appreciate it. Maybe I should drop off my cards at other mechanic shops in town."

His eyes always crinkled at the corners when he talked to me. "Sure, you should visit 'em all."

Would someone at L&B run me off the property if I showed up there again? I could just about smell Freddie Haag's cigarette breath, but I wasn't going to let Haag intimidate me. I said, "I might start with L&B since I have a connection to them, you know, Jeremy and now Axle. Hey, I found out Jeremy served time in jail. Do you think Dad knew?"

Byron polished his safety glasses with the rag. "He knew."

"You knew, too?"

"Yeah." He paused his polishing for a moment, then rubbed the cloth more vigorously over the clear plastic. "Del gave folks with a record a chance. He was a good man."

"He was?" My mother may not have had one pleasant thing to say about my father, but I had someone else to ask now. Someone whose opinions, I'd discovered, mattered to me. "Tell me about Del." I shuffled my feet and blushed. "I didn't know him very well."

"You didn't?"

I surprised myself by admitting, "He wasn't involved in my life." Byron seemed easy to trust with my history.

His eyes roved around like he searched for something to say. "Customers could count on him ta' do a good job."

"What was he like as a person?"

"Quiet. Didn't talk much, stayed ta' himself. Once you got him talkin' he was witty. Funny. But that only happened now and again." He scratched the top of his head, his thinning hair barely covering his pink scalp. "Hard ta' know what he was thinkin', even though he was smart, followed the news, read a lot…uh, anything else you want ta' know?"

I drank in his kind words. "No criticisms?"

"No, no." His deep, rich voice sounded reassuring.

"You know Tanner Utley pretty well, too, don't you?" I asked.

He gave me a hard stare. "Known him for a few years now. Why?"

"I'm covering private property lots for him because he's tied up on Tuesdays and Thursdays. Do you know what he does on those days? The reason he's busy?"

Byron's eyes darted to the left. "Nope. You'll have ta' ask him 'bout that."

The Old Man didn't want to tell me. Was Tanner in therapy…or at AA meetings? Maybe he had a standing date with his old girlfriend after all. Or a liaison with a married woman? That would at least explain his cold behavior.

I asked, "Do you have a problem with Tanner? 'Cause we went out for dinner a couple of times, but he never wanted you to know. And he acts strange."

Byron shoved himself to his feet, his hands forming into fists. "Strange? How strange?"

"Nothing perverted," I just about shouted, my heart kicking up. I knew a perv when I encountered one, like the guy at L&B Garage, and Tanner was as far as you could get from that dude. "I just meant he's real standoffish. I guess he's just not into me." I lifted my shoulders in a *can-you-believe-it* shrug but felt my cheeks pink up. "I've even flirted with him. Nothing. *Nada*. He can't stand me, actually. But, you know, I don't expect every guy to go for me. It's okay."

Byron put a hand over his eyes and sank his chin to his chest.

I asked, "What? What is it? Have you been talking to Tanner about me?"

His head went down farther between his shoulders. He said, "I warned him off. I told him he'd better watch himself 'round you. Ta' keep his hands to himself."

"What? You di-int!" I tried not to yell, since I knew Byron only wanted to protect me. Even so, I told him, "You need to back off."

He had the grace to appear ashamed of himself. "I'm sorry."

The Old Man acted like a dad with a sixteen-year-old daughter, but that was no reason for Tanner to behave like a conceited jerk, too good for the likes of me. Not knowing how real dads behaved, maybe I should cut Byron some slack. He was trying to be a good guy here. I hiked my purse onto my shoulder. "It's all right. I can tell you mean well. See you later, Old Man."

I headed over to the gas station. During the first few attempts at gassing up, I had trouble fitting the big rig between the pumps, but I was getting better at it.

My phone buzzed as I watched the dollars increase on the display, so I reached in my pocket and pulled out my cell. "Del's Towing."

"Did you recover the Jeep Wrangler?" This was the repo agent, Patrick Crump.

The gas flow shut off. I shoved the nozzle back into the pump and twisted the truck's gas cap on tight. "I told you the owner drove away before I could hook up." I didn't bother to explain the entire story. Byron didn't think Big Hal's fiasco amusing and neither would Crump. "Hey, I know another person named Crump. Are you related to Melissa Winslow?" Mom had told me her maiden name was Crump, not a common name.

"She's my sister."

So they were family, just like Kristen and Axle. Being an only child, it always surprised me when I encountered close relatives, but then everyone in a small town seemed connected in some way. Patrick had to have known Jeremy since they'd been in-laws. Here was an idea. What if he killed Jeremy on behalf of his sister? In *The Godfather*, the ruthless Michael Corleone had his brother-in-law bumped off. Patrick was a hard-nosed repo agent. A killer, too? All too possible, the scuzzball.

Crump's mean voice interrupted my thoughts. "Listen, you need to get that Wrangler picked up."

I scrambled in the glove compartment for a piece of paper. "What's the guy's address? I'll drive by and make an attempt."

"Don't bother. He always has the Jeep secured when he's home."

"Tell me anyway. And his name, too."

He read off the street and house number, and I jotted it down. Hot Head's name was Lou Frankel. I asked, "Aren't there onboard systems that track where the vehicle is at all times? I thought computers could even unlock doors remotely."

"The owners pay for those services. The dealership doesn't maintain service contracts on sold vehicles."

"Okay. How about his work address?"

"How should I know?"

“Isn’t that on his loan application?”

“He was fired from that job. He was a bouncer at one of the breweries downtown, but that won’t do you any good. I’ve exhausted that lead.” He puffed out an irritated sigh. “I’m only going to give you one more chance, then I’m getting another outfit to do the recoveries.” He hung up.

My heart cascaded a few inches to my stomach.

I didn’t want to deal with Patrick anymore, but my bank account was not where it needed to be. I just had to find that Jeep Wrangler. It would feel good to show up Lou Frankel, a/k/a Mr. Hot Head, the slimy, no-good, deadbeat bully who went to strip bars and threatened five-foot-two redheads with a tire iron. I wanted to squash both of these jackwads, Patrick Crump and Lou Frankel. I needed to recover that Wrangler *asap*.

And the repo money would be nice because the last call for Del’s Towing was from the old guy in the baggy suit who phoned in the middle of the night *five whole days* ago. The calls stopped after the negative comments were posted on the news site that practically accused me of murder. As the cops would say, not a coincidence.

Solving the homicide and silencing the internet rumor mill at the same time would be a plus.

Big Hal’s was not open today, but I may as well try Frankel’s house. Right now. I told myself, look on the bright side. Maybe Hot Head wouldn’t be home. Maybe his Jeep would be parked on the street. Maybe that would happen on the twelfth day of never.

I drove by the address. A ranch-style home of around a thousand square feet. Fake brown stone adhered to the front, and white fiberboard siding covered the rest. A couple of cement steps led up to a cracked stoop, with shades drawn at all the windows. The Jeep was there, but not at the curb. The sweet Jeep Wrangler was on the lawn, chained to a tree, along with a not-so-sweet, sixty-or-so-pound Rottweiler, with black paws, a brown muzzle, and most likely big, sharp teeth.

I rolled down my window. "Hey there, doggie, doggie, doggie…good boy." The dog wrinkled back his upper lip and emitted a low rumbling growl. And, yes, he had a mouthful of big, sharp teeth.

I called Axle. I'd bet he could cut the chain.

He answered on the first ring and his voice blared into my ear, "Delaney, I'm at the police station. They raided the garage."

I yelped, a hand over my heart, then told him, "I'm on my way." I shifted the engine into gear, smashed my toe to the pedal, and the truck jumped away from the curb. I sped down Oak Grove, hung a right on Pine, and zoomed over to Main. I slammed into a parking space, ran through the front door, and skidded up to the desk.

"I'm here for Axle Guttenberg," I said, all out of breath.

The duty clerk nodded, not in any hurry. A short, round woman in jeans and a tank top had come through the door after me with a chubby, barefoot infant on her hip. Mother and child lined up behind me. The officer said, "Everyone please be seated. They'll all be out in a minute."

Scattered visitors occupied the rows of orange plastic chairs in the low budget lobby. Baby mama and I both took seats, leaving a few empties between us.

Nobody wanted to associate with other people who had relatives or friends being questioned by the cops. She bounced the little one on her lap while he chewed on a fist. I took a moment to calm my breathing and pretended to examine an artificial Ficus tree in a wicker basket, black scuff marks on the polished linoleum, and photos with stern faces of the chiefs of police for the last fifty years. Waiting here was more uncomfortable than standing for long periods in four-inch heels.

After several minutes, a line of men shuffled out the steel door into the lobby, including the mechanic Freddie Haag, who gave me a narrow-eyed glare as he went past. Axle was the last one out.

Neither of us said a word until we got to the truck.

"Thanks for coming for me." He buckled his seatbelt. "Can you frickin' believe this?"

I hit the door locks and turned the ignition key. "Have you been arrested?"

"No, they didn't book us or nothing. They took copies of our IDs, and that was it."

"That's all?"

"I told them I didn't want to give a statement. They can't force you, you know." He slumped down in his seat.

"Was there an illegal operation going on, Axle?"

He had on a stubborn expression. "No."

"So, the police didn't find anything, then?" I turned the truck toward the trailer park.

He stared out the window.

I'd question our friendly Spruce Ridge police officer tomorrow. They must've found hot vehicles or they wouldn't have taken the work crew to the station.

****

The next morning, I told Kristen all about the police picking up her cousin. I kept staring at the door expecting Officer Bowers to show up for a coffee, and Kristen glanced out the front window several times as if she wanted Zach to walk in, too.

Around ten, Will called. “Delaney, I have some bad news.”

My heart slowed, like the sluggish drip, drip, drip of the percolator. “What? Is Mom okay?”

“No, no, it’s nothing like that.” He cleared his throat and I held my breath. “The sheriff told the insurance company there might be charges filed against you in the murder investigation.”

I shrieked, “The police said what?” A couple of customers lifted their heads from their laptops and stared at me.

“Let me start at the beginning. The insurance company denied your application because the underwriters felt it was too high a risk.”

“What does that have to do with the police?” I took a big swallow of coffee.

“You can be denied a tow carrier license if you have felony charges pending against you. You can be denied insurance if you don’t have a tow carrier license. The underwriters got wind of your involvement in the murder investigation and talked to the sheriff’s detective.”

My head spinning at that logic, I walked with my phone into the stockroom. “God, what should I do?”

Will answered, “I left a message for the sheriff to see if I can find out anything else. Listen, they could be blowing smoke, rattling cages. It might mean nothing. I’ve consulted a colleague who takes these kind of criminal cases and he's ready to jump in, if needed. In the meantime, don't answer any questions without me present. Understood?"

"Y-yes." This sounded stupid-serious.

"All right, as long as that's straight, let's talk about the insurance. You can apply with other companies, like one of the high-risk insurers."

I sank onto the chair at Kristen's work station. "What does that mean?"

He cleared his throat again. "High-risk insurers cost more. I'll dig around for different companies, but the estate administrator is going to cancel Del's policy by the end of the week, so you're running out of time."

"Tell me why I need it again? Apart from insurance on the truck, I get that, but you're talking about a business policy?" I twirled my hand around as if he could see me.

"Right. It covers general liability and everything else from property damage to inventory loss. What if a car you towed went missing? Or you dropped a car on someone's foot? Premium for that kind of coverage is expensive."

Okay, that was a lot of *attorney-speak.* What I needed insurance for was towing a car with a dead body in the trunk.

He continued, "You need a liability policy so you don't lose the company assets. You can't work without insurance. Remember, I told you this already."

"I know, I know." The only asset I had was the truck, but if I lost that, I'd be out of business. Then what would I do? Kristen was planning my replacement, and Guy couldn't wait to see the back of me.

"I'm still waiting for clear title," Will said, "but once I receive that, consider being done with this headache. You should sell. You'd have money in the bank."

I assured him I understood my options—the fear center in my brain was inclined to agree with him—and I hung up, but my cell rang again.

I punched the button so hard, the phone almost flew out of my hand. "Hello, this is Delaney."

"Delaney Morran?" Hailey's voice sounded in my ear.

Did Friendly Finance have work for me? Fingers and toes crossed that they did, I held my excitement back for a second before celebrating. "Yes."

"We didn't receive your payment for the Fiat. It was due last week."

All hope crumbled like a dried-out pastry. "Oh, yeah. My bad. I'll pay that online today."

"You can give me your bank account number now and remit the amount over the phone."

"Hailey, you know me. I signed up to help you with the repo work, remember? And, I've never been late before." Not with Friendly.

"Sorry, Delaney, this is standard procedure." There was a big sigh on the other end. "First, I call about a hundred times, then I send registered letters. You don't want one of those."

"Too true." I could so relate to the owners whose cars I was anxious to repossess. Even Hot Head? No, everybody but him.

"Over ten percent of our loans are in default. I'm trying to keep you from becoming one of our statistics."

"Is that a lot?"

"Yes. It eats up just about all our profits. You're a small business owner, you should understand that. Can you make the payment?"

My balance was low, but I had enough, just barely. "Sure, let me get my wallet." I fished for my debit card and gave her the account number, all the while wondering if standard procedure included sending an enforcer to collect.

Is that how Jeremy's body ended up in his trunk?

And how he ended up a murder statistic?

Chapter 14

I wandered out to the front of the coffee bar at the same time Officer Bowers strolled in.

Both Kristen and I rushed up to him and I asked, "What happened at L&B Garage last night?"

The Spruce Ridge officer crossed his arms and rocked back on his heels. "The police found one stolen car, nothing more. They brought the employees in for questioning, but no one gave anything up, not even why they were there on a Sunday night when the shop was closed."

Kristen laid a hand on Zach's arm. "Is my cousin in trouble?"

"A stolen car might be justification to suspect a chop shop, but there's no proof. They've all been told not to say anything. I do appreciate the tip, Kris. That's why we've been watching them all week."

Guy came out to hand Zach his drink. After the barista vanished back behind the espresso machine, I asked, "What's this about a hot car?"

"The mechanics told us they had no idea the car was stolen. They gave us a work order with a bogus customer name and a disconnected phone number. We impounded the car and it'll be returned to the owner." He pushed back out the door into the cool air, his to-go cup in hand. "I'll see you later, Kris."

"Wait." I held up my palm.

He stopped in midstride. "Yes?"

"Is the sheriff ready to file charges in Jeremy's murder?" I was reeling from Will's revelation that the police were still focusing on me, and my voice came out high-pitched, like a squeaky dog toy. "I heard they are."

"I don't know. And if I did, I couldn't answer that."

Kristen said, "Please let us know if you hear anything. Anything you can share."

I added, working on lowering my voice, "I hope the sheriff finds the real killer soon."

The Spruce Ridge officer wouldn't meet my eyes. He pivoted on his heel and powered out the door.

Kristen and I returned behind the counter. I wiped down the steam wand on the espresso machine with a hot rag, the heat burning my fingers. "Zach didn't let on who the sheriff is going to arrest. That's because they're going to arrest me. They're targeting me."

Kristen said, "No way."

"Word is out. I'm the one."

Her hands flew to her mouth. "What do you mean?"

I informed her, "The insurance company talked to the sheriff. They told Will I'm going to be arrested."

"That's ridiculous." My friend stood hand on hip, using her serious voice. "And why would the insurance people even talk to the police?"

I slumped my back side against the work counter. "They learned all about the murder. You know it was in the news that I towed Jeremy's car, so it was easy enough to read on the internet."

She raised her eyebrows in a confident look. "The

insurance company has it wrong. They shouldn't say anything inflammatory like that. Trust in the process, Delaney. God will take care of you."

A nice thought to fall back on, but I wasn't so sure. I said, "You need to tell your cousin to get another job. That garage is a chop shop even if the police can't prove it."

"He wouldn't take my advice. You're closer to him than I am."

"I'm worried about the big kahuna."

"Who?"

"The head of the crime syndicate." I sucked in my lips. Axle could be in danger. "What if they're shipping car parts to Mexico? Maybe L&B has connections to the Mexican drug cartel."

My friend gave me a grimace and an eye roll. "You've been watching too much television." Kristen pulled a lever and shot steam onto the spill tray below.

"You agree L&B is a chop shop, though?" I asked.

"I don't know anymore." She puckered her dark brows. "The best thing to do is pray for Axle."

"Pray about the murder investigation, too, that they'll catch the right guy." I scrubbed the sink as I told her about my visit with Jeremy's mother. "What can I do for her? You have any suggestions?"

"Send a card. Write down a couple of things you liked about Jeremy. Did he make you laugh? Was he kind?" My friend said, "Stuff like that. She will appreciate it."

I stood up straight and placed the sponge back on the rack. "That's thoughtful, Kristen. You always do the right thing."

"No, I don't." She let out a guffaw. "Nobody's

perfect." But she came close. She gave me a wide-eyed, hopeful glance and asked, "Changing the subject, are you ready to cut back hours? It seems like you've been doing a lot of towing, and Guy asked for more shifts."

Glancing at Guy, I saw him give me a superior once-over, eager to take my place, and my heart rate revved up. He hit the button on the grinder. I heard the blood pound in my ears, even above the noise of the gnashing machine.

Was I ready? No! That's a N! And a O!

I took in a calming breath to settle myself. I admit the goal was to move on from Roasters on the Ridge and work full time in the towing business, but the coffee shop was familiar and safe. The comforting smell of the brew, the relaxing music, even the repetitive work—all that had been my life for the past seven months. And more recently, a regular paycheck, even if it was small. Kristen might think so, but you and I know I hadn't been all that busy on tows and the business might not get off the ground. But working in my dad's truck…doing what he did…I didn't want to give that up. And I sure didn't want to go back into social work. And now my barista job was on its way out, too. But if I was arrested—perish the thought—none of this would matter.

"Delaney?" Kris had a concerned look on her face.

My gaze darted over to Guy and back as I thought of a way to accommodate everyone. "Sure. Take me off the schedule on Tuesdays and Thursdays. But I'd appreciate it if you'd give me three or four shifts a week for a little longer."

"That works." Her head bobbed up and down.

"And, Kristen, I'm going to pay rent as soon as I

can." The first of the month rapidly approached. That would be a good time to start.

She gave me a big smile. "Thanks, Delaney. That'll help me out. I've ordered a new espresso maker, the kind with a dual boiler that handles three shots at once." Even though it was badly needed, Kristen had gone without this expensive piece of equipment.

"That's great, Kris." I'd have to hustle up a lot more tows to come up with the rent money. If only those comments on the internet didn't tie me to Jeremy's murder. In a small town, most customers came to you through word of mouth. Were the townspeople shunning my business? That would explain why the phone didn't ring, and I was determined to fix that.

Kristen bustled to the backroom to order product, and I waited on the customer who'd sidled up to the cash register.

Noon arrived. I said goodbye to Kristen and tossed my apron into the bin. I drove my dad's tow truck down Mr. Hot Head's street—his Jeep was gone—then I jetted over to Big Hal's, but the Wrangler was not there, either.

Tanner pulled his tow truck into the lane behind me as I rumbled down Main. We both turned off onto a side street. A promising sun shone in a bright blue sky, a cerulean color, seen only at high altitude in Colorado. Pine scent from a nearby spruce wafted through my open window, along with discordant songs of birds hidden among the boughs. I nosed the self-loader to the curb, got out, and heaved myself up into his passenger seat.

I asked him, "You busy? I'm waiting for a call for

a tow myself." Yes, I was still hopeful.

"I just hauled a Subaru from one of the towaway zones. I'm ready for the owner to contact me."

"What model Subaru?"

"Forester."

"All-wheel drive, then."

"Hey, good job."

"I'm learning." I shoved my braid back and stared at the rear of Dad's truck. The big dent in the bumper reminded me of the metal dumpster behind the strip joint…but I couldn't make an insurance claim if I wanted to, since my application had been denied. From this angle, the cracked windshield and the hail damage were out of view.

Tanner gazed at the clock on the dash. "I have a Chamber meeting in half an hour. You should think about joining."

Good grief. He had a college degree, I remembered, was a homeowner, a business owner, on the Chamber of Commerce, strong, steady, beyond sizzling.

I was staring at him, so I tore my eyes away and gave myself a mental head-slap.

Byron may have warned him off, but the tow man should have a mind of his own. It was just too lame for me to believe Byron's over-protectiveness had kept Tanner from asking me out. What thirty-year-old male heeded that kind of advice? He was not interested in me, and I was no longer crushing on him. And the last thing I needed was a boyfriend to distract me, especially one I had to chase after. Why would I want to be with someone who didn't want to be with me? I had enough to deal with without adding Tanner to my worries.

"I'll let you go, then." I abruptly popped open the door and wiggled out. He gave me a *what-the-hell* look, but I just waved goodbye, then scrabbled into my truck. I sneaked a glance his way before he took off, and caught him looking at me, too, but he cranked his engine and left. It didn't take long before I'd parked behind the coffee shop. I trudged up the steps, pulling myself up the handrail, and locked myself inside the apartment.

The phone rang and the caller asked, "Is this Del?"

"Yes, Del's Towing." They always called me Del. "Can I help you?"

"My car broke down a couple blocks south of Main."

Yes! I was so happy to get a call on a job I almost levitated off the floor. "I can be there in ten minutes. How did you learn about me?" I wondered if the cards I was handing out were helping business.

"From the internet. Oh, wait. Are you the one who towed the dead body?"

I sucked in my breath. "I did tow a vehicle that was later implicated in an investigation, but I—"

The caller hung up. Blast it to hell. I should've denied it.

I'd started to peel a hardboiled egg when heavy pounding rattled my door. "Open up. Police!"

No shit? I mean, really? The cops were here to arrest me? No, just no. How could this be happening? I squeezed my eyes shut and tried to pull myself together, but the egg fell out of my fingers and cracked on the floor. If only I'd been out on that tow, then I wouldn't have been home.

Grabbing a paper towel, I wiped up the pieces of yolk, then threw back the deadbolt. I managed to ask, “Can I help you?”

A county sheriff stood on the top step. Not Sheriff Ephraim Lopez. “I need you to come with me.”

I didn’t want to be handcuffed and manhandled down the stairs, so I snagged my purse off the hook by the door and locked up. The officer followed me down to the parking lot and stuffed me into his pickup truck.

Once at the sheriff’s station, he sat me at the table in the cold interrogation room and asked if I wanted coffee or water. I said no, that I wanted an attorney.

“You need a lawyer?” His lips curled up in a sneer.

“You bet I do.” My voice sounded shaky.

“You haven’t heard any of the questions yet.”

“It doesn’t matter. I don’t like your attitude.” Where was Ephraim? He was so much nicer than this one. I was surely about to be arrested. Time to insist on legal representation. In other words, I required my stepdad.

“Do you need a phone?”

“I have my cell in my purse.” He let me retrieve it, then left the room while I made the call. I phoned my mother. “I’m at the sheriff’s station being questioned again.” A sob came out at the end.

“Laney! Are you okay?” Mom was alarmed, which made me feel worse. I suppose I should have called Will, but hers was the number I dialed automatically.

“I’ll be fine once Will gets here. Can you get a hold of him and tell him to come?”

“Yes, but it’ll take an hour to get to Spruce Ridge.”

“I know. Thanks, Mom.” I disconnected and tucked my phone away. The detective must have been watching from behind the glass because he came back into the room. I told him, "My attorney, Will Sharpton, is on the way. I'm not answering questions until he gets here, so don't bother to ask me any."

The officer left.

The gray walls seemed to close in. The iron chair at the metal table was uncomfortable and the room felt cold even though I was sweating. This was not a good time to feel claustrophobic.

With no windows it was impossible to tell the time of day, so I watched the clock on my phone as closely as if I was studying for the CDL exam. I couldn't believe the police brought me in. Me! They couldn't manage to arrest anyone at the chop shop, yet they were picking on the tow truck driver. Not fair. But effective if the police wanted to scare me. They did. I was scared.

Fifty minutes *slooowly* ticked by before the detective returned with Will. My tee-shirt was damp, and I'd racked my fingers through my hair until the strands frizzed out like Donald Trump's combover. My nerves were on edge, but Will gave me a tight smile and a nod and I wanted to believe that everything was going to be all right. Will was here. I wasn't alone.

After he grabbed the seat next to me, Will asked the detective in a voice much too calm for the question, "Are you going to arrest my client?" I glanced from Will to the man in uniform and waited for his answer.

He said, "Not today."

"Then, we're leaving. Come on, Delaney." Will stood up. *What?* That was too easy. My eyes ricocheted between the sheriff and Will. My stepdad stole a hand under my arm and lifted me to a stand. My legs had cramped into a bent position, and I held on to his sleeve as he led me on stiff legs down the hall and out the entryway. We marched over to his car and he opened the passenger door for me.

I found my voice. "Sorry about this, Will. It wasn't worth the effort for you to drive all the way here just for that."

"No problem. Next time, tell the sheriff you aren't going to the station unless you're under arrest, and if they arrest you, call me and I'll get a good criminal attorney on board. You did the right thing by not answering any questions without me."

Will helped me up the steps to my apartment and gave me a tight hug at the door. He said, "They don't have anything on you other than your connection to Jeremy and that's not enough."

"They told the insurance company they were going to arrest me, right?"

"No, they said they *might* file charges against you. *Might*. Rattling cages, remember? Try not to worry." He descended the stairs and hiked over to his Nissan Infinity, rear-wheel drive.

Not worry? *Fat chance*. This was too close of a call. I could just picture the handcuffs, the orange prison garb, the dirty brick walls of a jail cell. And what kind of footwear could I expect?

My apartment, as lovely as it was, felt confining, like I suffered the loss of my freedom already. Suddenly, I didn't want to be all alone again like I was at the sheriff's office waiting for Will. I wanted Tanner and was tempted to call him, but no, I'd had enough of his rejection.

I peeked out my window. A nondescript, white sedan, which I knew was an Acura—normally front-wheel drive, but possibly all-wheel if it had the larger engine—was tucked behind a stand of aspen. A man sat behind the wheel, wearing reflective, aviator sunglasses, reading a newspaper, thumbing the corners, casting glances up at my apartment. I ducked out of sight.

Who reads a paper anymore? And there was something familiar about the man in the aviator glasses.

I stomped down the apartment stairs and over to the car. The man lowered the printed sheet a fraction and pointed his face towards me. I leaned in his open window. "Ephraim?"

His eyebrows shot up over the top of his aviators. "Hello, Delaney."

"Why are you watching me?"

He tossed the Denver newspaper into the backseat. "Get in."

I opened the passenger door and toppled inside. "Your colleagues at the sheriff's department were pretty rough on me. Making me sweat it out until my attorney got there."

He gave me a tight smile.

I turned to face him full-on and leaned my back against the door. "Why are you here?"

He pushed his feet against the floorboards causing his seat to groan backward. "You know I can't say anything about an ongoing investigation."

"That's okay. I have a good guess. Tell me if I'm right." I rubbed a hand across my forehead. "I'm the number one suspect, but it took more force than I'm capable of to kill Jeremy, beating him with a chain like that. And I didn't have the strength to lift him into the trunk." I'd had plenty of time to think about this while waiting for Will. "So, the sheriff's office is putting pressure on me hoping I'll lead them to my accomplice."

Ephraim hid his reaction behind his sunglasses.

I swiped the requisite glasses off his nose, surprising us both. "Why do cops hide behind these things? You shouldn't cover up those brown eyes."

Did I just say that?

He squirmed a little, adjusting his position on the leather seat, then gave me a long steady regard. His aftershave hinted of something green, sweet, and warm, like the fresh scent of jasmine. *Dang*. He smelled fine. A flutter went through my chest and a heatwave hit my cheeks.

I asked, "Did you think I'd call my partner-in-crime and he'd come over so we could plan our big escape?"

His eyes darted away and back again. I was right. And, I had thought about calling Tanner and asking him to come over. I'm glad I didn't.

"So, your partner-in-crime is a 'he?' "

I levered myself out of the car. "Good luck. I hope you catch the real killer soon."

I planted my yellow peep-toes on the rough ground, aware he likely had his eyes on my backside. I couldn't resist darting him a glance as I ascended the stairs, and sure enough, he was gawking. He oozed his aviators back over his eyes and started up the car.

By the time I got to my door, he'd left.

That was fun in a way, but flirting with Ephraim hadn't accomplished much. I wasn't any the wiser. No new clues.

****

Waking up Tuesday morning without having to show up at the coffee shop was as gloomy as heavy rain. Guy had taken over my Tuesday shift. So, with nothing better to do, I called Jeremy's mom and asked her if I could stop by. The sympathy card I'd sent must have paved the way because she said, "I guess so."

She wasn't quite as reluctant to open the door this time, though she wasn't entirely welcoming either. "Thank you for the card. That was thoughtful." She gestured me inside as she continued to speak. "Jeremy did make people laugh. He was kind."

I blushed. Since I hadn't known what to write, I'd used Kristen's words…and she hadn't even known Jeremy very well. But then, neither had I, as it turned out. And, I suppose, I was lucky I hadn't known him better. I asked her, "Do you have Melissa's address? I'd like to send her a sympathy card, too. I know they were getting a divorce, but she must've cared a great deal for Jeremy at one time."

An intake of breath escaped Mrs. Winslow's mouth and disapproval appeared all over her face, but she said, "All right. I'll be right back." I waited in the doorway for a few moments until she returned with a sticky note.

I tucked the paper into my purse. "Do you know Melissa's family?"

"Not really." She was quiet today, tight-lipped and withdrawn, but I couldn't call her rude.

Should I ask about Melissa's brother? That mean repo agent, Patrick Crump? Get Mrs. Winslow to dish the dirt on the daughter-in-law she didn't like? Her shoulders were slumped, her hair uncombed, so I thought better of it. Maybe another time.

As soon as I got into my Fiat, I read the sticky

note.

913 Third Street.

That house. With that garage. Where we found that car with Jeremy's body.

Chapter 15

"Zach, why didn't you tell me Jeremy's car was at his wife's house?" I held a steaming, non-fat latte—his usual order—out of his reach. The Spruce Ridge officer stretched out his hand for his drink, but I drew back even farther.

"That information is part of an ongoing investigation." He snatched the cup from my grip.

"Meh." I pouted in a *so-what* look. How many times was I going to hear that line?

His gaze went to Kristen behind the checkout, but she was busy with a customer and couldn't help him. I, on the other hand, was here on my day off.

He took a sip of his latte, then blotted the foam from his mustache with a napkin.

I clicked my tongue. "Surely, Jeremy's wife killed him. Why are the police even considering anyone else? The woman who answered the door told me she didn't know him. I'll bet that was Jeremy's wife, the liar." I'd taken Jeremy's mom's cue. The wife, Melissa Winslow, had risen to the top of my suspect list.

Zach palmed his face in frustration. "Did you go to her house?"

"Yes. She's a liarmouth and a murderer. And I've seen her driving some expensive new cars around town. Where did she get the money to buy those, huh? Huh? The life insurance payout."

He threw up his hands. "Oh brother. Quit jumping to conclusions."

"I'm telling Kristen you won't help me." I glanced over at my friend behind the counter.

Zach stared at Kristen, too, and swallowed a couple of times. A bead of sweat appeared on his brow. "I'd help if I could."

He had it bad for Kris, and I wasn't above taking advantage. My very life's on the line here. And he didn't need to know I wouldn't actually complain to Kris or get in the way of their relationship.

I crossed my eyes with impatience. "Why hasn't Melissa Winslow been arrested? You know the sheriff picked me up again for questioning?"

With another glance at Kristen, he said, "Let's take this outside where we won't be overheard."

I hastened out after him, and he led me around to the back where I'd parked my Fiat near the dumpster. The parking lot was otherwise empty. I gave him a *just-spit-it-out* expression.

He pulled a hand down his face and stroked his mustache. "Melissa Winslow was out of town the entire week before Jeremy was killed and didn't return until two days after he was found. There's no evidence against her."

I deflated a little. "No evidence at all?"

"No. So you see, she didn't kill her husband. Leave her alone, Delaney."

"What about an accomplice? Was anyone living in the house with her?"

"Just Jeremy. It appeared as if he lived there."

A hot bolt of fury ran from my tight chest up to my choking throat and spit frothed at the corners of my mouth. Maybe it *was* better not to know the details of an investigation. I said, "What a dirtbag! So, that's why he broke up with me. He moved back in with the wife. He should've just told me."

Zach leaned against the brick building and crossed his arms. "She explained to the sheriff that they weren't together. He needed a place to stay and she helped him out."

I steadied myself with one hand against the building and swallowed down my anger along with the spit. Maybe Melissa was the reason why Jeremy dumped me. Maybe she wasn't. And did I care? *No!* Well, I did wonder why a loser like Jeremy would drop me, not the other way around. If I'd had all the facts, I would never have gone out with him in the first place. I was not going to take Melissa off my list, no matter what Zach said. Melissa Winslow was suspect number one. L&B was number two. There was also the guy in the mug shot, number three. Was there anyone else to consider? Yes, I remembered there was.

"Who discovered the body?" I pointed a finger at Zach. "Somebody from Friendly Finance, that's who. Did they kill him?"

"Delaney, stop." He pushed himself off the building, his shoulders stretched wide and back. "Now leave the investigation alone. No more questions, right?"

"Wrong."

He beat his temple with the heel of his hand. "I give up."

We walked back to the front and pushed through the door. Kristen was behind the bean roaster and didn't appear to have noticed we'd stepped outside. It took several more minutes before she arrived at our table. Zach had come in to see her, not me, so I headed for the espresso machine. A text arrived from Axle asking me for a ride to work. I made two espresso drinks to-go and swung out the door.

Maybe my little cuz' could help me brainstorm. I veered to a stop in front of his trailer and he folded himself into the Fiat. He fastened his seat belt, then grabbed his latte from my fingers.

"Axle, what can you tell me about Jeremy?"

"This again?" He took a pull from the steaming cup.

"Yes, again. Give me a crumb, here." The stretch of road leading out of the trailer park was empty of traffic. My Fiat jolted over a speed bump, then I left turned onto Fifth Ave.

"I know nothing about him."

I pretended to study the rearview mirror while I cast a few glances at Axle sitting inches away from me in my tiny car. "Did you know Jeremy was married?"

"No."

I gestured to my phone on the console between us. "Remember the mug shot I showed you? Did you know that guy?"

"No."

"Do you know L&B is operating a chop shop?"

"No."

"Good God. You don't know anything." I speared him with my elbow across the close space, and he dodged the blow, hitting his shoulder against the door. Then he gave me a shove, almost causing me to swerve into the other lane.

Hoping to get one straight answer, I asked, "How

do you get to work every day?" I really wondered. Hanging onto the wheel firmly in case he pushed me again, I turned the Fiat into L&B Garage.

"A couple of the mechanics live in the trailer park. I catch a ride with one of them." Axle gave me a half smile before inserting his earbuds. "Thanks for the lift, but this doesn't mean I owe you one."

"Yeah, right. You owe me." I returned his smile before he got out and slammed the door. When he entered the auto bay, snapping sparks from welders and the motoring sound of an air compressor shot out along with a sharp odor of burning metal. I watched Axle make his way across the bay into the reception area. He took the stool behind the counter and appeared to log in to the computer. Maybe he would get his driver's license back soon, then he could find another job. Thinking about work, it was time for me to quit procrastinating and start marketing. Yes, L&B might be a chop shop, but it had a legitimate enterprise going, too.

I entered the lobby and laid a stack of my new business cards on the counter in front of Axle. "I forgot to give these to you. Can you mention me if your customers need their cars towed?"

"I will, Delaney." Axle stacked the cards on the ledge where everyone could see them.

On the other side of the auto bay, Freddie Haag's head came out from under the hood of a car. He tossed down a tool and glared at me through the doorway. He called out, "Need any help, Axle?" as he walked over.

Axle drew his eyebrows together in a question but shook his head.

I said to Haag, "I gave Axle some of my business

cards in case any of your customers need a tow."

"We can't recommend anyone." He extracted a pack of cigarettes from a pocket and forced one out with angry tamps.

"Really? Because other shops in town told me they could." Well, Byron said he could.

He poked the cigarette in his mouth and the dry paper stuck to his lower lip. "Our policy is we don't. Understand? Or do I need to spell it out another way?" Axle's eyebrows almost disappeared under his knit cap as he stared between Haag and me.

"All righty. No problemo." I gave Axle two thumbs up to let him know I'm cool and shuffled out the front door fast. Did Haag's words sound threatening to you? They did to me and now I was even more worried about my lil' cuz'.

I drove over to the office park across the street from L&B and eased my car behind a tall pine. There wasn't much I could do about Freddie Haag. He didn't assault me or anything like that. I would never complain to Byron Oberly about him and wouldn't bring him up to Kristen's cop boyfriend, Zach, either. So…I needed to let it go. I dug out my list of auto repair shops. There were other places; L&B wasn't the only shop in town. As long as nobody called from the towaway zones and the repo agent didn't contact me about the Jeep Wrangler, I had no excuse not to tackle my business plan. Yes, I did have one.

Okay then. Just get started. I pictured Kristen standing behind me, giving me a whap on the head, saying, *Do it*.

But hold everything, look at this. A pearl-gray Ford Taurus, available in both front and all-wheel drive, had pulled into L&B, and Patrick Crump lunged out. Should I stick around and ask him about the Jeep Wrangler? Or about Jeremy Winslow? *Yes.* Plenty of time to visit auto shops later.

The repo man went inside. He faced the lobby window while he spoke with that mean man, Freddie Haag. The mechanic exhaled a puff of smoke and shook Crump's hand. They talked for a few minutes before Crump turned around and came back out. What was that all about? Was Crump hunting for one of his vehicles to repossess? Was he questioning Haag about his deceased brother-in-law, Jeremy?

I dialed Crump's number. I couldn't hear the ring from where I sat, but it must've made a sound because he lugged his phone out of his pocket. He tapped the screen and my cell dinged with a text received. It was from him.

—*Too busy to talk now.*—

More like, too bigheaded to bother with me now.

I texted back. —*I just have a quick question. Did you know Jeremy Winslow?*—

He stared at his phone. Seeing his reaction without him knowing was sneaky-fun. He replied. —*What a loser. My sister's ex. Why?*—

My fingers hesitated over the touch screen, but three little dots hovered in a conversation bubble, then his next text appeared. —*He was asking for trouble. Heard he went out with some hot redhead. I'm glad my sister took up with the cop.*— I jerked up in time to see him climb into his Taurus. He buckled his seatbelt, looked both ways for traffic, then turned in the direction away from Spruce Ridge.

Was I the hot redhead? Had Jeremy asked for

trouble because he dated me while still technically married to his sister? I wasn't exactly happy about that either. Interesting, though, that Melissa went out with a cop. I wondered which cop. And what was the repo man doing at L&B? Did Abington know his employee hung around car thieves? Should I mention this to Abington? A nice man like him shouldn't have such an unpleasant person working for him.

Nope. Tattling or complaining would not help anything. Besides, I was just inside the auto shop myself, and I was no criminal.

I started up the Fiat and aimed toward town. I might as well head over to the next car repair place on my list and drop off some business cards. Still no calls for tows had come in, and it'd been a week since my last tow. But who's counting.

Industrial Lane didn't have much traffic, but an SUV with dark windows exited L&B and got behind me. I turned right on Main and left on Pine. The SUV followed through each turn. I finally arrived at Spruce Ridge Auto Repair and steered into the lot. The SUV kept going down the street.

Just my imagination. I plunked the gear into park and got out. Took a deep breath. Said, *you can do this, you can do this*. Went inside.

"I'd like to introduce myself," I said to the man behind the register. "I'm a vehicle recovery technician and I've taken over Del's Towing. I respond quickly, you can read my reviews on the internet." *Oops*. I shouldn't have mentioned that. What if he saw the comments linking me to the murder? I fumbled in my purse, then set a small stack of my cards on the counter. "Please think of me next time you need a tow service."

The man glanced at the cards with the image of a tall stiletto and did a double-take. He picked them up and smiled. "I'll let the boss know, but we already have a tow man we use, so don't get your hopes up."

I thanked him and left, squashing those hopes down so low they were at a level somewhere below the pavement. The thought of another cold call made my stomach hurt, so I stuffed my list into the bottom of my purse and slumped down in the driver's seat.

My phone rang and I picked up. A call for a tow? Please, pretty please?

"This is Chérie. You left me your card, remember?"

"Yes?" I'd dropped off cards, but not to a Chérie.

"Chérie at Big Hal's. I helped you escape."

I sat up straight. "Oh, yes. What can I do for you?"

"That dangerous man is back. Just wanted to warn you in case you were close by."

"Thanks, Chérie. I'm so glad you called."

"Be careful."

"I will." I made a U-turn to head to Big Hal's. I passed by the front of the strip club, then turned into the alley. Mr. Hot Head had not parked the Jeep Wrangler behind the bar this time. I drove around the block again, then made a wider circle around the next few blocks, cutting through alleys, checking vehicles on the street. No Jeep Wrangler.

I called Chérie back. "This is Delaney. Is that man still at the club?"

"No, he's gone."

Darn. Darn. Darn. "Would you call me again the next time he shows up? I have a score to settle with him."

"All right, but are you sure?"

"Positive."

This Wrangler was costing me…burning up my gas, taking up my time, and keeping me from getting additional repo jobs. If I could only capture that stupid Jeep, it would surely lead to more work and I could forget about cold calling. I was going to get that Jeep yet.

But not at the moment, so I wormed my cold-call list out of my purse and flattened out the pages. The next auto shop was on the way to Melissa Winslow's house…and it wouldn't hurt to make a short detour, would it?

Procrastinate, much?

I ran inside the nearby grocery store for a small potted ivy.

This time when the same pretty woman answered the door of the house on Third Street, she had on a little makeup and her blonde hair appeared freshly washed. She wore a spring dress, and her thin legs ended in flip-flops.

"Melissa Winslow?"

She gave me a dirty look. "Yes, but I don't buy anything from door-to-door salesmen."

"That's not why I'm here. I'd like to give you this." I held out the plant, forcing her to open the screen to take it. "I'm sorry for your loss."

"Thanks. Who are you?"

"Delaney Morran. I dated Jeremy for a while. I got your address from Jeremy's mom."

"His mom?" She snorted.

I wished Kristen was with me. She would've smoothed things over in her gentle way. "I suppose the police have been by to talk to you? They've taken me in for questioning a couple of times now."

"Yeah?" She remained at the threshold, still holding the screen partially open. "So what?"

"I thought maybe we could compare notes."

A moment passed, then she said, "I don't think so," and started to step back inside.

"Come on, what do you have to lose?"

"Why should I talk to you?"

"Because we've both been questioned by the cops. Because we shared that experience. Because we both cared about him once. I know you helped him out, which was a nice thing to do, considering, uh, you know, the divorce."

"I remember you were here once before. Why do you keep bothering me? I already told the police everything. There's no reason to discuss it with you."

I dropped the bombshell, "Jeremy's mom thinks you might have been the one to kill him. That's why." Would that get her to talk?

"That bitch probably told the cops I did it." She stepped out, letting the screen bang shut, then set the plant on a ledge.

"That's what you get for trying to be helpful, am I right?"

She nodded with a slow bob of her head. "So, why were you talking to Jeremy's mom about me?"

"Jeremy broke up with me, probably to get back together with you." Even though Zach had told me that wasn't true, I still wondered.

"I let Jeremy sleep on the couch a few nights 'cause he had to move out of his apartment. That's all it was. We weren't getting back together or anything like that."

Okay. So, the jerk didn't break up with me to get back with his wife. Something else was going on. What was it? I asked, "Why did he need to move?"

She crossed her arms over her chest. "He was in some kind of trouble."

I raised my eyebrows. "Did he tell you what the problem was?"

"No, but it was something bad."

She got that right. Something bad. Real bad. Deep shit bad. Deep enough to get him killed. And I'd had no idea. He didn't confide in me and it seemed he hadn't explained it to Melissa either. I batted back the sudden moisture in my eyes. I didn't like Jeremy after the break-up, but I did feel sorry for the guy. "I heard you were out of town when it happened."

"I went to Denver to visit friends. When I got back, at first I thought he'd left, his car was gone, but then I saw his boxes and stuff still in the garage." She rubbed her forehead with the back of one hand. "Then the police knocked on my door and told me he was dead. They searched the house and garage. It was awful."

"I know. They combed over my place, too." I let my gaze drift to the street, empty of traffic. "Jeremy didn't tell me much. I don't even know who his friends were. You do, though, don't you?"

She gave a helpless shrug and sagged back against the door frame. "One of his buddies let him down big time, so he stopped hanging out with his old friends."

I showed her the mug shot on my phone. "Do you recognize this man?"

She pushed herself up to a stand and her eyes did a shifty thing. "Sure. That's Eugene Turnquil."

A name. I had his name now. "Do you have his number?"

She considered my request for a few seconds too long. "No."

I didn't press her for it, but had another question. "I'm surprised you let Jeremy stay with you if you thought he was in trouble, you dating a cop and all."

Her eyes widened in a look of *what the*...then she reached back for the door knob. "Thanks for the plant."

"One more thing. I know your brother, Patrick. Small world, huh?"

She paused with the handle in her grasp. "You know Pat?"

"We sort of work together, for Abington Auto Store. He's the one who told me you were dating a cop."

"Hunh. Well, goodbye." She darted inside and the door clapped shut. Then her hand reached back out, grabbed the plant off the rail, and slammed the door closed again.

Well, goodbye to you, too. If my words got back to them, I'd probably made enemies of Mrs. Winslow and Patrick Crump. What can I say? Neither liked me much anyway. I started the Fiat, turned in the alley, and cruised slowly past Melissa's garage. Were Jeremy's belongings still in there?

I tried to think of a motive for Melissa to kill her husband in spite of her excuse that she only wanted to help, and I knew of no compelling reason for Patrick to do the deed, either. His comments about Jeremy being a loser didn't exactly qualify as a motive for murder. On second thought, was the wife feeding me a load of bull? She could be lying about helping out her husband. She lied to me before about not knowing him. Don't forget she's the beneficiary of his life insurance policy. If Melissa had an incentive, then her brother Patrick had one, too, and he could be her accomplice.

While the engine idled at the end of the alley, I called the Sheriff's office and asked for Ephraim Lopez. When he picked up, I asked, "Is there anything new in the investigation? Notice, I haven't been arrested yet. So, I'm just wondering."

"There's nothing I can tell you."

"Really, nothing at all?"

"No."

I wanted to tell him a thing or two but held my tongue.

"We're releasing the evidence taken from your vehicle. You can come pick it up."

"Okay." At least this was something.

"Just tell the duty officer at the window, then pull around back. Someone will bring it out."

"On my way."

After stopping at the front desk at the sheriff's station, I followed the officer's instructions to the back entrance. A clerk buzzed me in, left and came back with a heavy carton, and slid a form toward me.

"Sign here."

I scanned the paper, an evidence property receipt. The box was open on top, and since the woman gazed at me expectantly, I examined the contents—heavy chains with hooks, some rusty rags, a small metal toolbox with wrenches and screwdrivers, and a well-thumbed, paperback, titled *Kelley Blue Book*—and I signed the form.

As I gathered the carton in my arms, the clerk said,

"The sheriff is going to call you. He said he forgot to tell you he has more questions."

I huffed out a breath. "Great," then caught myself. "I mean, that's fine."

I lit out for Byron's lot and parked in the back.

The *Blue Book* contained hundreds of pages of car descriptions, vehicle features, and estimated values based on mileage and condition, as good as or better than my car encyclopedia. The torn leaves were dirty like they'd been well read. I wasn't the only one who relied on such a guide for car information.

I fit the chains and toolbox in the compartment under the truck bed alongside the other gadgets. The *Blue Book* I tucked under the dash with my encyclopedia. I assumed the police examined the chains and tools to determine if any were the murder weapon, and I suppose the rust on the rags could've appeared to be blood, but who knew why they confiscated the book?

It was Tuesday night and five o'clock already, so I took the tow truck and drove around the no-parking zones. I was still a little nervous, but excited about this opportunity to haul cars and produce some income.

The sun set over the top of the mountain peaks, the orange and pink rays shooting through the gilded clouds, while I sat parked behind the antique store. Cars sped past the alley and kept going, people on their way from work, rushing to get home to family and dinner. I decided to drive up and down the alley rather than just sit there. After cruising around for an hour, I finally caught a violator parked unlawfully behind the brewery, and just as I was about to pull out with the car in-tow, a man flagged me down, arms waving, yelling, "Don't leave!"

My brakes squealed as I stopped the rig and powered down the window.

"Please?" He rifled his fingers through his hair, his eyes wide. "I'm late for work and I can't lose my job."

I almost teared up myself. "We can't let that happen. I could charge you a drop fee, you know, but I'll let it go this time."

"Thanks, miss."

With the controller in my hands, I launched out of the truck cab and lowered his car from the claws. Here was a marketing opportunity. "Please don't park in these towaway zones again. It's illegal." I handed him one of my cards. "If you ever need a tow, give me a call."

Gone was the grateful act. He tore the card with exaggerated effort and let the pieces fall to the ground. He said, "I would never hire someone who snatches cars for a living," then he unlocked his car door and catapulted inside.

I yelled, "If you change your mind, please recommend me to your friends," as he zoomed out of the alley.

That didn't go too bad. Much better than cold calling.

And here I was, in back of the brewery. Patrick had told me the Hot Headed Jeep owner had been fired from a brewery. A door yawned open a few inches, so I poked my head in and caught a whiff of stale barley and hops and the sound of voices. The hall appeared dark but led to a well-lit dining area with a crowded bar on one side. A startled waitress with an enormous, white apron wrapped around her waist appeared.

"Would you like a table?"

"No, thanks. I'm trying to find Lou Frankel. I think he used to work here as a bouncer."

Her brows creased together. "He hasn't worked here for a month or two."

"Do you know where he works now?"

"No." She waved the menu in her hand. "Do you want one of our beers on tap?"

"Does anyone else here know where I can find him?"

She glanced to her left then back at me. "The bartender is new and our manager's not here. Maybe if you come back another time."

"All right, thanks." I started toward the rear door, but she stopped me with a hand on my arm.

"Please don't go that way. Customers are supposed to use the front entrance."

I stepped out onto Main Street, then absconded to the alley where my dad's tow truck took up a lot of space. I'd bombed out, two for two. No towed vehicles, no intel on Frankel. But I had the truck. I had that going for me. This big ole hunk of metal had not let me down yet, always scooping up the target at the touch of a button. There was some satisfaction in that.

Learning how to operate the self-loader had turned out to be the easy part. Finding repos, generating business, that was the Rubik's Cube. Solving the murder was another hard puzzle.

Watching the clock, I drove around some more. A few minutes before the parking restriction ended, I found a car blocking the loading dock behind the art gallery, but I left it alone. Close enough. I tucked my card under the windshield wiper with a note that the vehicle was parked illegally and would be towed next time. And to think of me for future towing needs. I placed one of the stiletto key chains next to my card.

The swag was useful. I should have ordered more.

I knocked on Kristen's door when I got home and she pulled me inside for some chamomile tea and cookies from the coffee shop. She never sold day-old products and often gave the women's shelter the leftover baked goods and brought a few home to eat, too.

Nibbling on a cookie and blowing on my hot drink, I recounted my conversations with Jeremy's mom and wife. I said, "I have a name to go with the mug shot now, Eugene Turnquil. And, get this. Melissa and the repo agent I've been working with, Patrick Crump, *are* related, I found out."

"Tell me again why you want to talk to these people? You're torturing yourself trying to find out about Jeremy. You should be kind to yourself and let this go." Kristen folded her legs underneath her and relaxed into her gray chenille sofa with a black and white afghan. Kristen's apartment was all black and white.

"The sheriff wants to speak to me again, 'cause, you know, they're getting ready to file charges against me. So, that's why." I set my mug down on a coaster. "The police don't think the wife, Melissa, could've killed him, but she wasn't too far away at the time of the murder. She could've driven in from Denver without anyone knowing. She doesn't have an airtight alibi as far as I'm concerned, and she has a motive, the insurance money."

"You really think it's her?"

"Well…why not?" I wound my arms across my chest. "Melissa could've done it. Or her brother while she was out of town, so that she would have an alibi, as flimsy as it is."

"And what was his reason? To help his sister? That's not much."

I let my arms fall to my sides. "You're probably right. Maybe it wasn't Patrick."

Kristen took a sip of her tea. "I might as well ask, any other suspects?"

"Jeremy's mother told me someone he met in jail stopped by to see him. Maybe it was Eugene Turnquil, the guy in the mug shot. How creepy is that? I dated someone who served time and hung out with criminals." A shudder went up my spine. I had trouble wrapping my head around Jeremy and felons and armed robbery in the same sentence. And Jeremy, himself, being the victim of murder? I crawled under a corner of Kristen's afghan and she wiggled over to share.

She said, "He seemed like a nice guy to me. Everyone should be given a second chance."

"I don't think I would've given him a first chance if I'd have known he was a felon. You're a better person than I am, Kris." I put my head on her shoulder.

"Not true. You're more bleeding heart than me."

"No, that's you projecting on me." But I did tear up too easily.

Kristen said, "If anyone was a Good Samaritan, it was your dad. He helped out Jeremy by giving him a job when he had a criminal record."

"That's what Byron told me. There was a lot about Jeremy I didn't know. Boy, was I stupid." Really. You'd think by age twenty-eight I'd have better judgment when it comes to the opposite sex.

"Don't blame yourself. Besides, you'd broken up with him."

"He dumped me." This whole thing was so cringy.

"Makes no difference now." My friend bumped my shoulder and teased, "What about the chop shop kingpin? The Mexican cartel?"

Flicking the blanket so it hit her in the face, I said, "I haven't forgotten about them." She clutched the blanket and we had a tug of war.

I said, "There are a lot of suspects. Is it someone from L&B, someone with Friendly Finance, someone Jeremy knew from jail? Like Turnquil. Or was it Melissa? Or Patrick?" I twisted a corner of the afghan into a knot. "I wish I could just come out and ask them about their alibis. Melissa's is the only alibi I know about. I haven't found out anyone else's."

"Could be none of those people. Could be someone you don't know, have never met."

"Mm, hmm." I got up to stretch, letting the blanket fall over Kristen's knees, then walked my mug to the sink. I put my hand on the doorknob.

She said, "See you in the morning. Try not to think about the murder."

"Sure," I answered. Everyone told me the same thing, but me not thinking about the crime was as unlikely as world peace.

I ducked across the hall to my apartment, but before I prepared for bed, I called Axle. "Do you have a bolt cutter?"

"What do you need that for?"

"I have a chain I want to cut. About an inch or two thick."

"Yeah, I got something that'll work."

"Be ready. I'll pick you up in fifteen minutes."

Chapter 16

Idling in the truck across from Mr. Hot Head's Jeep Wrangler, Axle and I stared at the vehicle chained to the old tree and the vicious dog.

The motor went silent when I cut the engine. The night breeze was chilly enough for me to be thankful for my warm hoody. "Here's the plan. You snap the bolt, then I'll back up behind the Jeep." My voice came out unintentionally loud over the dead quiet of the neighborhood.

Axle peered out the cracked windshield. "I'm not goin' anywhere near that dog."

I spoke with a quieter voice. "Come on."

"You can't make me."

I hissed, "Don't be a scaredy-cat. He's sleeping." At least the brute appeared to be asleep. His head pointed down, his muzzle nestled between his paws, but he faced the other way.

Axle's eyes rolled back far enough he could probably see the knit cap covering his hair. "Okay, you cut the bolt and I'll back up the truck."

"I'm the tow driver, I'll back it up." I sighed. He was right. It was a dangerous thing to do. The dog laid curled in a ball, but would the beast turn into a snarling, barking, mouth full of sharp teeth if either of us approached the Jeep Wrangler?

I nudged my door open. I needed to find out.

Axle's eyes bugged out. "Where are you going?"

"I'll be right back."

He gave me a look that said *are-you-losing-your-mind?*

As I tippy-toed across the road, I tried talking myself out of a fright-induced cold sweat. A police cruiser turned the corner, its headlights throwing me in the spotlight. I wheeled around and dove for the truck.

"Oh, my God!" I lowered my voice. "Crap. Hide the bolt cutter, Axle."

"I'm impressed you can run that fast in those heels."

I shout-whispered, "Get rid of it."

The police car stopped alongside us, and the officer powered down his window. I took a deep breath to calm my heart and rolled my window down, too. The policeman stuck his head out. "Delaney, what are you doing here?"

"Zach?" Him again. I was so relieved I almost laughed. "See that Jeep chained to that tree?" He took in the sight at a glance, then his eyes came back to me. I explained, "It's a repo. I need to tow it."

His head lumbered side to side. "You can't touch it locked up like that on private property. You need a court order to do it."

"Like breaking into someone's garage?"

"Yes. Tell the finance company you need the order."

"I think they know. We're trying to catch the driver out on the street with the Jeep."

"That would be another way to do it."

I glanced over at Axle and he no longer held the bolt cutter. "Thanks, Zach. We'll be on our way." I gave him a wide, innocent smile and started up the truck.

"One more thing. You can't drive with your windshield like that. Cracked windshields are not safe. It's a DOT violation. I could place your tow truck OOS."

"Oh, oh what?"

"Out of service." Zach leaned farther out his window. "Can you get it replaced soon?"

"I will, Officer Bowers." After the insurance was paid, after the rent was paid, and after I was caught again. I revved the engine, but he remained stationed in front of Hot Head's house until I drove down the street and around the corner.

Axle punched my arm. "Thanks, Delaney, you almost got us arrested."

"Did not."

"Did, too. What if I'd had those bolt cutters on that chain?" He pulled the long tool out from under his seat.

"I'm sorry. You're right. But I need to recover that vehicle. If I don't bring this Jeep in, I'm not going to get any more jobs from the Auto Store."

"This is just one job, Delaney. They'll be more."

This one was hard. Did I really want another? I suppose so. That's what vehicle recovery specialists did. "Is every repo going to be like this, Axle?"

"Count on it." He laughed. "The life of a tow truck driver."

I let go of the steering wheel for a second and bounced both hands off my chest. "Yay, me, the badass tower." I wish.

Swinging Dad's rig onto Columbine Court, I narrowed my eyes at Axle. "Hey, I saw Patrick Crump, that repo agent, over at L&B Garage. Do you know what he was doing there?"

"Nah, not really."

"Was he asking about a particular vehicle? Maybe he was out on a job." The truck's headlights lit up Axle's mobile home as I brought the vehicle to a stop.

"Could be." He pried himself out of his seat. "Later." He sauntered across the drive in his indolent way, but opened the door and hurdled inside like he was glad to be home.

I made straight for home myself. Once there, I locked the door behind me, got ready for bed, retreated under the covers, and willed myself to sleep. A couple of hours later, I lay in bed, still alert, imagining breaking the chains, hauling away the Jeep Wrangler, over and over before finally drifting off to slumberland.

Bang. Bang. Bang.

I was startled awake.

Was Hot Head here for his Jeep?

Armed with nothing more than my cell phone, I rocketed out of bed and raced to the door. Kristen stood in my entryway, hands on hips. I was almost disappointed it was only my friend. That meant I hadn't actually recovered the Wrangler like I'd done a hundred times in my dreams.

I strained to see past her. "What's the matter?"

"You overslept. I still need your help, short-timer." She laughed and yelled over her shoulder as she clattered to the bottom of the stairs, "Get dressed and get down here."

I ran around to get ready. By the time I walked in, Kristen had brewed three urns of coffee, stocked the pastry case, and filled the creamers and sugars. We only had about two days' inventory of roasted beans remaining and had just received a shipment of the raw, green beans, so Kristen started up the roaster. A couple of customers in ski gear lined up at the checkout. I pulled shots as they chatted excitedly about slope conditions, a blue-bird day, perfect for skiing.

"I'll stay until closing, Kris." Guilt tugged at my gut. It was Guy's day off and Sierra wasn't scheduled to come in until noon, and I'd been half an hour late.

"No worries." She turned to greet the next customer—Zach. I hid with my back to the register and rinsed out measuring cups at the sink, hoping Zach wouldn't ask me about the chained vehicle or the cracked windshield. He and Kristen talked, several other officers stopped by, and our usual morning rush began. Popping sounds like microwaved popcorn and the pungent scent of roasting beans added to the comfortable chaos.

The day sped by fast. Wednesday, hump day. Near three o'clock, I wiped the tables with a rag soaked in vinegar, then I sponged off the chairs, all the way down the legs. Sierra squeegeed the windows and mopped the floor. Kristen worked busily behind the counter, scouring out the coffee machines and microwave, then tallying the receipts and preparing the deposit. I took the overflowing garbage sacks to the dumpster and wiped out the trash bins before tucking new bags inside. The last thing was bringing in the flower pots. Kristen left for the bank and Sierra took off for parts unknown.

My evening was free, but I needed to be ready in case anyone called for a tow. I was still hopeful, although I was now nine days out from my last call. Nine days! Counting the days was as bad as stepping on the scale every day you're on a diet.

I showered and made myself a burger and salad for dinner. I'd just sat on a stool to eat when my phone rang. A job, thank goodness. *Yes! Yes! Yes!* My no-call-streak was broken. My dinner was wrapped up in the fridge and I was out the door.

At the corner of Pine Street and Twelfth, a teenaged girl shivered in the cool evening air, wearing cutoff jeans and a tank top, leaning against a pale yellow VW Beetle with the hood up. The shorts were typical Colorado day wear, but this was the cold time of the evening in a mountain town. She faced me when I pulled to the curb, and I recognized Byron's niece with her cat-eye sunglasses in emerald green shielding her face against the last descending rays of the sun.

"Shannon? I didn't know that was you calling me."

"Hi, Del. I didn't think you'd remember me."

"Of course, I know you." I asked her, "Where's your jacket?"

"Show me your high heels."

I lifted the hem of my jeans so she could see my blush-colored ruffled stilettos. She said, "What's with the color? Not shocking pink or blood red."

"Boring, right? But I've been feeling uninspired lately. So, where's your coat?"

"Don't have one. I didn't know I was going to break down. The Old Man is going to get an earful when I tell him his repair didn't last long." We studied her Beetle, the newer model with a flower in the console, front-wheel drive, unlike older, collector models that were rear-wheel.

"Get in the truck." I made her buckle her seat belt and handed her an extra sweatshirt from the back. I slammed down the Beetle's hood, then pressed the truck's magic buttons. The T-Bar lowered the claws to the ground with several squeaks and clicks. I had to back up another foot before I hit the second button. The scoops went under and around the front tires and the yellow Beetle shot into the air.

"Wow. That's so cool." The young girl had swiveled around to watch.

"It is, isn't it?" We both had broad smiles. "Where do you want the car towed?"

"The Old Man's place, of course."

"Sure." I pulled the truck into the turn lane and the Beetle swung behind. "That's nice you're using your uncle to fix your car. Keep it in the family." Byron was probably the reason Shannon had called me.

"My dad doesn't care for Uncle Byron, but I think the Old Man's awesome."

Oh dear. Family trouble. Like I didn't know about that sort of thing. "Why doesn't your dad like Byron?"

"You know, him being an ex-con."

I almost missed the turn and swerved at the last minute, the Beetle lurching along in back of us. "Oh, I didn't know."

"Whoops. Maybe I shouldn't have said anything, but I thought you knew him."

"I do, but I didn't know that." What's with all these criminals cropping up everywhere? I'd never met a single one before all this happened. I trundled the truck with the Beetle in-tow to Oberly Motors. "Well, here we are." Should I forget about charging her since she's Byron's niece? Or give her a discount?

But she handed me her credit card. "Please put a tip on there, too. My mom pays on my balance for me, so don't worry about the amount."

"That must be nice." I ran her card through the reader on my phone and added fifteen percent. *Thanks, Mom, whoever you are.*

Byron pulled up in a white Ford 150, an all-terrain 4-wheel-drive…not that I would ever need to tow his rig. The three of us got out and stood by the Beetle. I couldn't meet Byron's eyes, now that I knew this about him. He asked me to reverse his niece's car into the auto bay, so I returned to the truck. I only jackknifed twice, having to pull forward and try again.

Everyone knew Del Morran hired felons. Even I knew now, and I should've expected something like this. Yet the news about the new owner of my dad's business still shook me with a rush of doubt.

Note to self—ask Byron a few pointed questions at the next opportunity. And practice backing up.

Her uncle leaned over the Beetle's engine with Shannon standing next to him. Now was not the time to confront him, so I climbed back in my dad's self-loader and started up the motor. I didn't know what to do with myself, I was that unsettled.

I dialed up Chérie at Big Hal's. "Have you seen that hot-headed, bald man again?" Since I was out and about, I might as well not miss an opportunity.

"Yes." She sounded hesitant. "He's here now, but you don't want to mess with him, Del."

Aww, she thought my name was Del, just like a lot of my customers did. "Can you keep him busy inside? I'm going to tow his Jeep away."

"Oh, that's funny. And just what he deserves, too. I'll do it. I'll give him a special dance and keep his attention."

"I need about twenty minutes." I thanked her and wended my way toward downtown. The sun had descended and the sky was steeped in darkness. Good cover for a stealth mission, even though, now that I thought about it, I wished I was shopping at the mall instead.

Hot Head had parked the Jeep Wrangler in the alley. *Yeah-ez. The arrogant dirt-bag.* I hustled out the dolly wheels. Stomped my heels on the ratchet bar and pumped up and down like the wind while the left tire rose off the ground. I started to push the other dolly around to the right wheel when my cell rang. I consulted the caller ID. Chérie!

"What's the matter?" I asked.

"Amber stopped him for a second, but he's on his way out. He's at the back door. Be careful."

I dropped my phone and swore at the crack that appeared across the screen. My heart pulverized my chest like beans in a coffee mill and my mouth went dry. I needed to get outta here right now. Forget the Jeep. No way I wanted a face to face with Hot Head again. My courage had disappeared like the last swallow of espresso in a sleepy man's cup.

I stowed the phone away and rushed the dollies into the mounts under the truck. Jumped back in the cab. Reversed right into the dumpster. *Again.* The clang of metal on metal could be heard for miles. Then I muscled the tow rig forward and banged against the Jeep.

Why not? I rocked the self-loader back and forth, crashing into the Wrangler again and again. Not really, but I wanted to.

I sped down the alley onto Main Street. My

breathing and heart rate leveled out the farther I got from Big Hal's. Hot Head hadn't caught me that time, but the effect was the same. Another failure.

I pulled over and dialed up Patrick Crump. "I just wanted you to know I made another attempt to recover the Jeep Wrangler behind that strip joint, but I'm going to need help."

"What kind of help?"

"Someone with a gun."

"I don't think so." His voice sounded as stiff as a new pair of man-made leather shoes.

"What about a court order to cut the chain when the vehicle is at his house?"

"That involves attorneys and legal fees. I have another idea."

"What's that?" I was open to suggestions. I just had to get that Jeep Wrangler.

"I'll get another tow company." He hung up.

He would, too. So much for showing up Patrick Crump. The repo work sucked big time, but *dang it,* I wanted the decision to quit to be my own. Besides, I needed the repo work until I could get established doing other kinds of tows. The repo agent wasn't going to edge me out, not if there was something I could do about it.

I glanced at my watch. Not quite nine, the Auto Store's closing time, so I called them and asked to be put through to Mr. Abington. I wanted to get to him before Crump did. I assumed Abington might be gone for the day, and I'd formulated the message I wanted to leave, but he surprised me by picking up.

"Delaney? How may I help you?"

"I, um, just wanted to let you know that I've run

into a few snags with my first repo, but I'm working on it and I promise to recover the vehicle."

"Thanks, but you don't have to report to me. Just work with Patrick on this."

"But he has not been very, uh, supportive." Did I want to complain? I hadn't thought this through.

"What do you mean? He's the best in the repo world. Just let him know what you need." His voice was kind. "Anything else?"

"No, that's it. Thanks, Mr. Abington."

"This is dangerous work, Delaney. Are you sure you're up for it? If you want to get out of the business, let me know and I'll find a buyer for your truck."

The phone slipped a few inches, but I grasped it tight. "No, I'm up for it. I won't let you down."

"All right. Good luck." He disconnected.

I narrowed my eyes and gave myself a determined head shake before punching in Will's number. "Have you talked to Mr. Abington about putting Dad's truck up for sale?"

"No, no, I haven't. Your mom and I had dinner last night with Rob and his wife and nothing was mentioned about selling. Are you still considering it?"

"I didn't know you were that good of friends. Did you talk about me?"

"Rob brought it up. All he said was that you came in to see him, that's it."

"He suggested selling the truck."

"Not a bad idea."

"But I still want to do the work."

"Sure, sure, but think about offering the truck for sale." Will was ever hopeful. The relentless optimist.

"Okay. Talk to you later." I hit end-call and tossed

my phone onto the passenger seat. I was going to get that rat bastard's Jeep Wrangler next time I saw it…he didn't deserve to have a cute Jeep like that.

I could be an optimist, too.

Chapter 17

Just after noon the next day, I was about to leave the ice cream parlor when Tanner pulled in next to my dad's truck. We simultaneously got out of our vehicles.

He smiled. "Hey, Laney. What's up?"

"Not much." All I'd accomplished that morning, other than sucking down a milkshake, was updating my phone's screensaver with the latest fashionable shoes. One day…those would be mine. But that day was a long ways off.

"No tows, huh?" He gave me a deep, steady look and I flushed up to my roots. "So, if you're not busy, you want to do some more training? You could probably use a little more experience." His voice had a low pitch that made a crackling shiver go up my spine like coffee over ice.

Wowzah. Was he flirting with me? Shock of ages.

He tucked a strand of my hair behind my ear. "I like your hair."

Yes, I think that counted as flirting. I said, "Thanks, I grew it myself."

He leaned toward me and I froze. Then—guess what?—he planted a kiss on me! His hands in my hair. His lips pressing hard. *Oh boy oh boy*, this was happening. This was not a drill. My heart revved up fast and a *ping!* went through my belly, like the rumbling, pinging feeling of the tow rig's engine. I found myself responding, my lips betraying me. He let go of me and flashed that sexy smile.

Why now? Right in the middle of the parking lot like a couple of teens? What game was Tanner playing?

I'd already decided not to take part in that sport; he'd blown his chance. I gave him a stern look. "Don't do that again."

He held out his palms. "Okay, okay, I respect your boundaries, but what's the matter?"

"Nothing. What's the matter with you?" Jeez, now I sounded like a teenager, too.

"I talked to Byron."

"So?" I gave him an eye roll.

"So, I made this promise to Byron, okay? He made me promise to leave you alone. Then after I met you, I wanted to go back on it, but I had to keep my word, you know?"

"What do you mean, keep your word? Why is Byron the boss of you?" My lips were still burning from his kiss. Why did I have to be such a stinker? I'd backed myself into a corner and didn't know how to get out.

He stared me down with those blue eyes until I looked away. He said, "I'm sorry. I guess I made a mistake."

"You could say that." I turned around and headed for my dad's truck. My hand missed the door handle and I just about fell trying to haul myself into the cab. I refused to glance back at Tanner. Almost jumping the curb, I had to concentrate to steer the self-loader onto the street.

What was Tanner's deal with Byron? I don't get it. I'd given this attractive tow man every opportunity to start a relationship. But he'd held me at arm's length and hurt my feelings, big time. Well, I would stick to my decision, my rules. He wasn't calling the shots anymore. If I let him, he'd only turn around and rebuff me again, and that wasn't happening. First Jeremy, then Tanner, jerking my chain. I deserved better than that.

And I'd grill Byron about their discussion at my next opportunity. Exactly what was said?

The air through the window cooled my face and the oxygen restored functioning to my brain as I drove over to Roasters on the Ridge. First things first. I needed my friend's take on *the kiss*. Kristen would back me up, I knew she would. She'd tell me I'm doing the right thing. I needed Kristen's encouragement because I was starting to get a sinking feeling. Think about it this way, I had come on to him first. He had no idea I wouldn't be pleased by the kiss and he'd even said he was sorry.

And, *dang*, his kiss was everything I imagined, like a double shot espresso that made my heart race.

I stored the truck on a side street in the next block and got out. I waited in the backroom while Kristen talked to Zach, who'd stopped by—again, didn't the guy ever work?—but there's no way this conversation was happening in front of the Spruce Ridge officer, so I grabbed myself a piece of fruit and cleared out. I would come back later when she wasn't so busy.

A dog barked from somewhere as I boogied down the block. I peeled the banana and took a big bite, then rounded the corner, mentally calculating my next steps. The barking jumped louder in decibels.

A big, black thing leaped around in the front seat of Dad's truck. I swallowed down my banana in one large lump, raced over, and was about to yank open the door, but pulled back. A Rottweiler brayed, steaming up the glass, throwing himself against the window.

I turned tail and ran back to the coffee shop. Thank goodness I wore flat gladiator sandals. And double thankful our police friend hadn't left for work after all.

"Can you give me a hand with something, Zach?" My words came out breathless.

His eyebrows shot up. "What's the problem?" At the same time Kristen asked, "You okay?"

I stuffed the banana peel into the trash can. "Someone put a vicious dog in the tow truck." I knew who, too. I must've left the rig unlocked because that idiot could not possibly have the skill set to jimmy the door open.

Zach stood up to follow me. Kristen stayed at the shop, but I rushed her boyfriend back to my dad's self-loader, and we both stared through the window at the black and brown, sixty-plus-pound beast baring his teeth.

"There's a dog in your truck." He pointed through the glass.

"Ya' think?" I stepped back as the Rottweiler barked and snarled. "What should I do?"

"Do you know this animal?"

"Remember that Jeep chained to a tree?"

"Yes." Zach's eyes went from the Rotty to me.

"This monster belongs to that guy. He's messing with me because he knows I'm after his vehicle."

The Rottweiler settled on his haunches and let out a low growl that ended in a pitiful whine. His nose twitched and he gave a whole-body shimmy and rolled out his tongue, long, flat, and narrow, with drool oozing off the tip. Was that a hopeful look in his eyes?

I said, “Maybe the poor dog isn’t as mean as he seems. Maybe he’s just scared.”

“Let’s find out. Stand back while I open the door.” Zach put his arm around my shoulders and directed me a few feet away. Just then, Tanner’s tow truck zoomed past. Tanner’s face was in the window, his mouth gaping, his eyes glaring at Zach’s hand on my arm. To be jealous of Zach was ridiculous, if that’s what he was. After all, Officer Bowers is a freaking cop and I needed help. Before I could wave him down and ask what he thought he was up to now, he’d made the corner.

With one hand on his duty belt, Zach unlatched the door. The Rottweiler cowered back and whimpered. Not the expected barking and baring of teeth. Another whine escaped and slobber hung from his mouth, pulling on my heartstrings.

The officer said, “Good buddy,” and let the brute sniff the back of his hand. “Do you want to return the animal to its owner?”

“I don’t think so.” Hot Head was not a nice guy, and he could very well be mistreating his pet, chaining him up to a tree all night, shutting him inside a stranger’s vehicle.

Zach said, “It’s against regulations to have a dog in your truck when you’re on a tow.”

“Why?” I’d missed that rule.

“I guess dogs can be intimidating to your customers.” Zach withdrew his hand and the black and brown Rottweiler hunched, trying to flatten himself even lower in the seat. “We should call Animal Control.”

I asked, “The pound?” That seemed a last resort to me. “Let him out and see what he does.”

“Wait here.” Zach went back to his patrol car while the dog and I stayed put. He returned in minutes carrying a long, flexible pole with a loop on the end. “You can’t be too careful. Many a cop’s gotten bitten trying to handle an unknown canine.” He snaked the loop around the Rottweiler’s neck and urged him to jump down. The Rotty gave a small cry as he bounded to the ground.

“What’s that on your steering wheel?” Zach pointed inside the truck.

“A note, looks like.” I snagged the white paper and read, “Leave me alone or next time I’ll do more than *sic* my dog on you.”

The officer’s hand went to his duty belt like he wanted to take out his gun and shoot somebody. Hot Head, for example. I felt the same way. Zach said, “Tell me again about this guy.”

“I don’t know him. I’m only trying to tow his vehicle.”

“You need to press charges against him for leaving that threat with this potentially dangerous animal in your truck.”

“I’ll think about it.” I went around to the back and dug in the bin for a short, thin chain. I slipped the links around the dog’s neck, and Zach slid the catchpole off the dog’s head.

The Rotty didn’t have on tags, probably didn’t have his shots or anything. He laid his ears back, tucked his tail down, and his limbs trembled. The poor beast didn’t act like a killer. More like a scared animal. He’d been throwing himself at the door in a fit of fear, not anger.

I said, “I know someone who will take him. The

owner clearly doesn't want him." Or deserve him. Besides, if the dog wasn't chained to the truck anymore, that would make the vehicle all the easier to recover.

Garbled words came over the police mic clipped to Zach's shirt, and he said to me, "I need to get going. Will you be all right, now?"

"Sure. Thanks, Officer." I rubbed his arm up and down and smiled at him. How nice it was to have a policeman in the family, so to speak. Tanner's truck sped past once more, so I fetched my hand back. I assume my face burned crimson with a guilty expression.

Zach said, "Call me if you need anything else," and took off.

I paced in a circle, flinging my arms in every direction. Was Tanner following me? Did he turn from a heartthrob into a nitwit? A nitwit who's a good kisser. What was up with that kiss anyway?

The Rottweiler let out a bark, so I stopped rushing around. "Get inside, buddy." I patted the seat.

The Rotty refused to budge. The seat was slobbery and the windows were all smeared with nose prints. What a drool bucket. I pushed the buttons to roll all the windows down and tapped the cushion again.

"Come on, sweetie. Up. Up." He wagged his tail with tight little wags, then leaped into the truck. Good. He knew a few commands, other than *kill* and *attack* evidently.

So, now I had to deal with this nervous animal.

I phoned Axle. "Hey, I have a surprise for you. Are you home?"

"Yes. What is it?"

"How would you like a puppy?" I started the motor and swung onto the street. The Rottweiler panted out the passenger side with a low hum in his throat that I'd come to know wasn't a threat at all.

"I can't have pets in my trailer."

"How did they let you in?"

"Aren't you a comedian?"

"Let me take a bow." After a few more verbal volleys, me the winner on the insult-tally, I arrived at Axle's house. I unbuckled my seat belt and opened the door to let the cute little monster out.

Axle emerged from his trailer. His first question was, "Did you steal that guy's dog?" He backed up a few steps. "Isn't he the one chained to the Jeep? The animal is mean, remember?"

"His owner, that rat bastard, locked this poor dog inside the tow truck. But I figured out he's not so mean after all."

"Inside your truck?" Axle let out a belly laugh. The Rotty whined and laid his ears back.

"You could use some protection, like a guard dog." I didn't add anything about the dangerous trailer park he lived in, so as not to be too impertinent. A feat when it came to Axle.

He asked me, "You got any more chains?"

"Lots." I showed him to the back of the truck.

He untangled a long length to make a tie-down cable and attached it to the short chain I'd put around the dog for a collar. The equipment in the tow truck was coming to good use. Then he went into his trailer and brought out a dish filled with water. The Rottweiler lapped up about a gallon, then plopped down in the dappled shade of an aspen tree. He licked his chops and settled his muzzle between his paws.

"Are you going to keep him? Keep him, please, don't get rid of him." I blinked back the annoying water in my eyes.

"You're a softy, Delaney. All right. I'll figure something out."

"What are you going to name him?"

"How about Boss?"

"Okay…why Boss?"

"He reminds me of you, bossy pants."

If the shoe fits…I glanced at my white gladiator sandals. They were adorable with my rolled-up skinny jeans. *Yes!* I was boss.

We discussed what Boss would need, a real collar for one, and dog food, and I volunteered to help Axle pay for his first vet visit. I inched out my hand over the top of Boss's head, then gave his ears some scrunchies. He opened his eyes, all round and anxious, and thumped his tail.

Axle fed Boss bites of cheese while I shut myself back in the truck. He said, "I'll let you know what the vet bill is." Nice, another expense I wouldn't be able to cover. But I promised, so there it was.

Because I was antsy, I took a quick detour to Melissa's house. I didn't have anything else going on at the moment. No calls for tows.

Leaning on the bell, I heard it ring inside, but no one came to the door.

After moving the truck into the alley, I got out and jiggled the garage door handle. It was still broken from a few short weeks ago when Zach had helped Tanner break in to recover Jeremy's Challenger. Here was a dilemma. If the door was unlocked, was that breaking and entering?

And that should concern me, why?

I raised the overhead door manually and it whirred up with a loud rumble. I ducked inside and shouldered it closed behind me, the rumbling ending in a silent bump, shutting out the cool evening breeze. The stale air within smelled like discarded tires, dusty cardboard, and dry cement. A line of brown boxes banked up against the back wall. A wheelbarrow and a lawnmower stood in the way, so I pushed them to the side, being careful not to make any noise over the concrete floor.

The first container held clothes and shoes, as did the next three. I recognized a couple of Jeremy's sweaters. He wore the blue one when he took me to see the latest superhero movie, and the beige one when we went to the Ale House a month ago. The clothing seemed personal and full of depressing memories. My eyes leaked a few tears and I wiped them on my sleeve. I went to the next stack of boxes. Old baseball trophies. Textbooks and school notebooks. A picture crammed in a corner—of me, with my red corkscrew curls tumbling down past my shoulders, giant green sunglasses perched on my freckled nose, smiling into the camera…a happy moment from those first carefree days of a relationship.

But the photo was ripped halfway through. A sticky substance gummed up the back side as if the snapshot had been taped to something, a mirror perhaps.

Why had Jeremy torn my photo? Had he been angry with me? Was I attracted to guys destined to break up with me? Treat me poorly? The *love-me-and-leave-me* types?

And here I was, poking through my dead boyfriend's—ex-boyfriend's—things like a stalker desperate for clues to the breakup. I was so pitiful. But, that's not what I was doing. I was investigating a murder and that sounds so much more awesome.

I tucked the picture into my pocket, sticky back and all, and folded the box shut. A glance out the small window in the overhead door revealed the coast was clear, so I disengaged the handle to roll the panels up, stepped out backwards, and dragged the door down to the ground.

"What are you doing here?" A man's voice behind me.

I whirled around and my hands flew to my chest. *Holy crapoli!* Eugene Turnquil!

My heart raced like I was on a caffeine buzz and that gave me a dizzy rush.

"Well?" He didn't look much like his mug shot, but it was him. His face was the same, thin and long, with a close-cropped beard. His broken nose had been fixed and his brown hair combed. At about six-foot-two, with bulging arm muscles from a lot of time spent on the weight machines, he was both superb and scary.

I thought my knees might buckle at any moment. "Eugene Turnquil." I'd said his name out loud this time.

"It's not EYEW-gene. It's u-GENE. Actually, I prefer Gene. What were you doing in Melissa's garage?" His hands went to his hips.

"Checking Jeremy's stuff. Why are you here?"

"Did you find anything?"

I held out the torn photo with trembling fingers. "Just this. I doubt Melissa will want it."

He glanced at the picture and grunted. "Yeah. She won't care. I've seen her with that sheriff a couple of times now, Lopez. And, you know what, you're annoying me." His hand shot out and yanked on my long braid like a bully in elementary school.

My head jerked back and my body just about bent double. Stinging pain hit me like a jolt of java through my veins. "Ow! Let go."

He sprang away and I fell to my knees, gulping in deep breaths of air. He charged down the alley, and I yelled, "Breaking news just in, you're an asshole," but he was already gone, having turned the corner out of sight. It took a couple more seconds to climb to my feet. I rubbed the back of my head, a headache coming on, then crawled into the truck on jittery limbs and started up the engine.

Should I file an assault charge, try to get Eugene's parole revoked? Or phone Sheriff Lopez? I could quiz the sheriff about his girlfriend, Melissa Crump Winslow, at the same time I reported Eugene Asshole Turnquil. And, I could report Lou Hot Head Frankel, too. But, no, I needed to stand on my own two feet since I'm a professional vehicle recovery specialist.

At least I learned something. Sheriff Lopez was a cool operator. He had even shown interest in me, told me to call him Ephraim and everything. *Sheesh.* Forget talking to him.

Resigned to do nothing, I drove over to the Main Street businesses to monitor the tow away zones. I stewed in my black thoughts as I cruised up and down the alley until the no-parking time period came to an end. No violators caught. No megabucks collected. Only a throbbing headache for my troubles. I returned the truck to Byron's lot and sat in the driver's seat while I opened a web browser on my phone to weigh in on reviews.

Don't call Del's Towing. Can't be trusted. Sic your dog on her if you've got one.

I balled my hands into fists and held my breath for a count of three, then blew it back out with a couple of choice words. Because this was "the most useful lowest-rated review" it had risen to the top of the page. I felt lower than a dirty napkin stuck to the coffee shop floor.

A light was on in Byron's mechanic's bay, so I wandered over.

"Hey, Old Man." I showed Byron the comments, hoping he'd make me feel better.

All he said was, "You gotta expect unhappy people in the towaway business."

I rubbed the back of my head and gave up a deep sigh, then produced my torn photograph. "See what I found in Jeremy's stuff." Recognition registered in Byron's eyes. I asked, "You've seen this picture before?"

His head seesawed up and down. "Jeremy had it taped ta' the dashboard in the truck. It mighta' gotten ripped when he took it down. That would be the day he was fired." Byron let out a low whistle between the gap in his two front teeth. "This explains a few things. I didn't put two-and-two together until just now." He stared at the tools scattered over the hood of a minivan, the paint faded from cherry red to tomato soup due to ionization. Dirty rags hung over the back of a folding chair. Diffuse fumes floated in the narrow space.

"What?" I twirled my hand in the air, like *get-on-*

with-it.

"Your dad told Jeremy he'd better break up with that girl. Meaning you. They argued about it, and Del fired him."

"Whaaaat?" Dad had recognized my picture? He knew what I looked like after all these years? Of course he did because I looked like him.

Byron tapped a finger to his chin. "Del must a' told Jeremy he didn't want him around his daughter."

Clutching the door of the minivan, I said, my voice soft, "Dad knew Jeremy had problems and didn't want him to date me?"

"At the time I didn't know it was you in this picture. I thought it was none a' my business, so I never asked who the girl was." He stabbed his finger toward the photo. "I should'a recognized you with that red hair, but I forgot all about the picture until just now."

The metal chair caught me when I lowered myself onto it. "I've been wondering why Jeremy broke up with me. Do you think it was because of Dad?" I stretched out a hand toward my friend and he took it in his rough, beefy grip.

"I don't know what to tell ya'."

"Byron, if Dad knew Jeremy and I dated, then he knew I was close by, but he never contacted me." Another snub, just like during my whole, entire childhood.

"Did you call him?"

"No."

"Did you stop by the shop?"

"No."

"Well, maybe he wondered why you didn't do any a' those things. And maybe he wasn't sure you'd welcome him in your life."

Mom didn't want anything to do with Del Morran, and she'd hinted that Dad had left us alone so she could get on with her life. Perhaps he was honoring her wishes all those years. He didn't know I would've been glad for the contact. How could he? And I'd blown the opportunity to tell him.

Byron was giving me a questioning look, so I squeezed his hand and let it go. Not wanting to address my little-girl-lost issues, I dug out my phone and asked, "Have you seen this man around here? Eugene Turnquil."

Byron gave the mug shot a glance. "I know who he is." He chugged off, his shoulders hunched, and returned with another folding chair. He scraped it over to me and settled down, lacing his fingers across his chest.

I'd been waiting, barely taking a breath. "How do you know him?"

"My niece told ya' I'm an ex-con. Gene and I have the same parole officer."

I flushed, my nose turning red, my freckles certain to be popping out.

He cast his eyes down. "I killed a man, Delaney."

Time went into that slow spin of dwindling down and standing still. I tried to absorb his words, wondering if I'd heard him right. Ex-con was one thing, but murderer was another. This blew my mind.

"I drank and hung out at bars. It was manslaughter because the other guy started the fight, but I killed him all the same. I punched him and he went down, hitting his head. Died the next day."

"Oh, Byron…" I sagged back and covered my eyes

with my hands.

"I did my time and got off the booze. Your dad gave me a break and a chance ta' earn a livin'. No one wants to hire a felon."

I dropped my hands. The Old Man gave me the *silent-question* stare, and I needed to say something. What would Kristen say? Something encouraging. "See where you are now. You have your own business and everything."

He ducked his head low. "I agree I owe your dad a lot."

My good intentions had missed the mark. "What I mean is, you've changed and made something of yourself."

"I'm workin' on it." The flimsy chair groaned under his weight.

No more words came to me, and for a long moment neither of us said anything. This news would take getting used to. I asked, "Did my dad know Turnquil?" Del Morran seemed to know quite a few guys coming out of prison, why not Turnquil, too?

"Yes, but he wouldn't hire him."

"Why not?"

"I think Gene was too far gone for even Del to take on. He's a real bad character. You want ta' stay away from him."

"I got that. I ran into him tonight. He was flippin' scary. He was at Melissa's house, the wife's." I massaged the skin under my braid.

Byron came back to life. "Whoa, whoa, Delaney." He sat forward, his hands gripping his knees. "Gene's dangerous. If you see him again, run. If he shows up, call the cops." His head gave a little jerk. "Wait, what'd you say about a wife?"

"Jeremy was getting a divorce. I didn't know about the wife, either. I only found out about her recently. Do you know a guy by the name of Patrick Crump?"

"No. Who's he?"

"Brother of the wife." I pushed myself to a stand. "One last question. Tanner said he talked to you about me. What did he say?"

Byron's fingers went to his mouth, then he let his hand fall away. "He likes you, Delaney."

"He does?" Before *the kiss* Tanner was disinterested. He practically fell off the trunk of his car to get away from me. "He sure has a weird way of showing it." My voice went high like a five-year old's.

The Old Man dropped his chin down, his face flushed, which was usually my reaction. "Give him another chance."

I thought I'd given Tanner enough chances already, but maybe I needed to quit letting my hurt feelings take over. "It's late and I have an early shift at the coffee shop tomorrow, so I'd better be on my way. Thanks for telling me all this."

"Sure, Delaney. Take care." His eyes were sad.

I wanted to clap my hand on the Old Man's shoulder and tell him he was okay with me, but I had a lot to think about. I needed to process this new info, so I just waved goodbye. As much as I liked and respected the Old Man, Byron had admitted to killing someone. If he was not who I thought he was—if he wasn't one of the good guys—then all the nice things he said about Del Morran might not be the truth either.

I didn't want to go there.

Chapter 18

After a long shift at Roasters on the Ridge, I locked up my apartment and turned the Fiat in the direction of Melissa's house once again. But I was more cautious this time. I glanced around before I got out of the car. No bully hiding in the alley. No monster at my back. In other words, no Turnquil.

No one answered my knock, either, and the house had a deserted appearance. The porch light was off, not left burning like when you're coming home later after dark. The curtains in the front window blocked the view so I couldn't see inside. Someone had stuck a crinkled-up, yellowed flyer in the screen door, and the mailman had delivered several Amazon boxes and stacked them behind a railing.

I made a beeline for Mrs. Winslow's, but I was unsuccessful there, too. She wasn't home, although Mr. Winslow greeted me at the door. I introduced myself since we hadn't met before. The only reason I was acquainted with Jeremy's mom was because I'd run into her one time when Jeremy and I had come over to pick up some of his things. But I'd never crossed paths with Mr. Winslow until tonight. After we got the polite, small talk over, he invited me in and walked me back to the kitchen.

"My wife's at her sister's, but she told me about your visits. She appreciated your card." He was a thin, wiry-looking man of medium height, wearing jeans that bagged at the knees and an untucked flannel shirt with a gray tee-shirt underneath. Black glasses covered his large, blue eyes, and a thick mop of gray hair capped his head. He had comfortable moccasins on his feet. "Do you want anything to drink? Coffee? Whiskey? Coffee with whiskey?" He chuckled and took a sip from a highball glass. Whiskey, I suspected.

"No, thanks." I slipped onto a stool at the kitchen counter. "Any news on the case?"

"I haven't talked to the police for a couple of days. Everyone says after the first twenty-four hours the investigation gets cold." He seemed more angry than grief-stricken.

"I've heard that, too." I propped my elbows on the counter and braced my knees against the wall underneath. "I've been asking questions of my own. I stopped at Melissa's before coming here, but she wasn't home."

He crossed both arms and leaned back against the sink. "She received a life insurance payout."

My whole body stilled, and I held my breath for a couple of seconds. "Did she?"

"Yes. A hundred thousand." His lips pinched together in a straight line.

"That's a lot of money, but not like a million."

"I don't care how much it is, my son's life is worth more than any amount of money."

My dry throat felt thick. I untangled my tongue and said, "Of course, you're right. So you think she had something to do with Jeremy's death?"

"Well, she's been driving around in a new BMW, already spending the proceeds."

"I know." I nodded in agreement. "I've spotted her in a Corvette once and some other fancy car that I can't remember now." I showed him the mug shot of Turnquil. "Do you know him?"

He grabbed the cell out of my hand and tapped the screen to enlarge it. "He's turned up here a few times. The cops questioned us about him, about both him and Melissa."

Oh good, not about me. I wasn't on the police radar after all. I blew out a sigh of relief.

"And they asked about you, too," he added.

Darn. I repressed a shudder.

He handed me my phone, grabbed his whiskey, and tossed back the contents.

I asked, "Since you're the parent, the detective would let you know how the investigation is going, right?"

He slammed down his empty glass and poured himself another measure. "Melissa made my son take out that insurance policy, so I know the police are very interested in her, as they should be."

"What about Turnquil, the man in the photo?" I gestured toward my phone.

"Jeremy told us he didn't want to see that man. Wanted to avoid him."

"Did he tell you why?"

"Isn't it usually over a woman?" He looked at me like I could be that woman.

I asked, "Or power or money or something that happened in jail?"

Pain flitted across his face. I could see bits of his son in his expression. He said, "Why don't you ask Oberly?"

I splayed my hand across my chest. I didn't see that coming. "Get out!"

"No, really, ask him."

"How do you know Byron Oberly?"

The man shrugged and took a swill of his fresh drink. Byron already told me he was acquainted with Turnquil. Byron seemed to know a lot of people, and quite possibly he knew the Winslows. And small town, no secrets. Maybe that's all there was to it.

"A better question is, how does a girl like you know a rough old man like him? How are you mixed up in all this, Delaney? The way the police asked about you, you'd think you were the prime suspect." Mr. Winslow's eyes now held a suspicious, narrow look. Not him, too.

Despite the fact I was aware the police wanted to pin this on me, I couldn't help the sick sensation in my gut. I said, "I need to get going."

He led me to the door and watched from the window as I pulled away from the curb. Sensing his eyes on me raised the hair on my arms and the back of my neck. I'd been flitting around town like I had all the freedom in the world, but was I about to be arrested? Was my liberty going to come to an end?

I returned to Melissa's house. Hey, I needed answers. Or at least a hint. A clue. Anything to take the heat off me. While I sat out front with the engine off, an older, sixty-something man gave me the evil eye from across the street like he was part of the Neighborhood Watch. I slammed the door and started toward him. He met me halfway.

Pointing my thumb over my shoulder, I asked, "I'm looking for Melissa Winslow. Do you know where she's gone?"

He gave me a squinty-eyed stare and countered with, "Do you know there was a murder at her house a couple of weeks ago?"

"Yes." I buttoned my lips, waiting, but we seemed to be having a stand-off. "About Melissa?"

"Well, she took off on a vacation. Mexico, she told me. I'm not sure how long she'll be gone."

On television the police always instructed suspects not to leave town. Maybe they didn't do that in real life. TV was not the place to learn about police procedure. I asked, "Did you know her husband, Jeremy?"

"No." He shook his head side to side, but his eyes were interested. "That's the fellow that was murdered. I heard about it on the news."

"I know, it's terrible, right?"

"Difficult to believe that happened here, right here in our neighborhood." He pointed down the street, his index finger out. "What's the place coming to? Used to be full of families, good, hard-working people, friendly folks who knew each other. Now it's turned to rentals." He swiveled his finger to point at Melissa's house. "Like that one. No one takes care of their yards anymore and the street is jammed with cars." He folded his arms over his sunken chest like he wanted to keep everyone at a distance.

I nodded and backed away. "Yeah, that's too bad." It was true that vehicles were packed in along the curb, bumper to bumper. And it was interesting that after Melissa had cashed in the big insurance payout, she'd taken off out of the country. Out of the grasp of the law? Certainly out of my reach. I'd have to rethink my surveillance plans until she got back.

****

"Is this Delaney Morran?"

"This is Del's Towing." I elbowed myself to a sitting position and rubbed the sleep out of my eyes. The clock showed nearly midnight.

"This is Friendly Finance Company. We need a tow operator right away. Can you do it?"

"Is this Hailey?" I recognized her voice now.

"Yes, it is."

I blurted out, "I thought you always used Tanner Utley."

"I can't get a hold of him. This was a hard car to locate, and we need someone right away before it's moved again. Are you available?"

"Sure. Give me the address and the type of car and the VIN." I nicked a pen off the bedside table and wrote the information down. "Will anyone meet me?"

"No. I don't get involved in the actual repo."

"Is there anything I should be aware of? Could this be dangerous?" I was learning.

"Not that I know, but repos are always risky, right?"

"You got that right." I hurled myself out of bed. "Do you want me to tow the vehicle to Tanner's lot?" His was the place where I towed vehicles from the no-parking zones and I didn't have another secure lot to use.

"Sure, that works. Text me when you've completed the recovery. Come by in the next day or two for the paperwork."

We both disconnected.

I scrambled into my jeans and a sweatshirt, grabbed my keys and purse, and locked the door on the way out. Few cars were on the road. Stars and a half-moon flowed in and out from behind the clouds, and the dark sky matched the dark circles sure to be under my eyes. I switched on the radio, then jumped when a song boomed into the silence. I must've left the volume on high, so I twisted the dial down low and glanced at my purse with my cell in the pocket. I pulled over.

The phone rang ten times before Axle picked up. "Delaney? Is that you? Is everything okay?"

I eased away from the curb. "I'm going on a repo. Maybe I'm not cut out for this business."

"Come and get me." Click.

I picked up the truck and zoomed over to Axle's to find him waiting on his stoop in his baggy jeans and tee-shirt with the name of the band, "Badflower," printed on the sleeve. His hair was covered by his knit cap. He crammed himself against the passenger window and dozed the short distance to the corner of First and Sims. He might be asleep, but he was also a living, breathing being, and I wasn't alone.

When I shifted the truck into park, Axle woke up and let out a low whistle. The new maroon Audi TT coupe was a beauty, a two-door sportscar worth over $60,000 according to *Kelley Blue Book*. This vehicle came in both front-wheel or "quattro" four-wheel drive, so I ran the numbers Hailey had given me through the VIN decoder app I'd downloaded and determined the coupe was four-wheel. I whispered to Axle, "You'll get to see your dolly mounts at work."

We scoped out the street. It was only a little past midnight on a Friday night, but in this residential neighborhood, all the houses were dark. No dogs barked. No televisions glowed behind curtains. No bathroom lights winked on or off. I cast my eyes all around, expecting a teenager in the family van to come barreling down the street any moment, but no one was about, not even any teens.

Axle gave me a quick nod and a thumbs up. "Let's rock and roll."

We tiptoed over and confirmed that the VIN matched. I reached under the truck bed and released the dolly wheels with a click, the sound ricocheting off the metal underbelly. Axle put a finger to his lips as if I needed to be reminded to be quiet. I launched out the first dolly wheel and Axle reeled out the second. He pumped up one while I blew up the other, and the tires lifted off the ground.

A car glided down the street. We froze, nonchalant-like, pretending we were just a couple of people who happened to be out standing next to a tow truck and an expensive car attached to dolly wheels. A dog barked and we glanced at each other. Was someone going to *sic* a beast on us, like a Rottweiler? When a window slammed, I flew about a foot into the air.

Axle mouthed, "Let's get moving." We jogged back to the truck. I used the remote controller to sweep the Audi's front end into the claws. Normally the iron bars only emitted a slight squeak, but this time the metal seemed to scream as the scoops slid into place.

The Audi's car alarm went off, whooping and wailing.

A porch light blazed on, illuminating the street.

We gave each other wide-eyed looks as if to say, *yikes!*

"Hang on," I yelled, tromping on the gas pedal. The Audi's beeping horn echoed off the pavement as we raced down the road. We crashed through the four-way stop at First and Main—empty of traffic, thank goodness—the Audi fishtailing behind us, scenery flying by outside the windows. We bowled along Main, then squealed into a left turn in front of the police station.

"You'd better slow down." Axle's voice came out excited and loud. "You shouldn't go over fifty using the dolly wheels."

My heart pounded away like engine pistons. I hollered, "I will," but didn't until we shuddered to a stop at Tanner's locked gate.

A black and white patrol car skidded up next to us.

"You again." Zach frowned on the other side of his open window. He had to shout above the alarm's racket. "Do you know how fast you were driving?"

My chest exploded, my fingers trembled, the alarm blared—*bweee-bweee-bweee*. I yelled, "Sorry. We were almost caught recovering this vehicle." I forced open the door and slithered out, my legs giving way, so I groped along the back of the truck and propped myself up against the bumper, the *bweee-bweee-bweee* singing its siren song, busting my eardrums.

We all crept over to the Audi. Axle bent underneath the front end, and his head disappeared from view. The alarm went silent with a final *beweept!* and an abrupt quiet took over, a welcome stillness in my relieved ears. Axle ducked back out.

I took a deep breath. We did it! It wasn't so bad. What was I worried about? I stood steadier and taller, as tall as I could at five-foot-two, and my heart slowed to a smooth ride. I told Zach, all casual-like, "I didn't mean to speed. Anyway, do you know Kristen's cousin?" I pushed Axle out in front of me, playing the relationship card to get out of a speeding ticket.

"Yes." Neither of the men met the other's eyes. *Oops*. The police officer's girlfriend's cousin had been involved in the raid on the chop shop, L&B.

To cover my clumsiness, I asked, "So, Zach, why are you working? Don't you patrol in the evenings, not this late at night?"

"I pulled a double shift." The Spruce Ridge officer ran a hand over the Audi. He gave out a whistle, just like Axle had done.

"Stand back until I get her inside the fence." I keyed in the combination and the gate began its slow sweep to open. I hauled the Audi through and the guys followed me in, watching as I released the car from the claws and the tires dropped to the ground. Luckily I didn't have to back up and the two men didn't have to witness me jackknifing. Axle helped me return the dolly wheels to the undermounts.

I asked Axle, "Why did the car alarm go off? That never happened before."

"I don't know. Contact with the wheels doesn't trigger the alarm. You have to mess with the doors or windows or bang into the fenders. I mean, if touching the tires set it off, the alarm would sound every time the car was driven down the street and the tires made contact with the road surface." Axle glanced at the police officer.

Zach agreed, "The owner must have added a more sensitive system."

"I need to let Friendly know I recovered the Audi." I sent a text to Hailey while the men stared through the windows of the beautiful sportscar. Hailey replied that she'd notify the cops, but I told her, with a glance at Officer Bowers, not to bother.

I was about to join the Audi's admirers when Tanner's black Volvo slammed to the curb. He got out and pointed at an apartment building across the street. "One of the neighbors over there called to tell me there was something in my lot making a bunch of noise." He scowled at Zach, then back at me. "This car can't be from the towaway zones, it's too late for that. Why did you bring it here?" The sportscar drew his attention, and he drifted closer to it.

"I recovered the Audi for Friendly Finance."

His eyes screwed up. "What?"

"A repo for Friendly."

Zach stepped forward and tapped my arm. "Delaney, no more speeding, okay. Next time it'll mean a ticket." The officer gave me a wink. "And get that windshield fixed."

Tanner kept his eyes narrowed, giving first Zach, then me, a foul look. No one said a word as the Spruce Ridge officer angled himself into his patrol car and drove away.

"Hey, Delaney, I need to get home." Axle tore open the truck door. "Let's go."

"All right." I turned to Tanner to explain why Hailey called me, but he stormed inside his Volvo and closed the door with a bang.

I asked Axle, "What's up with men?" as I walked around to the truck's driver's side. I thought I was over this, but my heart felt like it was stabbed in a million places with dry pine needles.

"I have no idea what you're talking about."

"No, you wouldn't."

I fired up the truck and accelerated out of the lot. I drove a couple of blocks down Fifth and left turned onto Columbine Court. Axle hadn't stuffed his earbuds in like he usually did. His mouth rattled on about the repo and he asked me for the third or fourth time, "Can you believe we stole that cool sportscar off the street?"

We both spoke at once. "We're *kewl*." "We're so bitchin'."

I brought the truck to a stop outside Axle's trailer. "How's Boss?"

"He chewed up a corner of my couch and some of the wood paneling, but he's okay. I'm teaching him to fetch. I don't think he's had a lot of attention before."

"You're a good man, cuz'. Thanks for going with me tonight."

"You want to come in? I've got some beer. We should celebrate." We'd shared an experience as cousins do.

"Sure." I killed the engine and beeped the truck doors before following Axle to the trailer. The click of the lock triggered a demanding volley of barking. The smell of stale beer and pizza and something else, skunky and strong, hit my nose. You know what I'm talking about.

"Did you have a party in here?"

"Ah, yeah. Couple of days ago." He dug around in the fridge and tossed me a can. A saggy couch and mismatched chairs reminded me of discarded freebies, and a big-screen television held up one wall, typical for a young, single guy.

I flipped the can open and Axle popped one of his own. Boss's whining sounded from behind a door, so he let the dog out. The baby came straight over to me, sniffed my shoes, then settled at his new master's feet.

"Are you old enough to drink, Axle?"

"I'm eighteen."

"Exactly, you're not old enough." He took me back to myself at that age. "So, who likes you enough to buy you beer?"

The insult went over his head. "A guy from work. He lives a couple of streets that way." Axle pointed to his right like I knew where he meant. "That was a sweet ride, that Audi TT coupe. When the alarm went off, I'd thought for sure we were dead meat." He was back to that. He hooted with laughter, then downed half his beer. I thought he might crush the can against his skull, but he didn't.

"That was great, wasn't it?" I drained my brew, then crushed my can against my forehead. Someone had to do it.

"Wow, Delaney, that's epic. You should play Detonator."

"What's that?"

"You know, a drinking game. And you have to take me with you on your next repo. That was wicked awesome."

"I'll give you a share of my recovery fee. You totally deserve it."

Axle yawned, causing me to yawn, and even Boss's jaws opened wide. It was time to go. Axle came outside with me, bringing his dog along for a potty break. They both watched me leave.

A hollow feeling lodged in my chest on the drive back, the thrill of the capture gone. It kept with me as I went up the stairs in the dark to my apartment. I recognized the loneliness, that familiar sense of abandonment. Axle was so young, in a different place from me, a time I could never go back to, nor would I want to.

I was all alone. I'd been with friends tonight—except for Tanner…I wasn't sure Tanner counted as a friend—but even so, this business was a solitary one.

Chapter 19

"Call Tanner."

I gave Kristen a *you've got to be kidding* look.

She said, "Phone him and explain why you did the repo."

"No, I don't think so."

We'd taken our morning break with coffees and muffins—mountain blend coffee and a new addition to the menu, jalapeño-cheddar mini muffins—while I'd caught her up to speed with the events of last night, but not about *the kiss*. I didn't want to discuss *the kiss*, after all.

"He has to contact me sooner or later, that is if he wants to take the private property lots away from me. I can explain then why Hailey called me. Not that I care what he thinks."

"Has he said he's taking the lots back?"

"No." But I worried he might.

My friend nibbled on her muffin. "Turn the other cheek. Call him."

"I might text him when I take a break, okay?" Should I tell Byron that Tanner kissed me and let the Old Man deal with him? I smiled at the thought, but there's no way I would tell Byron.

Kristen shook her head. "Well, texting's better than nothing, I guess."

We both got back to work.

I planned to suck it up and text Tanner, I swear, but even with Guy on the espresso machine the coffee shop got too busy for breaks. My shift ended and I hoofed it up the stairs to my apartment. What I needed more than anything was a nap. Once rested and thinking clearly, I would know how to deal with Tanner Utley. Better to wait.

I threw back the covers to climb into bed, but my cell rang. Tanner?

No. Chérie.

"That shaved-headed man was here."

"Is he still there?" I grappled with the phone.

"No, but he told me his aunt passed away. I thought you might be interested to know the funeral's today."

"Okay." My tired brain didn't register at first, then it hit me. "Oh, thanks so much for telling me. This helps." We disconnected. I rushed to my computer to locate death notices, hoping his aunt had his same last name. *Found it.*

I donned sneakers and grabbed my purse.

After leaving the tow truck a block away, I legged it over to the funeral home, a red brick two-story, built in the 1970s. Behind the building was the parking lot, and from there a narrow road topped with an antique-looking arch spelling out *Mountain View Cemetery* in scrolled metalwork, and beyond that a long, green lawn with an unobstructed view of flat grave markers and occasional taller tombstones. The parking lot was full, and a line of Fords, Lincolns, Hondas, and Subarus, front to rear, one behind the other, snaked out to the street. A black-suited man tied tiny black flags on each car's antenna.

I walked up to him. “Excuse me, could you tell me whose funeral this is?”

“Margaret Frankel.” He advanced to the next car, so I trotted over to the entrance.

White columns stood on either side of the double doors with a metal eagle over the lintel. Early American architecture. The door opened at my touch without a sound, and the foyer was hushed and empty. An enlarged photograph and a cardboard placard with the name, Margaret Frankel, balanced together on a tall easel. The deceased had a bouffant hairstyle and a stern expression. A stack of programs spilled over on a side table and I picked one up.

Margaret Frankel was survived by three children. Lou Frankel—Mr. Hot Head—being a nephew, was not listed. The ceremony had started a quarter of an hour ago.

I crept out the door and quick-stepped around to the parking lot. I stared at the back of the brick structure for a couple of seconds, there were no windows, then let my gaze wander over the asphalt pavement. The Wrangler was not in the line of vehicles being made ready for the funeral procession, so I threaded through parked cars to the far side of the building. There it was, out of view in a cracked, blacktopped area with a note on the dash, “Touch my Jeep and you die.”

Hot Head likely thought he’d hidden his vehicle well, but that if I found it, I’d be too scared to take it.

As much as I couldn’t stand the man, could I snatch his Jeep Wrangler out from under him at his aunt’s funeral? *Abso-freakin-lutely.* I was going to do this.

I sprinted to Dad’s truck and raced the truck back

faster than a Ferrari sportscar. The front of the Jeep was parked snug against the building, so I maneuvered the self-loader close to the rear bumper, swooped up the tires, and dragged the vehicle a few feet. Ear-splitting scrapping sounds echoed off the stonework as the front wheels, locked in place, skidded along the ground. I glanced left and right, then shunted out the dolly wheels, slid them around the tires, and ratcheted them up from the blacktop.

The last time I was at this funeral home was for my dad. A whole bunch of cars were lined up in a procession then, too, just like all these Fords, Lincolns, Hondas, and Subarus. A weight of sadness descended over me from out of the blue. I stood there, beating my forehead with my fist. *Do it, do it, do it*. But, I couldn't. It was his auntie's funeral for God's sake. At the same place where my dad's funeral had been held.

I rolled the dolly wheels back out from under the stupid Jeep and shoved them under the truck.

At the exit, I braked for traffic, and two thugs in suits ran up to the driver's door, pounded their fists against the glass, and yelled, "What do you think you're doing here?" One of them waved his phone around, and behind him Mr. Hot Head sprinted in my direction. The whites of his eyes showed and his bottom teeth stuck out like a bulldog's.

Panic pushed my heart into my throat where it jammed like heavy traffic on Main. I stomped on the accelerator and shot into the street. A car horn blasted and I swerved, narrowly missing a Chevy Impala, front-wheel drive. Hot Head gave me a stiff middle finger as I sped off. I made the corner and ducked into an alley.

Another failure. I'm such a loser. Shit! Shit! Shit!

You idiot! I was plenty mad at myself. I should have taken the jerk's Jeep.

What if I went back? Maybe Hot Head would not expect me to turn around and try again. But I hesitated for several minutes, drumming my fingers on the wheel. I needed to make up my darn mind and grow a pair. Finally, I nosed the truck out of the alley and coasted past the funeral home. The Jeep was gone. I slammed the heel of my hand against the steering wheel a couple of times. The opportunity was lost through no fault but my own.

My cell phone jingled and I picked up. "Chérie?"

"He's back."

I knew who she meant, of course.

"And he's bragging how he just ran off that silly tow truck driver. He's calling you stupid and chicken and worse."

Probably the names I'd just called myself. "I tried, but I just couldn't take his car at his aunt's funeral."

"He doesn't seem all that broken up to me."

"I'm on my way."

"You should have plenty of time. The bartender just poured his first beer. He usually has at least three."

I hung a left onto Main Street and crept past Big Hal's, turned the corner, and took the alley at the rear. There it was. The Jeep Wrangler. It didn't take me long to lift all four wheels off the ground. Heck, I'd had plenty of practice. The vehicle rose into the air with no Hot Head in sight.

I rocketed away with the Wrangler on the back, singing a song about being the champion of the world. It was almost anticlimactic not to be caught and chased with a tire iron. Laughing to myself, I sailed down the street on a euphoric high. How many times had I tried to recover the Jeep behind Big Hal's? I counted on my fingers…one, two, three…never mind. It was too many to count.

Just think, I'd never have to deal with Hot Head or his tire iron again. *I did it! Yay me!*

Once I got to Abington's, I dialed Crump. I cleared my throat a couple of times and tested my voice so I didn't sound too excited. This was all in a day's work, right?

"You did it? You recovered the Jeep?" He sounded shocked, but I couldn't blame him. "Bring the vehicle around back and leave it at the oil change department. Call the front desk to find out when you can pick up your recovery check."

I dropped the Wrangler in the back of Abington's as instructed and waited to see if someone would come out and shake my hand, pat me on the back, or something…but no one did. I called the police to let them know in case Hot Head reported his car stolen. He'd be the type who would.

I sped off with a beep of the horn and the wave of my hand. Goodbye, Jeep Wrangler.

Then guilt climbed over the back seat onto my shoulders.

What had I done? Funerals were for last goodbyes. Like Del Morran, Jeremy Winslow, and now Margaret Frankel. Too much grief surrounded funerals, and here I'd taken Lou's only means of transportation when he was at Big Hal's for some solace. I needed some consolation, too. The coffee bar had just closed, so I knocked on Kristen's apartment door. She answered wearing sweat pants with her hair in a ponytail.

"Kristen, I've done something bad, really, really bad." A tear ran down my cheek.

She pulled me in for a bear hug, then released me. "Everything's going to be okay. Now, tell me what's wrong."

I breathed in a ragged, shuddering breath and followed her inside. "I towed somebody's vehicle out from under them right after a funeral." That sounded even worse out loud.

"Was it a repo?"

Sniffing, I nodded.

"Was it that guy's Jeep you've been trying to get? The one behind Big Hal's?"

"Y-y-yes." Somehow the Audi hadn't affected me this way, possibly because I'd never met the owner. Hot Head and I knew each other now. I knew his name. Where he lived. Where he used to work. Where he hung out. He gave me his dog. It seemed too personal.

"I'll make hot tea." She led me to the couch and made me sit. On her way to the kitchen, she said over her shoulder, "Just concentrate on this, you had the authority from the lienholder to take the vehicle from that man. You are in the right. He's in the wrong."

My friend made sense, of course. Her words penetrated my self-reproach. I sank back into the sofa cushion and started breathing easier.

Her voice came to me from the other room. "It's good to feel compassion, but you don't need to feel guilt. This is your vocation and you're getting better and better at it." When the electric tea kettle dinged, I pushed myself off the couch and went to help. We both returned with our steaming mugs and sat down.

Kristen rubbed my back. "You doing okay now?"

I bobbed my head. The weight lifted as I swiped away a last tear. Lou Frankel was the bad guy here, not me. "I am better at the towing business, aren't I?" I wanted to hear her say it again, I was that insecure.

"You are. Look at you. Out on towing jobs all the time. Scoring great reviews on the internet." She gave me a happy smile.

This was embarrassing. Should I tell Kristen I wasn't getting calls? Not counting Byron's niece, who felt obligated to use me, I hadn't had a call for a tow in…I thought back…eleven days. And as far as reviews were concerned, my last one was negative.

"The owner of that Jeep posted a bad comment. He told people to *sic* their dogs on me." I made a stink-face. "I wonder what he'll say now."

"You have no control over what people think, so don't worry about it. Besides, he should be ashamed of himself."

I wasn't sure he would be ashamed, yet, she was right once again. What people thought of me for the most part was out of my hands.

"Guy asked for more shifts at the coffee shop." Kristen fiddled with the tea bag floating in her mug. "Now that you are so successful in your tow business, can I take your hours and give them to him? Starting next week?"

I gulped. "Next week?"

"The first of May?" She had on a hopeful, excited expression, like a proud parent at her child's graduation.

I reminded myself I just completed a successful recovery. The Jeep was a milestone. My first repo all on my own…without anyone else's help…and I would get checks soon from Friendly Finance and Abington Auto for the Audi and the Wrangler, both. And since my first was a success, Abington would send more repo jobs my way. Plus, on Tuesdays and Thursdays I had the towaway zones. So what…the Del's Towing phone line wasn't blowing up. So what…the on-line reviews sucked. My business was turning a corner.

I could do this. At least, I crossed my fingers and hoped I could.

Kristen went back to the kitchen for cookies, while I searched my reviews. Yes, I tortured myself again. A new review, only one star—*Never use Del's Towing. She'll repo your car and you'll be screwed.*

I suppose it was the truth. I'd finally captured Mr. Hot Head's Jeep. I had beaten him and he was screwed.

But he would just have to figure out his own damn problems.

****

Will phoned after I got back to my apartment, full of Kristen's Oreos and Oolong.

"Hello, Delaney. Just wanted to touch base. Del's carrier license has been transferred to you. The fee came to two hundred dollars."

"Two hundred?" At the time Will first told me I didn't think that sounded like much. It did now.

"I can float you."

"Thanks, Will." I hated owing my parents, but didn't have a choice until I received the repo checks and my last paycheck from Roasters. I couldn't wait. "Have you heard anything about the insurance?"

"Not yet." He paused for a moment, then continued in a wistful tone, "The title should arrive any day now. You could sell before spending any more money."

"I know." It was late afternoon and I had time enough, so I told Will, "I'd like to stop in and say 'hi' to Mom since I haven't seen her for a while."

"She'd like that."

"Okay. I'll leave now. Tell her I'll see her in a bit."

I set out for the expressway to Denver, making record time, my fun-sized Fiat humming along, keeping up with highway speeds.

My mind wandered to Tanner and what Byron had told me. I still hadn't spoken to the hot tow man. It felt like too much time had gone by. Even after *the kiss*, I really didn't know the guy well enough to say, *we need to talk*, ya' know? *Awkward.* I guess we'd remain distant colleagues now.

After setting the Fiat's parking brake, I got out in front of the much-loved beige and white two-story. Comfortable, homey feelings rose in my chest. Blue jays and house finches with peach-colored faces flitted among the tree branches, singing their last songs before the day's end. I went inside without knocking.

Mom folded her arms around me. "It's good to see you, Laney."

I returned the squeeze and followed her into the kitchen. The two of us sat together at the table. Will was still at his office downtown. A roast was in the oven, potatoes boiled in a pot, and Mom had the makings for gravy ready in a saucepan. My mouth watered just thinking of meat, potatoes, and gravy.

I asked, "You know Rob Abington, right?"

She got up to search the freezer. "Yes. What about him?" She extracted a bag of peas, then returned the package in exchange for broccoli.

"I just completed a vehicle recovery for him, a very

difficult one, too."

"Oh." She had on a vague expression. She had no idea about the difficulty. Best not to go into details. She volunteered, "I know his wife better than I know Rob. And listen to this, Nancy is thinking about leaving him, she told me so herself."

"Nancy? Abington's wife?" The woman with the fancy haircut and makeup in the photo on his desk? "That's too bad."

"The millionaire owner of one of those sports teams in Denver, I can't remember which, came into the dealership, and Rob sold him a new car at a discount. Nancy was really PO'ed." Mom would never use the word, pissed.

I felt obligated to ask, "Why would she be mad about that?"

"Nancy felt Rob missed out on money to be made. And on top of that, Rob didn't even try to introduce her to the guy. She wanted to meet him, get a selfie…"

I stifled a yawn and tuned out Mom's gossip. News of a failed marriage only made me feel bad. Soon Mom moved on to trash talk Will's sister's kids, then brought up the neighbors. Will walked through the door at five-thirty and we sat down by six.

Will said, reaching for the platter of meat, "Don't worry about paying back the two hundred right away." His eyebrows creased in. "I forgot to ask about your commercial driver's license. Have you taken the CDL class?"

"My temporary is good for six months. I've got plenty of time."

Mom asked, eyes narrowed, "Have you even signed up for the course?"

"Not yet. I will."

"Maybe you're thinking about selling?" Will leaned his elbows on the table, his fork and knife gripped in his fists, his voice happy with the idea.

I cleverly changed the subject by bringing up Will's nephews because talking about relatives was always important to the family, and for an added diversion I said, "Kristen's cousin lost his driver's license. He had too many speeding tickets. Can you help him, Will?"

"If he didn't dispute the tickets and the points were assessed already, he needs to wait out the suspension period. I might be able to get him a pink license, though."

"What's that?" I asked as I buttered a roll.

"For driving under conditions, like being permitted to drive to and from work for example."

"That would be great, Will. I'll talk to Axle. I have another legal question if you don't mind."

"Sure, what?"

"Jeremy's mother told me how he ended up with a robbery conviction, but his friend was the one who robbed the store. Jeremy was outside in the car and didn't know what the guy was doing." I hunched up my shoulders and let them fall back down. "He was just giving someone he knew from high school a ride. His mom said he was in the wrong place at the wrong time."

"I happen to know the other side of that story. I went to law school with the DA, so I called him and he told me what happened." He swallowed a drink of water, then continued in his courtroom voice. "Jeremy's classmate had a record dating back to age fifteen for street robberies and breaking, and Jeremy knew about it. He also admitted the bathroom stop took longer than normal, which was suspicious, and his friend ran out, and Jeremy received money."

"That does sound like a different story from what his mom told me." A slice of meat was on its way to my mouth, but I wasn't hungry anymore, so I set my fork back down.

"He was lucky to get only eighteen months of jail time, very fortunate to serve only twelve."

I asked, "Was the other guy Eugene Turnquil?"

Will said, "No, that wasn't his name. Who's Turnquil?"

I answered, "Just someone whose name came up." The convenience store robber would still be finishing his sentence.

My mom tapped my arm. "Jeremy may have been in the wrong place at the wrong time, but he also made some wrong decisions."

I agreed, leaving the rest of my food untouched on my plate. When Mom's right, she's right. We chatted over coffee and Mom told me about a television series she was binge watching. After that, I said my long goodbye and ducked out the door for the hour commute back to Spruce Ridge.

The sun sank behind the Rockies while the Fiat scaled the mountain road. My eyes drooped. I knew better than to drive when I was this tired, so I started hunting for a coffee shop. Signs on the mountainside warned, "Watch out for falling rocks," and others cautioned, "Wildlife crossing." The mile markers jumped out at me in the dark, the numbers fuzzy, but they drew my attention as they had done for the last month. Marker 418, then 419, then 420.

Mile 421 was where Dad went off this very road.

My headlights reflected off the white cross at the same time I was hit from behind, and the Fiat slammed down an embankment into a ditch.

Chapter 20

A bump formed above my brow where my head throbbed and I brushed my fingers against it. I closed my eyes and drifted off…

"Miss? You okay?" A police officer rapped on my window with a flashlight. His cruiser was pulled over at an angle with emergency lights blinking, the yellow glow causing shooting pains behind my eyeballs.

I pried open the door and tried to get out. After struggling, I realized I hadn't unfastened my seatbelt. *Duh.* I clicked it off and extracted my arm from the shoulder strap. "Someone ran me off the road."

The officer helped me to a stand. Not Zach for a change. He shone a light in my face and sniffed as if he was smelling my breath.

"I haven't had anything to drink." I was glad I hadn't had wine with dinner.

"Are you hurt?"

"I don't think so."

He held up a penlight and moved it to the right and left, asking me to follow the beam with my eyes. Seemingly satisfied, he led me around to the back of the Fiat and aimed the flashlight over the bumper. "I don't see where you were hit."

There wasn't a dent or a scratch.

Had I fallen asleep and imagined the whole thing? Had I relived Dad's accident in my sleep-deprived state?

"You'll need a tow truck to pull you out of this ditch."

I didn't know who else to call other than Tanner. The cop stood by while I sent the text, then he wrote down my driver's license number and filled out a form on a clipboard. It felt like only a little time passed before a black rig with a flatbed arrived, its set of emergency flashers joining the police cruiser's lights bouncing yellow off the roadway.

"Laney?" Tanner ran down the slope and enveloped me in his arms. *Oh my gosh*, he was worried about me. He really did care for me. I let him hold me for a couple of moments, then I took a step back.

The officer said, "I'm leaving now. You can get a copy of the incident report from the DMV." After the police car swung back onto the highway, the cruiser entered the median and turned to go in the opposite direction.

Tanner pulled me in again for another hug. "What happened?"

"I'll explain after we get out of here."

He led me several yards away and told me to stand there, then he got busy at my car attaching the winch to the undercarriage. After he put the car in neutral, the Fiat rolled slowly onto the flatbed. Then he secured all four tires with chains and came back to get me. I jumped inside his cab, he shut my door and walked around to the driver's side. Once in his seat, he reached across to fasten my seatbelt, then took my hand in his.

"Okay, tell me now." Tanner appeared all frenzied like his wheels were about to fall off.

Serious doubts about what had happened were

growing in the back of my mind. "I might've fallen asleep while driving."

"You fell asleep?" His voice had dropped low, as if in disbelief. He couldn't see my rubescent cheeks and nose in the dark.

"I thought someone came up behind me and then—" I pictured the Fiat's intact bumper without a scratch on it. "—and well, I may have imagined it, dreamt the whole thing. I didn't get a lot of sleep last night." I drew my hand out from his grasp and clutched my head. The bump was growing larger by the minute.

He studied me with concern. "I'd better get you home." He steered his truck onto the freeway and accelerated.

I said, "Friendly called me to recover that Audi when they couldn't get a hold of you. That's the only reason I took the job."

His eyes left the windshield to glance at me. "Forget it, Laney. It's all good. I'm more concerned about you right now. You could've been killed going off the road like that."

Like my dad.

On this same highway.

In the same spot.

That was too weird. But these thoughts weren't doing me any good, just freakin' me out all the more. I clutched a hand to my throat and a tear rolled down my cheek. Tanner tapped the brakes. "What is it? Should I pull over? Are you hurt?"

"No." I stared out my window, but only saw my own reflection in the black glass. "I'm just a little shaken up. Thanks for coming. It didn't take you very long."

"I wasn't far from here."

I leaned my head on the backrest, and let my eyes close.

Tanner jiggled my shoulder. "Here we are."

I opened my eyes and found myself sprawled out over the passenger seat. My Fiat was parked in my usual spot behind the coffee shop, and Tanner's flatbed was lined up alongside the Fiat.

His jaw muscles worked. "You might have a concussion. Maybe you should go to the ER."

"No, I'm all right. I just want to get inside and climb into bed."

****

When I woke up my head was on Tanner's shoulder, my nose pressed into his neck, his arm around me. He was sleeping. I'd fallen asleep as soon as my head hit the pillow, but I'd also tossed and turned all night, holding onto Tanner, breathing in his scent, soaking in his warmth.

I wore a sleep shirt, so when I got out of bed I yanked on a pair of yoga pants, then shut the door quietly behind me. I needed a cup of joe. It was Sunday morning, Roasters on the Ridge was not open, and I had to settle for making my own drip-brew. At that point, I would have welcomed anything resembling coffee. As soon as the machine dinged, I poured myself a mug. It was tongue-blistering hot but sent a jolt of much-needed caffeine into my veins.

While bacon sizzled in the pan, I stirred together some pancake batter, getting ready for Tanner to come out to the kitchen. Once he appeared in his jeans and tee-shirt, he wrapped his strong arms around me from behind, resting his chin on top of my head.

He said, "Morning. I smelled the coffee."

Leaning back into his hard chest, I noticed for the umpteenth time there was no flab on him anywhere. What did he do to get in this kind of shape? "Morning, Tanner. Thanks for everything."

"No need to thank me." He turned me around to face him. "How are you doing?"

I handed him a cup of coffee. "I'm okay." I pulled a curl down over the lump on the top of my forehead, then ran my hands down my arms. I crossed over to the stove, extracted the bacon with tongs, and poured a large dollop of batter into the skillet. I wrapped the bacon in foil. Bubbles appeared at the edges of the pancakes while I glanced at Tanner out of the corner of my eyes. "My accident happened right where Dad had his. It's so strange."

His worried expression was back. "You should sit down and let me make breakfast."

"I'm a lot better this morning. Really." I shifted the first couple of hotcakes onto a plate and poured more batter into the skillet. "I don't think I would've gotten any sleep at all if you hadn't stayed last night."

Tanner had been a gentleman. Nothing had happened. There was a deeper intimacy between us, though, which felt complicated, like something left unsaid. Like a lot left unsaid. I'd wanted him near me last night, but how did I feel this morning? What was going on with us?

I lifted the last of the pancakes onto another plate and carried both plates over to the counter where I'd laid out the silverware and maple syrup. I tore the foil off the bacon, still warm. Tanner sat watching me, his chin in his hand.

Taking the seat next to him, I raised the coffee cup to my lips, but couldn't take a drink, so I put it back down. The pancakes didn't have any appeal either. I asked him, "Tanner, what's the deal with you? Why did you kiss me?"

"Why did it bother you? Was it that bad?" He sat back on the stool with crossed arms.

I shook my head. "What kind of game are you playing?"

"You're the one playing games. You flirted with me like crazy, then when I made a move, you got mad."

"You don't like me. You made that clear."

"That's not true. I do like you, but Byron told me to keep my distance, so I did."

"Then why the kiss?"

"Why did you flirt with me, then do a runner?"

"I gave you three chances, then you were out."

"What?" He tilted his head and narrowed his eyes.

"I didn't want to subject myself to any more rejection." How much could a person take? Abandonment was my hot button.

He flicked his eyes closed a moment. "Let's start over. I told you about my promise to Byron."

"Yeah, so what?"

Tanner had on a sheepish look. "Well…it was like he was your dad or something."

"I know, I know. He's way too protective of me. What made you change your mind?"

"He released me from my promise."

I rolled my eyes. "What's that even mean?"

He frowned, his eyes sad, and fiddled with his coffee cup. Then he sighed and appeared to come to a decision. "You see, my mom made me swear to take care of my little brother and sister after she died. She knew she didn't have long to live. My dad passed away the year before and the kids had no one else. She told me my word was an oath that couldn't be broken. I'd been pretty irresponsible up until then, but all that changed." He took my hand in his and I let him. "Now, after that promise to my mom, I don't make promises I don't keep."

"Wow. I'm so sorry." I batted back tears, completely choked up. He had me there. A death bed vow would make anyone take promises seriously. "Why didn't you just tell me that in the first place?"

"Several reasons, but for one, I thought you'd think I'm lame. A promise to my mother and all that. And anyway, I did try to tell you."

"I think it's cool you had a tight bond." I was a little envious because there always seemed to be friction between my mom and me.

He gazed at the opposite wall, not meeting my eyes. "I never told anyone about the oath. It's hard to talk about. All this is kinda personal, and I don't know you very well."

Guys. They couldn't handle the emotional stuff.

"What I thought was lame was you going along with Byron. Keeping that promise to your mom, that's not what's lame. The promise to your mom's not the same kind of promise you made to Byron, you know that, right?"

He shook his head. "My word is my word. I live by that now."

"All right." I mulled that over, then asked, "Is there anything more?"

He gave me an intense look. "You seem like the

kind of girl who flirts with all the guys."

I flushed. "You're right, you don't know me very well."

"What about that Spruce Ridge cop?"

"He's Kristen's boyfriend. He's in love with her."

"He is?" A broad smile lit up Tanner's face. He entwined his fingers in my braid and tipped my head back. His lips landed on mine, lingering. Needless to say, I didn't mind this time. We broke apart and smiled at each other.

My appetite returned and I picked up a piece of bacon. "So, full disclosure. Are you seeing anyone else?"

He was quick to answer, "No." So, he didn't spend his busy Tuesdays and Thursdays in the company of another woman. He asked, "Are you dating anybody else?"

"No, but I'm not saying you can't see other people, I was only wondering."

He rubbed a thick strand of my tangled red hair between his fingers and gave me his sexy smile that made my toes curl. "I only date one person at a time."

I cut off a corner of pancake with the edge of my fork. "Can I tell Byron we're dating?"

He wore a satisfied grin. "Please do. Make sure he knows." He stuffed a piece of bacon in his mouth.

After breakfast Tanner helped me clean up the dishes—I said he was a gentleman—and I went to make another pot of coffee, but he said he had to work and needed to get going. He took his job as seriously as he took his promises.

I darted a glance out the window; Kristen's Prius was not parked in the lot, so the coast was clear. She was at church. Even though nothing had happened and Kristen wouldn't ask…and even if she did ask and I told her…I just didn't want to have that conversation.

Tanner grabbed his keys but stopped at the door. He reached for me, pulling me to him. His dreamy eyes closed and I shut mine too. Softly at first, then gradually more intense, his kiss caused my heart to beat faster and faster and my body to relax, to turn to mush. He seemed to have that effect on me. Our third kiss, and it was spectacular. And, yes, I was counting. Not three strikes this time, but three home runs.

Then he was gone, and the apartment felt empty and lonely.

I took a long shower and chose what to wear while my hair dried. My curls finally settled into waves that I wove into my usual plait.

I drove the Fiat over to get my self-loader. My car appeared not to have suffered any mechanical damage, but I wanted my truck so I could use the emergency flashers when I parked on the side of the highway. I pulled over at mile marker 421, hit the blinkers, and got out.

The wide shoulder led down to a grassy slope, and at the bottom of the hill, a thin stand of spruces. On the other side of the trees, the terrain took a slight incline back up then made a steep drop-off.

I picked my way down the verge, slipping on pine needles, and through the woods to an outcropping of rock. From there, the view of the valley was majestic with tall mountain peaks on the other side. The spruces provided only a thin barrier, and if my Fiat would've made it through the pines, it would've gone over the cliff. A dangerous, deadly spot. Even standing ten feet from the edge gave me a dizzy sensation, so I turned around and hiked back to the place my car ended up last night, right near where the white cross stuck up from the ground. The white cross I'd erected at the spot of my dad's fatal accident. Why had I gone off the road at this exact spot?

The Fiat's tire marks stretched down the highway onto the shoulder and into the grassy verge. Tanner's tow truck had forged another set of deep tracks in the grass. The police cruiser's tires had dug in the gravel.

But, there was no evidence of another vehicle.

****

On Monday morning Kristen and I had our usual coffee and muffin break. It was time to spill all.

"My car went off the road Saturday night, but I wasn't hurt."

Her eyes grew round and she clutched at my sleeve. "No! What happened?"

As I told the story, she gasped in all the scary places. I rubbed the tips of my fingers across my eyelids. "I thought someone hit me from behind, but maybe I dreamed it."

Kristen asked, going all-out big-sister, "Are you sure you're all right?"

"Yes, yes. There's something else I haven't told you."

"Is it Tanner? It's him, isn't it? You worked out your disagreement. I saw his flatbed parked outside all night."

Oops. I'd hoped she hadn't noticed. "He did stay overnight because I was wigged out, but nothing happened."

"I'm glad you respect yourself, and I trust your

decisions, Delaney." She believed in me like she always did. "So, what is it?"

"It's about Byron…he's an ex-con. He was in prison…for murder." I gulped down a mouthful of hot coffee, burning my tongue.

She sucked in a breath and sat up in her chair. "Do you think…did he…?"

I held up a hand and shook my head. "He didn't kill Jeremy. No, no, he couldn't've done it."

Her dark eyebrows soared up high, causing ridges in her forehead. "Maybe you should stay away from him. Find another place to park your tow truck. I know, ask Tanner if you can use his lot."

I chewed my lip for a moment. "I might, but not yet. Byron said he didn't mean to kill the guy. It was a bar fight. He genuinely regrets it, too." I usually followed my friend's advice because it was always spot on, but for some reason I wanted to trust the Old Man. Dad had enough faith in him to give him a job. Did I accept Byron because he had good things to say about Del Morran? Did I want to believe him because I wanted to believe in my dad? "It took a lot for Byron to tell me about it. He didn't say to keep his past a secret, but…"

"You know I won't breathe a word." Kristen made a zipping motion across her lips.

"Of course." I had a sudden thought. "Byron's record explains why he never tried to buy the self-loader from me."

Kristen's head drew back. "I don't understand."

"You can't have a tow carrier license if you're a felon."

"How could Jeremy drive the truck then?"

"Dad held the carrier license, but that didn't keep him from hiring people with criminal records to do the driving. Drivers with a criminal record can get a commercial license." That was a lot of information and I was proud of myself for knowing it. Maybe I was ready for the CDL exam after all, even though I hadn't studied.

My friend sat up even straighter. "That's why Jeremy didn't tell you he worked for your father."

I gave her a bugged-out look. "Why's that?"

"He thought you knew all about the ex-cons on your dad's crew, and he didn't want you to know he was one."

"You could be right, Kristen. He probably thought Dad talked to me about his business. I never told Jeremy my father and I didn't speak to each other. Jeremy and I didn't discuss our parents." It was an answer that made sense.

Guy unlocked the front door and flipped the sign to "Open." He saw me and said, "Oh, you're here."

"Time to get to work." Kristen rose from the table to wait on the customers streaming inside to line up at the cash register. I teamed up with her behind the espresso machine and the day began. The early rushes never seemed to let up that whole morning.

Just after noon, the handsome Spruce Ridge officer stopped in to see Kristen, who joined him at their favorite table. I brought over Zach's non-fat latte and noticed him give an uncertain glance at my friend.

Kristen nudged his arm. "Talk to her, Zach."

"What?" I loomed over him, my hands on my hips.

He fingered his mustache, then rubbed a hand over his salt-and-pepper hair. "I know you're curious about

Winslow's murder, and I know you talked to his wife, but Kristen said you've gone as far as questioning his folks and even the mechanics at the garage."

"Kris!" I gave her a look that said, *best friend betrayal.*

Kristen hung her head, her dark hair streaming down. "I'm sorry. I should've asked you before I shared that."

"You did the right thing, Kris." The officer rubbed her arm, then faced me. "She says you even talked to Eugene Turnquil. Listen, Delaney, you need to stay away from him."

I leaned forward. "Is he the prime suspect?" Or, was that still me?

Zach crossed his arms and scooted back in his chair. "No more questions."

I asked anyway, "Did Eugene and Jeremy have some kind of a problem, like a prison feud?" Zach pressed his lips together. I shook my finger in his face. "Come on, you're the one who brought the subject up." Jeremy's mom thought Turnquil had showed up at her house looking for him. Jeremy's wife knew Turnquil. But Jeremy's dad said his son wanted to steer clear of Turnquil. I tapped Zach's arm. "Tell me, what was going on between those two?"

Zach shook his head in a silent no.

"Kristen?" I presented her with a puppy-dog face, pleading for some help with her boyfriend. My friend gave him a helpless look, while I glared at him as if to say, *spill it!*

His eyes bulged out, but he said, "Look, everyone knows felons are not supposed to associate with one another."

"What happens if they do?" I asked.

"Sometimes the judge grants exceptions to probationary terms, but I don't know about their case specifically, so I can't tell you any more about it." He shrugged.

"That could explain why Jeremy avoided Turnquil." I chewed on a knuckle for a second, thinking about the next suspect on my list. "Melissa received the life insurance payout and she left for Mexico. She got a hundred-thou. That's a huge motive."

Zach sighed. "We're aware. Stay away from her."

"But you just said to stay away from Eugene Turnquil." I pronounced his name EYEW-gene. My bad. "Are they both persons of interest?"

He closed his eyes, appearing resigned. "I told you, Melissa is not a suspect. Just keep out of the investigation."

I pounded my fist on the table. "Is that because she's dating Ephraim Lopez? The sheriff."

"What?" Kristen's mouth dropped open.

"No, no. Sheriff Lopez made full disclosure. They only went out three times before he decided he wasn't interested in her." Zach held up both his palms. "He's a player, Delaney. Who hasn't he taken out in this town?"

"Oh, I didn't know that. But he hit on me, so I shouldn't be surprised, I guess." I secretly scolded myself for being disappointed. "What kind of a cop does that make him?"

Zach stuck out his big chin. "Lopez's a good sheriff, don't worry. He doesn't give the ladies any free passes for favors or anything like that. He takes his job seriously and he's above board."

"It's weird, though, that both Jeremy and Ephraim

had a thing for Melissa. I don't get it."

"Sounds like they each liked you, too." Zach's eyes swept me head to toe. "Don't you realize how much you look alike? Petite, pretty. Though she's blonde and you're a redhead." He grabbed the tail end of my braid and held it up as if to show me.

That's when the bell above the door rang and Tanner walked in.

Chapter 21

Tanner gave Zach a hard stare but his eyes went soft when his gaze settled on me. "Can I talk to you outside, Laney?"

"Sure."

Zach let go of my braid and I scraped my chair under the table.

Tanner took my hand and led me out the door and around the corner of the building, then he leaned me up against the brick wall. "You okay? You seem upset and you're all white."

Most of the time, I looked pink, so this was different. I put my hand on his chest. "I'm doing better, thanks. I notice you've been calling me Laney."

"That okay?"

I nodded.

He folded his hand over mine, covering my fingers in his, pulling me closer. "You know I'm working the towaway zones tonight, but call me if you need company and I'll come and get you. You can ride with me."

"I'll be fine." I clutched his shirt and pulled him in for the kiss this time. His lips pressed back, passionate, hungry for more. Even after all the craziness lately, I couldn't help feeling good about Tanner. He wanted me. We were dating now. *For real.* We'd already advanced to the pet names stage.

After he reversed his tow truck out of the parking lot, I returned inside. Making the coffee drinks, pulling the blank shots to preheat the mugs, tamping the grounds, and timing the shots were relaxing in their repetitive manner. Even Guy, racing to help the customers and elbowing me out of the way, didn't ruffle my feathers.

During the lull at around two, Rob Abington called me.

I was sure he would congratulate me on retrieving the Jeep Wrangler, but he said, "We won't be needing you for recoveries anymore, Delaney."

My heart fell straight to the floor like a heavy sack of espresso beans. I was so stunned, I stammered, "Wh-why? What did I do?"

"Patrick said you were difficult to work with, that you took four or five attempts to complete that recovery. He had to keep hunting for the Jeep over and over. He said you wasted his time."

A bead of sweat trickled down my hairline, so I lifted the braid off my neck and let it fall back down.

"Sorry, Delaney, but it didn't work out. You might want to reconsider getting out of the towing business. Remember, I can find a buyer for your truck."

I came close to groaning out loud. I'd been counting on a lot more business from the Auto Store. "I'll think about it. Thank you, Mr. Abington."

I darted to the backroom and massaged my thumbs into my temples. What bothered me the most? Losing the repo gig or having to admit to my stepdad, Will, that I lost the repo gig? I didn't care for the aggravation of it, but I needed the money. Maybe it would be a good idea to sell the truck. Reapply for my position as a social worker. I could handle the Social Services job if I tried harder, but that thought made my stomach hurt.

I tucked my phone in my pocket and ventured out front to help with closing, then after Kristen locked up, I trudged up the steps to my apartment. Not able to deal with a decision right away, I fell into bed, exhausted and headachy, the bump on my head still throbbing. I briefly thought about accepting Tanner's invitation to tag along with him that night so we could discuss my next steps, but sleep was calling me.

I didn't go into the coffee shop the following day because Kristen had given the last of my shifts to Guy, much to his satisfaction. I'd caught him cheering when he studied the new schedule.

I didn't have anything else to do, so I headed over to get my truck. At least I still had the private property impound lots and that work felt secure. Even though it was too early, I could monitor the towaway zones to keep me busy until I made a decision about my truck.

I spotted a vehicle, a new Cadillac Escalade, rear-wheel drive, nose-in, blocking a doorway, so I swooped up the back tires with the claws and got out of there fast. I dropped the Escalade off at Tanner's lot. I even made a good job of it. I didn't put any dents in the car. I didn't take too long. I didn't jackknife. Okay, so I did jackknife the vehicle, but no one was around to see it so it didn't count.

After locking the secure gate behind me, I returned to the towaway zones and brought out my phone to do some internet surfing.

My cell rang, Tanner calling. "Laney, what did you do?"

"What?"

"Did you tow a Cadillac out from behind the furniture store on Main Street?"

"Yes." My chest puffed out with a little pride. *Come on*…I was good at this, no matter what that repo agent or anyone else thought. Including me. "I didn't even wait for the call. I snatched it before they had to contact me."

"That's not how it's done. I told you the businesses would get in touch with you during the day when the stores are open, and you only needed to monitor the lots at night when the places are closed. Didn't I say that?"

"Yes, you did say that." So I didn't sit tight until they notified me, what was the big deal? "Did I do something wrong?"

"You towed the owner's car, the guy who owns the furniture store. He called me directly, and I had to stop everything and return his vehicle right away." He exhaled a deep breath into the phone. "He asked who towed it and I had to tell him. He said if I ever subbed the work out again, he would not renew my contract."

Well, this sucked. I was glad he couldn't see my *oh-no-what-else-can-go-wrong* expression. "I'm sorry to cause you so much trouble. I have no excuse. I should have followed your instructions."

Tanner said, "I'll take back the lots, starting now. Shoot. This is going to be hard."

Water hit my eyes and a tear escaped down my cheek. "What are you going to do about Tuesdays and Thursdays? I know you counted on me to free up your time."

"I'll have to arrange other rides for my little brother. I did it before, I can do it again."

"What do you mean?"

He paused, then gave out an aggravated sigh. "I have to drive Tate to therapy on those days."

I hadn't given much thought to Tanner's family responsibilities. "Is everything all right with him?"

"He's got some health issues, but he's getting

better all the time."

"I can take him to his appointments for you."

"Thanks, but I'll figure it out." He hesitated and I could imagine his brain working. "I'm sorry you can't have the lots anymore. It was an unlucky break." If he only knew the extent of it. His voice had gone soft and mellow. "You okay?"

I tried to keep my voice steady, not wanting him to guess I was about to have a meltdown. "I'm fine, and really, if you need someone to help with your brother, I'd be glad to do it."

Tanner seemed to have had his life in order before he met me. If he lost the contract, would he have trouble covering his bills? Like me. He wouldn't want my help if this was what my helping looked like. The tears dripped off my face now and locked up my nose making it difficult to breathe.

We said reluctant goodbyes. After the phone connection went dead, I allowed myself a good cry, the tears pulling black mascara streaks down my cheeks.

My ass was fired from the repo business. I could kiss the towaway zones goodbye. Kristen gave all my hours to Guy. Wasn't this just hilarious?

Why did I buy those new denim wedges? The innocent orange pedicure was a luxury, and I could've waited on the business cards, too. I fingered the stiletto keychain hanging from the mirror. Those purchases were minor compared to rent and car payments, but still…

I scrubbed my face with a tissue. Then I returned my tow truck to Byron's. Then I went home.

Decision time.

There were plenty of Fulcan Xtruders for sale on

the internet. I scribbled down the average asking price, then subtracted what I owed on my credit card and Friendly Finance for my Fiat and the bank for my student loan. Didn't mention that before, did I? But we all have school debts, that's a given. The other bills to pay, of course, were the two hundred to Will and the rent to Kris. My stepdad should've received my truck's title by now. Selling was doable and an easy way out, a responsible plan, well researched and financially sound.

No more deranged customers. No more embarrassing jackknives. I was over it. I couldn't work without liability insurance anyway.

The internet ad was simple to create and so was hitting the button to post it. My truck, that ole hunk of metal, that dented beauty with Del's Towing painted on the door, was now for sale. I wasn't going to let Abington sell it for me. *Screw that*. I'd sell it myself.

I'd have to scrape the money together to make the windshield repairs or give a concession to the buyer. Even so, once my truck was sold there would be a healthy amount in the bank to live on for a couple of months while I contemplated what to do with my life.

Move back to Denver.

Find a cheap apartment.

Search for a position in social work.

Or…without a job and putting my truck up for sale, the world opened up and I could go where my heart took me. I could leave the country and disappear like Melissa did. Maybe move to the coast. Except, I'd never considered living anywhere other than Colorado. Grew up here. Went to college here. My parents reside here. My best friend owns a business here. And I'm starting a relationship with Tanner…here. Bummer, my heart wanted to stay here in Spruce Ridge.

And do what?

Job prospects in this small town were limited.

If only I would get a call for a tow. That would be an indication I should keep the truck, right? If no one contacted me to buy the self-loader, and someone phoned me for a tow, that would certainly be an omen. I stared at the ceiling as if the answer could be found there, but no words appeared magically written in the plaster. Where else could I look for a sign? I read over my ratings on the internet. People had posted several comments on Hot Head's negative review: *Tow truck drivers are jerks. I won't use Del.* Okay, I needed a different sign.

I stared at my phone…ring, ring, ring, please ring. Please, someone call for a tow…I concentrated hard. The cell didn't buzz, but Kristen banged on my door, and when I didn't answer, she shouted, "Delaney, are you all right?"

I rushed into my bedroom and crammed the pillow over my head until the pounding stopped. Man, I couldn't believe I ignored my friend. I guess I'd explain later I was in the shower. *Liar, liar.* I was really in the pits. At an all-time low, I laid on my bed feeling crummy.

Buck up, I told myself. Snap out of it. So, what if I lost the business? I didn't have my self-loader a month ago, never even knew I'd inherited a tow truck. And I had to be realistic, I wasn't very good in this hauling business.

I started to feel better about selling. It was no use brooding, although I couldn't help feeling sad.

****

Kristen had gone back to her apartment, so I made my escape. I eased myself behind the wheel of the Fiat. God still hadn't given me a sign, but maybe talking to Byron would help.

I turned the key and the vehicle came to life. I coasted down Pine Street and hung a right on Fifth. Bringing the Fiat to a stop behind my parked truck, I cut the engine. Byron strolled outside wearing his usual oil-stained overalls with a red rag tucked into the pocket.

Getting straight to the point, I said, "Hey, Old Man, I put my self-loader up for sale."

His mouth turned down at the corners. "Now, what'd ya' do that for?"

I forced my eyes away from my truck. "I lost the repo work." I almost told him Tanner took away the impound lots, too, but then he'd be mad at Tanner.

"You didn't really like doin' those repos."

"True that, but I can't get any of the mechanic shops to use me for tows, either." I rolled my eyes. "Not even L&B Garage, that chop shop."

"What's this?"

"The police raided the place and found a stolen car."

"Gosh, I'd never a' guessed." He took his rag out of his pocket and wiped his forehead. "If they're doin' something criminal, you want ta' stay away from that place anyways."

"But getting random calls for tows isn't enough. I haven't received any calls for two whole weeks now other than from your niece. I wonder how Dad brought in business." It probably helped that Del Morran didn't have bad reviews about dead bodies and murder investigations.

Byron said, “People liked him and he was well known around here. It won’t take long for people ta’ get to know you, too.”

“I’m not so sure, Byron. I’ve been waiting for some kind of omen telling me to stick with it, but maybe I’ve already received the sign.” I tugged on my braid. “Maybe towing a car with a dead body in the trunk was the clue for me to quit. And the police think I’m their main suspect. That’s got to be an indication I should give it up.”

“Now, Delaney, don’t think that.”

I folded my arms around my middle. “Who killed Jeremy, Byron? Who?” His murder was the thing I could not get past. If I could figure out that, maybe I could figure out what to do about the business.

We both stared up at the waving tops of the pine trees behind the auto bays and the snowy mountain peaks on the horizon to the west. The wind was chilly with an undertone of rain.

Okay. A thought had been bothering me for a while now. Time to trot out my conspiracy theory. “What if Jeremy was involved in the chop shop? What if he used Dad’s rig to do it?”

Byron’s eyebrows drew together in a fierce scowl. “No.”

I stared down at the ground. “Did Dad know Jeremy delivered stolen cars with his tow truck?”

Byron’s spine stiffened. “Del would never of allowed that.”

I threw up my hands. “Maybe that’s why Dad fired Jeremy, and it had nothing to do with me.” That was more likely the case. The logic made sense.

The Old Man appeared to consider my idea, then shook his head side to side. “I don’t think Del knew ’bout any chop shop. He never said a thing.” His expression changed to deep seated-concern. “I worry ’bout you, Delaney. You’re getting mixed up in somethin’ dangerous and your dad’s not here ta’ protect you anymore.”

My stomach curled in on itself, tight like a chain around a winch. “Dad was never around to protect me.”

“How could ya’ think such a thing? How can you believe your dad didn’t look out for you?” Disappointment threaded through his words. Byron pictured my dad as the kind of father he would’ve been. But Del Morran was as distant as they come.

I gave Byron a *yeah, right* expression.

“Think what ya’ want to.” He tore open the door and stormed inside the auto bay.

“Hey, Old Man?” I hollered at his retreating back. “Byron? What’s your problem?” He didn’t know Dad the way I did. Dad never made contact after the divorce. Doesn’t Byron get that?

Guess not, since he lowered the overhead door to the ground with a solid thunk. Not a word goodbye or even a wave. The Old Man was loyal to the man who gave him a job and a second chance.

I crawled up into my truck and bowed my head, a tear dripping off the end of my nose. I started up the engine, my toes barely touching the pedals, even in my black stilettos.

Black to match my outlook.

Chapter 22

If this was my last day as a tow driver, and I had to believe it was, I might as well wrap up everything. I cut over four blocks and chugged up to the curb in front of Friendly Finance Company. After I checked my face in the mirror, I dabbed the edge of my sleeve under my eyes.

Hailey sat behind her desk staring at her computer. Classical music played in the background and fluorescent lights buzzed overhead. She gave me a welcoming smile. "Hey, Delaney. What can I do for you?"

"Do you have my repo check?"

"I happen to have the checks prepared, just waiting to go out on the first of the month." She rotated her chair around and sorted through a stack of envelopes. "Here's yours." She handed me a white, business-sized envelope with my name and address on the outside. "The authorization for possession of the Audi is included. Thanks for handling the repo so late at night."

"I appreciate you giving me the job." I plastered a smile on my face. "I don't suppose you have any more work?"

"No. Tanner's handling everything."

"Okay." I wasn't interested in taking jobs from him anyway. I kidded, "You're the only one I ever see working here. Do you run the whole company?" Was it possible Hailey was the office manager, the loan officer, and the repo agent all in one? She seemed very capable. Maybe she was even the owner. Was she also the enforcer? I imagined her pointing a gun at me and growling, "Pay up, or else." Yes, my thoughts were that dark.

Hailey just said, "It sure seems that way."

We laughed together.

"Thanks again, and I'll see you around." I went out the door without telling her I'd quit. I'd ask Will to disconnect the business line from my phone. Customers, if I had any, would soon learn Del's Towing was out of operation.

Money should be waiting for me at Abington Auto Store, too, so that's where I set out for next. Only I discovered once I'd arrived that the check hadn't been drawn up yet. The blonde receptionist told me my fee would be mailed within the week.

I went back out to the parking lot and sat in my truck. There was no great inspiration as to what I should do after this. What was it going to be? Tow truck driver? Barista? Social worker? Or the fall guy for a murder? I stared through the super-colossal windows into Abington Auto's showroom.

The sun started its descent behind the mountains, the slanting rays lighting up the spacious lobby filled with the latest car models in the prettiest, gleaming colors. On the other side of the window, Mr. Abington, in his smart suit and wire-rimmed glasses, ushered a man across the polished parquet floor. Abington patted the hood of a red BMW sports coupe, rear-wheel drive. They shook hands and the customer left, a smile on his face. It's possible he'd purchased one of the BMW coupes.

Mr. Abington chatted with the receptionist, whose head went unceasingly up and down in deferential agreement. Her gaze followed him as he strode across the showroom and out of sight. A few moments later, he emerged from a side door and strutted up to a Jaguar in a prime parking spot, a rear-wheel-drive vehicle in lemon yellow, not a color that could be pulled off by just any car. Above the parking space was a notice painted on the side of the building, "Reserved for Robert C. Abington." He reversed out of his space and turned north on Pine.

If only I could get the repo gig back, then I'd make the towing operation work. Forget signs and omens. Just get the business back. I could talk to Abington and explain how difficult Mr. Hot Head was. Certainly Lou Frankel was the exception rather than the rule. I'd play the *you-know-my-stepdad* card, and Abington would understand and give me another opportunity.

I followed half a block behind the Jaguar.

A few minutes later he turned into the golf community and stopped in a circular driveway in front of a white-pillared, red-bricked mini-mansion. I pulled up to the curb and got out. I gave him a cheerful wave that said no hard feelings.

Abington braced himself against the side of his car. "Delaney, what are you doing here?"

"I know some people who live a few blocks over." I flapped a hand in the direction of the Winslows' house. "That way." I didn't want to admit I'd tailed him home. "Do you have a second?"

"What do you need?"

"I, um…" Now was my chance. No doubt my nose

turned red and my cheeks pinked up. "I'd, uh, like an opportunity to explain what happened with the repo job you gave me. It was a challenging situation, the owner dodged the capture, and he was quite aggressive." I stopped to suck in a quick breath. Abington seemed dumbfounded, so I went on. "And Patrick Crump didn't like me, probably because his sister was married to my ex-boyfriend." I needed to quit babbling. I flashed him what I hoped was a confident smile. "Please give me another chance to prove myself."

His gaze swerved left and right. I'd trapped the poor guy, cornering him, asking for my job back.

"No, I can't." His words came out clipped. Gone was the kindly Santa-like look behind his gold-rimmed glasses. Gone was the booming gentility in his voice. His tone was cold, cutting through me. He pointed a finger down at my black stilettos. "What a ridiculous tow driver you are, showing up in high heels. I told you to give it up."

I gasped out loud. Did he just call me ridiculous? Tears pricked my eyes and my heart felt as heavy as an engine full of lead.

The front door flew open, and a blonde woman stomped out wearing high-end, furry boots and a brand-name leather jacket I happened to know was priced at two thousand dollars. Funny the details you notice at the weirdest times. She dragged a designer suitcase behind her, bumping down the brick steps.

Abington's shoulders hunched up and he cringed as though preparing for a blow. "Where are you going, Nancy?" He'd gone rigid like he was waiting for the other shoe to drop. I didn't dare move a muscle either, except for my eyes darting back and forth between the two of them.

She held out her hand. “Give me the keys to the Jaguar, Rob.” She snapped her fingers. “Hurry up.”

He handed them to her.

“I’ll be at my sister’s, but don’t bother to contact me. My lawyer will be in touch.”

Even with his neat, white hair and smart business suit, he appeared to deflate like a flat tire. “What is it you want? More money? Is that it?”

She laughed, a cruel sound. “I’m taking the Jaguar. I’ll be back tomorrow with the moving van.”

“Take it all, what do I care?” he shouted in a blustery way to make it seem like he didn’t mind, but it was obvious he did.

“Oh, I plan to.” A smile twitched at the corner of her mouth. She propelled the suitcase over his toes on her way past him. He sprang aside when she shouldered open the driver’s door and shimmied behind the wheel. It was a beautiful car. I’d want it, too.

She sped out of the driveway and down the street.

I wished I could disappear as well, and let him be alone. If I just drove away, like Nancy, would that be even more humiliating for us both? I said, “I’m sorry, Mr. Abington.”

“I gave her everything she wanted.” His voice was a whisper.

“She’ll realize she made a mistake. She’ll come back.” I tried to give him some hope and help him save face. I could just about picture myself in his shoes, rebuffed and cast aside, all alone. Abandoned. Yup. I knew what that felt like.

His face remained pointed at the horizon, his eyes peering intently through his glasses as if he were longing to see the Jaguar turn around.

I was attempting to salvage my livelihood here, so after the purr of the Jag's engine faded, I made one last effort. "I'll take your advice and quit wearing the high heels if you think I should. I'd like to keep working for you, Mr. Abington." I felt so bad for him, I was even willing to give up my trademark high heels.

But he had on a preoccupied expression, his eyes glued to the end of the street.

"Now's obviously not a good time. Can I call you tomorrow?"

"Call me?" A dark crease appeared between his eyebrows. "What for?"

"To talk about the repo work." I shuffled my feet. "I understand how you feel. I've had my share of bad news, and really, I can identify. I'll give you a few days, then I'll be in touch." This was embarrassing and I was talking too much. I took a few steps back. Time to leave this man in peace.

He swiveled to face me. "No, you can't understand how I feel. And what are you still doing here? You never go away. I assigned you the repo from hell and told Patrick to give you a hard time. Between the two of them, Lou Frankel and Patrick Crump, I thought for sure you'd quit and move back to Denver. But you didn't."

I stared at him in total disbelief. How could he do something so mean? And Will knows this guy. And Abington knows Will! And I did think about quitting and moving.

The red ball of the sun dipped halfway behind the mountain peaks, and twilight turned a darker blue with a ridge of pink over the purple summits. Night approached fast, not my favorite time of day. I wanted to run and hide even more, but I would not, could not, beat a retreat now. I was here to get my job back and, by God, Mr. Abington owed me an explanation.

I shook his elbow. "I know I was getting on Patrick's nerves…and I…" I let out a nervous laugh. "Well, I guess I could've tried harder with Patrick, but I thought he might have something to do with my boyfriend's death. Jeremy Winslow. That, or he was involved with L&B Garage. I never told you this, but I saw Patrick at that chop shop. Man, they were nasty…they had the worst attitude toward customer service, ever. But you…I hoped you were in my corner." *I know, I know*, I couldn't stop my motor mouth, but I was reaching, still unable to wrap my head around this.

Abington jerked his arm away from me and his eyes shrank to slits.

"What did I do now?" I could taste and smell the wound-up tension in the man beside me, upping the creep factor, but why? I'd asked, what had *I* done. But, what had *he* done? What was *he* hiding? The puzzle pieces didn't fit.

Think, think, think.

His wife just left him. He was a desperate man. Even though he seemed a success, he was broken. The notable Robert C. Abington of Abington Auto Store.

I clasped my hand over my mouth. I had it! Mr. Abington—the man with the gold rings and the diamond watch and the wife with the expensively coiffed hair, the man I'd once thought generous and kind—was he the one Freddie Haag phoned from L&B Garage the night I'd spied on the chop shop? Was

Robert C. Abington the man Freddie referred to as RC?

He must have noticed the wheels in my brain turning because he asked, his voice a growl, "What is it?"

I had to make sure before I said anything else. Mom's words came to me. Listening to her gossip about his wife paid off. "Nancy wanted to rub shoulders with the millionaires in this town. The dealership provided a good living, but not that good. What lengths were you prepared to go…what were you willing to do to save your marriage? Who were you willing to do business with? Who calls you RC?"

"This is none of your business."

True, that. I took a few steps toward my truck and groped around in my front pocket for the keys.

"Wait. Why'd you bring up L&B Garage?" he asked.

I stumble-halted. "No reason. *Nada*. Diddly squat. The police only found the one stolen car that time."

Abington's upper lip broke out in a sweat and a sliver of fear passed over his face. "You guessed it. You figured it out."

"All right, I did. You're the chop shop kingpin, not the Mexican cartel." I almost shouted those last words.

He barked out a laugh. "Mexican cartel? You watch too much television."

"Only the shopping channel." Where were the keys? Darn, where were they? My hands faltered as I hunted through my jacket.

He *tssked* and shook his head. "It's all on account of that Mustang."

My mind spun like wheels on an icy road. "The Mustang? The one Jeremy towed?"

He nodded through clenched teeth. "When Jeremy brought the Mustang in, the owner called up Del. The idiot actually thought Del would return his money for the tow because his car was stolen. Jeremy was careless, stealing the Mustang on the same day he towed it for Del. He should've waited."

"That was risky." I patted my top but there wasn't a place for keys there.

"Well, Del fired Jeremy over it, told him to stay away from his precious daughter, too."

I found the keys. The fob was in my jean's back pocket. I wheeled around and grabbed onto the truck door. Wait. Time out. Had I heard him right? *Precious? Me?* Precious to Dad?

"What did you say?" My ankles wobbled in my stilettos and I felt like I should go sit down somewhere.

"After Del fired him, Jeremy told me he'd broken up with you to get his job back with Del. Jeremy didn't know this, but Del informed me he'd never hire Jeremy back. It didn't matter because Del had his accident the next day and that opportunity went bye-bye." He chuckled like it was a joke.

"Dad talked to you about Jeremy?" I could barely breathe. Was it because of me? Or was it because of the stolen cars? "Why would Dad talk to you about Jeremy?"

He shoved his hands into his suitcoat. "You're asking all the questions, but I have one for you. How in the world did you find that one tow receipt? The one for the Mustang?"

"It was in the truck compartment. Maybe Dad had it out to talk to Jeremy about it." My stomach clenched like sharp, cracked espresso beans that jumped around in my belly. This was proof Dad knew Jeremy was using his tow truck to steal cars. This was also proof Dad knew I was in town, knew I was dating Jeremy. My chest tightened like a wrench on a lug nut. "So, about Dad…"

"Your boyfriend was scared after what happened to Del, and he had reason to be."

"Why's that?" I asked.

"Jeremy threatened me, said he was going to tell all. I knew he was serious because he'd moved out of his apartment and was getting ready to disappear. I couldn't let him just walk away, even if he was family."

"Family? He was family? Wow. Is everyone related in this town?"

"Nephew by marriage only. His mother is Nancy's sister. He was going to tell his mom and his mom would've told my wife. I couldn't have that. Between Del finding out and Jeremy threatening me, I had to do something." Abington's eyes flashed fire and the hairs on my arms stood up.

I told him, "Even with them out of the picture, the police will figure out about the chop shop. They're already all over it." I reached for the truck's door handle once more, still gripping my keys.

"No, they won't. I don't own L&B. My only connection is Freddie and he won't let me down."

That's right, Freddie Haag hadn't said anything when questioned by the Spruce Ridge Police. None of the mechanics had. "Axle didn't know about the chop shop, did he?" I asked.

"No. I almost told Freddie to fire your little friend when you started chumming around with him, but he was clueless. Jeremy and Freddie knew about the source of the cars, but not Axle."

My lips trembled. "I did tell Axle to get another job."

"Yeah, you're the one who should've gotten another job." Abington's voice went deeper and his eyes glinted. "You really shouldn't've kept asking questions."

Everything fell quiet. The trees stopped rustling, birds ceased chirping, as if the earth knew something bad was about to go down.

Abington whipped out a gun from his jacket. Tendrils of horror swirled up my spine. My breath caught and sputtered, like an engine that wouldn't turn over. *Yup*, I hadn't guessed that, but it was bad. I couldn't speak. I couldn't move. I couldn't breathe. Abington killed Jeremy and now he was going to finish me off, too.

"Get in your truck. We're going to head to the highway where you'll have a deadly wreck of your own." He aimed the gun at my chest. "I said, get in."

It took me a long moment, but I forced myself to calm down, take a few swallows, and bluff an answer. "I'm leaving now." I waggled my keys to show him. "I'll just be going."

"That's right." He gripped the weapon steady in his hands, the metal shape of the barrel pointing my direction. "Only I'm going with you."

"No need. I'm heading out." More key waggling.

"Not without me. Get in." There was no reasoning with his gun, so I stumbled up into the cab. Before I had my door shut, Abington jerked open the passenger side, keeping his gun aimed at me. He settled in his seat. "Step on it."

The keys wouldn't go into the switch at first, but finally I managed to get the engine started. I turned on the headlights and angled away from the curb. My feet shaking on the pedals, I crept my truck along the web of winding streets until we came out on the main road.

Abington rasped out the order, "Head toward the highway."

"Okay." Maybe I could escape, but how? My purse with my cell phone and mace lay on the floor near Abington's feet, not doing me any good. He'd shoot me before I could reach it.

Note to self—keep the phone and pepper spray in my pocket.

Whoops. I'm sure I'd made this same note to myself before.

Abington shifted his weapon to speak into his phone. "I'm in Del's tow truck. We're almost to the highway at the Red Hawk Road entrance. Call me back when you get close." He concentrated on the pavement ahead.

I still had trouble lining up the facts or maybe facing the facts. It was all so shocking. Dad found out about the chop shop and fired Jeremy; Jeremy broke up with me the same day. Dad was killed the next day in an accident and Jeremey was killed two weeks later, murdered in a violent way.

And Abington was a killer. And a car thief.

Let's start with that.

I gave him the side eye. "I can't believe you stole cars, Mr. Abington."

He said in glacial tones, "What about you? You steal the vehicles from the buyers who don't pay."

"Hey! It's not stealing if the owners renege on their

payments."

"Yeah, yeah, yeah." He flapped his palm.

"Tell me about Dad's accident."

Abington turned to face me, his right hand on the gun in his lap, his left hand on the back of the seat, and his gaze first darting out the rear window then out the front windshield. "Nothing to tell. Shit happens."

"Did you have something to do with Dad's car wreck?"

"No." Abington's expression was cloaked in the dark of the night.

"But you admit you got rid of Jeremy?"

"I told you, quit asking questions." He wasn't going to confess like killers did in books.

"And now you're going to get rid of me. Why didn't you just kill me right away instead of torturing me with the Jeep Wrangler?"

"All right, all right. Quit nagging me. I thought at first you were only a nuisance, like you're being now, not a genuine threat. I'd convinced myself you were too stupid to figure anything out, but then you brought the Jeep Wrangler in." He sat forward to peer into the side mirror and watch traffic behind us. "Maybe you were just lucky with that recovery. Or unlucky, depending on how you look at it. Or jinxed, since you were the one to tow Jeremy's Challenger." He barked out a laugh. "Who knew Jeremy was behind in his payments? What irony."

It was a coincidence after all that I'd towed my ex-boyfriend's car with him in the trunk.

"You're just a ditzy redhead, trying to operate a tow truck in high heels." He snickered. "But you're a pain in the ass, too, bothering me right when I needed to talk to Nancy. What'd you have to show up for? I'm never going to get rid of you unless I take care of you myself."

Headlights appeared in my rearview mirror, then a Chevrolet Silverado quad cab with dual rear wheels and six-wheel drive caught up to us. Abington leveled his gun at me. "Pull over."

"Onto the shoulder?" My fear jumped up a notch more, to engine-rattling shakes. The white cross at highway marker 421 glowed in my headlights.

"Yes, this is the spot."

"Why here?" I asked, "Did you run me off the road Saturday night?" Was he returning to the scene of his previous crimes?

He only grunted in reply.

Should I yank on the wheel and roll the truck? Slam down the embankment into the trees? Or swerve into the median? No. I was too scared to do any of that.

Sweat ran down my face as I moved my foot over to the brake pedal. I kept slowing until the front wheels hit the dirt shoulder and we came to a complete stop under a bright street lamp where the light cut a circle. The Silverado muscled right up behind us, our bumpers almost touching. Both trucks idled alongside a standing of tall spruces that grew toward the mountain run-off.

Abington whirred down his window and the earthy scent of pine wafted in. He waved his arm outside at the other driver, then lowered himself out of the cab. His gun remained pointed in my direction while he came around to stand on the other side of my door.

Right near where the white cross stood sentinel as the last witness to my impending demise.

He held the gun steady and spoke through the

glass, "Turn toward the trees."

I cranked the wheel, but didn't touch the accelerator. My pulse revved up, but my mind stalled out. The Silverado lunged at me and rammed my bumper. My truck shot a few feet forward down the hill towards the cliff on the other side of the pines.

Abington made a flying leap into the Silverado.

I stomped both of my feet down on the brakes and stood on the pedal in case the Silverado rammed me again. I couldn't take my hands off the steering wheel to get to my phone. I couldn't!

But the controller for the T-bar dangled from the dash. Within reach. I grabbed it and hit the magic button.

The claws snatched up the Silverado's front tires, shooting the cab high in the air, even though the heavy-duty work truck's weight was likely over the limit of my light-duty tow truck. I'm such a professional for thinking of it at a time like this.

I could see Abington in the Silverado from my rearview mirror. He had on a shocked expression, his eyes bulging wide behind his glasses. The man in the driver's seat next to him was the mechanic from the chop shop, Freddie Haag.

Abington popped his door open and dangled one foot out, so I shoved my truck into reverse, the Silverado went into a jackknife, and he scrambled back inside. As he slammed his door shut the gun flew out of his hands. The Silverado sliced through the pines and the truck cab became wedged, stuck fast between the dense evergreen trees.

I'd trapped Haag and Abington in their vehicle, hammering on their doors trying to get out.

Ha! So, who's stupid and can't operate a tow truck now?

I wrestled open my door and fell out of my seat, but had to go back for my purse, then I fumbled around for my phone. After about a dozen jabs at the keypad, I got the numbers right, and the 9-1-1 operator came on the line. At first, my words tumbled out too fast for her to understand. When she got it, she told me a passing motorist had already called in what appeared to be an accident between a tow truck and a pickup, and the cops were on the way.

The *whoop-whoop* sound of the siren came from the opposite direction, so I hung up. When the police cruiser came into sight, I flagged him down, running back and forth, my three-inch stilettos sinking into the damp pine mulch.

The policeman drove his patrol car right up on the grass, his headlights illuminating the night, and yelled, "Are you all right? What happened?" Zach again. The Spruce Ridge officer always seemed to be handy.

"I'm okay." Which nobody would believe for a minute. My knees weakened and my heart still whaled about in my chest. Zach jumped out of his cruiser and put one arm around me to keep me from falling. Two more police cars careened to a stop and teams of officers poured out. I yelled, "That man in the Silverado," and gestured wildly, "he's Rob Abington, and he was going to shoot me."

One of the policemen asked, "He has a weapon?"

"I think he dropped it."

The officer switched on a searchlight and pointed it toward the Silverado. The three other policemen, guns out, approached the truck where the occupants had fallen silent.

Just then, Tanner's tow truck skidded to a stop on the verge. "Laney," he shouted as he ran up. He tore me away from Zach and folded me in his strong arms, but Zach grabbed Tanner by the shoulder and jerked him back.

The Spruce Ridge officer warned Tanner, "You need to step away. This is a crime scene."

They stared each other down, so I said, "Please, Tanner, do as he says."

He gave me a slanted look that indicated, *okay, since you're the one asking.*

As Zach led me away on shaky legs, I asked Tanner over my shoulder, "How come you're here?"

"Heard about an accident with Del's Towing truck on the police radio."

I said, while walking backward, "This was no accident. Rob Abington tried to kill me. He's a murderer."

Chapter 23

Right after my narrow escape, as they say, my mother drove to Spruce Ridge to see for herself that I was all right. A week later she was still staying with me. Fun times.

We'd all gathered at the usual spot, Roasters on the Ridge. Mom sat at the table with a non-fat latte in her hand, Zach perched on the chair to her left, and Tanner had the stool on her right. Sheriff Lopez sat across from her.

The sheriff had just finished explaining that Abington had lawyered up, but Haag had confessed to killing Jeremy and said that Abington had paid him to do it. Haag had ratted out Abington after all and both were going down for the crime.

The District Attorney obtained a warrant and found the murder weapon, a v-bridle, in Haag's toolbox. Those of us in the towing business are familiar with v-bridle chains. That includes me, now. I never noticed Haag was lefthanded, but I was not surprised he was Abington's hitman.

Eugene Turnquil hadn't known about the chop shop, but he'd tried to talk Freddie Haag into hiring him. He'd also begged Jeremy for help in getting a job, but Jeremy didn't want to associate with a felon. The Sheriff convinced Turnquil it was in his best interest to stay away from other felons and seek employment elsewhere.

Melissa Winslow and her brother Patrick Crump didn't have anything to do with Jeremy's murder. Upon her return from Mexico, Melissa put a down payment on a condo not far from the coffee shop. She decided against one of the fancy new cars she'd been test-driving around town.

I'd heard all this before, so when Kristen motioned me into the back room, I went with her, even though I didn't like leaving the men alone with Mother. I kept darting glances out the doorway until my friend patted my arm. "Listen, Delaney. I didn't know you were struggling to make the rent payment. You should've told me instead of stressing out about it. I'm sorry I was so focused on helping Guy when I should've been helping you. You will only start giving me the money when you can afford it, and no sooner, do you hear me?"

"Thanks, but I'll be good to give you the rent in another week." It wouldn't be easy to pay the rent along with the high-risk insurance premium, but money had started coming in.

I'd taken down the tow truck from the internet site and put up dozens of my barely worn high-heeled shoes, the ones that just clogged up my closet. I'd bought most of them at a huge discount from a friend at the mall, so I hoped to make several hundred dollars from the sales. That, and Tanner had given me back all the towaway zones on Tuesdays and Thursdays, except for the furniture store. Plus, I'd received some nice publicity for bringing the head of the chop shop to justice and solving the mystery surrounding stolen vehicles in Spruce Ridge—a crime spree that shouldn't have been news to me where everything is known in this small community—so the comments on my reviews were looking up. And I'd had seven tows this week. Must be an omen.

The one thing that was still hazy and a big question in my mind was the extent of Dad's involvement in all of this. Had Dad's accident been intentional or was it simply an accident? Add those questions to every other question I had about Del Morran and it was a long list.

I said, "I'm going to be all right, Kris. The tow business is working out after all."

"Told you so. Where is your truck?"

"Byron has it at the autobody shop. It got pretty dented up when I jackknifed the Silverado."

"Did you get the windshield fixed?"

"Yes, and the hail damage. The Old Man took care of everything."

"Why is he doing that for you? It's sure nice of him."

"Oh, he's trying to make it up to me. Listen, I'd better get out front. Mom has Tanner's ear and you know how destructive she can be." I made a *pee-yew* face.

Kristen grimaced. "Go on. I'll help Guy behind the counter." She swished past me, then stopped and turned. "And if you ever need extra cash, I'll give you some hours. I love working with you, Delaney, you know that."

"Okay. I appreciate it." I gave her a big hug. Guy shot me an angry look behind her back.

Tanner stood up and pointed toward the window. "Look what's outside."

My tow truck!

New windshield. No dents. New paint. No white.

My truck was a gorgeous red with my stiletto logo and "Del's Towing" scripted in black. My heart soared seeing my rig appearing brand-spanking new. It felt as though my baby was home.

We all rushed through the door. Mom, too.

Byron got out of the driver's seat, Axle threw open the passenger door, and the Rottweiler, Boss, hopped to the ground and sat on his haunches at Axle's feet. My lil' cuz' was not wearing his usual hoody or knit cap, and his hair stuck up all over, dark and thick like Kristen's.

Tanner punched Byron's shoulder. "Great job. The truck's beautiful."

I couldn't agree more, but stood there speechless, blushing like I always did.

Tanner asked me, "Why didn't you change the name to 'Delaney's Towing' or 'Laney's Towing?' "

"Everyone knows me as Del."

"But you're more of a Laney."

I glanced at my mom, who was the only other one to call me that, and answered, "I'm more Del than you know."

When Byron and Axle started a conversation about…whatever it was that mechanics discussed…I ran my hand over the hood of my truck and kicked the tires with my pointy-toed shoes. Not too shabby. I threw open the door and clambered inside, and Tanner got in the passenger seat. He ran his fingers through my hair, loosening the braid, the red waves tumbling down past my shoulders. I just laughed. I didn't mind. His face came near my own, and I smelled his woodsy scent with the familiar hint of gas and oil. He pulled me in for a kiss, even though Byron watched from a few feet away.

When my phone vibrated in my pocket, Tanner released me and I answered it.

I disconnected and turned the ignition switch, the dangling stiletto on the keychain making a jingling sound.

"Someone needs me. Want to come along on a tow?"

A word about the author…

Karen C. Whalen is the author of two cozy mystery series, the Dinner Club Murder Mysteries and the Tow Truck Murder Mysteries. The first in the dinner club series, Everything Bundt the Truth, tied for First Place in the Suspense Novel category of the 2017 IDA Contest. Whalen loves to host dinner parties, camp, hike, and read.

Thank you for purchasing
this publication of The Wild Rose Press, Inc.

For questions or more information
contact us at
info@thewildrosepress.com.

The Wild Rose Press, Inc.
www.thewildrosepress.com

CPSIA information can be obtained
at www.ICGtesting.com
Printed in the USA
LVHW051541250623
750731LV00010B/1038

9 781509 241064